THE BEST
HORROR OF THE YEAR

VOLUME NINE

Vol. 9 2017

8-17

WITHDRAWN

Also Edited by Ellen Datlow

THE BEST
HORROR OF THE YEAR

VOLUME NINE

EDITED BY ELLEN DATLOW

NIGHT SHADE BOOKS
NEW YORK

The Best Horror of the Year Volume Nine © 2017 by Ellen Datlow
The Best Horror of the Year Volume Nine © 2017 by Night Shade Books, an imprint of Skyhorse Publishing, Inc.

All rights reserved. No part of this book may be reproduced in any manner without the express written consent of the publisher, except in the case of brief excerpts in critical reviews or articles. All inquiries should be addressed to Night Shade Books, 307 West 36th Street, 11th Floor, New York, NY 10018.

Night Shade books may be purchased in bulk at special discounts for sales promotion, corporate gifts, fund-raising, or educational purposes. Special editions can also be created to specifications. For details, contact the Special Sales Department, Night Shade Books, 307 West 36th Street, 11th Floor, New York, NY 10018 or info@skyhorsepublishing.com.

Night Shade Books™ is a trademark of Skyhorse Publishing, Inc.®, a Delaware corporation.

Visit our website at www.nightshadebooks.com.

10 9 8 7 6 5 4 3 2 1

Library of Congress Cataloging-in-Publication Data is available on file.

Interior layout and design by Amy Popovich
Cover art by Kevin Peterson
Cover design by Amy Popovich and Lesley Worrell

Print ISBN: 978-1-5107-1666-7

Printed in the United States of America

ACKNOWLEDGMENTS

Thanks to Michael Kelly, Alvaro Zinos-Amaro, and Gardner Dozois for recommendations.

Thanks to all the publishers and editors who sent me their books and magazines.

Thanks to *Video Watchdog*, *Rue Morgue*, the *British Fantasy Journal*, and *Locus* magazine for reference and reviews that pointed me to cover books I might not have been aware of.

And thanks especially to Kristine Dikeman, my stalwart reader, and to my patient editor Jason Katzman.

TABLE OF CONTENTS

SUMMATION 2016

Here are 2016's numbers: There are twenty-one stories and novelettes in this year's volume, ranging from 500 words to 14,400 words. They were chosen from anthologies, print magazines, webzines, single-author chapbooks, and single-author collections. Eleven of the contributors live in the United States, one lives in Canada, and eight in the United Kingdom. One writer grew up in Indonesia, one in New Zealand (as well as England). Six contributors are female, fourteen male (two novelettes are by one male writer). The authors of eight stories have never appeared in previous volumes of my year's best.

AWARDS

The Horror Writers Association announced the winners of the 2015 Bram Stoker Awards® May 14, 2016, at the Flamingo Hotel in Las Vegas, Nevada. The presentations were made during a banquet held at the inaugural Stokercon. The winners:

Superior Achievement in a Novel: *A Head Full of Ghosts* by Paul Tremblay, (William Morrow); Superior Achievement in a First Novel: *Mr. Suicide* by Nicole Cushing (Word Horde Press); Superior Achievement in a Young Adult Novel: *Devil's Pocket* by John Dixon (Simon & Schuster); Superior Achievement in a Graphic Novel: *Shadow Show: Stories in Celebration of Ray Bradbury*: by Sam Weller, Mort Castle, Chris Ryall, & Carlos Guzman (editors) (IDW Publishing); Superior Achievement in Long Fiction: "Little

Dead Red" by Mercedes Yardley (*Grimm Mistresses*, Ragnorak Publications); Superior Achievement in Short Fiction: "Happy Joe's Rest Stop" by John Palisano (*18 Wheels of Horror*, Big Time Books); Superior Achievement in a Screenplay: *It Follows* by David Robert Mitchell (Northern Lights Films); Superior Achievement in an Anthology: *The Library of the Dead* edited by Michael Bailey (Written Backwards); Superior Achievement in a Fiction Collection: *While the Black Stars Burn* by Lucy A. Snyder (Raw Dog Screaming Press); Superior Achievement in Nonfiction: *The Art of Horror* by Stephen Jones (Applause Theatre Books and Cinema Book Publishers); Superior Achievement in a Poetry Collection: *Eden Underground* by Alessandro Manzetti (Crystal Lake Publishing).

The Specialty Press Award: Borderlands Press.

The Richard Layman President's Award: Patrick Freivald and Andrew Wolter.

The Silver Hammer Award: Michael Knost.

Mentor of the Year went to Tim Waggoner.

Life Achievement Awards: Alan Moore and George R. Romero.

◄◦►

The 2015 Shirley Jackson Awards were given out at Readercon on July 10, 2016, in Quincy, Massachusetts. Jurors were Robert Shearman, Bev Vincent, Livia Llewellyn, Simon Kurt Unsworth, and Kaaron Warren.

The winners were: Novel: *Experimental Film* by Gemma Files (ChiZine Publications); Novella: *Wylding Hall* by Elizabeth Hand (PS Publishing-UK/Open Road Media-US); Novelette: "Even Clean Hands Can Do Damage" by Steve Duffy (*Supernatural Tales* #30, Autumn); Short Fiction: "The Dying Season" by Lynda E. Rucker (*Aickman's Heirs*); Single-author Collection: *The Bazaar of Bad Dreams* by Stephen King (Scribner); Edited Anthology: *Aickman's Heirs* edited by Simon Strantzas (Undertow Publications).

◄◦►

The World Fantasy Awards were presented October 30, 2016, at a banquet held during the World Fantasy Convention in Columbus, Ohio. The Lifetime Achievement recipients, David G. Hartwell and Andrzej Sapkowski, were previously announced. The judges were Laird Barron, Rani Graff, Elaine Isaak, Kay Kenyon, and Konrad Walewski.

Winners for the best work in 2015: Novel: *The Chimes* by Anna Smaill (Sceptre, UK); Long Fiction: "The Unlicensed Magician" by Kelly Barnhill (PS Publishing); Short Fiction: "Hungry Daughters of Starving Mothers" by Alyssa Wong (*Nightmare* magazine, October 2015); Anthology: *She Walks in Shadows* edited by Silvia Marino-Garcia and Paula R. Stiles (Innsmouth Free Press); Collection: *Bone Swans* by C.S.E. Cooney (Mythic Delirium Books); Artist: Galen Dara; Special Award, Professional: Stephen Jones for *The Art of Horror* (Applause Theatre Books and Cinema Book Publishers); Special Award, Non-Professional: John O'Neill for *Black Gate: Adventures in Fantasy Literature*.

NOTABLE NOVELS OF 2016

Stiletto by Daniel O'Malley (Little, Brown) is the long-awaited sequel to the brilliantly entertaining *The Rook*, about the Checquy, a top secret group of supernatural operatives working out of the British government. In this book, Mythwany Thomas, who is The Rook, plays a secondary role to two young women who couldn't be more unalike. One is a member of the Checquy. The other is a Grafter, the Checquy's centuries long enemy. Although deeply distrustful of each other, the two are forced to work together when the tenuous peace is seemingly being sabotaged. Murder, mayhem, humor, and a fascinating look at diplomacy on a supernatural scale.

The Everything Box by Richard Kadrey (HarperCollins) is the first in a new dark fantasy series by the author of the celebrated Sandman Slim novels. One thing is immediately apparent: angels are assholes. The plot revolves around a box that a low-ranking but ambitious angel is ordered to use to destroy the world. Alas, the angel loses the box and has been stuck on Earth for thousands of years, searching for it. But the book is really about Coop, a thief immune to magic who is coerced into stealing the box back. Violent and full of action, the novel is also very funny.

The Perdition Score by Richard Kadrey (HarperCollins) is the eighth Sandman Slim novel about Stark, a Nephilim (half human/half angel), who has saved the world multiple times, escaped from Hell more than once, been Lucifer, and continues on his merry way to wreak havoc in our Los Angeles, and the one underground. Stark is forced to deal with the Wormwood Corporation when they cook up a little something called Black Milk, which makes angels into Berserkers and can make mortals immortal. Entertaining and violent dark fantasy.

Lovecraft Country by Matt Ruff (HarperCollins) combines the harrowing horror of 1950s Jim Crow America with the supernatural horror of the Lovecraftian Mythos. In 1954, an African American man goes missing and his war veteran son sets out from Chicago with two companions to search for him. Each chapter tells a separate story that builds into a complete whole exuding an acute sense of dread—almost more from the rampant racism than the monsters conjured up by a cult of sorcerers. But even so, this is most definitely a Lovecraftian story, with all the paranoia, conspiracies, family secrets, and cosmic horror that readers could hope for.

It's the perfect companion to Victor LaValle's novella (see under chapbooks), *The Ballad of Black Tom*.

Mongrels by Stephen Graham Jones (William Morrow) is a gorgeous dark and moving coming-of-age story about a young, not-yet werewolf being brought up by his grandfather, aunt, and uncle who are all tasked with teaching him how to *be* a werewolf—what a werewolf can and can't do, what can harm or kill it. Moving gracefully back and forth over a period of several years, clues are sprinkled throughout to the history of the family.

Flicker by Theodore Roszak (Summit Books) was published in 1991. It's one of those books I should have read when it first came out but never got around to. Friends have been urging me to read it for years and I've bought more than one copy since it was published, forgetting I have one. So . . . I finally decided to take a break from 2016 novels and see what all the fuss was about. A movie lover's dream, *Flicker* just might be the lost movie/ auteur/secret history/conspiracy novel that started the subgenre. Told from the point of view of a film critic who in the 1960s becomes obsessed with a minor filmmaker named Max Castle and where this obsession leads—to an exploration of the hidden depths beneath the surface of film, the Knights Templar, the Cathars, and a group of death cultists named the orphans of the storm, who are intent on the destruction of humankind.

Hard Light by Elizabeth Hand (Minotaur) is the third noir novel featuring Cass Neary, a former New York punk known for her transgressive photography, not to mention her very bad behavior. After fleeing Reykjavik on a stolen passport, she waits in London for her lover, and when he doesn't show up, is easily enticed to attend a party hosted by a gangster, becoming involved in dirty dealings in antiques, ancient instruments of movie making, beautiful and dangerous losers, and, of course, drugs and alcohol. The plot is complicated, but even if the reader might occasionally become lost in the intricacies of who did what to whom, the experience of reading this gorgeously written novel fully makes up for it.

Hex by Thomas Olde Heuvelt (Tor) is one of the most *unnerving* novels I've ever read. A small town in upstate New York is cursed by a witch from the seventeenth century—a witch with her eyes and mouth stitched up. What is especially unnerving is that the witch mysteriously appears and disappears around town at will: in the street, in shops, in homes. Everyone in town knows there are rules that must be obeyed or harm will come to them or those they love. One of those rules is that outsiders must never know of the curse, so the town is basically quarantined from the rest of the world. When a new family ignorantly moves into town despite all attempts to discourage them, a string of events begin to drive the whole town batshit crazy.

Most novel-length supernatural horror doesn't work for me, as my suspension of disbelief usually falls away at some point. *Hex* manages to avoid this—perhaps because it's both supernaturally and psychologically horrific.

The Fisherman by John Langan (Word Horde Press) is the terrific second novel by an author who has been making his reputation in the horror field by producing consistently powerful and literate stories for the past several years. In a perfect origami of stories within stories, a fisherman relates a tale of another kind of fisherman, who is seeking more than mere fish.

The Loney by Andrew Michael Hurley (Houghton Mifflin Harcourt) was originally published by Tartarus Press in 2014 and won the prestigious Costa First Novel Award in 2015. It's a gorgeously written, powerful gothic novel about events that take place during three Catholic families' religious retreat to the wild northern coast of Lancashire, an area known as the Loney. They go to find a cure for the disabilities of the narrator's brother, as the area is known to be ghost-ridden, full of Mystery, and sometimes the provider of miracles. But there's a cost. There's always a cost. Literary horror at its best.

Fellside by M. R. Carey (Orbit) is a ghost story about a severely burned junkie sent to prison for murder after her apartment went up in flames, killing a child in the building. The woman's prison is privately run and corruption reigns. Wracked with guilt, the woman initially tries to starve herself, something the administrators would love as they really don't want this high profile monster/celebrity to bring attention to Fellside. But the ghost of the dead child appears and changes everything.

I Am Providence by Nick Mamatas (Night Shade Books) is a biting satire about convention-goers and fans, particularly those of H. P. Lovecraft. A writer is murdered during a horror convention. Is it related to the mysterious and rare copy of a book he was planning to sell? Or did he just annoy the wrong person one time too often? A fast, entertaining read but the best thing about the book is the commentary by the faceless murder victim/narrator, whose body is decomposing in the morgue.

Only the Dead Know Burbank by Bradford Tatum (Harper Perennial) is about a young girl who survives her death from the Spanish Flu only to be cursed with an immortality that keeps her the same age as when she died. In Berlin, she becomes obsessed with the new technology of movie-making and with her experience of death and the dark, homes in on emerging horror cinema—becoming involved with the early German expressionists and later moving to Hollywood where she meets some of the actors and directors we consider icons from that period of horror. Moving and entertaining, although it occasionally feels too contrived, as it touches on every flashpoint of early movie history. Maddy Ulm is Zelig-like in her ubiquity—never noticed but always present.

Stranded by Bracken Macleod (Tor) is an engrossing horror thriller that immediately pulls in the reader with its foreboding atmosphere in the arctic cold. A resupply ship en route to a drilling platform is caught in a storm that leaves the crew stranded within a weird fog, instruments useless. Several men leave the ship to find help, encountering something that cannot be—a ship very like the one they came from.

The Grief Hole by Kaaron Warren (IFW Australia) is a wrenching horror novel about the despair and paralysis caused by grief. The "grief hole" is both a place and a state of mind. A social worker sees ghosts showing how people will die, and she attempts to prevent these deaths. After one disastrous intervention, she quits, hoping to find peace. But when she discovers that a teenage cousin who died had been hired by a charismatic singer to draw dying youths in a derelict building, dubbed the grief hole, she's forced to take action. The novel won the Australian Shadows Award.

We Eat Our Own by Kea Wilson (Scribner) is an absorbing imagining of the making of the infamous movie *Cannibal Holocaust*. A struggling actor is lured to the Amazonian jungle in civil war–torn Colombia for a movie about which he is told nothing. Revolutionaries have infested the jungle, along with drug dealers. The director is a maniac obsessed with verisimilitude and at a certain point in the narrative the movie crew and the reader are forced to wonder how far he's willing to go for it.

Down on Your Knees by Lee Thomas (Lethe Press) is a short, brutal, and entertaining supernatural crime novel with a gay gangster as the anti-hero. Denny Doyle gets out of prison, expecting to take up where he left off, but there's a new big boss in town—a sadistic, formerly low-level thug who seems to have more than gun power to aid in his rise to power.

ALSO NOTED

In late 2015, Penguin Classics reissued three titles of supernatural weird fiction with forewords by contemporary writers in the genre. The three were Ray Russell's short novel, *The Case Against Satan*, with a foreword by Laird Barron; a collection by Charles Beaumont, *Perchance to Dream*, with a new afterword by William Shatner; and Thomas Ligotti's collection containing both *Songs of a Dead Dreamer* and *Grimscribe*, with a foreword by Jeff VanderMeer. *Paper Tigers* by Damien Angelica Walters (Dark House Press) is a first novel about a young woman mutilated in a fire who becomes obsessed with an antique photo album that makes promises she finds difficult to ignore. *The Binding* by Nicholas Wolff (Gallery Books) is the first supernatural novel written pseudonymously by a "*New York Times* bestselling" novelist about a cocky psychiatrist in a small Massachusetts town who is approached by a frightened father whose children have manifested odd behavior, leading all but one to commit suicide. *Disappearance at Devil's Rock* by Paul Tremblay (William Morrow) is about a thirteen-year-old who vanishes in the woods of a state park and the slowly revealed secrets that hint at what happened to him. The plot takes a while to get going but picks up steam in the last third of the book. *The Last One* by Alexandra Oliva (Ballantine) is about a reality show contestant whose life changes irrevocably when devastation occurs in the real world unbeknownst to her and her fellows. Zombies continue to terrorize us with *Day by Day Armageddon Ghost Run* by J. L. Bourke (Gallery Books) and *Everybody Dies Tomorrow* by Matt Howarth (The Merry Blacksmith

Press). *Good Girls* by Glen Hirshberg (Tor) is a worthy sequel to *Motherless Child*, a novel about how a couple of regular young women get caught up in a deadly nest of vampires as a result of an unfortunate encounter with one of them. The climax was shocking. Although *Good Girls* is a sequel, it can stand on its own. The aftermath takes off from those events, with the survivors of the final conflict left with grievous wounds, both physical and psychological. *The Devourers* by Indra Das (Del Rey) is brutal and bloody with moments of grace. Horror readers would do best to ignore the American cover which is a bit too placid and *pretty* to do justice to this powerful horror novel about shapeshifters known by different names around the world: ghuls, werewolves, et al., and their relationships with humans. *Lost Gods* by Brom (Harper Voyager) is about a young man who journeys to Purgatory to save his wife and child. Includes illustrations by Brom throughout. *Certain Dark Things* by Silvia Moreno-Garcia (Thomas Dunne Books) is a fast-paced novel about a Mexican street kid who encounters a vampire on the run from a rival family that wants to kill her. The introduction of various nationalities/myths of vampires from around the world into one setting is intriguing. *Shadows in Summerland* by Adrian Van Young (ChiZine Publications) is a promising first novel about spiritualism and murder in 1859 Boston. Keith Donohue's *The Motion of Puppets* (Picador) is a weird little thing about a newlywed who, after falling in love with a marionette in a shop window, is herself transformed into a marionette. Her husband searches for her while she learns about life as a puppet. *Beneath Ash & Bone* by D. Alexander Ward (Bedlam Press) is a short, supernatural novel taking place just before the Civil War in the Blue Ridge Mountains. A boy disappears during a winter storm and the sheriff is tasked with finding him. *The Apartment* by S. L. Grey (Blumhouse Books/Anchor Books) is about a South African couple traumatized by a break-in, who swap apartments with a couple in Paris in order to get away. But their ideal vacation goes horribly awry. *Phantom Effect* by Michael Aronovitz (Night Shade Books) is about a vicious serial killer being stalked by the ghost of one of his victims. *The Vampires of Dreach Fola: A Non-Narrative of Extreme Horror* by Scáthe Beorh (JWK Fiction) is a mixture of letters, notes, lists, and essays that allow the reader to experience the book in any order they like. *The Harrowing* by Robert E. Dunn (Necro Publications) is a dark fantasy about a biker recruited by an archangel to rescue the innocent from Hell. *Heartsnare* by Steven B. Williams (Lethe Press) is about a town in Yorkshire,

England, plagued by monsters. *A Brutal Chill in August* by Alan M. Clark (Word Horde Press) is a fictionalized portrait of Mary Ann "Polly" Nichols, the woman believed to be the first victim of Jack the Ripper. *Under the Harrow* by Flynn Berry (Penguin Original) is a first novel about a woman traveling from London to visit her sister in the country only to discover her murdered in her home. *The Wretch of the Sun* by Michael Cisco (Hippocampus Press) is a complex tale about a haunted house, written in Cisco's unique style. Weird and dark. *Almost Dark* by Letitia Trent (ChiZine Publications) is about the aftermath of an accident in an abandoned textile factory that kills one twin and leaves the other wracked with guilt. *Lily* by Michael Thomas Ford (Lethe Press) is about a young girl who can see how others will die, by touching them. This ability makes her a target for those who want to take advantage of it. *The Devil's Evidence* by Simon Kurt Unsworth (Doubleday) is a sequel to Unsworth's fine first novel, *The Devil's Detective*. Thomas Fool, a man with no memory of what damned him to Hell, has been promoted to command the Information Office of Hell, and must track down those setting a series of deadly fires there. *The Fireman* by Joe Hill (William Morrow) is about a plague of spontaneous combustion triggered by strange gold and black tattoos that are highly contagious. *The Feast of Souls* by Simon Bestwick (Solaris) is about a woman who after having gone through traumatic life changes, returns to the house outside of Manchester, England, where she spent her student years, hoping to find peace. She does not. *The Hidden People* by Alison Littlewood (Jo Fletcher Books) takes place in rural England during the mid-1860s where superstition is rampant, in contrast to cosmopolitan London. A young woman is killed by her husband, who is only trying to save her from the fairies. Her cousin decides to investigate what actually happened, putting his own wife in danger.

MAGAZINES, JOURNALS, AND WEBZINES

It's important to recognize the work of the talented artists working in the field of fantastic fiction, both dark and light. The following artists created dark art that I thought especially noteworthy in 2016: Steven G. Gilberts, Lynette Watters, Matt Bissette-Johnson, Sandro Castelli, Vincent Sammy, Adam Katsaros, Dave Senecal, Richard Wagner, Martin Hanford, Ben

Baldwin, Vince Haig, Steve Santiago, Rod Julian, Kirsi Salonen, Jeffrey Collingwood, Bill Rutherford, Yana Moskaluk, Paul Lowe, Tran Nguyen, Natalia Drepina, Victor Stepushkin, John Coulthart, Harry O. Morris, Michael Bukowski, Maggie Chiang, Kim Lennard, Cindy Mochizuki, Brenda Bailey, Mikio Murakami, Marcela Bolivar, Ian MacLean, George Cotronis, Andrew McKiernan, Steve McDonald, and Daniele Serra.

BFS Journal edited by Allen Stroud is a nonfiction perk of being a member of the British Fantasy Society. It's published twice a year and includes reviews, scholarly articles, and features about recent conventions. *BFS Horizons* is the fiction perk. Issue #3 was edited by Jared Shurin and #4 was edited by Helen Armsfield. During 2016, there was a strong dark story by Archie Black.

The Green Book: Writings on Irish Gothic, Supernatural and Fantastic Literature edited by Brian J. Showers used its first issue in 2016 to publish contemporary writings about Ireland's 1916 Easter Rising—the violent, controversial rebellion for independence. There's no genre slant in the works published by Rudyard Kipling, Arthur Machen, Dorothy Macardle, and others but there are the usual book reviews.

Black Static edited by Andy Cox continues its reign as one of the best horror magazines in the field. In addition to fiction, the bi-monthly regularly includes interviews, book and movie reviews, and commentary by Stephen Volk and Lynda E. Rucker. In 2016, there were notable stories by Ralph Robert Moore, Robert Levy, Kristi DeMeester, Michelle Ann King, Priya Sharma, Harmony Neal, Stephen Hargadon, Steve Rasnic Tem, Charles Wilkinson, Lisa Tuttle, David Hartley, Simon Avery, Carole Johnstone, Mark Morris, V. H. Leslie, Tyler Keevil, Stephen Graham Jones, and Damien Angelica Walters. The Levy is reprinted herein.

Nightmare magazine edited by John Joseph Adams publishes online monthly and by email subscription. Each issue includes two original and two reprinted stories plus nonfiction. During 2016, there were good dark stories by Lisa Goldstein, Adam-Troy Castro, Livia Llewellyn, Sandra McDonald, David Tallerman, Dennis Etchison, Gavin Pate, Nadia Bulkin, and Marc Laidlaw. The Bulkin is reprinted herein.

Supernatural Tales edited by David Longhorn is a regularly published repository of supernatural fiction with both fiction plus book and movie reviews. In 2016, three issues were published, with notable stories by S. M. Cashmore, Jane Jakeman, Tom Johnston, Keith Colman, and Kathy Stevens.

Cemetery Dance edited by Rich Chizmar brought out two issues in 2016. They included notable stories by Amanda C. Davis, Glen Hirshberg, Ian Rogers, K. S. Clay, JG Faherty, Joe Hill (novella), Bruce McAllister, and Keith Minnion. On the nonfiction side, there was an interview with Ray Garton, plus book reviews and regular columns (one column by me).

The Dark edited by Jack Fisher and Sean Wallace was a quarterly until May 2016, when Fisher left and Wallace took over the helm, moving the webzine onto a monthly schedule. Two of the four monthly stories are original, the other two reprints. The fiction runs more to dark fantasy than horror. In 2016, there were strong dark stories by Amber van Dyk, Kali Wallace, Cassandra Khaw, Carrie Laben, Gregory Bossert, Rhonda Eikamp, A. C. Wise, and Kristi DeMeester. The Bossert is reprinted herein.

The Lovecraft eZine published by Mike Davis and edited by Alex Kreitner and Matthew Carpenter published one print issue during 2016, with notable stories by Michael Griffin, Raven Daemorgan, Marcus Grimm, Jonathan Raab, and a collaboration by Benjamin Knox & Toby Bennett.

Weirdbook edited by Doug Draa published a second year in its new incarnation of the long-running magazine published for many years by W. Paul Ganley. It concentrates more on dark fantasy than horror but, in 2016, there were notable horror stories by John R. Fulz, Taye Carroll, P.R. O'Leary, and Kelda Crich.

The Horror Zine edited by Jeani Rector is a monthly zine that has been publishing since 2009, and includes fiction, poetry, art, interviews, and news. The fiction features reprints by prominent horror writers and original stories by newer writers.

MIXED-GENRE MAGAZINES

Shimmer published by Beth Wodzinski, edited by several people, comes out every other month and usually contains a good mix of fantasy and dark fantasy, with the occasional science fiction story. During 2016, there were notable dark stories by Megan Arkenberg, Kay Chronister, K. L. Morris, Nicasio Andres Reed, Jessica May Lin, and Gwendolyn Kester. *Dark Discoveries* is meant to be a quarterly edited by Aaron French, but only brought out two issues in 2016. There was a good poem by Linda Addison and notable stories by Nick Mamatas, Angela Slatter, and Cameron Pierce. There was also an interview with Laird Barron. One issue was Bizarro themed. *Not One of Us* edited by John Benson is one of the longest-running small press magazines. It's published twice a year and contains weird and dark fiction and poetry. In addition, Benson puts out an annual "one-off" on a specific theme. The theme for 2016 was "Go Now." In 2016, there were strong dark stories by Erik Amundsen, Tim L. Williams, Nicole Tanquary, and Patricia Russo. *Aurealis* edited by Dirk Strasser, Stephen Higgins, Annika Howells, and Michael Pryor is one of only a few long-running Australian mixed-genre magazines. In 2016, there were strong dark stories by Si Wang, Annika Howells, Michael Johnston, and Marlee Jane Ward. *The Magazine of Fantasy and Science Fiction* edited by C. C Finlay is bimonthly, and always provides a generous mix of science fiction, fantasy, and horror. The best of the darker stories published in 2016 were by David Gerrold, Bruce McAllister, John P. Murphy, Bennett North, Sarah Pinsker, Steven Popkes, and Joseph Tomaras. *Conjunctions 67: Other Aliens* edited by Bradford Morrow and Elizabeth Hand includes interviews of Samuel R. Delany, Kelly Link, and John Crowley, a selection of letters by James Tiptree, Jr. written to Joanna Russ, plus original science fiction and horror by a varied assortment of mainstream and genre writers including Brian Evenson, Lavie Tidhar, Jeffrey Ford, Valerie Martin, Leena Krohn, Joyce Carol Oates, Peter Straub, and others. The Straub is included herein. *Shock Totem: Curious Tales of the Macabre and Twisted* edited by K. Allen Wood published one issue in 2016, and announced it was folding. There were notable stories by Thana Niveau and Paul H. Hamilton. *On Spec*, Canada's best known genre magazine, is published quarterly by a revolving committee of volunteers since 1989. The only story from the three 2016 issues that I'd consider horror was by Lynne MacLean. Tor.com publishes new sf, fantasy, and horror weekly edited by several in-house editors and several consultants (I'm one). In 2016, there were notable horror and dark fantasy stories by Brian Hodge, Theodora Goss, Melissa Marr, Angela Slatter, Stephen Graham Jones, Glen Hirshberg, and David Nickle. *Uncanny* edited by Lynne M. Thomas and Michael Damien Thomas is a monthly ezine publishing sf and fantasy mostly, but occasionally darker stories. In 2016, there was notable dark fiction by Brooke Bolander, Kat Howard, Alyssa Wong, E. Lily Yu, Carmen Machado, Seanan McGuire, Sarah Pinsker, JY Yang, and Catherynne M. Valente. *Asimov's Science Fiction* magazine edited by Sheila Williams is a staple in the sf field but occasionally publishes quite dark fiction. In 2016, there were notable dark stories by Esther M. Friesner, Bruce McAllister, Ian Rogers, and Sandra McDonald. *The Audient Void: A Journal of Weird Fiction and Dark Fantasy* edited by Obadiah Bird is a new small press print zine that brought out two issues in 2016 (I only saw one). Its featured artist for that issue was Allen Koszinski. It publishes poetry, prose, and nonfiction, and there was notable work by Daniel Pietersen, K.A. Opperman, and David Barker.

ANTHOLOGIES

Lovecraftian fiction still rules with several mythos-inspired anthologies published in 2016.

Tomorrow's Cthulhu: Stories of the Dawn of Posthumanity edited by Scott Gable and C. Dombrowski (Broken Eye Books) features twenty-nine sf/h Lovecraftian stories. The strongest are by Clinton J. Boomer, A. C. Wise, Kaaron Warren, Damien Angelica Walters, Lynda E. Rucker, Samantha Henderson, and Desirina Boskovich.

Cthulhu Lies Dreaming: Twenty-Three Tales of the Weird and Cosmic edited by Salome Jens (Ghostwoods Books) has some fresh takes on the mythos with strong stories by Matthew Chabin, Gethin A. Lynes, Brian Fatah Steele, Lynn Hardy, Lynnea Glasser, and Matthew J. Hockey.

Autumn Cthulhu: Tales of Lovecraftian Horror edited by Mike Davis (Lovecraft eZine Press), with eighteen new stories and one reprinted poem, has notable work by Laird Barron, Gemma Files, John Langan, Orrin Grey, Daniel Mills, Scott Thomas, Damien Angelica Walters, Joseph S. Pulver, Sr., S. P. Miskowski, and Robert Levy. The Files is reprinted herein.

The Mammoth Book of Cthulhu edited by Paula Guran (Robinson) has twenty-four Lovecraftian-influenced stories (all but one original) and a nonfiction piece. The best stories are by Laird Barron, Brian Hodge, Amanda Downum, Lisa L. Hannett, Usman T. Malik, Helen Marshall, Norman Partridge, John Shirley, Michael Wehunt, and A. C. Wise. The Hodge is reprinted herein.

Children of Lovecraft edited by Ellen Datlow (Dark Horse Books) is an all original anthology of fourteen Lovecraftian stories by a variety of writers including Laird Barron, Livia Llewellyn, Siobhan Carroll, Brian Hodge, Brian

Evenson, Richard Kadrey, and nine others. Stories by Llewellyn, Hodge, and Carroll are reprinted herein.

Tales of Cthulhu Invictus edited by Brian M. Sammons (Golden Goblin Press) features nine dark fantasies about battling Cthulhu in ancient Rome.

Black Wings V: New Tales of Lovecraftian Horror edited by S. T. Joshi (PS Publishing) continues the series created by Joshi, a major Lovecraft expert. There were notable stories by Cody Goodfellow, Darrell Schweitzer, Caitlín R. Kiernan, John Reppion, and Donald Tyson.

CthulhuSattva: Tales of the Black Gnosis edited by Scott R. Jones (Martian Migraine Press) features fifteen stories, mostly new.

Gothic Lovecraft edited by Lynne Jamneck and S. T. Joshi (Cycatrix Press) features thirteen Lovecraftian stories (all but one, new) based on classic gothic tales. A gimmick that works some of the time, although too many stories stay closer to the original then they should. There was good work by John Shirley.

The Hyde Hotel edited by James Everington and Dan Howarth (Black Shuck Books) is a mostly original (with one reprint) anthology featuring eleven stories taking place in a nondescript hotel in an unnamed British city. I would have preferred more variety in the tales, but there are notable ones by Simon Bestwick, Amelia Mangan, and Ray Cluley.

Black Candies: Gross and Unlikeable Guest edited by Natanya Ann Pulley (SSWA Press) presents twenty-eight horror stories by women, all but one new. Although quite short, many of the stories pack a punch. The best are by Jennifer Manalili, Danielle Renino, Cait Cole, Marie Johnson Parrish, Kayla Miller, and Jeanette Sanchez-Izenman. This latter, the author's first publication, is quite impressive.

Fright Mare: Women Write Horror edited by Billie Sue Mosiman (DM Publishing) has twenty stories, four of them reprints. The best of the originals are by Lucy Taylor, Kathryn Ptacek, and Loren Rhoades. The book itself is one of the most poorly produced anthologies I've read: no page numbers in the table of contents and the actual stories aren't in the order of the contents. Also, there are bios for only some of the contributors.

Peel Back the Skin edited by Anthony Rivera and Sharon Lawson (Grey Matter Press) is an all original anthology of fifteen stories, broadly themed around monsters, some of them supernatural. There are notable stories by Yvonne Navarro, Durand Sheng Welsh, Joe McKinney, Lucy Taylor, Jonathan Maberry, William Meikle, and Erik Williams.

Borderlands 6: An Anthology of Imaginative Fiction edited by Olivia F. Monteleone and Thomas F. Monteleone (Borderlands Press) is a non-themed anthology of twenty-one new stories and one reprint. There were notable stories by Steve Rasnic Tem, Bob Pastorella, Peter Salomon, Rebecca J. Allred, and Jack Ketchum. The Tem is reprinted herein.

Gutted: Beautiful Horror Stories edited by Doug Murano and D. Alexander Ward (Crystal Lake Publishing) is a loosely themed anthology (beauty at the heart of darkness) featuring fifteen stories and one poem, three of the stories reprints. There are notable darker stories by Amanda Gowin, Richard Thomas, and Brian Kirk.

Great British Horror 1, Green and Pleasant Land edited by Steve J. Shaw (Black Shuck Books) is a strong, all-original anthology of eleven horror stories taking place in rural areas and small towns of Great Britain. There are notable stories by A.K. Benedict, Adam Millard, Jasper Bark, V.H. Leslie, James Everington, Ray Cluley, and Simon Kurt Unsworth. It's the first in a proposed annual series of anthologies featuring ten British writers and one international contributor. The Cluley is reprinted herein.

Eternal Frankenstein edited by Ross E. Lockhart (Word Horde Press) features sixteen original stories paying tribute to Mary Shelley's novel. The best stories stray furthest from the original, as with many anthologies influenced by a specific piece of fiction. The strongest stories are by Siobhan Carroll, Michael Griffin, Damien Angelica Walters, and Kristi DeMeester. The DeMeester is reprinted herein.

The 3rd Spectral Book of Horror Stories edited by Joseph Rubas (Spectral Press) is the third volume in the British non-theme, all original anthology series inspired by the Pan Books of Horror. This volume has twenty stories and one poem. The best are by Lisa Morton, Richard Farren Barber, and Dan Wellington.

Lost Signals edited by Max Booth III and Lori Michelle (Perpetual Motion Machine Publishing) presents twenty-four stories (three reprints) about radio and other kinds of transmissions. There are notable stories by Josh Malerman, George Cotronis, John C. Foster, Michael Paul Gonzalez, and Tony Burgess.

The Cold Embrace: Weird Stories by Women edited by S. T. Joshi (Dover Publications) features nineteen stories originally published between 1830 and 1922.

Murder Mayhem Short Stories (no editor credited, Flame Tree Publishing) presents a generous helping of forty-five stories (eight originals). The reprints include stories by Doyle, Hodgson, Poe, Bierce, Chesterton, Dickens, and Nesbit. The best of the originals is by Dean H. Wild.

What the #@&%% is That? edited by John Joseph Adams and Douglas Cohen (Saga Press) is an entertaining all-original anthology of twenty stories, mostly about monsters. There's a gimmick—each story has to use the phrase of the title. Luckily the gimmick doesn't get in the way of the stories. The best of the darkest stories are by Alan Dean Foster, Christopher Golden, Isabel Yap, Terence Taylor, Seanan McGuire, John Langan, Laird Barron, and Maria Dahvana Headley. The Golden is reprinted herein.

Five Stories High edited by Jonathan Oliver (Solaris) is an anthology of five dark novellas, all related to one building that at various times has been an asylum or a private home, always haunted. The novellas are by Nina Allan, Tade Thompson, K. J. Parker, Robert Shearman, and Sarah Lotz.

I Can Taste the Blood edited by John F.D. Taff and Anthony Rivera (Grey Matter Press) contains five varied dark novellas based on the eponymous graffito found on a wall. The strongest is by Josh Malerman.

Now Playing in Theater B edited by Adrean Mesmer (A Murder of Storytellers) is an anthology of twenty-seven brief tales written in the style of B horror movies.

All That Darkness Allows: Thirteen Tales of Horror and Dread edited by Anton Umali, Maggie Adan, and Lio Mangubat (Summit Books) is an anthology of thirteen new dark stories by Filipino writers.

The Beauty of Death edited by Alessandro Manzetti (Independent Legions Publishing) is an un-themed anthology of forty-one stories, seven of them reprints. There's notable work by Mike Lester, Tim Waggoner, Daniel Braum, Erinn Kemper, Thersa Matsuura, Kathryn Ptacek, Daniele Bonfanti, and a collaboration by Bruce Boston and Marge Simon.

Cemetery Riots: A Collection of Dark Cautionary Tales edited by T. C. Bennett and Tracy L. Carbone (Awol From Elysium Press) is an anthology of twenty-one stories, four reprints. There are notable stories by Lisa Morton, Chet Williamson, Karen and Roxanne E. Dent, and Dennis Etchison.

Into Painfreak edited by Gerard Houarner (Necro Publications) is an original anthology inspired by a story written by Houarner twenty years ago about an international club dedicated to fulfilling people's deepest sexual needs and appetites. Pain as entertainment. Sexual horror to the extreme. While some of the stories are merely tableaux of gore lacking much plot, there are some notable stories by Edward Lee, Lucy Taylor, Colleen Wanglund, Chesya Burke, Jeffrey Thomas, and a poem by Charlee Jacob and Linda Addison. *Year's Best Hardcore Horror Volume 1* edited by Randy Chandler and Cheryl Mullenax (Comet Press) collects nineteen stories of extreme horror, originally published in 2015, many featuring graphic violence and gore during torture and mutilation. *The Best Horror of the Year Volume Eight* edited by Ellen Datlow (Night Shade Books) has twenty stories with a list of Honorable Mentions and an extensive summary of the year in horror. *The Year's Best Dark Fantasy & Horror 2016* edited by Paula Guran (Prime Books) has thirty stories originally published in 2015, plus a list of Honorable Mentions and a summary of the year. Three stories overlapped with my own *Best Horror of the Year Volume Eight. Year's Best Weird Fiction Volume Three* edited by Simon Strantzas and series editor Michael Kelly (Undertow Publications) reprints nineteen stories published in 2015. Some are dark, some are not. Only one story overlaps with my anthology, and only one with Guran's. *Best New Horror #27* edited by Stephen Jones (PS Publishing) has seventeen stories, with two overlapping with my anthology and two overlapping with Guran's.

Mixed-genre Anthologies

New Orleans Noir: The Classics edited by Julie Smith (Akashic) contains eighteen reprints, with the authors ranging from Tennessee Williams, O. Henry, and Eudora Welty to Poppy Z. Brite, James Lee Burke, and Nevada Barr. *Clockwork Phoenix 5* edited by Mike Allen (Mythic Delirium Books) is a crowd-funded, un-themed anthology of twenty stories, mostly sf and fantasy. There are a few notable darker stories by A. C. Wise, Barbara Krasnoff, and Sonya Taaffe. *Dead Letters: An Anthology of the Undelivered, the Missing, the Returned . . .* edited by Conrad Williams (Titan Books) is built around an intriguing idea. Each contributor was sent something in the mail and was asked to write about it. So we have seventeen stories of fantasy, science fiction, or horror. The best dark stories are by Adam L. G. Nevill, Kirsten Kaschock, Ramsey Campbell, Steven Hall, Christopher Fowler,

Angela Slatter, Lisa Tuttle, Nicholas Royle, and Joanne Harris. The Nevill is reprinted herein. *The Dragons of the Night* edited by Nick Gevers (PS Publishing) is an un-themed anthology of twenty-three mostly new stories of fantasy, dark fantasy, and a bit of horror. The best dark stories are by Stephen Bacon, Scott Edelman, Robert Guffey, Cate Gardner, John Grant (two good ones), Andrew Hook, and Darrel Schweitzer. *In Sunlight or in Shadow: Stories Inspired by the Art of Edward Hopper* edited by Lawrence Block (Pegasus Books) has seventeen original stories by mostly crime and mystery writers—some are dark, with the best by Stephen King, Joyce Carol Oates, Kris Nelscott (a pseudonym for Kristine Kathryn Rusch), and Robert Olen Butler. *The Shadow over Portage and Main: Weird Fiction* edited by Keith Cadieux and Dustin Geeraert (Enfield & Wizenty) has fifteen weird and sometimes horrific stories inspired by Winnipeg. Unfortunately, one doesn't really get a feel for the capital of Canada. The strongest stories are by Zacharie Montreuil, Keith Cadieux, Richard Crow, and Brock Peters. *Clowns: The Unlikely Coulrophobia Remix* is a really good one-shot from Bernie Mojzes and A. C. Wise, the people who bring you the magazine *Unlikely Stories . . .* of twenty-two strange tales and interstitial bits for clown lovers—and haters—everywhere. Most are new, a few are reprinted from the webzine. *Grave Predictions: Tales of Mankind's Post-Apocalyptic, Dystopian and Disastrous Destiny* edited by Drew Ford (Dover Publications) is an anthology of sixteen science fiction (and sometimes horror) reprints by authors ranging historically from Eugene Mouton's "The End of the World," published in 1872, to Carmen Maria Machado's "Inventory," published in 2013. With an introduction by Harlan Ellison. *The Worlds of Science Fiction, Fantasy and Horror Volume 1* edited by Robert Stephenson (Altair) is an all original anthology of eighteen stories from around the world (although most are from the US). There's one very good dark story by Sarah Totton. *Chiral Mad 3* edited by Michael Bailey (Dark Regions Press) is the third entry in the series. This volume is un-themed and a mixed bag featuring twenty poems and twenty-one stories. The strongest dark stories are by Richard Thomas, Michael Paul Anderson, Ramsey Campbell, Mort Castle, Scott Edelman, Erinn L. Kemper, Josh Malerman, Max Booth III, and a poem by Marge Simon. *The Starlit Wood: New Fairy Tales* edited by Dominik Parisien and Navah Wolfe (Saga Press) presents eighteen retold fairy tales, fantasy and dark fantasy. There are notable dark stories by Seanan McGuire, Stephen

Graham Jones, Margo Lanagan, and Jeffrey Ford. *In Your Face* edited by Tehani Wessely (Fablecroft Publishing) features eighteen original and four reprinted science fiction stories intended to be provocative. Some are, but a few are retreads of themes considered provocative thirty years ago. The best of the stories evoking horror are by Craig Cormick, Claire McKenna, Jason Nahrung, Cat Sparks, and Kaaron Warren. *The Valancourt Book of Horror Stories Volume One* edited by James D. Jenkins and Ryan Cagle (Valancourt Books) features fifteen strange and sometimes horrific tales chosen from the publisher's catalog of classic collections, which span two hundred years, plus two new stories. *Out of Tune Book 2* edited by Jonathan Maberry (JournalStone) presents fifteen original dark fantasy and horror stories based on traditional folk songs and murder ballads. The strongest are by James A. Moore, Rachel Caine, Dan Abnett, Laura Anne Gilman, and Nik Vincent-Abnett. *Something Remains: Joel Lane and Friends* edited by Peter Coleborn and Pauline E. Dungate (The Alchemy Press) is an anthology tribute to the late British writer Joel Lane. The stories and poems within were all inspired by fragmentary notes Joel left behind when he died unexpectedly in 2013. More than thirty writers took these notes and spun them into a worthy tribute. Some notable dark stories are by Steve Savile, Terry Grimwood, Chris Morgan, and John Llewellyn Probert. *The Madness of Dr. Caligari* edited by Joseph S. Pulver, Sr. (Fedogan & Bremer) features twenty-two original stories of weird and dark fiction inspired by the 1920 expressionistic classic movie, *The Cabinet of Dr. Caligari*. There are notable stories by Orrin Grey, Gemma Files, John Langan, Michael Cisco, Richard Gavin, Robert Levy, Maura McHugh, Damien Angelica Walters, David Nickle, and Paul Tremblay. *Asian Monsters* edited by Margrét Helgadóttir (Fox Spirit) follows the 2015 anthology *African Monsters*. This one features twelve stories and illustrations plus two illustrated texts. All but four appear in English for the first time. The best of the new stories are by Eve Shi, Eliza Chan, and Yukimi Ogawa. *The End: The Extinction Event* edited by Anne C. Perry and Jared Shurin (Jurassic London) is a fitting farewell to the five-year run of this small press. It's a mix of reprints and new stories, and while none of the new stories are dark enough to be considered horror, there are reprints by Robert W. Chambers, Mary Wilkins Freeman, and contemporary writer Sophia McDougall. Nicely illustrated by an array of fine artists. *Ghost Highways* edited by Trevor Denyer (Midnight Street Press) has fourteen stories (three reprints) on the theme of roads and highways (occasionally using a *very* broad definition) and an introduction by Paul Finch. The best of the dark stories are by Ralph Robert Moore, David Surface, and Thana Niveau. *Uncertainties Volume I & II* edited by Brian J. Showers (The Swan River Press) are two beautifully produced volumes of deliciously strange tales focusing on the fragmenting of reality, which actually provides a broad range of dark fantasy and horror. The first volume of eleven stories has a foreword by John Connolly and notable dark fiction by Maura McHugh, Lynda E. Rucker, Sarah LeFanu, Martin Hayes, and John Reppion. The second volume is introduced by the editor and features fourteen stories. The most notable dark fiction in it is by Reggie Oliver, Peter Bell, R. B. Russell, Steve Duffy, Mat Joiner, Gary McMahon, and Adam Golaski. The McMahon and Duffy are reprinted herein. *Dreaming in the Dark* edited by Jack Dann (PS Australia) is an all-original anthology showcasing the variety of contemporary Australian science fiction, fantasy, and horror with twenty-one stores, following up the World Fantasy Award-winning anthology from 1998, *Dreaming Down-Under* co-edited by Dann and Janeen Webb. There are three notable dark stories by Richard Harland, Simon Brown, and Kirstyn McDermott. *A Midwinter's Entertainment* edited by Mark Beech (Egaeus Press) is a charming mix of twenty-one old and new tales and poems of dark fantasy and occasional horror. There's notable new horror by Tina Rath, Alison Littlewood, and Avalon Brantley. *Heroes of Red Hook* edited by Brian M. Sammons and Oscar Rios (Golden Goblin Press) is an anthology of eighteen cleverly entertaining Lovecraftian stories taking place during the jazz age. Although there's not much horror in the volume, the best of the darker tales are by Edward M. Erdelac, W. H. Pugmire, and William Meikle. Also from Golden Goblin Press is the very pulpy *Dread Shadows in Paradise* edited by Brian M. Sammons and Oscar Rios and consisting of nine stories taking place in the Caribbean. *The Ghosts & Scholars Book of Shadows 3* edited by Rosemary Pardoe (Sarob Press) has twelve stories intended to be sequels of a kind to classics by M. R. James. A fascinating project that when it works, works quite well, although some of stories suffer from a bit too much ambiguity. Each story stands on its own without having read the original. There are notable dark stories by Peter Bell, David S. Sutton, Mark Valentine, Steve Rasnic Tem, and John Howard. *Finnish Weird 3: Enter the Weird* edited by Toni Jerrman is a sampler of five Finnish sf/f, and dark fantasy stories. *New Worlds, Old Ways: Speculative Tales from the*

Caribbean edited by Karen Lord (Peekash Press/Akashic/Peepal Tree) has a good mix of eleven sf/f/dark fantasy and horror written by Caribbean writers and infused with the spirit of the land. *The Bestiary* edited by Ann VanderMeer (Centipede Press) is a gorgeous little hardcover book illustrated throughout by Ivica Stevanovic and with an introduction by Jeff VanderMeer. It's a fantastical bestiary of non-existent animals, with contributions by writers including Karen Lord, China Miéville, Rikki Ducornet, Stephen Graham Jones, Brian Evenson, Karen Tidbeck, and many others. Only a few of the entries are dark, but it's still a fun book (published late 2015). *Pagan Triptych* by Ron Weighell, John Howard, and Mark Valentine (Sarob Press) is a mini-anthology of three stories written in tribute to "The Ghost Man" by Algernon Blackwood. A wonderfully haunting book, with some words about each story by its author. *Iraq + 100: Stories from Another Iraq* edited by Hassan Blasim (Commapress) is an anthology of ten mixed-genre stories by Iraqis living in Iraq and those in diaspora, imagining what life in their country might be like in 2103, after a century of invasions by the US and Great Britain. *Nightscript II: An Anthology of Strange & Darksome Tales* edited by C. M. Muller (Chthonic Matter) is a nicely packaged all-original anthology of twenty-one weird tales, some of them quite dark. The strongest are by John Reppion, Charles Wilkinson, Gordon White, Matthew M. Bartlett, Kristi DeMeester, Malcolm Devlin, Ralph Robert Moore, Gwendolyn Kiste, and Eric Guignard.

COLLECTIONS

Shadow Games and Other Sinister Stories of Show Business by Ed Gorman (SST Publications) collects the 1993 novel *Shadow Games* along with four stories originally published between 1990 and 2007.

Furnace by Livia Llewellyn (Word Horde Press) is the author's second collection, featuring fourteen stories, one new. Llewellyn is in the forefront of contemporary writers excelling in the horror short form. Psychosexual, provocative, sharp, and complex.

Wrapped in Skin by Mark Morris (ChiZine Publications) is this British horror writer's third collection. It includes fourteen powerful stories, three new, one reprinted in an earlier volume of my *Best Horror of the Year*.

Interior Darkness by Peter Straub (Doubleday) is a compilation of sixteen stories and novellas published over twenty-five years and culled from Straub's three collections. Three of the stories and novellas are previously uncollected.

All the Dark, All the Time: The Complete Short Fiction of Brian Keene (CreateSpace) is the second volume in a series collecting all of the author's short fiction.

Malevolent Visitants by C.E. Ward (Sarob Press) is the author's fine third collection of ghost stories, containing eight tales, two new. The author admits to being strongly influenced by M. R. James and, truly, his work could be considered more traditional than modern in outlook and in tone—not a bad thing in this case. One is reprinted herein.

A Collapse of Horses by Brian Evenson (Coffee House Press) contains seventeen stories reprinted from a range of venues including *McSweeney's*, *Granta*, and *Conjunctions* to horror anthologies (including one of my own). One story first came out in 2016.

Zoopraxis by Richard Christian Matheson (Gauntlet Press) is a gorgeous looking new horror collection of primarily short-shorts by a writer known best for that form. Twelve of the twenty-two pieces are new, and although not all work, enough do to show off Matheson's talent. Illustrated and with jacket art by Harry O. Morris, interior design by Dara Hoffman-Fox.

Arkham Nights: Tales of Mythos Noir by Glynn Owen Barrass and Ron Shiflet (Celaeno Press) is a co-written collection of eight Lovecraftian hardboiled detective stories, all reprinted from various anthologies originally published by Rainfall Books.

Some Will Not Sleep: Selected Horrors by Adam L. G. Nevill (Ritual Limited) collects eleven early stories, originally published between 2002 and 2011. These have never been collected before. Several were chosen by me for the *Year's Best Fantasy and Horror* and *The Best Horror of the Year*.

Ragman & Other Family Curses by Rebecca Lloyd (Egaeus Press, Keynote Edition I) is a limited edition mini-hardcover collection of four impressive new novelettes. "Ragman" and "For Two Songs" are both disconcertingly horrific. The former is reprinted herein.

Sylvan Dread by Richard Gavin (Three Hands Press) is the author's fifth collection of uncanny weird and dark fiction. This excellent volume has twelve stories most originally published between 2009 and 2016. Two are new.

Phantasms: Twelve Eerie Tales by Peter Bell (Sarob Press) is an excellent selection of seven reprints and five new stories by a formidable writer of ghostly tales.

Rapture of the Deep and Other Lovecraftian Tales by Cody Goodfellow (Hippocampus Press) has twelve stories, ten reprints dating from 2005 and two of them new. Some are more obviously infused by Lovecraft than others, but Goodfellow makes each tale his own.

The Travelling Bag and Other Ghostly Tales by Susan Hill (Profile Books) is a strong mini-collection of four new creepy, well-told stories.

The Parts We Play by Stephen Volk (PS Publishing) reprints twelve strong horror stories published between 2006 and 2015. With an introduction by Nathan Ballingrud and story notes by the author.

The Doll-Master and Other Tales of Terror by Joyce Carol Oates (Mysterious Press) reprints six stories, three originally published in *Ellery Queen Mystery* magazine, and one (providing the title of the collection) which first appeared in my anthology *The Doll Collection*.

You Can Never Spit It All Out by Ralph Robert Moore (Createspace) is the author's fourth collection, this one containing ten novelettes, three of them new.

All That Withers by John Palisano (Cycatrix Press) is a debut collection of twenty-one stories, most first published between 2008 and 2015. Four are new, and a few were published in 2016. With a foreword by Lisa Morton and an afterword by Gene O'Neill.

And Death Shall Have No Dominion: A Tribute to Michael Shea edited by Linda Shea and S. T. Joshi (Hippocampus Press) is a moving posthumous volume of fiction and verse (with three previously unpublished stories from the early eighties) by the late, much missed, award-winning author. There are also reminiscences and testaments to Shea's influence by Laird Barron, Cody Goodfellow, W. H. Pugmire, Jessica Amanda Salmonson, and other writers and friends. With illustrations.

Winter Children and Other Chilling Tales by Angela Slatter (PS Publishing) features twelve stories, one new, by this prolific writer of fantasy, dark fantasy, and horror. With an introduction by Conrad Williams.

Lovecraft Alive!: A Collection of Lovecraftian Stories by John Shirley (Hippocampus Press) contains ten stories, one new. The reprints were originally published between 1993 and 2016, mostly in anthologies.

Splatterspunk: The Micah Hayes Stories by Edward Lee and John Pelan (Necro Publications) includes five "humorously disgusting, erotic horror stories" about a sexually over-endowed police deputy. In perfect, bad taste.

The Devil Will Come by Justin Gustainis (Edge) has twenty-two stories about evil, three original to the collection.

Darkness, My Old Friend by John Pelan (Fedogan & Bremer) is a collection of eighteen pulp stories, two new. It includes all of the author's non-collaborative short stories from 1998. With an introduction by Ramsey Campbell and cover and interior art by Allen Koszowski.

Lethal Birds by Gene O'Neil (Omnium Gatherum) collects five stories and novellas focusing on birds. With story notes by the author and an introduction by Eric Guignard.

Earth-Bound and Other Supernatural Tales by Dorothy Macardle (The Swan River Press) is a beautifully produced little hardcover reissue of nine stories originally published in 1924. Four additional stories are included in this new edition. They were written by the author while she was a political prisoner in Dublin, Ireland.

Swift to Chase by Laird Barron (JournalStone) is the author's fourth collection, featuring twelve stories and novellas, one new. Barron's short fiction ranges from horror and sword and sorcery to noir and dystopic, never moving too far from the dark, dark core he writes about so well.

The Monster, the Bad and the Ugly by Alessandro Manzetti and Paolo Di Orazio (Kipple) is a collection of twenty grotesque, supernatural western stories, tenuously interconnected, several solo, some collaborations. These two Italian writers create some impressive work.

13: A Collection of Horror and Weird Fiction by Michael Boatman (A Mystique Press Production) is the second collection of stories by the author (who is also an actor), and most of the stories focus on different dark aspects of the "American Dream." Eleven of the stories are reprints from 2005–2013, and two are new.

Concentration by Jack Dann (PS Publishing) reprints seven harrowing horror stories taking place in Nazi Germany or emanating from the Holocaust. There is one new story. With an introduction by Marleen S. Barr.

Amaranthine and Other Stories by Erik Hofstatter (Createspace) has nine horror stories with notes on each by the author. Five of the stories are new.

Mixed-genre Collections

The Bone-God's Lair and Other Tales of the Famous and the Infamous by A. R. Morlan (Wildside Press) features twelve reprints by the late writer of sf/f/h. *Djsturbia* by David J. Schow (Subterranean Press) is the always entertaining author's eighth collection, containing thirteen pieces of fiction and twelve nonfiction pieces. Five of the short stories are new ones. Within you will find monsters, ghosts, and nasty humans, plus critical essays, interviews, and editorials. *Almost Insentient, Almost Divine* by D. P. Watt (Undertow Publications) contains sixteen odd stories, all weird, some dark. Five were published for the first time in 2016. *The Night Marchers and Other Strange Tales* by Daniel Braum (Grey Matter Press) is an impressive debut collection of twelve dark and weird tales, three new. *A Long December* by Richard Chizmar (Subterranean Press) is a thirty-five story retrospective of almost thirty years of Chizmar's short dark fiction, much of it crime/psychological rather than supernatural. There are four new stories and one dynamite new novella. The book includes author notes on each story. Chizmar is also publisher of the long running *Cemetery Dance* magazine and press. *Greener Pastures* by Michael Wehunt (Shock Totem Publications) is a debut collection of eleven weird, often dark stories by a promising new voice. Five were first published in 2016. *You'll Know When You Get There* by Lynda E. Rucker (The Swan River Press), the author's second collection, is mostly concerned with haunted houses. Of the nine unsettling stories, two appear for the first time. With an introduction by Lisa Tuttle. *The Unheimlich Manoeuver* by Tracy Fahey (Boo Books) is a debut collection of fourteen uncanny stories, half of them new. *Tough Guys* by Adrian Cole (Parallel Universe Publications) has three new novellas and a short story on dark themes. *Echoes of Darkness* by Rob Smales (Books and Boos Press) has thirteen horror stories, six of them new. *A Feast of Sorrows* by Angela Slatter (Prime Books) is the Australian author's first collection published in the US. Of the fourteen dark tales, two are new and one of those is a novella. *A Haunting in Germany and Other Stories* by Darren Speegle (PS Publishing) contains six new stories and novellas, a few with the same protagonist. Literate and haunting, but not all that dark. *Dead on the Bones: Pulp on Fire* by Joe R. Lansdale (Subterranean Press) collects eight stories he wrote in tribute to the pulp tales he loved as a youth.

Illustrated throughout by Timothy Truman. *The Lure of Devouring Light* by Michael Griffin (Word Horde Press) is a very impressive debut collection of weird, surreal dark fantasy and horror. It includes six reprints, four new stories, and one new novella. With an introduction by John Langan. *Out of the Dark: A Storybook of Horrors* by Steve Rasnic Tem (Centipede Press) features around seventy of the author's previously uncollected stories. The book also included five new stories. *Green Thoughts and Other Stories* by John Collier (1901–1980, Tartarus Press) collects twenty-six stories in a limited hardcover edition. *The Felicity of Epigones* by Derek John (Egaeus Press, Keynote Edition II) is a limited edition mini-hardcover collection of six tales of decadence and the supernatural, one new. With seven illustrations by Hans Rigo Kluger. *Meet Me in the Middle of the Air* by Eric Schaller (Undertow Publications) is a debut collection, with nineteen stories of fantasy, dark fantasy, and horror originally published since 1995, with a few new stories. One story in the collection was reprinted in *The Year's Best Fantasy and Horror: Sixteenth Annual Collection*. *Singing with All My Skin & Bone* by Sunny Moraine (Undertow Publications) is the mixed-genre debut collection of nineteen stories, published since 2011, two new. *The Spider Tapestries: Seven Strange Stories* by Mike Allen (Mythic Delirium Books) is the editor/publisher's second collection of fiction. Six stories were originally published between 1999–2015, and one is new. *Death After Death* by Edmund Glasby (Shadow Publishing) has eleven supernatural stories inspired by the pulps. Eight appear for the first time. *Brutal Pantomimes* by Rhys Hughes (Egaeus Press) is another, wonderfully quirky collection of ten very weird (sometimes dark) tales by a master of them. Seven of the stories are new, and the book itself is a beautiful hardcover, lovingly produced with spot illustrations. *American Nocturne* by Hank Schwaeble (Cohesion Press) is the author's first collection, with twelve dark fantasy and horror stories, seven published between 2007 and 2015. Five new. With an introduction by Jonathan Maberry. *The Hidden Back Room* by Jason A. Wyckoff (Tartarus Press) is the second collection of weird, and sometimes dark tales by the author. It has fourteen stories, ten of them published for the first time. *The Winter Hunt and Other Stories* by Steve Lockley and Paul Lewis (Parallel Universe Publications) contains fifteen dark fantasy stories, six of them new. *Seven Sins* by Karen Runge (Concord Free Press) is a debut collection with seven mixed-genre stories, four of them new. *Haunted Graves* by Ezeiyoke

Chukwunongo (Parallel Universe Publications) contains eight stories of sf/f/h by a Ghanaian writer who uses the folklore of his country prominently. Four stories are new. *Fables and Fabrications* by Jan Edwards (Penkhull Press) features fourteen dark fantasy and horror tales and a handful of haikus. The stories are reprints; the haikus are new. *The Secret of Ventriloquism* by Jon Padgett (Dunhams Manor Press) nicely combines weird fiction with horror in eight stories, two new. *First Communions* by Geoffrey Girard (Apex Publications) collects fifteen dark fantasy and horror reprints and one original tale. *What Is Not Yours Is Not Yours* by Helen Oyeyemi (Riverhead Books) is the first collection by the acclaimed author of *White is for Witching* and *Mr. Fox*. It contains nine stories (several new) revolving around keys, literal and figurative. *Tribulations* by Richard Thomas (Crystal Lake Publishing) is the author's third collection of sf, fantasy, dark fantasy, and horror. It includes twenty-five reprints originally published in a variety of magazines and anthologies. *The Girl with the Peacock Harp* by Michael Eisele (Tartarus Press) is an impressive debut collection of fourteen weird stories and one poem, all published for the first time. *A Natural History of Hell* by Jeffrey Ford (Small Beer Press) is the author's fifth collection. He's one of the best writers of short sf/f/h short fiction today. I'm a huge fan of Ford's work, which will be obvious to anyone who checks out the copyright page. Although he only occasionally writes horror, his dark fiction—always strange, always intriguing—might very well be of interest to horror readers. One of the thirteen stories in the collection is new. *Creeping Waves: Broadcasts and Blasphemies* by Matthew M. Bartlett (Muzzleland Press) is a novel of interconnected stories about Leeds, Massachusetts, and its inhabitants. With an introduction by Nathan Ballingrud. *Black Propaganda* by Paul St. John Mackintosh (H. Harkson Productions) is a debut collection of weird and dark fiction with thirteen stories, all but three new. *A Twist in the Eye* by Charles Wilkinson (Egaeus Press) has sixteen weird tales originally published in a variety of anthologies and magazines specializing in the weird. Some of the stories are dark, one is new. With an introduction by Mark Samuels. *The Kissing Booth Girl and Other Stories* by A. C. Wise (Lethe Press) is the author's second collection, with fourteen stories of fantasy, dark fantasy, and horror. Four of the stories are new. *Five Feathered Tales* by Alison Littlewood and illustrated by Daniele Serra (SST Publications) is a lovely hardcover package of four new stories and one reprint. However, the only horror story is the reprint, "Black

Feathers." *Bonsai Babies* by Mary Turzillo (Omnium Gatherum) contains twenty-three science fiction, fantasy, and horror stories, several of them new. *Tough Guys* by Adrian Cole (Parallel Universe Publications) presents three novellas, and one short story, all previously unpublished. Cole only occasionally writes horror but I picked one for reprint in my *Year's Best Fantasy and Horror: Fourth Annual Collection*. *Damage* by Rosalie Park (PS Publishing) has twenty stories, some dark, many mainstream or fantasy. Six are new. *When the World Wounds* by Kiini Ibura Salaam (Third Man Books) is the author's second collection (her first, *Ancient, Ancient*, won the James Tiptree Jr. Award). This one features five stories and one novella, all but one new.

POETRY JOURNALS, WEBZINES, ANTHOLOGIES, AND COLLECTIONS.

Underwater Fistfight by Matt Betts (Raw Dog Screaming Press) collects more than sixty pieces, more vignette-like than poetry, more whimsical than dark. *What I'm Afraid to Show You* by Michael Tugendhat (Five Oaks Press) features twenty-four dark poems. *Verses from a Deeply Darkened Mind* by Mary Genevieve Fortier (JWK Fiction) is a prolific poet whose work has been published in a variety of magazines and anthologies. More than sixty are collected in this volume. *The Seven Yards of Sorrow* by David E. Cowen (Weasel Press) collects thirty-seven poems about death, all centered around the city of Galveston, Texas. *Sacrificial Nights* by Bruce Boston and Alessandro Manzetti (Collana Fuori) is a strong, mostly new collection of poetry and some prose in collaboration by Boston and Manzetti and occasionally singly. *Brothel* by Stephanie M. Wytovich (Raw Dog Screaming Press) contains almost two hundred brief poems about sexuality. Interesting, but only a few could be characterized as horror. *Field Guide to the End of the World* by Jeannine Hall Gailey (Moon City Press), the poet's fifth collection, is filled with some wonderful dark poems with sf themes and about fairy tales, werewolves, vampires, and witches. *Corona Obscura: Sonets Dark and Elemental* by Michael R. Collings (Createspace) is a strong dark collection of forty-nine sonnets, twenty-three of them new. With an introduction by Linda D. Addison and an afterword by Michaelbrent Collings. Collings also published *Dark Designs: Forms and Fantasies: Speculative Poetry* (Createspace) covering ninety modes of poetry in 175 poems. *In Favor of Pain* by Angela Yuriko Smith (Createspace) presents twenty-seven short, dark poems, most published for the first time. *Poems of My Night* by Cynthia Pelayo (Raw Dog Screaming Press) is a masterful collection of all new poetry written in response to the work of Jorge Luis Borges. *Rhysling Anthology 2016: The Best Science Fiction, Fantasy, and Horror Poetry of 2015* selected by the Science Fiction Poetry Association edited by Charles Christian (Science Fiction Poetry Association), is used by members to vote for the best short poem and the best long poem of the year. The volume includes seventy-three short poems and forty-four long poems originally published in 2015. *The Horror Writers Association Presents Poetry Showcase Volume III* edited by David E. Cowen (HWA) presents more than fifty new pieces of poetry chosen from HWA members in a juried competition in celebration of National Poetry Month (the first two volumes were open). *Spectral Realms* edited by S. T. Joshi is an important showcase specializing in weird and dark poetry. Two issues came out in 2016. In addition to original poems, there's a section with classic reprints and a review column. There were notable poems by G.O. Clark, Jeff Burnett, Jennifer Ruth Jackson, Mary Krawczak Wilson, John J. Mundy, D.L. Myers, Darrell Schweitzer, Scott Thomas, K.A. Opperman, and W. H. Pugmire. *Star*Line* is the official newsletter of the Science Fiction Poetry Association. The journals regularly publish members' poetry. Three issues came out in 2016.

CHAPBOOKS/NOVELLAS

The Tor.com novella program started publishing science fiction, fantasy, and horror in 2015, but the first actual horror novella was *The Ballad of Black Tom* by Victor LaValle (acquired and edited by me). The author, who in his dedication relays his conflicted feelings about Lovecraft, reimagines "The Horror at Red Hook" with a young African American protagonist. Charles Thomas Tester is hired to deliver an occult book to an elderly woman in Queens, New York. By doing so he becomes involved in arcane, mythos-inspired doings. Other dark novellas published under the Tor.com novella imprint were by Cassandra Khaw, Seanan McGuire, and Kij

Johnson. The LaValle, McGuire, and Johnson were nominated for the Hugo Award. Dim Shores is publishing a chapbook line, with each story illustrated by a different artist. During 2016, there were chapbooks by Cody Goodfellow (art by James Quigley), S. P. Miskowski (art by Nick Gucker), and Kristi DeMeester (art by Natalia Drepina). Borderlands Press continued its "Little Book" program with *A Little Ochre Book of Occult Stories* by Karl Edward Wagner and *A Little Blue Book of Bibliomancy* by Chet Williamson. The Wagner, edited by Stephen Jones, is very personal. Jones introduces the book with a lovely letter to his absent friend and includes poetry, stories, and one previously unpublished article about H. P. Lovecraft. The Williamson is all nonfiction except for one original story. *Shadow Moths* by Cate Gardner (Frightful Horrors) is a two-story chapbook, with two strong horror stories, each very different from the other. With an introduction by Simon Bestwick. Nicholas Royle's Nightjar Press brought out four new story chapbooks in 2016: *Rounds* by Wyl Menmuir, *Jackdaws* by Neil Campbell, *The Numbers* by Christopher Burns, and *Fury* by DB Waters (the latter two reprinted herein). White Noise Press published the Victorian tale "The Winter Tree" by Alison Littlewood as a chapbook. Earthling Publications has been publishing a series of Halloween specials for a number of years now. Briton Sarah Pinborough's short novel *They Say a Girl Died Here Once* is the twelfth. It's about a teenage girl and her family moving to a new town, after a traumatic event. *Man with No Name* by Laird Barron (JournalStone) has two reprints, a supernatural crime novella which gives the chapbook its title, and a story originally published in *The Mad Scientist's Guide to World Domination*. *The Grieving Stones* by Gary McMahon (Horrific Tales Publishing) is a novella about a grief therapy group that, during a special weekend meeting, stirs up something ancient. With an introduction by Nathan Ballingrud. *Muscadines* by S. P. Miskowski (Dunhams Manor Press) is a nasty little brew about a monstrously dysfunctional family with a secret recipe for wine. *Bloody Hull* is a chapbook of three winning entries to the Dead Pretty City writing competition inspired by British crime writer David Mark's novels taking place in Hull. Each story uses the phrase "dead pretty." *The Wrath of Concrete and Steel* by John Claude Smith (Dunhams Manor Press) is a chapbook of three weird and dark tales set in cities.

NONFICTION

Hobgoblin Apollo: A Life of My Own, The Autobiography of Donald Sidney-Fryer (Hippocampus Press) covers the poet and author's life and relationships and includes almost fifty poems, most previously unpublished. *Cult Cinema: The Arrow Video Companion* edited by Anthony Nield (Arrow Films) is an illustrated book of thirty essays, more than half on horror with five chapters encompassing key cult movies, directors, actors, and an historical overview of the history of cult film. *The Kaiju Film: A Critical Study of Cinema's Biggest Monsters* by Jason Barr (McFarland) is a critical examination of Kaiju considering the entirety of the genre—the major franchises, along with lesser-known films. The author discusses how Kaiju has crossed cultures from its original folkloric inspirations in both the US and Japan and how the genre continues to reflect national values to audiences. *Sudden Storm: A Wendigo Reader* curated by Larry Fessenden contains thirteen essays exploring Wendigo mythology from a cryptozoological point of view. Included is full-color artwork by prominent illustrators.

   H. P. Lovecraft: Letters to J. Vernon Shea, Carl F. Strauch, and Lee McBride White edited by S. T. Joshi and David E. Schultz (Hippocampus Press) presents letters covering a wide range of subjects, from movies, books, and stories to Lovecraft's racism and anti-Semitism. *The Age of Lovecraft* edited by Carl H. Sederholm and Jeffrey A. Weinstock (University of Minnesota Press) includes eleven critical essays including work by scholars such as Gothic expert David Punter, historian W. Scott Poole, musicologist Isabella van Elferen, and philosopher of the posthuman Patricia MacCormack. Also with a foreword by Ramsey Campbell. *A Strange Little Place: The Hauntings and Unexplained Events of One Small Town* by Brennan Storr (Llewellyn Publications) is about the author's family's hometown in British Columbia, Canada. *Haunted Bridges* by Rich Newman (Llewellyn Publications) showcases over three hundred bridges in the United States that are known for strange happenings occurring on or near them. *Italian Horror Cinema* edited by Stefano Baschiera and Russ Hunter (Edinburgh University Press) covers the heyday of Giallo between 1950s and 1980s. *In the Mountains of Madness: The Life and Extraordinary Afterlife of H. P. Lovecraft* by W. Scott Poole (Soft Skull) acts as a biography of

Lovecraft and a discussion of his place in history and culture. *Scored to Death: Conversations with Some of Horror's Greatest Composers* by J. Blake Fichera (Silman-James Press) is a compilation of interviews with composers John Carpenter, Fabio Frizzi, Claudio Simonetti, Jeff Grace, Charles Bernstein, members of the band Goblin (which scored for Dario Argenti), and others. The interviews include the composers' musical background, the process of scoring film, and the relationship between the composers and directors. *Beware the Moon: The Story of An American Werewolf in London* by Paul Davis (Cult Screenings) is a textual adaptation of the author's 98-minute documentary on the making and legacy of the movie. Interviews galore and over 300 photographs throughout. *Guillermo Del Toro: At Home with His Monsters: Inside His Films, Notebooks, and Collections* by Roger Clark, Guy Davis, and Paul Koudounaris (Insight Editions) is a companion volume to a traveling exhibition of Del Toro's work and collections. *Euro Gothic: Classics of Continental Horror Cinema* by Jonathan Rigby (Signum) analyzes more than one hundred key films, starting in the aftermath of World War I and winding up with the video revolution of the early 1980s. *The Gothic Works of Peter Straub* by John C. Tibbets (McFarland) is the first biographical/critical work on Peter Straub since William Sheehan's 2000 volume *At the Foot of the Story Tree: An Inquiry into the Fiction of Peter Straub*. With a foreword by Gary K. Wolfe. *The Monster Book: Creatures, Beasts and Fiends of Nature* by Nick Redfern (Visible Ink) is an almost four-hundred-page compendium of monsters, presented in sections such as "Unearthly Cats, Deadly Dogs, Werewolves," "Nature Gone Mad," "Reptilians, Amphibians, Dinosaurs, and Worms," "Flying Beings," and several others. It presents monsters from around the world and includes some first-hand reports of monster sightings. A fun book to dip into. *Ghostland: An American History of Haunted Places* by Colin Dickey (Viking) is a rarity: a fascinating, well-written, remarkably uncheesy book of reported hauntings around the country. *Something in the Blood: The Untold Story of the Man Who Wrote Dracula* (Liveright Publishing Corporation) is a hefty biography of the Irishman who created a monster for the ages (possibly) based on his own anxieties and fears. It includes new material such as some of his sexually ambiguous poetry and letters to Walt Whitman, printed in full for the first time—one letter that he waited four years to send. *Guillermo del Toro's The Devil's Backbone and Pan's Labyrinth: Studies in the Horror Film* edited by Danel Olson (Centipede Press) is the study of these two movies in relation to each other, with essays, interviews with those involved in making each film, photographs, and concept drawings. With a preface by Ivana Baquero (Ofelia in *Pan's Labyrinth*), introduction by del Toro, and an afterword by Fernando Tielve (Carlos in *The Devil's Backbone*). *Shirley Jackson: A Rather Haunted Life* by Ruth Franklin (Liveright Publishing Corporation) is only the second biography of Jackson. The first, *Private Demons* by Judy Oppenheimer, was published in 1989. This new one adds to our knowledge of Jackson with newly found correspondence and interviews. It contextualizes her life within the time she lived and her work firmly within the gothic tradition.

ART BOOKS AND ODDS AND ENDS

The Damage Museum by Vincent Sammy (SST Publications) is the first book of this South African artist's art, which has appeared in publications such as *Black Static, Interzone, Something Wicked,* and on book covers during the past ten years. He specializes in beautiful dark and often macabre art in both color and black and white.

In Fairyland: The World of Tessa Farmer edited by Catriona McAra (Strange Attractor Press) is a book about the artist and her work, which incorporates various (dead) insects as participants in her brilliant, often grotesque art. I first came across her insect tableaux at a special exhibit of her work at the Brighton World Fantasy Convention, and they're astonishing. The critical essays connecting her vision to Arthur Machen and fairy art are okay, but the black and white and sixteen color photographs of her work are what's important. The only thing missing is an interview with the artist.

The Anatomical Venus: Wax, God, Death & the Ecstatic by Joanna Ebenstein (The Morbid Anatomy Museum/Dap) is a detailed investigation of wax female figures used for teaching anatomy, particularly the marvelous life-sized wax figure dubbed the Anatomical Venus, created 1780–1782 by Italian sculptor Clemente Susini. She was given human hair and glass eyes and created so as to avoid regular dissection of dead bodies, with seven anatomically correct layers, including a fetus curled in her womb. There are several models made in late eighteenth century Florence that can still be found in medical museums. The book intersperses plentiful illustrations with the history of these renderings of "slashed" female anatomy. Beautiful and disturbing.

Black Dog: The Dreams of Paul Nash by the great Dave McKean (Dark Horse Books) is a gorgeous (of course) rendition of the life of surrealist painter Paul Nash, who was traumatized by his time of fighting during WWI and made art out of those experiences.

Sirenia Digest has been published by Caitlín R. Kiernan for several years and might be considered an early iteration of Patreon. Sponsors pay a set amount for this monthly digest of excerpts, new stories, vignettes, and other bits springing from the mind of this excellent writer. Subscribe and enjoy.

Atlas Obscura: An Explorer's Guide to the World's Hidden Wonders by Joshua Foer, Dylan Thuras & Ella Morton (Workman) is a beautifully rendered travel guide to some of the most interesting places on Earth. It includes (with pictures) natural and architectural wonders and events. This is a book to cherish and dip into whenever you feel like escaping out of everyday life.

Animal Kingdom: Stereoscopic Images of Natural History by Jim Naughton (Prestel) is a beautiful book of animal specimens photographed by Naughton from two different angles, which when looked at through the viewer included with the book, appear as 3-D. Included is a brief history of stereoscopy (the original word for 3-D viewing) and commentary about many of the images. The book is divided into five chapters: sea creatures, reptiles, birds, mammals, and primates.

NESTERS

SIOBHAN CARROLL

They killed the last calf that morning. Ma wanted to hold off, give the poor thing a chance, but Pa said it were cruel to let a body live like that. He cracked the hammer on its head—a sick, sad sound. Later he slit the calf open and showed Sally the animal's stomach, choked with dust. "Suffocated from the inside," he said.

Sally cried, or would have cried, but her face was too caked with dirt. The Vaseline in her nostrils couldn't keep it out. She wondered how much dirt was in her stomach and whether her body was already full of it, like the calf, her tears and blood just rivers of dust. But when she asked, Ma said, "Jaisus, quit nattering and help the bairn." So Sally did, even though her baby brother was curled up like the calf had been, under a skin of dust that never went away no matter how they cleaned.

Sally followed Ma round the dugout, stuffing rags into the cracks where the dust had trickled through. Alice toddled after her. Ben watched from the bed, his feverish eyes glistening. At fourteen, he was taller than Sally and better at reaching the upper cracks. But what could be done? The dust-lung had him. If Ben were to move, Ma said it would be to her sister's place in Topeka, away from the land that was killing him. Better still, Ma said, would be to head out to California, where there was still work to be had.

But Pa had heard about the cities. Many who went there came home poorer than before. They told tales of Hoover camps, the shame of being spat on by city-dwellers. At least here they suffered together. At least here they had the land.

To lose your land was to lose yourself, her father had warned her and Ben. This was in the early years, when folks still thought next year would bring the rains back.

"This here's the first thing our family's ever owned in this country," he'd said, showing Sally the dark soil between his fingers. "Mackay land." His eyes had shone with the wonder of it.

Now the earth was hard and brown and dusters turned the sky the same color, choking and fierce. "Still," said Pa, "we have the land. We lost it once to the English. We won't lose it to the wind."

◄◦►

Two strangers were at the gate. Sally could see right off they weren't farmers. Too pale. Too well-fed.

The taller man leaned forward, dangling his hands into the yard in a way Sally didn't like. "Your father at home, sweetheart?"

Sally looked the stranger up and down, the starving chickens pecking at her feet. "You from Washington?" There was talk of Mr. Roosevelt sending folk to tell the Nesters how to run their farms. This man, with his clean suit, seemed like he could be one of them.

A glance from the leaning man to his companion. "What d'ya think, Bill? Are we from Washington?"

The older man looked like a schoolteacher, one of the impatient ones who rapped kids' knuckles. "We're on official business," he said. "We're looking for the man of the house."

Sally knew Ma would scold her if she let a government man pass by, even rude ones. There might be a dime in it, and a dime could buy bread.

"I'll fetch him then," she said. "Best come out of the blow."

At the dugout's entrance, Ma's face already showed the strain of a smile. Sally knew Ma was thinking of rusted cans of water instead of tea, the assistance bread gone hard by week's end. At least they had some milk to offer, thanks to the dead calf. Still, it was as much her mother's smile as the need to fetch her father that made her run so quickly.

She found Pa fixing up the old John Deere D, trying to get work done while the air was clear.

"Government men come."

Pa nodded and wiped his hands, reluctant to leave a task half-done. "You take over here."

Sally took Pa's place as he strode off. She checked the front tires for cuts, wiping off a grease splatter with a gasoline-damped rag. Everything on the farm depended on the tractor. If it broke, they'd be beat.

Sally thought instead about the government men. Maybe they brought work with them. Maybe it'd be a good day after all.

◂◦▸

Stepping inside the dugout, Sally realized something was wrong. Ma stood stiffly in a corner. Pa sat beside the older man, his shoulders squared. The younger government man looked at Sally as she entered, then back at Pa.

The older man spoke, an edge to his voice. "Did no one go out to the farm to look for him?"

Pa's face was closed. He shook his head.

"Why not?"

Pa glanced at Ma, who folded her arms tightly against her chest. Reluctantly, Pa said, "They say the Dubort place's cursed." Pa shrugged as if to remind them he didn't hold with superstitions.

The Dubort place! Sally watched the strangers with new interest. The abandoned farm was the only site for miles with greenery to spare. Tom Hatchett said if you passed too close to the Devil's Garden—what the kids called it—one of the monsters living there'd gobble you up. Tom Hatchett was a liar, but still.

The man flipped through his notebook. If he was trying to frighten Pa with that flapping paper, he didn't know nothing. "Stories of strange vegetation? Odd lights and noises? Animals disappearing? That kind of thing?"

Pa's gaze was stony. He shrugged again.

"And all this happened after the meteor fell?"

"I don't know nothing about no meteor," Pa said. "One of Dubort's fields caught fire. We went to fight it, like good neighbors. Some folk said a falling star started it. Don't know more than that."

"Good neighbors," the government man said. "But nobody went looking when Frank Dubort disappeared?"

Pa blinked. Looked away. "Place got a bad reputation," he said. "No one wanted to borrow trouble. It was a wrong thing," he admitted, quietly, to himself.

Rage blossomed in Sally. Couldn't these men see how tired Pa was? He had enough to deal with, without these men asking him to feel bad for a stranger, a weekend farmer who couldn't take the hard times.

But Sally remembered that day at Ted Howser's farm, the man scuttling out of the barn on his back, like an upside-down beetle. Mr. Howser had put his hand over his mouth. Sally's Pa had stared like he hoped what he saw wasn't true. Sally thought the scrabbler looked like Howser's neighbor, Mr. Dubort—or like some hobo wearing one of Mr. Dubort's famous blue-checked shirts, all stained and tore-up. But Pa stood in front of her, blocking her view.

Pa told her and Ben to go home. He'd stayed behind to talk to Mr. Howser about what needed to be done. What *had* they done? Pa had refused to speak of it. He'd said it was settled, and to ask no questions.

Dread crept through Sally. She wondered what had happened to bring these government men here.

"We'd like to go out there, Mr. Mackay," the government man said, "To have a look around. Your name was mentioned as one who could take us there."

Sally wanted to know who'd given them Pa's name. She suspected Pa did too. But the less said to these folk, the better.

"There's money in it." The younger man pronounced the words carefully, as though he knew the effect they'd have in this dusty, coughing dugout. "Fifteen dollars, for a guided trip, there and back." He smiled at their astonishment. "We're . . . scientific men, Mr. Mackay," he said reassuringly, "We need to see this site close up."

Sally thought the older man might be angry with his companion for offering money straight off, but he seemed to be taking Pa's measure.

"If we find Frank, that'll put this thing to rest." The young man added, slyly, "It's the right thing to do."

Pa's face was tight. His gaze slid over to Ma. But Ma didn't know what to do either, Sally saw. She was caught between fear and worry and the promise of fifteen dollars.

"Alright then," Pa said. "But you pay upfront."

The older man got up from the table. "Five now, the rest later."

"Ten." There was a determined glitter in Pa's eyes. The government man flicked a bill onto the table. Ten whole dollars.

"We appreciate your help." The younger man smirked, like he'd known how this was going to go all along.

Sally hated him, she decided. She hated them both. She itched to give the nearest one a kick on his shins as he passed. It was the sort of thing she'd have done last year, never mind the manners. But she thought of Ma and the remaining five dollars. She let the men go.

Pa glanced down at Sally as he put his hat on. "Take care of your Ma." He patted her head, messing up Sally's hair. Sally smoothed it back as she watched Pa leave.

It was a funny thing to say, she thought. Ma was the one who took care of everyone else. The strangeness of this kept her standing there, while the men got in the car and drove off.

◄◦►

The duster rolled in a few hours later. Sally crouched into the grating wind and kept one hand on the guide rope, the other over her eyes as she traced her path back from the chicken coop. She struggled along blindly, feeling her bare skin scraped raw. She tried not to think of Pa out in this duster, guiding strangers on someone else's land.

In the dugout, they huddled together with cloths over their faces. There was no point in burning the kerosene lamp. No light would get through. They sat silently, trying not to breathe in too much of the dust, while the wind raged outside.

The duster lasted the rest of the day. When its blackness cleared, the night was there to take over, and the cold. They lit the lamp and looked at each other, her and Ben and Alice and Ma.

Ma said, "Let's clean up," and so they did. Sally tried not to wonder about Pa. He'd have to see the government men back to town. He'd probably stayed there.

But in the morning, Pa still wasn't back. Sally forced the door open and trudged to the chicken coop to count the survivors. There were two dead, dust-choked. She took the bodies out, feeling the lightness of their scrawny bodies. They needed more food.

It was Sunday and Sunday meant church. Pa wouldn't miss church, Sally was sure. She put on her "nice" dress—still made out of feed sacks, but cleaner than the others—while Ma got Alice ready.

Ben's eyes opened when Ma put a hand on his forehead. "Keep an eye on the bairn. And if you see Pa, make sure you tell him to stay put till we get back." Ben closed his eyes. Sally wasn't sure if he'd heard them.

But Pa wasn't at church. Sally kept turning around, scanning the pews. Ma pinched her arm to make her stop, but Ma kept glancing backwards too, every time they had to stand up.

The service was one of the usual ones, about the end times and how the dusters were the Nesters' fault for ignoring the Lord's will. Inwardly Sally was having none of it. It was a pretty poor God who visited misery on folk for drinking too much and taking his name in vain now and then. Maybe it was true what the ranch hands said, that they'd done wrong by taking the grassland from the Injuns and turning it to the plow. But even so, where was the good in little kids dying? If that was God's will, then she hated him, Sally thought, and felt a flash of fear.

After the service Ma caught Ted Howser by the arm. "I need to talk to you about Pat."

Sally wanted to hear the rest of it, but Ma told her to mind Alice didn't hurt herself. Sure enough, Alice took a spill. The dust cushioned her so she wasn't even crying when she looked up. Well, that's one thing it's good for, Sally thought, offering the toddler her fingers to grab.

She looked back. Ma was at the center of a ring of old ranch hands and farmwives, their faces grave.

"Come on," she said, tugging at Alice's hand. "Back this way."

"Paddy's a good man and I'd walk to hell for him," Jake Hardy was saying, "but if the wind stirred something up, we'd best not get too close."

Someone else snorted. "Walk to hell but wouldn't go in it, would you?"

"Facts are," Mr. Howser said, "the Dubort place is off-limits. Pat knew that when he headed out there." He looked round the circle. "You saw what it did to Frank. We can't go there. Can't let anyone go there," he said, looking back at Sally's Ma. "Who knows where it'd end?"

"He's probably holed up at another farm," Dan Giss said. "Roads are tough. Duster's closed a lot of 'em. He's probably holed up with Schmitt, minding those damn fool government men."

Sally's Ma seemed to sway on her feet. Sally let go of Alice to run towards her.

Margie Fisher, the schoolteacher, reached Ma first. She put an arm around the younger woman.

"There now," she said, glaring at Ted Howser. "We need to organize a search party. Knock on every door. Chances are, Pat's not the only one who could use a hand."

Sally heard a wail behind her. She turned to see the abandoned Alice sitting in the dust, blood running down her forehead. Somehow the toddler had found the only uncovered rock in the yard and fallen smack into it. Of course she had. And it was Sally's fault for leaving her.

"Shush," Sally pleaded, stroking the toddler's sweat-damp hair. "It'll be okay." But it wouldn't be, Sally knew, the dread rising in her. It wouldn't be.

◄◦►

Ma and Mrs. Fisher would search along the road, Mr. Howser would take a horse up Fincher's lot. Jake and Dan would go to the Dubort place. Everyone was worried about this plan, but Jake and Dan swore they'd leave right quick if they felt they were stirring things up.

Stirring things up, Sally thought, remembering the giant vegetables Mr. Dubort had brought to town. Turnip skins so bright they hurt your eyes, apples that glistened like they'd been dipped in water, and huge! One turnip was as big as Ben's head—he'd put it on the table so Sally could measure before Pa had slapped them away.

"Don't you do that," Pa had said, angrier than Sally had ever seen him. "Don't you touch those things, no matter what."

Sure enough, when Mr. Dubort sliced the turnip open, dark gray powder crumbled out.

"Must be some kind of blight," Mr. Dubort had said, pushing his hat back on his head. He was a city man, unused to farming. "Have you seen anything like this before?"

The Nesters said nothing. Their silence hung around them like a sky empty of rain, waiting for the dust to roll through.

Now Sally walked behind Alice as the toddler clung to Mrs. Fisher's furniture. Mrs. Fisher had a proper house, with tablecloths and everything. Sally noted the dirty film on Mrs. Fisher's table with satisfaction. She reckoned it must take a lot of sweeping to get dust out of a place this size.

The tick-tocks of Mrs. Fisher's clock reverberated through the house. Each one felt like a burning pin pushed into Sally's flesh. Why couldn't someone else watch the babies? If Ben was here, she reckoned they'd let him go.

She imagined herself wandering across the dust-dunes, finding Pa in a place no one had thought to look. Not hurt, of course. Her mind shied away from that. No, Pa would be fine but helping one of the government men, who'd gotten his fool self hurt. The younger one, Sally decided, viciously. She imagined Pa's grin when she clambered up the dune that hid them from the road. "I knew I could trust you to figure it out," he'd say. And the government men would pay them thirty whole dollars for the trouble they'd caused. And—

There was a noise outside.

"Stay there," Sally told Alice. She didn't want to pull away the sheets the Fishers had nailed over the windows, so she headed to the door instead.

There was a scramble of people in the yard. Jake was trying to hold a flailing man by the shoulders. "Don't let him go!" Mr. Fisher, the mortician, grabbed the man's other arm.

It took Sally a moment to recognize the flailing figure, all covered in dust. It was the older government man. He lips were pulled back from his teeth, his eyes rolled to the sky. As Sally watched he arched his back and howled, a long hard sound that raised all the hairs on her scalp. A string of gibberish babbled out of him: *grah'n h'mglw'nafh fhthagn-ngah . . .*

She shut the door, closing out the sight. It was as though God had heard Sally's foolish dream of finding Pa and had sent the government man back to punish her vanity. *Please, please,* she thought frantically, hushing Alice, *please let them have found Pa, please let him be all right—*

When Ma came back her face was strange. "Make sure you thank Mrs. Fisher for letting you stay here."

Sally obediently repeated the words, even though Mrs. Fisher was standing right there. Ma and Mrs. Fisher stared at each other like they were having a silent conversation above Sally's head. Normally Sally would hate that. Now it made her more scared than ever, because something was really wrong if nobody was talking about Pa.

◦

Ma's silence carried them back to the dugout. It filled the air there when Ben tried to gasp out a question.

"Others are seeing to that," Ma said shortly. And, "Jaisus, get the broom, will you?"

Sally got the broom and swept the dust about the place, while Ben wheezed and the babies coughed and Ma tried not to cry. *If only the dust would leave the place, they'd be alright*, Sally thought wildly, knowing it wasn't true.

Next morning, Sally was up before cockcrow. Her head was buzzing as she cast the hard, dried-up corn into her bucket and went out to face the chickens.

"I'm going to school," she told Ma at the door. Ma hesitated, then nodded. Ma was always on at Sally and Ben to keep up their lessons. In truth, Sally doubted there'd be any kids in the school. The morning had that hard-light look to it that threatened dusters, and there was too much work to do just to get some food through the door.

But today Sally had other things on her mind. If there was a duster coming, she needed to move fast and early.

She packed her water and the scrap of hard-bread that Mam set aside for her. She'd also take the shovel from the back of the tumble-down barn, in case she needed to dig her way out. That's what Pa would do.

Ben watched her tie the strings up on the rucksack, his eyes angry. He knew what she was doing.

"Just . . . don't say nothing. Unless I'm not back by sundown," Sally whispered. Then she threw the rucksack on and left, before Ben could muster the air to call her back, before anyone changed her mind about what needed to be done.

◦

The sky above her was blue, blue, blue, dotted with the occasional cloud. No point trying the local road over to Dubort—that would be drifted over. She'd cut across land, avoiding the big drifts except when it came time to climb the fences.

It was hard going. Sally's feet sank into the sand, her boots filling with grit. *Mackay land,* she thought, *turned against us.* The spade was heavy on her shoulder.

About halfway to the Dubort place she started to feel she'd made a mistake. The sun was fully up now. In its glare she could see the green strip of land away in the distance. The Devil's Garden, some called it. It'd been so long since there'd been green in these parts, Sally couldn't tell if it was the drought or whether there was actually something wrong with the color.

The animal-sounds dropped away as she approached the Dubort place. You'd think the jackrabbits and birds would flock here, given that no one hunted at the farm. But the air out here was stiller than the desert.

Sally walked along the side of the giant dune that had piled up over Dubort's old fence. She saw the white bones of some animal poking through. Probably a starved cow, tangled in wire and Russian thistle. Beyond the bones was a place where the dune dipped a little. As good as any spot for a crossing, she thought, and waded up.

It was strange being surrounded by green again. Sally remembered the color from the old days, but here it was everywhere. Dubort's fruit trees had grown large and tangled. Between them, vines draped and alien flowers gaped at the sky. A nearby bush dangled huge, glossy fruit. They looked like they would quench the thirst that was beginning to rasp her throat. Sally looked away, remembering the powdery vegetables.

The lurid greenery stretched everywhere on the Dubort-side. There was nothing for it. "Pa!" she shouted. "Pa!"

Silence. Sally took a swig from her bottle and kept walking.

The Dubort house stood on the northern part of the property, close to Mr. Daverson's fence. Surely, if Pa was in trouble—if a duster was bearing down on them—that's where he'd head. For shelter. And he hadn't had the shovel that now ground into her skinny shoulder. They could be stuck in there, underneath the grit.

At a certain point the trees thinned and she saw a hard-pack section where nothing grew, a burned-looking hole at its center. She figured that must be where the rock had hit. There was something blue standing by the crater—a human color.

Sally didn't want to walk into the clearing—it seemed strange to her somehow—but she figured if she were looking for Pa, she had to check out every clue. So she walked quietly over to the blue thing. A couple cans of gasoline and a man's hat, filmed with dust.

Sally tested the weight on the gas cans. They were full. The young man had been wearing a hat.

A screeching sound jerked her head up. It was probably some kind of buzzard, she told herself, walking quickly back to the dune line. She had the uncomfortable feeling something was watching her, its gaze focused just between her shoulder blades. It was a relief when she left that clearing behind her.

She knew she should yell for Pa again, but after the screech she couldn't work up the nerve. Pa had to be at the house. The sooner she got there, the better everything would be.

When she finally reached Dubort's house, her stomach sank. It didn't look like a house at all these days—more like a sandy hill, with a strange gray vine growing up its side. As with the clearing, the forest that had claimed the rest of the property seemed to have left this part alone.

Sally circled the house, afraid of what she'd do if it was empty. She saw a dark square opening in the leeward wall. The black square of a window, or door. Someone had recently been inside.

Sally lowered the shovel. "Pa?" She tried the word out, scared of speaking too loud. "You there?" The air itself seemed to be listening to her.

Sally closed her eyes, thinking of Pa and his tobacco smell and his graceful fingers as he patched up a gunny sack. She had to see.

She walked slowly up to the dark square and peered inside.

◄○►

The first thing that hit Sally was the smell. It was horrible, and faintly familiar, as though she'd encountered it many years before. It was the smell of rot, the kind of thing you might find in a wet place, not here on the plains.

She stared hard at the darkness, trying to make it form shapes. She had matches in her pocket, swiped from the old kerosene lamp. She struck one, but a faint stir of wind guttered it out too quickly. She needed to do better than that.

She slung her leg over the windowsill, gulping what clean air she could. The wooden sill moved beneath her hands. *You're doing a dumb thing,* she thought, and slipped inside.

The ground was soft sand. Grimacing, she put her hand up against the wall. She'd follow the wall around, in the dark. Figure out how far she could go.

But she hadn't gone very far at all when she heard the breathing.

Sally froze. She wanted to believe she was imagining things. She held her breath, to prove it. A wheeze in. A wheeze out. Too regular to be the wind.

Fear pressed on her. She didn't want to call for her father. If he hadn't heard her earlier, he wouldn't hear her now. And if it was something else there breathing, she didn't want to know.

Don't try to solve all the problems at once, Pa always said. *Break them up. Deal with each one in order.*

So Sally groped her way back to the window, with its bright patch of light. She was glad, now, to see the lurid green outside. She fumbled the matches out, holding them in the light. Ten left. *I am going to do this,* she thought, *I am.*

She struck the match.

At first she could see nothing in the orange circle of light. She cupped the flame and extended her arms. There was one shadow that was stranger than all the others, taller than any man should be. Something was there.

Sally moved forward. She had to get the circle of light closer before the match went out. The soles of her feet crunched onto uneven sand piles, miniature dunes that hissed out of place as she stepped on them.

Yes, there was definitely something there, in the jumping flame. A line of vine, of leaves, a reassuringly normal shape. The vines fed into the bulky mass growing out of the wall, a

>*—gaping incomprehension of seeds and veins and flesh and*
>*interiors that were exteriors yawning backwards into dark*
>*[consumed] the dirt the air the vine the stone the bird the man the*
>*the—*

It had her father's face.

It used that face as a hand, reaching for her, sensing maybe the kinship between them. It reached for her with its

>*—fused body that bulked vegetable animal*
>*a cuff link from the other agent still on its cuff oh god the—*

Sally ran. Quick as sight, she was out the window, her disconnected self not feeling the stones that slammed and cut her knees and saved her life because the father-thing stopped to drink her blood, the jeweled red pools that clustered in the stone—

Sally ran, feeling her body again when the evil not-vegetation tried to clutch her legs her arms but she was an arrow loosed from a bow. She thought of those crusts of bread her mother had saved *eat this you must stay strong,* and here was why, this flight this stumble towards sand, the sand would save her. Even the *gnaiih*-thing behind her could not grow in the dust the choking otherness would slow it down while she, a Nester, fleet, could reach the fence, could stagger *ch'*it while *h'*followed her on what kind of legs? Dear god *h'ah'olna'ftaghu*—

She was over the fence, running across the dust to the end of the horizon.

When her legs gave out, Sally forced herself to look back towards the house. This was maybe the bravest thing she'd done, because she knew if [it] was coming for her, there was nothing she could do but watch her death walk up. Not death, no: [it] was worse than that, her father's face absorbed into some amalgamation of life and used as a tool to probe the world. At least [it] didn't look human, because if [it] did—

But [it] didn't. She hoped [it] never did. She hoped that along with those pieces of her father and the government man, [it] had not taken their memories: the pattern of her mother's dress, the creak of the old well, the words the government man had used to get her father, oh, her father, to come trudging out here to die.

Except he wasn't dead.

Sally understood now what the screaming government man had tried to tell them,

—the exterior turned interior the reaching dark the—

and knew also there was no words to contain [it]. She had to force her mind back, to here, to the soil on her hands and the gleam of life that was Sally because

—the howling light a rage of knowing—

if she didn't, she would become like one of those wizened stock, tangled in the wire. No. She was a Nester. She would not die like that.

But her Pa.

If she told, they would come out here. If she lied and said she'd found nothing, they might come anyway.

She'd lost the shovel, dropped it somewhere. That wouldn't do. A fire. She remembered the red can of gasoline by the crater.

I've cracked, she thought, brushing her face. But that was all right.

When her legs started working again, she got up and went back to the clearing.

◄◦►

Sally struggled over the dunes, the sun high in the sky. No birds, no clouds, only infinity staring her down.

When she was actually at Dubort's fence, seeing again the drift, the body of the cow ominously absent, she felt fear thrill through her. It was that fear that finally brought her back to herself, no longer one with the sky and the—

down in the dark, in the deep

—but back in her shaking, dry-throated body.

She didn't want to die. She was sure the calf hadn't wanted to die either, no matter how its stomach hurt or how short its life would be. It had struggled even as the hammer came down, with Sally's fear reflected in its eyes.

It's like riding a horse, she thought. *Like riding a horse somewhere it doesn't want to go.* With that in mind she coaxed a foot forward. Then another one. And another.

She watched her feet. If this was all she saw, maybe it wouldn't be so bad.

But it was bad. The hideous green jangled her mind. The wind breathed wrong, whispering things. Why had she come, after all? Why had she come?

There was a stubbornness in Sally that went down through the soil and past that, through the rock and its layers of time. She was a Nester, wasn't she? She belonged here, or at least—(remembering the Comanche, remembering the English with their guns)—at least she *was* here, and she would not easily be moved.

It was a long hot way. She had to keep switching the gas can from one arm to another when the pull got too much. As she walked she became more and more herself, these tired muscles lugging a sloshing burden through an ugly glare of green. She should have brought Ben. If Ben could walk, he would have helped her. But then he would see the thing and she did not want anyone else in her family to see [it]. That would be too much.

At last the house swam into the tunnel of her vision. She expected her legs to balk again, but they didn't. It was as though, having crossed the fence, all of her options were gone.

She did not bother wasting a match outside this time. She slung her leg over, and stepped inside.

◄◦►

When she lit the match, she saw only awful greenery. The father thing had vanished.

[It] couldn't have gone far, she thought. Of course she wasn't sure if that was true or not. Maybe the thing was faster than it seemed. Maybe [it] was already advancing through the township, swallowing stray passersby into its madness.

No. The thing was here. Somewhere.

Perhaps [it] was deeper in the house.

The hairs on the nape of her neck rose. Of course the house had more rooms. It was a wealthy house. Now that the outgrowth on the wall had torn itself away, she could even see the gap where the door had been. Might not that be a sign, then? That something had gone through?

Between her and the door was a mess of tangled growth. It was dangerous to step through, and not just because of the smell of rot that rose with every step. She had the notion that the vines and [it] were all connected. She was like an ant walking on [its] arm letting [it] know where she was.

If [it] found her, she could kill it faster, she reminded herself. She walked through the door.

◄◦►

The air inside this room was moist and sweet-smelling. The rot-stench was thick here, and something else, something indescribable, and bitter-edged.

She struck a match. There was a dark square in the floor. A rusted ladder curled out.

Sally peered into the black hole and thought about dropping the match. But what would happen if the flame lit on part of [it]? The thing would know what she intended.

So she blew out the match. In darkness she found the creaking, terrifyingly mobile rungs of the cellar ladder. She climbed down.

◄◦►

At last Sally had come to the end. She knew that even before she opened her eyes, before she struck the second match. She could hear the breathing around her. Synchronized, from many points. A sucking in and out.

She stepped down. Fumbled the cap off the gasoline.

A puff of air on her leg. She carefully pulled that leg away, trying to stand close to the ladder. They were all around her.

And they were.

The jumping orange light revealed twisted bodies—humans, cows, birds, plants, all merged together. Bird wings fanned air around the room. Human faces twisted on vine stems. A flower opened around an eye. She placed the match carefully on the ladder, letting it burn.

The antenna/vines/fingers quested forward. She looked for her father's face. That was the only one that mattered. The prickle down her leg told her that one of the vines had caught her, was latching on.

Then she saw Pa. It helped that he didn't look like her father anymore, but like a sack that had been stretched over a different shape. Something appeared to be growing under his eyelids.

She hurled the gasoline at him. It missed, soaking a good portion of the vine-wall instead. Heart clutching, she felt the slight slosh of some remaining gasoline. Nothing to do but this. She strode forward and poured, the awful, wonderful smell of gasoline filling her nostrils.

She could feel the latch of the vines on her arms and hands, could feel them burrowing into her skin. But what mattered, what truly mattered, was that she get the other match free, and out, and—stepping back, despite the tearing pain at her legs—struck.

The whoosh of flame knocked her backwards. Now there was heat to get away from and the screams of [it] as flowers, vines, hands stretched up in pain and terror. She stumbled away from the father-thing, crawling with flame. Her hand found the cold rungs of the ladder. Up.

Eyes streaming Sally stumbled towards the thin light of the window—a different window this time, she'd come out wrong. The house was filling with smoke and blackness, like a duster. She didn't want to die like this. She tore vines away from the old window frame, pushed her way through the rotten wood. She fell outside, into the sunshine and the merciful air.

Sally choked on the ground. There was not enough air in the whole world for her. The sun dazzled overhead, a hot stare, and black trekked above her in a column of smoke. Behind her, the vines were screaming.

Let them scream. Sally rolled on her side, scrabbled blindly away from the noise, going somewhere else.

◄◦►

They found her on the road. Her mother grabbed Sally, a relief of human skin pressing against hers. "Sally what happened to you, your face—my God—"

All of these words were tiresome. Sally leaned her smarting face against her mother's shoulder, breathing in the smell of flour. One of the adult men was shouting but Sally ignored him. "It's okay Ma," she tried to say. The words came out as a croak.

"Hold on, Sally," Ma said, "You hold on." And Sally lowered her head as though Ma's words would keep her safe.

◄◦►

Later, when the doctors finally let Sally come home, she helped Ma look for dimes. The funeral had come and gone when Sally was in her fever. About it, all Ma said was, "Your Pa was a good man." She added, staring at the pile of bills, "He would have wanted us to stay here."

Sally knew Ma was talking about the hardware men who were calling in their debts, and who Ma refused to look at when they were in town. It wasn't fair of Ma, really, Sally thought. What choice did the hardware men have about eating? They needed the money.

But something seemed to have changed for Ma, since the day Sally had come stumbling back to them on the road. She didn't care so much about politeness now. That part of Ma seemed to have been lost somewhere. Sally missed it.

Ben, on the bed, was trying to do his part. He held up the coin he'd found—or hidden, Sally thought, a long time ago.

"Found one," he gasped. He looked away from them. Ma added it to the small pile on the table. Sally remembered the ten dollar bill sitting there and turned her head away. That money was long spent.

"Are we going to be okay, Ma?" Ben couldn't see the coins from where he lay. He didn't know how few there were.

Baby Alasdair snuffled in his box, his breathing low and ragged. Ma adjusted his blanket, then scooped up Alice, who was getting underfoot as always. She went over to Ben and sat on the bed beside him, motioning Sally to join her. Sally sat gingerly on the end of the bed. Sometimes she thought she could still feel the vines squirming under her skin, and then she was afraid to let folk touch her.

"Now you listen, all of you," her mother said. "This is Mackay land. We've worked for it and we're going to keep working for it." She squeezed Ben's hand and threw a hard, half hug around Alice and Sally. Sally found herself returning the painful embrace, as though she was hanging on to her family as they slid off the face of the world.

"We won't be moved," her mother repeated into Alice's hair, like it was true.

From the nick of her eye, Sally could see the future coming for them: baby Alasdair dead from dust pneumonia by year's end, the land foreclosed, her mother half-mad at losing another loved one in a land not even good for graves any more. They'd be moved, alright, the way you had to move, when the only other choice was to die.

Sally felt that future and it terrified her more than the thing she'd seen at Dubort's. But she said nothing. Instead, she reached out and took hold of Ben's arm, like it really could work, like they really could make it.

Head bowed, she told the lie that was asked of her.

"We'll hold on, Ma," she agreed. "You'll see."

THE OESTRIDAE

ROBERT LEVY

White dust rises from the road like tobacco smoke, followed by the grinding of car wheels on dry Pennsylvania dirt as a silver compact rumbles into view, up the hill on its way to the house. "Who's that?" I say, but Dara only shakes her head and continues to chew at her hair. The spit-wet strands fall from my sister's lips, her gaze lifting until she rises, pulled from the Adirondack chair as if hefted on a rope. It's an August scorcher, the space between us and the road shimmering with heat as we wait for the sky to shift like a sieve and let the rain tumble through, the air a thick wool blanket. It's been humid like this for a month now, ever since our mother disappeared. And just when I think I've finally run out of hope, one last drip of it leaks out to ruin everything.

Near the end of the drive the car stops, about thirty yards from the house. We move as one to the porch steps, the windows of the compact filthy with bone-gray dirt, windshield so impenetrable it's hard to believe the driver can see at all. The car door swings opens and a woman emerges, her tangled mane of tight blond curls tamed by a lime green scarf wrangled over her hair and tied underneath her chin like a golden age movie star. She wears oversized shades as well, big black lenses in lacquered Hollywood frames. Her tattered red t-shirt and cutoff blue jeans, though, they're pure country, lean browned limbs bent in two sickled crooks like a grasshopper's legs before she straightens and turns her face toward us.

She lowers her sunglasses, just as Dara gasps beside me. Beneath the headscarf and blond hair, the large glasses and down-home getup, the woman appears to be our mother.

"Billy," Dara says in a whisper.

"Don't." My hand slides in front of her, but she brushes past me and down the steps. The woman, still as a scarecrow, waits beside her car, the sky and distant mountains behind her a matte pane of gray against her vibrant clothing. A soft smile forms upon her achingly familiar face as we approach.

"Hi there," she says. "You're Marlene's babies, aren't you? William and Dara." It's only once she speaks that I'm sure it's not Mom, not really. But this stranger's voice, husky and damp, it looks to be spoken between our mother's lips, and I feel Dara tense on the other side of the dulled silver car. "You must be wondering who I am."

"Are you going to tell us?" I say, and she laughs, really throws her head back and lets it rip.

"I figured *you* wouldn't remember me. What about you?" she says, and looks at my sister. "Might you have a guess?"

"No," Dara says, but I can see her searching the woman's face, dredging the shallows of her memory for an answer. "But you look just like our mother . . ."

"Yes. Well, I'm not surprised by that one bit. Although it sure has been a while." With a swift blur of motion she unties the scarf and pulls it artfully from her head, a cascade of long tendrils springing out in a bottle-blond wave. "I'm your mother's sister. Your aunt."

"Our aunt?" I say, the words foreign to me. "Mom's an only child."

"Wait." Dara chews at a split end, and she's nodding now, only a little but it's there all the same. "I think I do remember hearing something once about a sister. An older one."

"Younger, thank you very much. But only by a year. The neighbors used to call us Irish twins. Not real ones like you two." She presses a palm to the side of her skull, makes a couple of curls bounce. "My proper name is Lydia Leigh. But you can call me Aunt Lydie."

"Aunt Lydie," I repeat, as if commanded. It doesn't sound as wrong as I would imagine.

"So, where's your mother at?" She looks toward the house. "I traveled a long way to get here. She'd sure be a sight for tired eyes." Dara and I stare at each other, then away, at the car, the road, the trees and mountains beyond.

"What is it?" Lydie says. "She not here? Don't tell me I came all this way for nothing."

"Our mother . . ." Dara starts, then stops and looks toward the fence and the road beyond.

"She's missing," I finish. "Twenty-eight days now. She works at a store at the mall, and her manager said she never came back from her lunch break. No one knows what happened to her, or where she might have gone." That sweltering afternoon I pictured her passed out in her car, overtaken by the humidity, but her hatchback was found in the mall parking lot unoccupied.

"Dear lord." Lydie pales and lists, her hand releasing the headscarf as she leans on the hood of the car for support. "Oh my dear sweet lord."

Dara goes to her, puts her arm around Lydie's shoulders and holds her firm. "Come," my sister says, sounding sure of herself for the first time in weeks. "Let's go inside and I'll get you something to drink."

As we mount the porch steps, Aunt Lydie stares over her shoulder at me, her black eyes hard like the lenses of the glasses that had obscured them. Her irises are like polished stones, like our mother's eyes. They're tough to look into so I turn away, toward the lawn and Lydie's scarf as it snakes across the grass, the wind newly baleful.

The hot breeze lifts the scarf into the air before dropping it to the earth once more, where it continues to slither through the dry turf until it catches on the bottom of a fence post and coils there, dead. The screen door snaps closed behind us with a clap, just as it begins to rain.

◄◦►

Dusk settles over the mountains. It will soon be time for dinner, and for three, no less. Storming bad now and I head out back before it gets any darker, soaked through by the time I fetch the hatchet from the woodpile at the side of the house and make for the board-and-wire coop out back. "Shhh, don't worry, okay," I say, "it's going to be okay," the chickens screaming and kicking up pine shavings and running wild from my reaching fingers until I manage to snag one and wrestle it from its cage. I place the bird between my knees, stroke its soft brown feathers until it calms a bit; I cradle it in my arms like a tender thing and walk the green mile to the hemlock stump. Still, I can smell its fear. I stun it with the axe handle and cleave its head off, hold its jerking body up by its feet until it's done fighting, done bleeding out. Mom used to do all this, but now it's down to me.

By the time I've dried myself off and plucked and prepped the chicken, Dara and Aunt Lydie have set the table and parked themselves there over beers and a summer salad of greens from our mother's garden. As I cook they chatter about Lydie's cross-country trip to New York to visit an old cosmetology school friend who opened her own salon, and how Lydie had to make the detour to stop in on her only sister, her only niece and nephew, whom she'd never even met. How startled she is to see them grown, and to learn her sister has vanished.

Once we've had our fill, we let the weight of the meal sink us back in our seats. Aunt Lydie lights a cigarette, and I glance at my sister; Mom never lets anyone smoke in the house, but Dara appears unfazed. I was supposed to leave yesterday for college, but I decided to stay here instead. Me and Dara, we take care of each other. And in the four weeks since Mom went missing, I've imagined the most terrible things.

"Four weeks," Lydie says from the head of the table. She taps the lip of her empty beer bottle against her front teeth. "I can't believe it."

"No trace, no nothing," Dara says. "She just walked on out of the mall and never came back. There's security camera footage of her heading down the road on foot in the direction of the river, but that's all we have."

"I still can't believe Mom has a sister," I say, then flinch, not meaning to say it out loud. I stand quickly to collect the dishes, avoiding Lydie's too-familiar face, afraid of meeting her head-on.

"So, Lydie," Dara says, all her attention on our new aunt, "tell us more about Los Angeles."

"Oh, it's a grand place. Just grand. The people though . . . They aren't quite up to snuff, if you ask me. They aren't *real*. Some of their parts aren't, neither." She huffs out a smoke-ringed laugh. "Take this one fella I was dating. He was real nice, real generous too. But what an ego! He was a *general practitioner*," she says, enunciating the words with disgust. "You know doctors. They all think they poop out angel feathers. Every last one of them."

I swallow hard and turn from the kitchen area. "I'm actually studying to be a surgeon," I say with as much calm as I can muster. "I'm supposed to go pre-med this semester."

"Well look at you!" Lydie smiles, her teeth stained yellow, like antique ivory buttons. "So it turns out this doctor is still married. Has a wife and family out in Pasadena. Can you imagine? And here I am, sitting there like a fool just waiting for him to make an honest woman out of me. *Actors.* All of them actors out there, even the ones that aren't."

"Really coming down now," I say as I peer out the little window over the sink, and make a point of rattling the stack of dirty dishes against the tiled counter, turn the tap on loud to cause more of a racket, anything to disrupt her nattering. "Aunt Lydie, you should get a move on before it gets much worse. The flooding around here is brutal. I'd hate for your car to get stuck on your way out of town."

"Billy, that's rude." Dara places her beer bottle down on the table. "She's come a very long way, and had a terrible shock."

"It's true," Lydie says, her head wobbling in a gyroscopic shimmy, a bobbleheaded doll. "The shock has been terrible."

"Aunt Lydie," Dara says, shifting closer to her, "I'd like you to stay the night with us. It would be lovely to catch up some more."

"Oh. Oh, honey, that would be swell," Lydie says. "Just the night, and I'm gone."

"You can stay as long as you want. Isn't that right, Billy?" Dara says, her face turned away. Lydie, though, she looks up at me, her stare penetrating, the electric glow of the overheads forming two crescent moons in her shark-black eyes. I feel her on my skin, trying to crawl inside my head. I turn back to the window over the sink and the darkness beyond.

"Sure." What else am I supposed to say? I go back to doing the dishes, scraping away the remains with renewed aggression as they return to their small talking.

"Dara, honey," Lydie says after some time, "when was the last time you washed your hair?" She reaches for my sister but stops. "It's so beautiful, but honestly . . ."

"What, this?" Dara takes a shoot of her greasy locks in her fingers and stares at it appraisingly, as if through new eyes. "It's been a while," she admits.

"Well, tonight's your lucky night. Because I am going to do it for you. I'm gonna use a deep treatment that will bring its natural rich luster to the surface, where it will really shine. Show me where your bathroom's at, will you?"

"Okay." Dara smiles, really smiles, something I haven't seen in too long. "But it's not going to be pretty."

They rise and glide across the room. Dara disappears up the steps, while Lydie turns back for a moment, clutching the banister with the sinewy talons of a nighthawk.

"Nice to meet you, Billy," she says, her voice sickly sweet. There's no joy in her face, though, her expression as unreadable as her eyes of hard jet. "And thanks for letting me stay. Looks like it might rain for quite some time."

She lengthens and continues her ascent, leaving me and the night to ourselves.

◄◦►

It rains for three days straight. Mostly I spend it in my musty bedroom, playing video games or thumbing through the moldering Introduction to Anatomy textbook I bought at a tag sale a few years ago, the one that first made me curious about how a person looks when he's been opened wide for the world to see; after I showed interest, Mom made sure I got a scalpel set for Christmas, and a model skeleton for my next birthday. I'd bring home things to dissect, frogs from the pond or stillborn rabbits from my friend Barry's hutch. The only thing my mother warned me never to mess with were the botflies that gather in black clouds around the chicken coop, particularly during an Indian summer. It's bad luck to kill those.

Lydie and Dara shut themselves up in Dara's room. I don't know what they get up to exactly, except sometimes at night I can hear them both laughing behind the closed door, the only real laughter we've had in the house since Mom went away. I've stopped saying vanished, or disappeared, or went missing, because it doesn't feel like that anymore, not to me; now it feels like she knew something bad was on its way, and took off before she had to meet it face to face.

On the third night of rain, we gather for a dinner of rice and beans. Heavy bags have swollen under Dara's glassy eyes, dark and brown circles ringed like bird nests. Her mood is buoyant, however, almost manic, and I start to wonder if my sister is sleeping at all. "Tell us more about California, Lydie!"

she shouts. "Tell us everything!" Dara claps her hands hard enough to put out the tapers, the ones in the silver candlesticks Mom got at work for next to nothing. And Aunt Lydie is happy to oblige. She's all saucy stories and little winks and butter-scented smiles, but it's hollow, so hollow. I want to say something is very wrong, but I don't. I know no one wants to hear it.

Just before dawn it's finally not raining for one goddamned minute, although it's already hot enough in the day to bubble the paint on my bedroom wall. I head down the hallway to pee, and on my way back I notice my sister's door is cracked open. Just beyond is her bed, three lumpy and worn mattresses piled atop a fiberboard platform. Bent at its foot is Aunt Lydie. She's wearing a blood-red slip dress and hunched over so I can't see her face, only the corkscrews of her near-white hair. She lifts herself into a sitting position and unfurls a black stocking on her long tanned leg, her red lacquered toenails visible through the sheer. I can't imagine why she wants to wear stockings in this weather; even shirtless I feel the first slick of perspiration as it forms on my skin.

"Like what you see?" Aunt Lydie says, and it takes me a moment to realize she's talking to me. She teases the second stocking up her thigh, then faces me with her same put-on smile, her same eyes of glossed black onyx, familiar but not. "I'm guessing the answer is no."

"Where's Dara?" I step closer to the doorway but Lydie leaps up and makes it there before me.

"Dara's busy right now. Girl stuff." She steps into the hall and shuts the door behind her. "Is there something I can help you with?"

"It stopped raining, at least for now. I was wondering . . ."

"Whether I was going to hit the road anytime soon?" Her smile remains, but if there was ever anything behind it that's gone now. "It's not that simple. Your mama has something of mine. A very special thing. And I'm going to need it to get better."

"Are you sick?"

"Something like that." She stretches her hands above her head; her arms tremble, they shake.

"Maybe she left it here. We can help you look for it."

She laughs a little laugh. "You don't understand. That's why she went away. She knew I was coming, and she put it where I couldn't get at it. Maybe she took it. Or maybe not."

"What is it that's so important to you? Or to her?"

"It's a real piece of me. One I can't be whole without." She gives me a strange look. "You can't comprehend," she says. "It's not a matter for men. Let alone little boys."

"Who you calling boy?"

"You, Jack-be-nimble." With a sharp flick of her wrist she slashes a fingernail across my left cheek. I put my hand to my face, stunned. "Play with fire and you just might find a candlestick up your ass."

Before I can speak, she spins on her heel, scuttles back inside and eases the door shut once more, this time with a clicking of the lock.

I stagger back and down the hall to the bathroom, where I grip the edges of the sink to stare at my reflection in the mirror. My face is shocked and pale but there's no mark, and I appear to be unmarred, as if never scratched to begin with. But I feel the wound nevertheless, just beneath my sweat-coated skin. I press the meat of my palms to my stinging eyes as I try to steady my breath.

❖

I wait for them to show for dinner, but they never come. So I remain downstairs at the table until long past midnight, a bottle of beer warming in my hand as I listen to the rain pelt the tin roof. Eventually a door creaks open overhead, followed by the groan of wood risers as a body gradually descends the stairs, its gait awkward with the provisional unsteadiness of the infirm.

"Dara?" I squint through the gloom at the figure, and she stills at the bottom of the stairs, her nightgown pale pink and hung lifeless over her narrow frame. She's too tall to be Aunt Lydie, but she doesn't move like my sister, not at all.

"What? Oh, yes," she replies, my sister's voice after all but spoken in a scratched-vinyl rasp. "I was just going to . . ." She points toward the kitchen with a spindly arm, skin pale blue in what little diffuse moonlight manages to filter inside the room. "May I?"

"Please." I wonder why she's asking permission, it's her house as much as mine.

She shuffles over to the refrigerator and reaches inside for the water pitcher, the spout of which she brings directly to her lips. Dara drinks for an interminable length of time, until the pitcher is drained and returned empty to its shelf.

"Thirsty, huh?" I chuckle lamely.

"Yes," she says, "thirsty," and laughs in vague imitation. Her black hair shines in the dim, but not her eyes, which are hooded and obscured as she turns toward the stairs.

"Hey." I rise from my seat, which makes her stiffen, as if I were a wild animal she knows she can't outrun. "Don't you ever wonder why Mom never said anything about Aunt Lydie?"

"But she did, she did." My sister slowly nods, and continues to do so. "She told me something once, about how you can't ever stop what's coming. That when it's your time, you have to open yourself up to it and let it do its work. She said those exact words."

"And you think she was talking about Aunt Lydie?"

"Of course, silly," she says and gives another little chuckle, her head still nodding, nodding. "What else would she be talking about?"

"Dara . . ." I step closer and she steps back, but now I see just how skinny she is, her nightgown soaked through and clinging to her chest like a false skin. "You look like you've been having night sweats. Are you feeling okay?"

"Yes. Oh yes." She smiles, her teeth gray in the moonlight. "Oh yes."

Her wet eyes swim with glaze before she turns away again and heads up the stairs, the sound of bare feet padding against wood steadily diminishing until the only sound is the beating of the rain.

I ease the screen door closed and step onto the porch, breathe in the steaming wet smells of late summer as it continues to pour, the rain a thick curtain off the eaves and overflowing gutters just this side of the vast darkness beyond the house. A snap and a flare of light and I start: Aunt Lydie, seated beside me in one of the two Adirondack chairs. She lights a cigarette, her dark eyes trained on me.

"Lovely weather we're having, isn't it," she says and smiles, but it's not a question, just like it isn't a smile. "Here." She flicks her chin in the direction of the second chair. "Have a seat."

"I'm good standing, thanks." Looking down on her from this height I note how tiny she really is, almost roachlike, and she repulses me just the same. "Probably should get to bed, so . . ."

"You think you're pretty clever, huh?" She ashes her cigarette with an angry jab of her finger. "Little doctor man. A real Doogie Howser MD, am I right? *Night sweats.* That's a good one." She leans forward in her seat, and her face widens, eager, its own kind of collection plate. "You don't like me very much, do you? No, I can tell. You don't think very much of me at all."

I shrug, but my skin goes cold. I have no choice, I see that now. I've got to get her gone from here.

"You know that piece of yourself you said you were looking for," I begin, "that one that you said our mother took with her?" I stare out into the dark night, in the direction of the main road. "If you want it so bad, why don't you go look for her or something? It's not here, you said it yourself."

"You see, little boy, that's the thing," and she taps the tip of a sharp fingernail against her lower lip. "I'm starting to think that all I need is right here after all." Lydie reaches for her beer, her fingers skittering over her black plastic lighter and across the arm of the chair like a spider. "Mothers and daughters, they share certain gifts. Certain secrets."

"Like how Dara had heard of you before and I hadn't."

"Something like that." She watches a spiral of smoke snake upwards in the muted light. "Besides, your mother might come back some day. And I want to be here when she does."

"She's not coming back," I say, and as soon as the words come out of my mouth I know that they're true. Our mother is never coming back. And as soon as I know this, I also know that Aunt Lydie isn't all she says she is, and that she's not going to leave, not ever, even if she does get what she's come for. She's an evil thing that's found a dry and deep hole to move into, found a dark void in our tragic little lives that was all too primed for the filling, made her way into a place she was never meant to be. Just like the botflies do, out by the coop. After the chickens peck at each other the flies move in, lay their eggs beneath the feathers, in the scratched and broken skin.

Aunt Lydie, she's just like those flies. She's crawled inside our open wound, here to stay unless I do something about it, and fast. She's a dirty little liar is what she is. I bet she's never even been to Los Angeles.

My stomach contracts so hard that my legs buckle and I fall to my knees, the porch wood and roof tin and rainy night sky all spinning out around me. I can't breathe, not enough air to take in, nowhere near enough. I can't breathe. I bring a hand to my chest, open and close my mouth like a fish flopping on the floor of a boat, and in a flash she's right beside me.

"You feel that, little Billygoat?" she whispers in my ear, and all I can do is moan in response. "That's the pain your mama felt when she shat you out into this world, the pair of you good-for-nothings. And ever since, all the both of you have done is take. That's probably why she ran off. Who the hell would want to stick around this dump with you two?"

"You may look like her," I manage to get out, my eyes fixed on the porch's scored surface. "But you're nothing like our mother. Nothing at all."

"But I'm the one who's here."

I swear I can hear her smile. "Lydie," I say between wheezes. "Aunt Lydie, listen."

She puts the side of her head against the floorboards, her eyes inches away from mine and peering inside me, hollowing me out. "Yes?"

"I think there's something you should see. It's where our mom keeps her most special things."

"Oh yeah?" Her eyes turn to honeycombs, her lips quiver and part in pleasure.

"It's around the side of the house, by the woodpile. I'll show you . . ."

"Finally." She rises and straightens, the sound of her dusting off the front of her dress before the clack-clacking of her heels as she crosses the porch. Nausea seizes me in its contracting fist, and I roll onto my side, use one of the chairs to pull myself up into something resembling a standing position.

"Well?" she says from the porch steps, her bright hair already sparkling in the rain. "You coming or not? And you better not be screwing with me."

"Don't worry, okay?" Lydie turns and heads down to the lawn, and I slip her plastic lighter from the arm of the chair, its deceptively insubstantial weight solid in the palm of my hand. "It's going to be okay."

◄◦►

I take the hatchet to Dara's bedroom door, its blood-stained edge making a pulped mess of the wood around the beveled glass knob so I can reach through and open the door from the inside. I tuck the handle of the hatchet into my waistband and search the room, overturn the bed and move the dresser away from the wall before I find my sister on the floor of the closet. She's skin and bones, her naked body sticky all over with what feels like cobwebs. As I pull away the wet strands, however, it begins to feel more like damp thread or hair. "Dara," I say, "we've got to go," and I haul her up into my arms, her eyes shocked wide and haunted, face sheened with sweat. "Listen to me. Can you hear me?"

"Something hurts," she says, wincing. She puts a hand to her chest and coughs. "Right here, inside of me. I can feel it . . . moving."

"I'm going to get you better. I promise. But you're going to have to come with me."

Dara nods a little, but then she pushes against me, tries to twist from my grasp and back toward the closet. She's weak, though, and I pull her in close, hustle her out of the room. We head down the stairs and through the kitchen, out the front door and down the porch steps, dodging loosed chickens as we make our way to Aunt Lydie's car. I wonder if my sister smells the meat cooking above the scent of cindering pine shavings, the savory odor of burning flesh. It's not raining anymore, but still it threatens.

"Chickens," Dara says in a dazed whisper, as I lay her down in the back seat. "Someone let the chickens out."

"Looks like." I toss the hatchet onto the passenger seat and run back inside the house for a few last things before I climb behind the wheel.

Dara stares up at me. "What about Aunt Lydie?" she asks, her lips cracked and bleeding.

"She's going to stay here for a while," I say, my voice pitched to soothe in my best bedside manner. "As long as she wants, like you said. She's going to hold down the fort."

I start the ignition just as a terrible moaning pierces the damp wet air, a deep and mournful wail that causes me to shake so violently I slam on the gas pedal before taking the car out of park. No, not mournful. Injured. Spiteful. I had hoped dissevering her head from her body, her tongue from her mouth, her limbs from her torso would have brought us some quiet. But even dismantled into pieces and locked up in the chicken coop, the entire structure doused in lighter fluid and set aflame, even that hasn't managed to fully shut her up.

I wanted it to have been easy; instead I bit down hard on my tongue as I worked, wished myself less timid and more bold, more cruel, like her. That I could reduce her to specimen alone. But that's not in my nature, and I know that now as well. What I don't know is why I turned out different from Aunt Lydie, where the branches of our family tree parted and made us into two separate kinds of things. But I am different from her. And I have to believe my sister is as well. We can't all be monsters, can we?

"That sound . . ." Dara shivers and sits up. "What's that sound?"

"It's only the wind, playing tricks. Close your eyes and sleep, okay? We'll be there soon."

We roll out into the night. The hood of the car is glossed with rain and shimmers in the starlight as we leave our home in the rearview, the bright flicker of flames from the coop burning yellow and blue as we continue down the drive. We reach the bottom of the hill, and I make the turn away from town.

"Where are we going?" Dara asks.

"In the direction of the river," I tell her. That's all we have to go on.

I glance at the hatchet on the passenger seat, where it sits atop my anatomy book, beside my scalpel set and surgical tools, all the things I'd hoped would bring me closer to being the person I wanted to be, the one who could make everything better. But that's probably over now. I've messed where I shouldn't have, and now I'm on call. All that's left to do is finish the work I started.

The scalpels, those are for Dara; if Aunt Lydie left something inside of my sister, I'm going to have to cut it out of her. I'll do the same for myself if I have to, and I touch at the invisible wound upon my cheek. Who knows how deeply she's burrowed inside of us? And the hatchet, that's for our mother if she abandoned us, not to mention any other bad relations we may meet along the way. There might be more of them.

THE PROCESS IS A PROCESS ALL ITS OWN

PETER STRAUB

I have this thing I do because the thing reminds me of you know. You use these little deals, like the hearing aid batteries that go into that thing deaf guys put in their shirt pockets, the thing with the wires that come out. You dump these batteries out of the pack and swish them around in 3-4 inches of water. Little bubbles begin to come up: in fact, little bubbles show up almost immediately. Why, I don't know, but they do. Maybe for reasons we will get into later. The batteries rest like little machine turds down there on the bottom of your ashtray or whatever. (I use an ashtray, mainly.) Then what you do, is you sniff the bubbles.

Huh.

If you push your head right down next to the water, the bubbles open up right under your nose. Which is the point here, O Unseen. They give off this strange little smell. Those bubbles from Ray-O-Vac hearing aid batteries smell like what happens when you shove your nose right into the middle of an old dictionary, the gutter where the two pages come together, and inhale. That's the smell at you get from the bubbles out of hearing aid batteries.

If the odor you get from the bubbles from hearing aid batteries has anything in common with the odor you get from thrusting your nose deep into the seam of an open dictionary, particularly a dictionary of some vintage, then it cannot be inaccurate to say that the odor must be that of words. One comes across the odors of words in many, many contexts, and the odors of words are usually the same from one context to another. Only the strongest, most distinctly individuated, if that's a word, of individuals can control the colorations of the words that pass through them.

Nothing in this situation is odd, actually, odd given that we are dealing with words. Words are produced within the medium of air, and balloons and other empty spaces that produce bubbles do so because they themselves are filled with air. Air itself must be thought to be laden with words, to be word-packed, word-jammed. In fact, words tumble out of every orifice, panting to be born, screaming against the resistant membrane, trying their best to . . . . Here's the deal. Words have plans. Ambitions. Goals. They are always trying to veer around us & zoom away. They wish to leave us in an abysmal darkness. You can think what you like about this.

Try the following experiment. Choose any old balloon you happen to see lying by the side of the path in a public park, even a balloon that may have been blown up for a child's birthday. (But make sure it's a *balloon* balloon, or you might not like the results!) When you thrust these poor old things underwater, pierce their hides with your knife, your hatpin, whatever, and then inhale the fragrance of the hazy penumbra-substance that escapes into the water and bursts above it in bubble form, nine times out of ten, five out of six anyhow, there may be heard the off-key delivery of birthday songs, the chanting of inane good wishes, on top of these frequent invocations of the birthday child's name, and distributed through all of the intermediate spaces the names of his wretched friends and, guess what, lists of the silly birthday presents given and acquired on this date. *And* this tired, tired smell. All this verbal information can be detected within the exhalations to be had from these semi-deflated pastel colored balloons. Once you really commit to this process, pretty much the same goes for gadgets like tape recorders, typewriters, old over-under cameras, headphones, microphones, everything like that. Once they have been plunged under water and agitated crushed berated abused destroyed, one can detect beneath the more prominent odors of distressed metal, rubber, and plastic, the ambitious stench of words that once passed through these various windows.

To a casual observer, dear little friend, all of the above may seem over-specialized, in fact obsessive. I can scarcely pretend that I am a casual onlooker. To illustrate the exact nature of my function, which at the moment I am perhaps a bit reluctant to do, I might allude to the properties of another set of bubbles and the nature of the inhalations contained within, which is to say, getting at last to the point, well, *one* of my points, the bubbles found in blood. Blood is particularly given to the formation of bubbles. Those with the stomach to lean over bubbles of blood and inhale their messages will find that they have in the process acquired a complex detailed subtle record of the life from which that blood emerged. It is one of the most delicate and moving instance of information-transmission that I can imagine. It is certainly one of the most beautiful experiences that I have ever known—the catching of the deep, particular inflections within the bubbles of blood that issue from the human throat. Voices contain smells: all human structures carry—on their backs sides bellies feet cocks pussies scalps—stinks and perfumes. We cannot escape into any goddam odor-free realm. Any such realm should scare us right out of our you know. Odors fasten us to our common world. Rot, fragrance, bud and bloom exude the physical aura of the process that animates them. It does not take a scientist to detect a verbal motion, a verbal smell, within the bubbles of blood of a recently deceased beast or human. It is, however, perhaps only one given my particular history who may with a reasonably good assurance of being believed claim that when words are detected within the blood of human beings they generally have an English smell. It is the odor, and I understand that what I am telling you might seem arbitrary, of fish and chip shops on barren High Streets, of overcooked roast beefs, of limp, glistening "chips," of blank-eyed mackerel reeking on the departing tide, of dull seaweed and wet wool, of humid beards, of crap Virginia tobacco, of damp hair, likewise of cheap cologne and hair oil, also of flowers sold three days past their prime in Covent Garden, also of similar flowers wilting in the hair of neglected women—all of these structures are to be detected in the bubbles that form when blood is released from *any* human being, cart man, prince-regent or vicious greedy poxy trollop.

Those kind of people I was talking about before, they do not produce these English smells. With them, it's all different, you don't know what you're going to hear. Fortunately they are very few in number.

Am I being fanciful? All right, perhaps I'm being fanciful. And yet what I tell you is on the nose. Most of the time, an English accent is what you get. What's more, it's usually a Cockney accent—turns out, words are blue collar guys.

I don't want you to think that I mess around smelling blood bubbles, for God's sake. Nobody has that much time. Time is a luxury. And what human beings do with luxuries is very much their own business, thank you very much.

T.H., June 1958

⟶

A man named Tillman Hayward wrote these words in a Hardy & Badgett leather-bound notebook, 5" x 4", with pale blue lined paper. He had purchased the notebook, along with three others like it, on-sale for $9.95 at Ballantine and Scarneccia, a high-end stationery store in Columbus, Ohio. He "lived" in Columbus. His real life took place elsewhere.

Tillman Hayward, "Tilly," did not work in Columbus. He earned his reasonably substantial salary as a property manager in Columbus, but his real work—his "work"—was done elsewhere. This separation was self-protective.

Tilly was writing with a German-made mechanical pencil purchased for $8.99 at the same store. Faber Castell, its manufacturer, described it as a "propelling pencil." He liked the word "propelling": to propel sounded madly up-to-date. A propeller-pencil. (It, the word not the pencil, smelled a great deal of Elmer's Glue.)

Tilly Hayward had been married for nine years to a blonde woman named Charlotte, nee Sullivan. Tilly and Charlotte had produced three blonde daughters, each of them the replica of both her mother and their sisters. They looked like triplicates born in different years. These perfect girls were named Edith, Hannah, and Faith. The Hayward family lived in one of the apartment buildings owned by Charlotte's father, Daniel Sullivan, a flinty Irish immigrant in a flat cap, who had never known a moment's warmth or sentimentality. Tilly's job was to oversee the properties, keep them in satisfactory condition, check out whatever new might come on the market, and to make sure the rents came in. He deployed a full range of subcontractors to deal with the tenants' demands. With his father-in-law's approval, Tilly also had taken it upon himself to search for other properties to add to his holdings. He had convinced his father-in-law that the city of Milwaukee, his birthplace, was an excellent location for the long-planned expansion of the Sullivan company. Six or seven times a year, sometimes way more than that, Tilly either drove took the train, or flew to Milwaukee (the handsome old General Mitchell Field, where his tricky old Dad used to take the kids to watch the planes take off and land). There, he sometimes stayed with his brother, Bobby, and Bobby's wife Mags, in the old brown-and-yellow duplex on West 44th Street, where Bobby, Tilly and their sister Margo, then Margaret, had been born and raised. At other times, he planted himself in hotels, not always under his real name. "Jesse Unruh" and "Joe Ball" spent a few days at the Pfister, "Leslie Ervin" at the funkier, less expensive Plaza. Although Tilly appeared to be, and sometimes actually was, dedicated in his search for commercial properties, he had as yet to purchase a single one of these buildings for the Sullivan real estate empire.

It was in Milwaukee and under conditions of rigorous secrecy that Tilly's real "work" was carried out.

Tilly Hayward was one of those men in possession of two lives. Either he was a dark, disturbing criminal sociopath who wore a more conventional person around him like a perfectly fitted suit of clothing, or he was a conventional person who within himself concealed a being like a wild animal. Tillman's response to his duality was not simple. He wondered sometimes if he were really a person at all. Perhaps he had originated on some far away star—or in some other, far distant time. Often, he felt *other*.

Many of the words whose odors Tillman caught as they emerged reeked of death and corruption. There were some words that almost always stank of the graveyard, of death and corpses. (These were words such as happiness, fulfillment, satisfaction, pleasure, also joy.) Tillman understood that these words smelled foul because the things they referred to were false.

In Tilly's sensitive nostrils, the word "job" often smelled like fresh vomit. People who spoke of their jobs evoked entire butcher shops filled with rotting meat. Tilly knew that if he ever permitted himself to speak in mixed company, away from his family, of the job he did for Sullivan Real Estate Holdings, the same terrible stench would attach itself to his vocabulary. Therefore, he never did speak of these matters except to his wife, who either did not notice the stinks that accompanied these words or, having grown accustomed to them during childhood, pretended that she did not. Words like sorrow, unhappiness, grief, these words which should have carried perhaps the worst stenches of all, did not actually smell so bad—more like rotting flowers than rotting meat, as though what had once been fresh about them was not so very distant. When Tilly went out in search of the people that he dealt with as part of his real "work," he deliberately sought women who uttered the foulest words of all. He had an unerring instinct for women whose vocabulary betrayed a deep intrinsic falsity. He often thought that other people could do the same. He thought that a kind of politeness kept other people from speaking of this power, so out of uncharacteristic politeness he himself remained silent about it. There were times when he wondered if he alone could detect the odors that clung to the spoken words, but if that were true, and the power only his, he could never figure out what to do with it. Apart from being perhaps another indication of his status as an alien from a sphere far different, the power seemed a mere frivolity: like so much else, it had no relevance beyond its own borders.

Funny thing: the word "remorse" actually smelled pretty good, on the whole. The word remorse tended to smell like wood shavings and sunburnt lawns, at its worst it smelled of ant hills, or something sort of like ant hills, sand dunes, Indian burial mounds. He never objected to the smell of the word remorse. In fact, rather to his surprise, Tilly tended to like it a lot. It was a pity that the word was heard so seldom in the course of ordinary conversation.

Tilly, of course, tended not to have ordinary conversations.

◄o►

In October of 1958 Tilly once again found himself in Milwaukee. He had come not in pursuit of one or more of his many private obsessions, but because he had a genuine interest in a real estate property. Two years before, Tilly had acquired a real estate license. It had required considerable effort, but he managed to pass the qualifying exams on his first attempt. He wanted to be able to justify his trips out of town, especially those to Milwaukee, on commercial grounds. Now, at the end of September, he had come to inspect a building a four-story mixed-use building on Welles Street. Its only problem was its single tenant: a 65-year-old woman who had once worked for the Mayor and for the past six years of her life had claimed to be dying from cardiomyopathy. Tilly had come to see if might be possible to resolve this tenancy problem by means of certain efficient measures never to be revealed. Yet when he looked at it again, the building had become far less attractive—he saw the old lady, intractable, seated on her unclean old sofa, skinny arms extended as if for hundreds of feet, and chose not to negotiate in any way.

Late in the afternoon of the same day, Tilly decided to take a walk through downtown Milwaukee. He wanted to uncoil, perhaps also to allow passage into the attentive atmosphere some portion of his rabid, prancing inner self. Around the corner on Wisconsin Avenue stood the vast stone structure of the Central Milwaukee Library, and across the avenue from this big, dark building was a bookstore called Mannheim's.

Tilly had no interest in these buildings and could imagine no circumstance that would persuade him to enter either one. No sooner had he become conscious of this fact than he took note of someone, a young woman, who had no problem being in both. Through the slightly sunken and recessed front door of Mannheim's she floated, unencumbered by handbag, not to mention doubt, fear, depression, or any other conventional female disorder—perhaps thirty yards away, and already, instantly upon her entrance into his frame, rivetingly, infuriatingly attractive.

The girl was in her mid-twenties, and perhaps five and a half feet tall, with dark brown hair, and long blue eyes in a decisive little face with a flexible red mouth. She wore a green cardigan sweater and a khaki skirt. Her hair had been cut unusually short, to almost the length of a boy's hair, though no one could mistake her for a boy. He liked her suntanned fox-face and her twinned immediate air of independence and intelligence. The girl glanced at him, and before continuing on displayed perhaps a flicker of rote, species-reproductive interest. (Tilly had long felt that women capable of bearing children came to all-but-instantaneous decisions about their willingness to do so with the men they met.)

She came up the stairs to the sidewalk, moved across the cement, and with a side-to-side flick of her eyes jumped down into the traffic moving north and south on busy Wisconsin Avenue. Delightful little twirls of her hands directed the cars that coursed around her, also to dismiss the few drivers who tried to flirt with her. It was like watching someone conducting an orchestra that moved around the room. She looked so valiant as she dodged through the fluid traffic. Who was this girl: her whole life long, had she never been afraid of anything? At first not entirely aware of what he was doing, Tilly began to move more quickly up the block.

The young woman reached the near curb and flowed safely onto the sidewalk. Without the renewed glance he felt he rather deserved, she sped across the pavement and proceeded up the wide stone path to the Central Library's massive front doors. Tilly began walking a little faster, then realized that she would be inside the building before he had even reached the pathway. He suffered a quick, hell-lit vision of the library's interior as a mazy series of tobacco-colored corridors connected by random staircases and dim, flickering bulbs.

Once he got through the main door, he looked both left and right in search of the girl, then straight ahead down the empty central hallway. At the end of the hallway stood a wide glass door, closed. Black letters painted on the pebbled glass said FICTION. This was almost certainly where she had gone. She was imaginative, she was interested in literature: When the moment came, she'd have things to say, she would be able to speak up. Tilly enjoyed flashes of spirit in his playmates.

At the you know. During the. Maybe. If not then, what a pity, never.

Tilly strode through the glass door into the fiction room. The girl could have been bent over a book at one of the wide tables or hidden behind some of the open shelves at the edges of the room. He did a quick scan of the tables and saw only the usual library riff-raff, then moved toward the shelves. His heart began to beat a little more quickly.

Tilly could taste blood; he could already catch the meat-sack stench of "please" and "mercy" as they slid through the girl's sweetheart lips. Better than a meal to a hungry man, the you know . . . except the you know *was* a meal, finer than a T-bone fresh from the slaughterhouse and butchered on the spot . . .

Tilly stopped moving, closed his eyes and touched his tongue to the center of his upper lip. He made himself breathe softly and evenly. There was no point in letting his emotions ride him like a pony.

Twice he wandered through the three stacks of books on the fiction floor, going in one end and out the other, along the way peering over the cityscape tops of the books to see if his target were drifting down the other side. Within a couple of minutes, he had looked everywhere, yet had somehow failed to locate the girl. Girl walks into room, girl disappears. This was a red-line disappointment, a tremble, a shake-and-quiver. Already Tilly had begun to feel that this girl should have had some special place in his grand scheme—that if she were granted such a place, a perfection of the sort he had seldom known would have taken hold. The grand scheme itself borrowed its shape from those who contributed to it—the girls whose lives were demanded—and for that reason at the moment of his fruitless search the floating girl felt like an essential aspect of his life in Milwaukee. He needed her. The surprise of real fulfillment could be found only in what would happen after he managed to talk her into his "special place" out in the far western suburbs.

After something like fifteen minutes, Tilly finally admitted to himself that somehow she had managed to escape from the fiction room. Baffling; impossible. He had kept his eye on the door the whole time he'd been in the room.

Two people, both now bent over their reading, had entered, and only three people had left—a pair of emaciated women in their fifties and a slender Negro girl with glossy little curls in her hair.

For a moment, Tilly considered racing out and following the wide central hallway wherever it went. He saw, as if arrayed before him on a desktop, pictures of frantic Tillman Hayward charging into rooms where quiet people dozed over books or newspapers. No part of balance and restitution could be found in the images strewn across the desk. Something told him—everything told him!—that none of these people half asleep under the library lamps could be his girl.

He had lost her for good. This wonderful young woman would never be permitted to fulfill her role in the grand design of Tillman Hayward's extraordinary life. For both of them, what a tragic diminution. Tilly spun around and dropped himself into an empty chair. None of the pig-ignorant people reading their trashy books even bothered to glance at him. He continued to try to force calm upon himself, to take control of his emotions. Tilly feared that he might have to go outside, prop his hands on his knees, and inhale deeply to find calm. Eventually his body began to relax.

The girl was gone. There was nothing to be done for it. It would always be as if he had never seen her. For the rest of his life he would have to act as though he had never sensed the possibilities with which this young woman, so alive with possibility, had presented him. Tilly knew himself to be a supreme compartmentalizer, and he did not doubt his power to squeeze the girl down into a little drawer in his mind, and there quite nearly to forget her.

◄◦►

Two nights later, he had planned to get some rest before going back to Columbus, but the idea of Mags and Bob sitting in their miserable living room thinking God knows what and remembering too much of what he might have said made him edgy. Probably he should never have given that *True Detective* to poor little Keith. It was like a secret handshake he could not as yet acknowledge. It was like saying, *This is my work, and I want you to admire my achievement, but it is still too soon to for you and me to really talk about it. But you're beginning to understand, aren't you?* Because that was true: the kid was beginning to put things together.

Tilly tried stretching out on the bed and sort-of reading his book, which was a novel based on the career of Caryl Chessman, the Red Light Bandit who had been sentenced to execution in the gas chamber at San Quentin. Tilly loved the book. He thought it made Chessman seem at least a little sympathetic. Yet his attempt at reading did not go well. The image of Bob and Mags seated stiffly before their television, and that of Keith doing God knew what with *True Detective* in his bedroom kept dragging his concentration away from the page. Finally he decided: One last night, maybe one last girl. Good old Caryl kept himself in the game, you had to give him that.

He checked his inner weather. A sullen little flame of pure desire had flared into being at the prospect of going out on the hunt one last time. He tucked the book beneath his pillow, took his second-favorite knife from its hiding place, then put it back. He would play it All or Nothing: if he could coax a girl out to his Special Place in the suburbs, he would use his favorite knife, which was stashed in a drawer out there; if he failed, there'd be one less corpse in the world. All or Nothing always made his mouth fizz. He lifted his overcoat off the hook on the back of the door and slipped his arms into the sleeves on the short distance to the living room.

That coat fit him like another skin. When he moved, it moved with him. (Such sensations were another benefit of All or Nothing.)

"Why do you do that, Tilly?" Mags asked.

"Do what?"

"That thing you just did. That . . . shimmy."

"Shimmy," a word he seldom used, stank of celery.

"I have no idea how to shimmy, sorry."

"But you are obviously going out. Aren't you?"

"Oh, Mags," sighed Bill.

"Last-minute look at a property. I shouldn't be super late, but don't wait up for me."

"Where would this property be, Tilly, exactly?"

He grinned at her. "It's on North Avenue, way east, past that French restaurant over there. The next block."

"Is it nice?"

"Exactly my question. Be good now, you two."

"What time is your train tomorrow?"

"Eleven in the morning. I won't be home until midnight, probably."

When he got outside and began walking down the street to his rented car through the cool air, he felt himself turning into his other, deeper self. It had been months since he had last been in Lou's Rendezvous.

Formerly an unrepentant dive, Lou's had recently become a college joint with an overlay of old-time neighborhood pond-scum. Ever optimistic about the possibility of having sex with these good-looking youngsters, the old-timers kept jamming quarters into the jukebox and playing "Great Balls of Fire" and "All I Have to Do is Dream of You." That the neighborhood characters never got disgusting made for a loose, lively crowd. Supposedly a businessman from Chicago, a man who had been at Lou's several times before, the Ladykiller dressed well, he was relaxed and good-looking. Knew how to make a person laugh. The man wandered in and out, had a few drinks, talked to this one and that one, whispered into a few ears. Some thought his name was Mac, maybe Mark. Like a single flower in a pretty vase, the girl from the library was parked at the corner of the bar. Her name was Lori Terry. She called him Mike and slipped out of the bar with him before anyone had time to notice.

So not Nothing. All. A final present from the city of Milwaukee.

After he had driven west some fifteen minutes she asked, "So where are we going, anyhow, Mike?" (Young avocado, peppermint.)

Like very few people, he had observed, Lori Terry had the gift of imbuing words and even whole sentences with fragrances all her own. His nephew had a touch of this ability, too.

"This place a little way out of town," he said.

"Sounds romantic. Is it romantic?" She'd had perhaps two or three drinks too many. ("Romantic" kind of hovered over a blocked drain.)

"I think it is, yes." He smiled at her. "Tonight wasn't the first time I've ever seen you, you know. I was in the library this morning. I saw you walk from Fiction right through into Biography."

"Why didn't you say hello?"

"You were too fast for me. Peeled right out of there."

"Must have made quite the impression." (Some lively pepperminty thing here, like gum, only not really.)

"I looked at you, and I thought, That girl could change my life."

"Well, maybe I will. Maybe you'll change mine. Look what we're doing! Nobody ever takes me out of town."

"I'll try to make the trip extra memorable."

"Actually, isn't it a little late for going out of town?"

"Lori, are you worried about sleep? Because I'll make sure you get enough sleep."

"Promise?" This word floated on a bed of fat green olives.

He promised her all the sleep she was going to need.

Trouble started twenty minutes later, when he pulled up into the weedy dirt driveway. As she stared first at the unpromising little tavern next to his actual building, then at him, disbelief widened her eyes. "This place isn't even open!" (Rancid milk.)

"Not that one, no," said the Ladykiller, now nearly on the verge of laughter. "The other one."

She swiveled her head and took in the old storehouse with the ghost-like word clinging to a front window. "Goods?" she asked. "If you tell me that's the name of the place, you're fulla shit." (Gunmetal, silver polish.)

"That's not a name, it's a disguise."

"Are you really sure about this?"

"Do you think I brought you all the way out here by mistake?" He opened his door, leaned toward her, and smiled. "Come on, you'll see."

"What is this, an after-hours joint? Like a club?" With a gathering, slow-moving reluctance, she swung the door open on a dissipating cloud of rainwater and fried onions and moved one leg out of the car.

"Private club." He moved gracefully around the hood and took her hand to ease her delivery from the car. The temperature of his resolve was doing that thing of turning hot as lava, then as cold as the flanks of a glacier, then back again, in about a second and a half. "Just for us, tonight."

"Jesus, you can do that?"

"You wait," he said, and searched his pocket for the magic key. It glided into the lock and struck home with the usual heavy-duty sound effects.

"Maybe we should both wait." (Chalk-dusty blackboard.)

He gave her an over-the-shoulder glance of rueful, ironic mock regret. "Wait? I'll get you back into town in plenty of time."

"We just met. You want me to follow you into this old building, and it's already past twelve . . ."

"You don't trust me?" Now he was frankly pouting. "And after all we've meant to each other."

"I was just thinking my father would be really suspicious right now."

"Isn't that part of the whole point about me, Lori? That your father wouldn't like me?"

She laughed. "You may be right."

"All right, then." He opened the door onto an absolute darkness. "Just give me a sec. It's one flight down."

"A basement? I'm not so . . ."

"That's how they keep the place private. Wait, I'll get the light."

He disappeared inside and a moment later flipped a switch. Watery illumination revealed floorboards with a sweeping, half-visible grain. She heard the turning of another vault-like lock. He again appeared in the doorway, took her hand, and with only a minimum of pressure urged her into the building. Shivering in the sudden cold, she glanced around at the barren cell-like room she had entered. It seemed to be perfectly empty and perfectly clean. He was drawing her toward a door that opened onto a rectangle of greater brightness. It gradually revealed the flat, dimpled platform and gray descending handrail of a metal staircase. No noise came from the dark realm beyond the circle of light at the bottom of the steps.

"Ladies first," he said, and she had reached the fifth step down before she realized that he had blocked any possibility of escape. She turned to look at him over her shoulder, and received, as if in payment, a smile of utmost white bedazzlement. "I know, it looks like no one's here. Works in our favor, actually. We'll have the whole place to ourselves. Do anything we like, absolutely everything."

"Wait a second," she said. " I want to have a good time, Mike, but absolutely everything is not in the picture, do you hear me?" What he had here, Till realized, was a clear, straightforward case of a specific fragrance emerging from a sentence as a whole, instead of blooming into the foreground of a lot of other, lesser smells. And in this case, the fragrance was that of a fresh fruit salad, heavy on the melons but with clean, ringing top notes of lime, just now liberated from the grocer's wrapping. Dazzled, he felt momentarily off-balance, as if his weight were on the wrong foot.

"Loud and clear. I don't have those kinds of designs on you."

"You don't?" In spite of everything, it was a kind of shock. He could smell it, too: the fruit salad had been topped with a layer of thin, dark, German pumpernickel. From *two words*. He was going to kill this wonderful girl, but part of him wished he could eat her, too.

"Just wait at the bottom of the stairs. There's another door, and I have to get the light."

The habit of obedience rooted her to the floor as he squeezed past and pushed a third key into a third lock. Again Lori took in the heaviness of the mechanism, the vault-like thunk of precision-made machinery falling into place. Whatever made Mike happy, he had taken pains to keep it safe. Mike grasped her elbow and drew her after him into the dark room. The door closed heavily behind her, and Mike said, "Okay, Lori, take a gander at my sandbox, my pride and joy."

He flipped up a switch and in the sudden glare of illumination she heard him relocking the door. In all the sparkle and shine she thought for a moment that she was actually looking at a metal sandbox. When her vision cleared, she glanced over her shoulder to see him tucking a key into his pocket.

"Oh my God," she said, and stepped away from him through a briefly hovering cloud of old saddles and baseball mitts.

"Lori Terry. Here you are."

"You're him."

"I am?"

"You're the Ladykiller guy. God damn." (Concrete sidewalks. Steel girders, plus maple syrup. She imprinted *her own* odors upon the words that issued from her, and she had the strength of character to shape entire utterances within that framework. He was still reeling.)

He spread his arms and summoned a handsome smile. "Like what I've done with the place?"

"I'd like you to take me home, please."

He stepped toward her. "In all honesty, Lori, this could go either way. Whichever path you choose, you're gonna end up in the same place. That's the deal here."

She moved about three inches backward, slowly. "You like blowjobs, Mike? I'll make you come like a fire hose." (Oh, exquisite, in fact almost *painfully* exquisite: when she must have been dropping into terror like a dead bird, her sentences came swaddled in clove, and ginger, and yet again the kind of maple syrup that came from trees bleeding into pails way up in Vermont and Maine, that area.)

"I always come like a fire hose. Of course, most of my partners aren't alive any more. I like it that way. Come to think of it, they probably do, too."

"You think a woman would have to be dead to enjoy making love to you? Let me prove how wrong you are."

He was inching toward her, but the distance between them remained constant.

"You're an unusual girl, Lori."

"What makes me 'unusual?'" (Marshmallow and chocolate: Smores!)

"You're not cowering on the floor. Or sniveling. All the other girls—"

She took one fast step backwards, spun around, and sprinted toward the center of the room. Amused by this display of nerve, he lunged for her playfully and almost deliberately missed. Lori ran around to the other side of the second steel table and leaned on it with stiff arms, her eyes and mouth open, watching him closely, ready to flee in any direction. For a couple of seconds only, she glanced into the corners of the shiny basement.

"To get out, you need my keys," he said. "Which means you ain't gonna get out. So are you going to make a break for it, or wait for me to come get you? I recommend the second one. It's not in your best interest to piss me off, I promise you." From across the room, he gave her the open-hearted gift of a wide, very nearly genuine smile.

She kept watching him with the close, steady attention of a sailor regarding an unpredictable sea. On every second inhalation, she bent her elbows and leaned forward.

"Because right at this moment? Right at this moment, I admire the hell out of you. All kinds of reasons, honest to God."

He waited for her to break for either the right or the left side of the metal table so that he could at last close the distance between them and finish the gesture he had begun at Lou's Rendezvous, but she did not move. She kept on leaning forward and pushing back.

He shook his head as though to clear it. "Say something. Say anything. I love what happens when you talk."

"Oh?" Not enough to be measured: something about peanuts in a roaster . . . peanuts rolling in an oiled pan . . .

"You know how words have these smells? Like 'paycheck' always smells like a dirty men's room? You know what I'm talking about, yeah?"

"You smell what I'm saying?" Without relaxing her attention, Lori leaned forward and narrowed her eyes. "How would you describe the smell of what I'm saying now?"

"Like butter, salt, and caramel sauce. Honest to God. You're amazing."

Lori exhaled and straightened her arms, pushing herself back. "You're a crazy piece of shit."

Something dark, something unstable flickered in his mind and memory and vanished back into the purely dark and fathomless realm where so much of the Ladykiller was rooted. Once again he shook his head, this time to rid himself of the terror and misery which had so briefly shone forth, and after that briefest possible moment of disconnection saw that Lori had not after all been waiting to bolt from the table. Instead, she had jerked open the drawer and snatched out a knife with a curved blade and a fat leather handle wrapped in layers of sweat-and-dirt-stained tape. He loved that knife. Looking at it, you would be so distracted by its ugliness that you'd never notice how sharp it was. You wouldn't fear what it could do until it was already too late.

"Oh, that old thing," he said. "What are you going to do, open a beer can?"

"I'll open you right up, unless you toss me those keys." (The worse it got, the better it smelled: a bank of tiger lilies, the open window of a country kitchen.)

He pulled himself back into focus. "Jeez, you could have picked up one of the scalpels. Then I might be scared."

"You want me to swap it for a scalpel? It must be really lethal."

"*You'll* never find out," he said, and began slowly to move toward her again, holding out his hands as if in supplication.

"No matter what happens, I'm glad I'm not you." (Dishwashing liquid in a soapy sink, a wealth of lemon-scented bubbles: in his humble opinion, one of the world's greatest odors.)

Lori Terri moved back a single step and assumed a firmer grip on the ugly handle. She was holding it the right way, he noticed, sharp side up.

"You're a funny little thing." He straightened up, laughed, and wagged an index finger at her. "You have to admit, that is pretty droll."

"You have the emptiest, ugliest life I can imagine. You look like you'd be so much fun, but really you're as boring as a cockroach—the rest of your life is a disguise for what you do in this miserable room. Everything else is just a performance. Can't you see how disgusting that is?" This whole statement emerged clothed in a slowly turning haze of perfumed girl-neck gradually melting to a smellscape of haystacks drying in a sunstruck field. This was terrible, somehow shaming.

"I thought I heard you trying to talk me into a blow job."

"That's when I was scared. I'm not afraid of you any more." (Spinach, creamed, in a steakhouse.)

"Oh, come on." He moved across the room on a slanting line, trying to back her into a corner. "I know you're scared."

"I was afraid when I thought I had a chance to get out of this cockroach parlor. But I really don't, do I? I'm going to die here. At best, I'll cut you up a little bit. Then you'll kill me, and it'll all be over. You, however, will have to go on being a miserable fucked-up creep with a horrible, depressing life." (Who knew what that was—horses? A rich man's stables?)

"At least I'll have a life," he said, and felt that he had yielded some obscure concession, or told her absolutely the wrong thing.

"Sure. A terrible one, and you'll still be incredibly creepy." (Incredibly, this came out in a sunny ripple of clean laundry drying on a line.)

"I believe you might be starting to piss me off."

"Wouldn't that be a fucking shame." An idea of some kind moved into her eyes. "You thought I might change your life? I think you were right, I think I will change your life. Only right now you have no idea how that'll happen. But it'll be a surprise, that I can tell you."

Amazed, he said, "You think you're better than me?" (*And you just said four or five sentences that smelled like cloves and vetiver.*)

"You're a disgusting person, and I'm a good one."

She feinted and jabbed with the curved blade. It was enough to push him backward.

"I see you're afraid of this knife."

He licked his lips, wishing he were holding a baseball bat, or maybe a truncheon, a thing you could swing, hard, to knock in the side of someone's head. Then, before he could think about what he was going to do, he ducked left and immediately swerved to his right. Having succeeded in faking her off-balance, the Ladykiller rushed forward, furious and exulting, eager to finish off this mouthy bitch.

Before he could get a proper grip on her, Lori surprised him by jumping left and slashing at him. The blade, which had been fabricated by a long-dead craftsman in Arkansas and honed and honed again a thousand times on wet Arkansas stone, opened the sleeve of his nice tweed jacket and continued on to slice through the midriff of his blue broadcloth shirt. In the second-and-a-half it took him to let go of her shoulder and anchor his hand on her wrist, blood soaked through the fine fabric of the shirt and began to ooze downward along a straight horizontal axis. As soon as he noticed that the growing bloodstain had immediately begun to spread and widen, he heard blood splashing steadily onto the floor, looked for the source, and witnessed a fat red stream gliding through the slashed fabric on his sleeve.

"Damn you." He jerked her off-balance and threw her to the ground. "What am I supposed to do now? Hell!"

She looked up at him from the floor. Crimson stains and spatters blossomed on her opened skirt and splayed legs. "The sight of your own blood throws you into a panic," she said. "Figures, I guess." (Tomato soup, no surprise, with garlic. Was she actually controlling the smells she sent out?)

"You *hurt* me!" He kicked her in the hip.

"Okay, you hurt me back. Now we're even," she said. "If you give me the keys, I'll bandage you up. You could bleed to death, you know. I think you ought to be aware of—"

Both her words and the renewed smell of laundry drying in sunshine on a backyard clothesline caused rage to flare through all the empty spaces in his head and body. He bent over, ripped the knife from her loose hand, and with a single sweep of his arm cut so deeply through her throat that he all but decapitated her. A jet of blood shot from the long wound, soaking his chest before he could dodge out of the way. Lori Terry jittered a moment and was dead.

"Bitch, bitch, damn bitch," he said, "fuck this shit—I'm bleeding to death here!"

He trotted across the room to a pair of sinks, stripping off his jacket as he went and leaving bloody footprints in his wake. Though his wounds bled freely, and when first exposed seemed life-threatening, a matter that made him feel queasy and light-headed, soon he was winding bands of tape around a fat pad of gauze on his arm. The long cut on his stomach proved less dangerous but harder to staunch. While simultaneously stretching toward his spine with one hand and groping with the other, he found himself wishing that Lori had not been such a colossal bitch as to make him kill her before she could help him wrap the long bandage around the middle of his body. Of course, had she not been such an unfeeling bitch, she would have obliged him by curling up in whimpering terror even before he explained in free-spending detail precisely what he was going to do to her. The tramp had escaped the punishment she had craved, down there at the dark center of her heart. She got to fulfill her goal, but she had cheated herself of most of the journey toward it! And cheated him of being her guide!

While he was mopping the floor with a mixture of bleach and soapy water, the Ladykiller remembered his admiration of Lori Terry—the respect she had evoked in him by being uncowed. Instead of bursting into tears and falling down she had offered him a blow job! He had approved the tilt of her chin, the steadiness of her voice. Also, the resolute, undaunted look in her eyes. And the odors, the odors, the odors, in their unfathomable unhurried march. In farewell to her spirit, he dropped to his knees at the edge of her pooled blood, pursed his lips and forcefully expelled air, but although he managed to create a row of sturdy little ripples, for only the second or at a stretch maybe third time in his life as the Ladykiller he failed to rise up even a single bubble. He nearly moaned in frustration, but held back: she had refused to speak in Cockney, she had held to her dignity.

For the first time in his long career, the Ladykiller came close to regretting an obligatory murder, but this approach to remorse withered and died before the memory of her ugly dismissal of his life. Why, he wondered, should a sustained, lifelong performance be *disgusting*? Couldn't the cow see how interesting, how clever his whole splendid balancing act had been? After this consoling reflection, his pain, which had been quietly pulsing away, throbbed within his lower abdomen and left forearm. This was a sharp reminder of her treachery. When the floor shone like the surface of a pond, he rinsed and stowed the mop, reverently washed the curved knife in a sink, and approached the long cold table where Lori Terry's naked body, already cleansed and readied, awaited the final rites.

Two hours later, with everything, tables, walls, floor, switches, the dismembered body—rescrubbed and doused yet again in bleach, he stacked Lori's remains in a cardboard steamer trunk: feet and calves; thighs; pelvis; female organs from which his traces had been washed; liver, heart, lungs, stomach, and spleen in one bag, the long silver ropes of her intestines in another; hands and forearms; upper arms; ribcage; spine; shoulders; and as in life the open-eyed head atop all in a swirl of pale hair. At the end, she had smelled of nothing but washed corpse. He locked the trunk, lugged it up the stairs, dragged it to his car, and with considerable effort wedged it into the car's trunk.

On his journey back into the city, he found that the care he had given her body, the thorough cleansing, the equally thorough separation of part from part, its arrangement within its conveyance, brought back to him now the respect he had learned to feel for her once the final key had turned in his serial locks. For respect it had been, greater and more valuable than admiration. Lori Terry had displayed none of the terror she, no less than his other victims, felt when she saw the pickle she was in: instead she had fought him from the beginning, with, he saw now, offers of sex that had actually promised something else altogether. She had wanted him exposed and vulnerable, she had wanted him open to pain, *in* grave pain—she had intended to put him in agony. It was true, he had to admire the bitch.

A momentary vision of the dismembered body arrayed like an unfolding blossom in the cardboard trunk popped like a flashbulb in his mind. He heard words begin to flow through his throat before he realized that he was talking out loud—talking to Lori Terry.

As he spoke, he had been removing the girl's remains from the cardboard trunk and placing them this way and that on the cobblestones of back-street downtown Milwaukee. It took a while to get them right. By the time he was satisfied, gray, early light had begun to wash across the cobbles and the garbage cans behind the clubs. Lori Terry's porcelain face gazed up at him like a bust in a museum. Then he was gone, yessir, the Ladykiller was right straight outta there, clean as a you-know-what and on to pastures new.

THE BAD HOUR

CHRISTOPHER GOLDEN

The hiss of the hydraulic doors dragged Kat Nellis from an uneasy sleep and she came awake with a thin gasp of hope. Her neck ached from the way she'd been huddled in the corner of the bus seat, her skull canted against the window, but at least the dream had come to an end.

The same fucking dream.

It wasn't an every-night sort of thing, but frequent enough that whenever she went a few days without having it, she began to feel not relief but a creeping sort of dread. Ironic, because what made the dream verge on a nightmare was that same feeling, the inescapable knowledge that something terrible was about to happen.

The dreams were always of Iraq, of the time she'd spent escorting convoys along the worst stretch of highway in the world. In the dream, she would hold her breath as the truck rumbled over ruined pavement, waiting for a tire to smash down on top of a mine or for a broken-down car to explode with a planted IED, or for an old woman or a child on the side of the road to step aside to reveal a suicide bomber. Kat had done hideous things in the war—things that would haunt her waking hours for the rest of her life—but when she slept, it was the dread of the unknown, of *waiting*, that plagued her dreams.

"Come on, honey," the bus driver called back to her. "If you're gettin' off, this is the place. Wish I could get you closer."

Kat stretched her stiff muscles and felt her joints pop as she stood. She'd kept fit in the years since she had left the army, but there were some wounds the human body could heal but never forget. Down in your bones, you would remember. Blown fifteen feet by a roadside explosion, she had survived with little more than some scrapes and bruises and a wrenched back. Kat felt grateful that she still had all of her working parts, that she hadn't been closer to the explosion, but her back had never been the same. She had no shrapnel, no bullets lodged in her body, but her spine always ached, and in warm weather, she had a tinny buzz in her brain that kept her company everywhere she went.

It was autumn now, though. No more buzzing.

She slipped her backpack over her shoulder and walked to the front of the bus. Passengers studied her curiously, wondering why she would be getting off in the middle of nowhere. A seventyish woman in a head scarf squinted at her, and Kat smiled in response, unoffended by the scrutiny.

"How far is it from here?" she asked when she reached the front of the bus.

The October morning breeze blew in through the open door and a man in the first row muttered something, half asleep, and tugged his jacket tighter around his throat as he nestled back in his seat.

"Gotta be eight or ten miles," said the driver. He took out a handkerchief and blew his big red nose, then sniffled as he tucked the rag away. "Sorry I can't run you down there."

"No worries. I could do with the walk."

She stepped down onto the road and the door closed behind her. The bus rumbled away, the morning sun hitting the windows at an angle that turned them black. Kat inhaled deeply, calming herself. The bus was on its way to Montreal, but she had gotten off about twenty miles south of the Canadian border. She stood on the side of Route 118 and glanced around at mountains covered in evergreens and patches of orange and red fall foliage. Most of the leaves that were going to fall this far north had already fallen.

October, Kat thought. She'd grown up in Montana, and though the landscape looked different, the chilly breeze and the slant of autumn light made Vermont feel like home.

Across from the spot where the bus had dropped her, a narrow road led through the trees. The morning sky might be blue, but the trees cast that street into dusky shadow. No sign identified this as King's Hollow Road, and the bus had already pulled away. No way to confirm her location with the driver. A quick check of her phone confirmed her expectation of crappy cell service out here in the middle of mountainous nowhere.

Kat pushed her fingers through her short blond hair, rubbed the sleep from her eyes, and set off into the shadows.

For the first few miles, she doubted she had found King's Hollow Road at all. She passed several farms and spotted a handful of people collecting pumpkins from a field. No cars went by, but she did pass two narrow roads heading off to the southwest. If the bus driver had left her in the right place, this road should take her right into Chesbro, Vermont, if the town still existed.

Not a town, she reminded herself. Chesbro was officially a village, or it had been the last time anyone had noticed there had been a village at the end of King's Hollow Road. She'd had no trouble finding its location on the Internet, confirming its existence on Google Earth and studying three-year-old satellite photos of its small village center. But her Internet searching had turned up virtually nothing else—no local newspaper, no listing of obituaries. Nothing of note had transpired there in the past forty years.

At the bus station in St. Johnsbury, she had found only one person who could tell her anything about the town, an old man who ran the kiosk that sold candy and magazines. The skinny fellow had stroked his beard and told her that there'd been a mill in Chesbro once upon a time, but it had been closed for ages and most of the locals had drifted away. That sort of thing happened more often than people knew. Kat understood that, but the only address she had for Ray Lambeau was in Chesbro. If she intended to find him, that was where she had to begin.

An hour after she'd set out from where the bus had dropped her, Kat rounded a corner and came to a stop on the leaf-strewn pavement. Half a dozen massive concrete blocks had been laid across the road and onto the soft shoulder. The blocks on the left and right had steel hooks set into the concrete, and heavy chains looped from the hooks to enormous pine trees on either side of the road. A dirty signpost reading STOP HERE FOR DELIVERIES had been plinked with bullets, some of which had punched right through the metal. There was no other hint that Chesbro lay ahead—only the certainty that whatever might be down that road, outsiders weren't welcome.

"Fuck it," Kat said, moving between two of the concrete blocks.

She had spent her life going places she wasn't welcome.

-o-

The pavement over the next five miles was broken and rutted, weeds growing up from the cracks. Nobody had cut back the trees in years and they had spread into a canopy over the road. Most of the people in the region seemed to have forgotten Chesbro, and the story she'd heard of the whole place being abandoned seemed more plausible with every step. Then she crested a rise in the road and paused to stare at the little village that lay before her.

A white church sat on one end of an idyllic village green with a bandstand at the center. On the other end of the green was a main street with brick buildings, little shops, town hall, and a little diner on a corner. There was even a little theater with a marquee overhanging the sidewalk, the sort of place she had only ever seen in old movies. If not for the large gray building that sat on the edge of a narrow river farther up the road, it would have looked like a New Englander's idea of Heaven. In contrast to her expectations, the village seemed well cared-for, certainly not abandoned.

As she walked toward the green, Kat felt her pulse quicken. Chesbro might not look empty, but it certainly felt that way. She passed several large houses and a brick building that might once have been a bank. Unsettled by the silence, Kat had begun holding her breath, but now she heard the squeak of hinges and saw motion in her peripheral vision. She swung around to see a bearded man in green flannel and blue jeans exiting Chesbro Hardware with a small plastic bag in one hand. The other held a can of paint.

The man's eyes went wide and he dropped the can, which plunked to the ground. His reaction—as if *she* were the ghost—struck her as odd, but not nearly as odd as the way he closed his eyes and took several deep breaths. He pressed his fingers against his wrist as if checking his pulse. When he opened his eyes, he had a wary smile on his face.

"You gave me quite a fright," he said, picking up the paint can and starting toward her. "Looks like I startled you as well."

"That's all right," Kat found herself saying. "I'm guessing you don't get a lot of visitors around here."

The man picked up the paint can, shifted it into the hand holding the plastic bag, and put out his free hand to shake.

"Elliot Bonner," he said. "And that's one way of putting it. If you came down King's Hollow, I'd guess you know we haven't exactly laid out the welcome mat."

Kat shook his rough hand and introduced herself. She stood five foot nine, taller than the average woman, but Bonner was half a foot taller. Another day, somewhere else, she suspected she would have found him quite attractive, but something about the set of his eyes made her uneasy. Elliot Bonner looked worried.

"Sorry," she said. "I'm looking for someone and I guess I was too focused on that to pay much attention."

"Not too late to turn around," Bonner said quietly. "Not yet."

Kat frowned. "Are you being funny? 'Cause I've come a long way and maybe I'm too tired to get the joke."

The man laughed nervously. "Just joshing ya. Who are you looking for? Might be I can help."

"His name's Ray Lambeau. We served together in Iraq. We've been keeping in touch the old-fashioned way for a while, writing letters. Ray said there was no Internet and not much phone service up here. But I haven't heard from him in six months or so, and that didn't seem right. So, here I am."

"Ray," Bonner said, as if the name tasted like shit in his mouth. He sighed, and his smile vanished. "Listen, miss—"

"Kat," she said. "Or Sergeant Nellis."

Bonner narrowed his eyes. Looked her up and down like he was sizing her up, wondering if he could take her in a fight. Kat had seen that look a hundred times before.

"I'm gonna make a suggestion, Sergeant," Bonner said, and he pointed to a split-rail fence on the other side of the road. "If you go and sit there and wait for me, I'll run over to the diner up the street and get you something to eat, packed up all nice for your trip back to the main road. On me. Trust me when I say that accepting my hospitality and my advice would be the smartest decision you ever make."

Something in Bonner's eyes, a frightened animal skittishness, reminded Kat of Iraq in the worst way. The guy felt to her like an IED packed into a broken-down truck on the side of the road, ready to explode if you nudged him wrong.

"I guess I'll find Ray myself," she said, and strode toward the village green.

The diner seemed like the most obvious place to start. This late in the morning, there wouldn't be many customers, but there had to be at least one server and a cook. In a tiny community like this, odds were good they would know pretty much everyone in the village.

Bonner caught up with her as she stepped onto the green, still carrying his purchases from the hardware store.

"Hold up, Sergeant," he said tersely. "You need to listen."

"I don't think so."

An elderly woman came out of some kind of clothing shop a couple of doors up from the diner. She had a fall knit scarf around her neck, and when she spotted Kat and Bonner, she clasped it to her chest like a church lady clutching her pearls. As Kat started to cross the street, she could see the old woman's lips moving in a silent mutter. Fearful, the woman pushed her way back into the shop and Kat heard her calling out to someone inside.

"Damn it," Bonner murmured as he caught her arm from behind.

Kat spun, tore her arm free, and stood ready for a fight. "You want to keep your hands off me."

Bonner held up his hands and exhaled, uttering a small laugh. "I don't want trouble—"

"I didn't come here to make any," Kat said, studying his face. "I'm just looking for my friend."

Bonner's mouth pinched up like he'd been sucking a lemon. He exhaled loudly. "I know how crazy this must seem, but you have to leave right now. For your own safety."

It was Kat's turn to laugh. "Are you threatening me?"

"Please calm down—"

"I'm plenty calm," she said, and meant it. In combat, she'd earned a reputation as an ice queen. "When I'm not calm, you'll know it."

"Lot of that going around," Bonner said.

Kat cocked her head in confusion. Then she heard voices behind her and turned back toward the diner. A waitress in an apron had come outside with a silver-haired man in a brown suit. Other people had come onto the street, and as she glanced around, she noticed a pair of teenagers crossing the village green in her direction. They paused at the bandstand and draped themselves over its railings in classic American teenager poses. Studying her, like there was a show about to start.

"Get her out of here, Elliot," the waitress called from in front of the diner.

Kat could only laugh. What was wrong with these people?

"Look!" she snapped. "I'm trying to find Ray Lambeau. If he's here, I just want to talk to him. If you hate outsiders so much, I'm happy to be on my way as soon as I've talked to Ray."

Bonner grabbed her by the backpack and shoulder, turning her toward the road out of town. "I'm sorry, but you just need to—"

Kat twisted and pulled him toward her even as she hammered a fist into his face. Bonner staggered backward, arms flailing, and went down on his ass.

"I told you not to put your hands on me," she said, a trickle of ice along her spine.

Bonner's lips curled back in anger as he scrambled to his feet. "You little bitch," he said, stalking toward her, fists raised, "all I wanted to do was—"

She stepped in close and hit him with a quick shot to the gut, followed up with a left to the temple, and then a knee in the balls. Bonner roared as he went down.

"Kat, no!" a voice cried out.

She turned to see Ray Lambeau running across the green. Her first thought was that he looked like shit, pale and too thin and with dark circles under his eyes.

"Sarge, please," Ray said, rushing up to her and grabbing her arm. "You don't know what you're doing. You can't be here."

He started hustling her away from Bonner and she let him, startled and hurt by his reaction to her arrival. Her backpack felt much heavier all of a sudden, and she looked over at the hardware store and the beginning of King's Hollow Road and realized that Ray was propelling her back the way she'd come, just the way Bonner had. Corporal Ray Lambeau wanted her out of his hometown.

Behind her, Kat heard cussing and shouts of alarm.

"Kat—" Ray began, his breath warm at her ear.

She shook loose and turned to stare at him, saw the fear in his eyes. "You're all insane. . . ."

"Go," he pleaded with her, shaking his head in frustration as he glanced toward the village green. "Please, just go."

More shouts came from that direction, but she kept her gaze fixed on Ray. His eyes had begun to moisten and he seemed to realize it the same moment she did. Letting out a breath, he struggled to keep his emotions in check the same way Bonner had. Then they both heard a clanking of something metal, followed by the unmistakable sound of someone cocking a rifle.

Ray lowered his head. "Kat, *please* . . ."

She'd been so wrapped up in her hurt and irritation that she had focused entirely on him. Now she turned toward the spectators again and saw that they had lost all interest in the spectacle of her little drama with Ray. They had surrounded Bonner. The man hunched over and a keening wail began to issue from his lips. He dragged his fingers through his hair and tugged at his beard and bent over further, arms folding inward.

One of the spectators stepped forward, a rifle hung in his arms.

"Jesus," Kat whispered.

The teenagers who'd been loitering by the bandstand dragged a net across the grass, its edges weighted with cast-iron pans and a hodgepodge of other metal objects.

All these people had wanted her to leave. For the first time, she wished she had.

"Ray?" Kat said, taking several steps back onto the village green.

People were talking to Bonner the way they would talk to a toddler holding a gun, or a loose dog with a penchant for biting. Nobody wanted to go near him, but the guy with the rifle took a bead and then nudged the teenagers forward.

"Listen—" Kat said.

At the sound of her voice, Bonner whipped around to snarl at her.

She froze, her mind trying to make sense of what she saw. Bonner's mouth opened impossibly wide. Rows of needle-sharp black teeth glistened in the morning light, viscous saliva drooling onto his beard. His skin had turned a bruise-yellow leather, run through with thick crevices and dry cracks in the flesh. His eyes were sickly orange and they fixed on her as he opened those deadly jaws and hissed wetly.

Jaw slack, body numb, Kat flinched and reached for her hip, where she would've had a gun if she were still in the army. Her fingers closed on empty air and she blinked, understanding that all of this was real.

As Bonner took a step toward her, Kat stumbled back.

"Ray," she mumbled, "what the fuck is that?"

Bonner leaped at her. Kat twisted out of the way, let him sail right by, and punched him in the back of the head. As people shouted, she followed through with a blow to the kidney. Ray called to her to get back, but she kicked the back of Bonner's leg and his knee buckled. She felt the familiar sensation of ice sliding into her veins, the calm that always came over her on the battlefield.

She drove a fist into Bonner's skull, then pistoned her arm back for another blow. He turned on one knee and lunged, tackled her around the waist, and drove her to the grass. Kat hit hard, all the air bursting from her lungs. Bonner threw back his head and roared in savage triumph, and she saw those black teeth again. Pink spittle hung in webs from his jaws and dripped onto her face. Kat bucked against him, kidney-punched him again, but Bonner slapped her arms away.

The crack of a rifle shot echoed across the village green and off the main street façades. Bonner jerked. Blood sprayed as the bullet punched through his right side and kept going. Enraged and off-balance, the berserker turned toward the man with the rifle. Kat bucked harder, reached up, and threw him off, scrambling away as Bonner roared again, trying to recover.

The teenage boys were there with the net. They threw it over him and Kat wanted to shout at them, thinking no way could a simple net hold a man so monstrously strong, even with the metal weights tied around its circumference. But Bonner cried out and smacked against the ground. He thrashed once and then was still, wide-eyed and panting like a dog, as if something about the cast-iron pans and other weights caused him pain.

A second passed as they all stared.

Kat turned on Ray. "What the *fuck*? Shit like this does not happen in the real world."

Ray put his hands out. "Kat, calm down—"

"Don't tell me to calm down! Talk to me about this!" She gestured toward Bonner, netted and moaning on the grass. "This isn't just a freak-out. Look at the guy's face! Look at his skin!"

In combat, her ability to remain calm could be eerie. But with the fight over and the reality of what she'd just seen sinking in, panic began to unravel her. Kat could practically feel her self-control shattering.

Ray approached her, hands still up. "Kat, stop. Just breathe and listen to my voice—"

"I'm listening!" She looked over at Bonner again, glanced at the bloody fissures in his leathery skin, and saw the murder in his eyes, trying to match this visage up with the man who had walked out of the hardware store with a can of paint.

Ray put his hands on her arms. "Kat—"

She recoiled from his touch. "What is he? What is . . ."

Kat felt it then. Panic, fear, and anger had all been roiling inside her, and now the anger surged upward in a wave of malice. She snapped around to glare at Ray and her lips peeled back in a snarl. His eyes widened in alarm and he stepped backward, but she pursued him, swinging a fist. Ray tried to block, but too slow. She struck him in the cheek and heard the bone crack, then followed up with a left to the gut that sent him reeling across the grass.

She ran her tongue over her teeth and felt their sharpness . . . and their number. Horror seized her. Thick drool ran out over her bottom lip and dribbled down her chin. Raising her hands to lunge at him, she saw that her skin had darkened and split, and she understood, but Kat could do nothing to stop herself. She grabbed a fistful of Ray's hair, and she laughed as she dragged one yellow fingernail across his cheek, opening up a bloody furrow.

When the gunshot rang out and the bullet punched through her back, she felt only relief.

⟨⟩

Kat woke with a groan. Her throat felt parched and she ached all over. When she shifted on the hard cot, bright pain seared a place on her back just below her left shoulder blade. She rolled onto her side and opened her eyes to see metal bars and flickering fluorescent lights.

A jail cell.

She shifted on the cot and saw Ray leaning against a desk out in the room beyond her cell. *Village jail,* she thought. *Police chief's office, one cell. Fucking Mayberry.* Sitting up, she felt like she might pass out again, but she forced herself to sit there and she stared at Ray . . . at this man who had been her friend under fire. More than a friend.

"It started in Iraq," he said quietly.

"Say again?"

Ray gestured toward the door and whatever lay beyond it.

"That. Out there," he said. "It started in Iraq. Since then, I've done some research. Different stories come from different parts of the world, Greece in particular, but the name translates pretty much the same in Arabic as in Greek. Both call it 'the Bad Hour.'"

Kat tried to clear her head. "Are you making zero sense or am I just not—"

"You remember the day I lost it?"

She stared at him, a hard knot in her gut. Images slid through her mind of a shattered door and a dead family, a grandmother with her head caved in, two little bloodstained boys full of bullet holes, and a grief-mad mama shot for trying to take revenge. Kat had seen worse in her time in Iraq, but not at the hands of a friend, someone she trusted. After that day, it had been weeks before she had let Ray touch her again.

"I remember."

"That wasn't the only time something like that happened. Just the only time you were there to see it." His voice was a guilty rasp. "A couple of days before the incident you remember, Harrison picked me for a squad to search a little enclave on the outskirts of Haditha for insurgents. Local informants told us the place was off-limits—nobody ever went there and nobody ever left. Merchants brought supplies up from the city and left them at a drop point. People from the enclave came out to get them after the delivery men had gone."

Kat blinked, alert now, remembering her walk into Chesbro and the sign she'd encountered at the roadblock. The parallel was not lost on her.

"I don't know if we got intel that insurgents were hiding there or if we just figured what better place for them to hide than somewhere considered off-limits, but we went in hard," he continued.

Ray stared at her, his eyes so damn sorry. She remembered those eyes well, even that look, and she hated him for making her remember how she'd felt on those dark nights in the desert.

"What you saw out there with Bonner?" he said. "We saw it with everyone in the enclave. Killed every last one of them because once they went rabid like that, killing them was the only way we could stop them. When it was over, Harrison told us the rest of what the locals had fed him, the story about the enclave and the Bad Hour. It's like an infection. You let yourself get too angry or too emotional in general, and it just . . . takes over. The people around Haditha said the Bad Hour was a demon, that once it touched you, it stayed with you always, ready to take over if you couldn't control yourself."

"Bullshit," she whispered, the weight of the story crushing her. If she had heard about it before coming here, she'd never have believed it. But now?

"They also said it was contagious," Ray went on. He closed his eyes and breathed evenly, and she recognized the effort he made to stay calm. Remembered him doing the same earlier, and Bonner as well.

The ice in her gut grew heavier. Kat stood and grabbed the bars of her cell. "Let me out of here, Ray."

"In a while."

She smashed an open palm against one of the bars of the cell. "Let me out, asshole. I can't stay here!"

Ray pushed away from the desk and walked toward the cell. He stopped a few feet from the bars and studied her with those I'm-sorry eyes.

"You can't leave, Kat. We'll let you out in a little while, but the Bad Hour's in you now. Harrison's squad killed everyone in that enclave, but we brought it out with us. Some of the guys in that squad are dead. Others are probably out there infecting people the way I did in Chesbro. I didn't mean to. Even after the times I lost it in Iraq, I chalked it up to the war. PTSD, maybe. But once I came home . . . once I was in one place long enough . . . I started to see it happen to other people."

Kat remembered Bonner's face, the way he'd changed, and the strength and rage that had filled her when she had turned on Ray. Then she remembered the day she had seen him go berserk, the day he'd killed that family.

"When you lost it, you didn't look like Bonner," she said. "Yeah, you were a fucking lunatic, but—"

"At first, none of us looked any different when it came on. The way I've got it figured, once the Bad Hour takes root in a place, it gets stronger. The people in the enclave looked like Bonner when they went rabid—"

"But I . . . This *just* happened to me. If you don't look like that at first . . ."

Ray grabbed one of the bars. "I'm explaining this badly. It's the Bad Hour that's getting stronger, taking root. Maybe it's one demon or maybe it's a bunch of little ones, like parasites, but it gets stronger. Doesn't matter if it's your first time giving in to it . . . it's the strength of the Hour that matters. Not always an hour, either. The stronger it gets, the longer it can hold on to you."

Kat laughed softly, but it wasn't really a laugh at all.

She rested her forehead against the bars. Impossible. All of this was simply insanity. For a moment, she wondered if she had fallen asleep on that northbound bus and still sat there, dreaming with her skull resting against the window. But that was mere fantasy.

"What you're talking about . . . it can't be," she said softly.

Ray wrapped his fingers around hers, him on one side of those bars and her on the other. "I've seen the way you can rein in your fear, Kat. You can do this. You have to."

Kat began to tremble. She pressed her lips together, trying to stay in control, but tears welled in her eyes.

"You don't know what you're saying. I have to . . ."

Ray squeezed her hand sharply, and she snapped her head up and stared at him.

"Stop. You know what will happen," he said. *"Calm down."*

Kat pulled her hand away and wiped at her eyes. She nodded, took a shuddery breath, and straightened her spine. Another deep breath. Terrified of the Hour taking her over again, that madness . . . She didn't want to believe, but she could not erase from her mind the things she had seen. The things she had felt.

"I'm all right," she told him firmly. "But you can't keep me here. I have to go home, Ray."

"Kat—"

"I have a daughter."

He frowned, staring at her.

Kat inhaled. Exhaled. Felt that familiar battlefield chill spread through her. This was an altogether different sort of combat.

"I have to leave," she said, "but I get it, Ray. And I'll come back."

Ray held onto the bars from the outside as if worried he might fall over if he let go. "How old is she? Your girl?"

Kat embraced the combat chill in her bones. Met his gaze. "She's four."

"Four," he said, a dull echo.

"I wanted to raise her myself," Kat said. "You were my friend, but I'd seen what kind of man you could be. What kind of father you might be. I thought it would be better—"

"You started writing to me," Ray said, gaze pinning her to the floor inside her cell. "Then when I stopped replying, you came looking. If you didn't want me to know—"

Kat approached the bars again. This time, it was she who put her hands over his.

"At first, I just wanted to reconnect. I guess I figured someday I'd tell you. Then later . . . I needed to talk to you," Kat said. Breathing evenly. "Her baby teeth started falling out at the beginning of this year. That's early. *Really* early. The new ones have been growing in ever since . . ."

She breathed. Steadied herself.

"Tell me," Ray said through gritted teeth, and she saw that he was doing it too. The both of them just breathing. Slow and steady. In control.

But they couldn't stay in control every second of every day. Not forever.

Nobody could do that. Especially not a toddler.

"The new teeth are coming in and she has too many of them, Ray. They're tiny things, sharp and black, and there are too many—"

"Kat, no."

She let the cold fill her, stared into his eyes.

"And, Ray," Kat said. "Your little girl has such a temper."

RED RABBIT

STEVE RASNIC TEM

H e found her on the back porch again, watching the yard through the sliding glass door. He didn't want to spook her, so he made some noise as he left the kitchen, bumped a chair, and made a light tap with one shoe on the metal threshold that separated the porch from the rest of the house. Then he stopped a few feet behind her and said, "What are you looking at, honey?"

"The rabbit. Matt, have you seen that rabbit?

"That was yesterday, Clara. Remember? I went down there, and I scooped it up with a shovel, and I dropped it into a trash bag. Some wild animal got to it. Rabbits can't protect themselves very well. That was yesterday."

"But it's back." Her voice shook. "Can't you see it?"

He followed her gaze to the lower part of the lawn, where it dipped downhill to the fence. Shadows tended to pool there, making the area look damp even though it hadn't rained in almost two months. Beyond were a field of weeds and wildflowers, and the line of trees bordering the old canal. Beyond that was the interstate. You couldn't see it, but you could certainly hear the traffic—a vacillating roar that you could pretend was a river if you really tried.

The skinned and bloody rabbit had appeared there yesterday at the bottom of the yard, eased out of the shadows as if from a pool. And here was another one, its front legs stretched out toward the house, its body gleaming with fresh blood. This must have just happened. They must have had some sort of predator in the yard.

"I see it," he said. "Something got another one."

"Something terrible is happening," she said. "I've been feeling it for weeks. And now this rabbit—I see it every day. Sometimes just after sunrise, sometimes just before sunrise. I thought I was going crazy, but now you see it too. What do you think it wants? Can you tell me what it wants?"

Matt looked at her: her eyes red and unfocused, lips trembling. She was somewhere else inside her head. She was wearing this old green tube-top thing. She'd never looked good in it. Her back was knotted, her shoulders pushed up, her arms waving around as she spoke. He figured she must be crazy tense if he noticed it—he never noticed things like that.

He felt sorry for her, but he also felt scared for himself. The woman he had loved had been gone for years, and now he was left with this. He wasn't a good enough person to handle something he hadn't signed up for.

"It's not the same rabbit, Clara. There must be a predator loose in the neighborhood. Probably just a big cat or maybe a dog. It's just a dead rabbit. I'll go get the shovel and take care of it. There's nothing to get upset about."

He didn't really understand how her mind worked anymore. But maybe his being logical helped her. No one could say he hadn't tried.

"There's blood all over him," she said. "He's all torn up. Can't you see that something terrible is going to happen, that something terrible *is* happening? Can't you see it?"

She continued to stare at the rabbit in the yard. She wouldn't turn around and look at him. It felt creepy, talking to her back all the time. He didn't dare touch her when she was like this, like a fistful of nerves. He didn't think she'd looked at him full in the face in days.

"It was a wild animal. It had a savage life. And something got to it. It's not like a cartoon, Clara. Rabbits can't protect themselves very well. Real rabbits in the wild, their lives are short and cruel."

They hadn't had sex in a long time. He'd been afraid to touch her. You can learn to live with crazy, but you can't touch it. He couldn't let her drive, and when he left her alone she called him at work every hour to complain about some new thing she'd suddenly realized was wrong. Their GP kept prescribing new pills for her, but he was just a kid, really. Matt was sure the fellow had no idea what was wrong with her.

"I haven't been feeling right, Matt. Not for a very long time. Something terrible is going to happen—can't you sense that?"

"I know that's what you feel, but just go lie down. Let me take care of this, and then I'll come join you." But he knew she wasn't hearing, the way she stared, glassy-eyed and the edge of her upper teeth showing. He stood in front of her and whispered, "Go inside now. Please." When she didn't respond he stepped closer to block her view of the yard and put one arm around her, gave her a bit of squeeze.

"Honey, just go inside and lie down. I'll join you in a few minutes. Maybe I can even figure out what's killing these rabbits, and I'll deal with the thing. You just go inside." Hopefully she'd be asleep when he was done. When she was asleep he could grab a drink, watch some TV, relax and unwind for once.

He grabbed a shovel and a trash bag and some gloves and started down the slope of the lawn. He'd generally neglected that part of the back yard. The ground there had always been mushy, unstable. He didn't know much about ground water, septic systems, any of that stuff. But he figured it must be some sort of drainage issue, maybe because of the old canal, or maybe because of an old broken septic system, something like that. It didn't smell too bad, just a little stagnant most of the time, a little sour. Only sometimes it stank like rotting meat. But they couldn't afford to fix it whatever it was, so he'd just tried to ignore it.

The carcass wasn't where he had seen it. In fact he couldn't find the rabbit anywhere. He thought about that mysterious predator, and went back to the house and grabbed the rake that was leaning against the wall by the sliding glass doors.

He stood still, the rake held in both hands in front of him, raised like a club. He still didn't see the rabbit. He felt unsteady, and shortened his grip on the handle. He imagined that the predator, whatever it was, had dragged the body off somewhere. Some of the more dangerous animals in the region—coyotes, a wildcat or two, once even a small bear—had been known to wander out of the foothills and follow the canal into the more populous suburbs. He crept down the lawn toward the fence, afraid he might lose his footing. The grass looked shiny, slippery, as if the earth beneath were liquefying.

He detected a subtle reddish shadow as he got closer to the fence, and then saw that it was a spray of blood. The body had been pushed up against one of the fence posts, eviscerated, but still clearly some version of rabbit. He was glad Clara couldn't see this. It must have suffered terribly, ripped and skinned alive, all gleaming, bright-red muscle, damp white bone, strings of pale fat. But the muscle had no business being bright red like that, like some kind of rich dyed leather. He'd skinned squirrels with his dad—he knew what a dead, skinned animal looked like, so dark and bruised. But this? This looked unreal.

He bagged it and trashed it, then brought out the hose to wash away the blood and any loose pieces of meat. That's what you did with this sort of thing. That's how you handled it. You cleaned up the mess and then you went on with your life. Later he grabbed his binoculars and studied the field and the trees beyond, checking for any signs of movement. He saw nothing. If he had been ambitious he would have climbed over the fence and walked through the field to the row of trees that bordered the canal. He could have followed that canal into some other place. The water might not be running through the canal anymore, but it was still a passage to something, wasn't it? But he wasn't ambitious. And he didn't want to go there.

Matt drank and watched TV until about midnight. The house was a mess—Clara hadn't cleaned in weeks. He couldn't abide a messy house, but he worked all day—he didn't have the time. But if he had the time he knew he'd do a great job. It wasn't that hard keeping up a house—you just had to understand how to manage time and not let it get away from you. He hadn't signed up for this. He'd tried—and you owed your wife at least to try. But everybody had limits. You couldn't expect a man not to have his limits.

She didn't wake up when he crawled into bed with her. Good thing—she'd ask about the rabbit, and he didn't want to talk about that damn rabbit anymore.

He woke up once and saw her standing at the window, looking out onto the back yard. He started to say something, started to ask her what was wrong, but he stopped himself. He was tired, and he knew what was wrong.

He woke up alone. He didn't like waking up alone, but he didn't want to answer any of her questions. He fell back asleep, and when he woke up again the room was bright from the sun coming through the window. He'd overslept, but at least it was the weekend. Nothing important ever came up on the weekend. They'd stopped doing the important stuff a long time ago.

"Clara, you up here?" She didn't answer. "Clara!" Nothing. He got his pants and shoes on and went downstairs. He still couldn't find her. He felt a little panicky, and he was mad at himself for feeling a little panicky. He made himself be methodical. He went back upstairs and searched each bedroom as he went down the hall. He wasn't sure why they had all these bedrooms—they didn't have any kids. They had way too much house, but he'd gotten such a good deal on the place.

He felt a pressure building behind his eyes. He tried to shake it off. He went back into their bedroom and looked in the closet and in the master bathroom. He got down on his knees and looked under the bed. There were several socks, another larger, unidentifiable piece of clothing. He made a note to sweep under there later.

He called again from the top of the stairs. "Clara! Are you in the house?" Nothing. No steps, no rustle, just the soft hum of the refrigerator. He went downstairs and jerked open the front door, a little too hard. It banged against the rubber bumper mounted on the wall. He hadn't realized it before, but he was beginning to feel pretty angry. Maybe she couldn't help it, but this was ridiculous.

She wasn't lying on the front lawn again, thank God. And the Subaru was still there, which was a big relief. Matt thought about getting in his car and driving around looking for her. But she could be anywhere, and besides, he knew that once you started chasing after someone like that it never ended, not until you'd given yourself a heart attack. She was a grown woman—he shouldn't have to be searching for her.

He made himself stop. Most things got better that way: taking a break, waiting. People needed to be patient, not make such a big deal out of everything.

He went out to the porch and sat down. That's when he saw her kneeling down at the bottom of the yard, her back turned to him. Just like she always did. Her shoulders were heaving.

He slid open the door and stepped outside. "Clara?"

She didn't speak, but he could hear her crying. Then he saw the blood streaks on her sleeves. He started running. "Clara!" Not again. Not again.

He came up behind her and grabbed her by the shoulders, twisting them to stop her from whatever she was doing. He grabbed both of her hands and raised them, trying to get a good look at her wrists. Her forearms, his hands, everything slick with blood. "Where's the knife, Clara!"

She looked up at him, wide-eyed and dull. "No knife. I didn't see a knife."

He couldn't find any cuts on her wrists, her arms, her hands. He looked down at her knees, and then the grass, and then the bloody bits he was standing on. He jumped back in alarm. It was another rabbit, skinned and gutted, its flesh weeping fresh blood.

"It's *back*!" she said, her voice rising. "It's back!"

"Dammit, Clara. It's not the same rabbit!"

She stared at him, her face tilted. "But how can you tell it's a different rabbit? How do you know for sure?"

He started to explain, but what was there to explain? "Because this is real life. We live in real life, Clara! Just stay right here. I'll get something to cover it with, and then we'll go wash you up, okay?"

He ran into the garage and grabbed a drop cloth, and on his way out he grabbed the rake, too, just in case of, just in case he needed it. But when he got back Clara was gone. The rabbit was still lying there, but there was no sign of Clara in the yard. How could she have moved so quickly? He stared down at the rabbit. It looked like all the others, as far as he could tell. One huge eye, pushed almost out of its socket, stared up at him.

He looked around the yard, the edge of the house, inside the house. He couldn't find her anywhere. He gave up. He imagined her walking around the neighborhood, her shirt bloody, her arms and hands bloody. Somebody would call the police. Well, the hell with it. He'd done everything he could.

Matt left the rabbit and went back inside. At least he could clean himself up. At least he could get that much done.

After his shower he grabbed a jar of peanut butter out of the fridge and stood at the kitchen window digging two fingers into the jar and eating the peanut butter right off them. Looking through the window into the porch and then through the sliding glass doors made the yard seem a pretty safe distance away. He could still see the fields and the line of trees beyond, and he was sure he'd be able to see any movement out there if there was any. But there wasn't any. After a while he collapsed into that old chair on the back porch and sat watching the yard for a couple of hours. It was midafternoon by then and he hadn't had any lunch. He supposed he could find something in the fridge to heat up, but then maybe Clara would come home. Fixing him something might occupy her, keep her mind off things.

He was actually pretty surprised she hadn't shown up yet. If the police had picked her up they would have come by now. He was used to her being anxious, but she usually snapped out of it after an hour or so and managed to get going on whatever needed to be done. He'd call some of her friends but that woman Ann had moved away six months ago and he didn't know any of the others, if there were any others. Clara never made friends easily, at least not since he'd known her.

He couldn't get over those damn rabbits. Whatever had gotten to them, it must have wiped out an entire den. Why had the thing left its kills in his yard anyway? Like a house cat dropping the mouse it slaughtered at your feet. But you had to trust your eyes—most of the time it was the one thing you could trust.

Clara needed to be back soon. She'd always been this timid thing, couldn't protect herself worth a damn. Terrible things happened to timid creatures like that. She knew. That's why she kept saying that. Well, terrible things do happen, Clara. It wasn't too hard predicting that.

He must have dozed, because the back yard suddenly looked dimmer. That shady bit down by the fence had grown, spread half-way up the yard toward the house. Lights were popping on over at the neighbors'.

He sat up suddenly as a chill grabbed his throat. "Clara!" he yelled as loud as he could to scare it away. Still no answer. He listened hard now. The refrigerator still hummed. It was like he was living by himself again.

He could check with all the neighbors, but the last thing he needed was for everybody to know his business. He could call the police, but would they even take a report? Maybe if he told them Clara was a danger to herself. She'd cut her wrists more than once, but she'd always botched the job. Timid people like that, he reckoned they intended to botch the job.

He thought about talking to some young policeman, trying to explain how Clara was, trying to explain about the skinned rabbits, how they must have a predator in the neighborhood, and how the cop would act deliberately patient, and condescending to this older guy who had just called in about his missing wife, who'd only been gone a few hours, probably on some impulsive shopping trip. Matt couldn't bear it.

She'd been a lovely girl when he'd met her—pretty, and shy. She'd made him feel like he was about the greatest man in the world. Then she got nervous, and then she got old, and surely she was crazy now. Maybe if he was truly a good man he could handle that—he'd stick with her and make the best out of a sad situation. But people had to be realistic. Good men were few and far between.

Flashing red lights broke through the trees on the other side of the field. They made it look as if parts of that line of trees bordering the old canal were on fire. But then the wind shifted the branches a bit and he could see that he was mistaken. There were scattered fires on the interstate beyond. And many more lights and faint, but explosive noises. People shouting maybe. Or cars being pried open like clamshells to get to the meat inside. The Jaws of Life, that's what they called them. But only if the people inside were still living. If not, then they were the Jaws of Death, weren't they?

The radio was right by the chair, so he could have turned it on. But he'd rather wait until Clara showed up and then they could learn together what terrible thing might have happened over on the highway. Matt supposed it was an unhealthy thing in people, how listening or watching together as the news told the details of some new disaster tended to bring couples and families together.

He sat and watched the red flashes and the burning and listened hard for the noises and the voices until it was dark enough for the automatic yard lights to come on. The gnawing in his belly was painful but he had no interest in eating, assuming eating was even the sort of remedy required.

He could see everything, except for that shadowy region down near the fence. He could see the rake where he'd left it, and the folded-up drop cloth. But there was no sign of that rabbit. Something had moved it, or maybe—and the idea made him queasy—it hadn't been completely dead. Skinned, but not dead. Crawling around suffering.

As Matt's eyes grew weary he found himself focusing on that area of shadow. It had always seemed odd that the longer you stared at a shadow the more likely you were to find other shadows swimming inside it. Something moved out of the edge. In the border between dark and light a skinned body lay in the slickened grass. Bleeding heavily, and this one much too large for a rabbit. Stripped to muscle and bone, it was an anatomical human figure made real. The skin over part of one breast remained. And when it reached its scarlet arms toward the house it called his name.

IT'S ALL THE SAME ROAD IN THE END

BRIAN HODGE

The roads all looked the same again, along with the dried-up little towns they led to. They'd all looked the same again for the last couple of years, the way they had at the beginning.

Funny thing—there was a stretch in the middle when they hadn't. Two or three years when Clarence's and Young Will's eyes had grown keen enough to pick up on the subtle differences that, say, set Slokum apart from Brownsville. Here, the peculiarities of a water tower, with the look of an alien tripod; there, the way a string of six low hills undulated across the horizon like the humps of a primordial serpent.

But now they'd let the distinctions slip away. From place to place, it wasn't that different after all. They'd seen it all before and forgotten where. Everything was the same again.

This was how things hid in open daylight, beneath the vast skies, out here in the plains of western Kansas. There was no need for mountain hollows or fern-thick forests or secret caves tucked into seaside coves. The things that wanted to stay hidden would camouflage themselves as one more piece of the monotony and endless repetition.

The worst thing Clarence could think of was that he and his brother were now a part of it too. That the land was digesting them so slowly they didn't even realize it.

Five days into this trip, the latest of many, all the Brothers Pine had to show for it was another gallon of gas traded for another dusty roadside hamlet that, until this moment, was just a name along a blue line on the most detailed map they'd been able to buy. Gilead, this time. Sometimes there wasn't even enough town to land on the map.

Another stop, another chance for the truth. More or less, it always went this way:

They started with a feed-and-seed store a block away from a grain elevator. From the moment they stepped in, they drew looks from the old man on one side of the counter and the farmer on the other. No hostility, just curiosity, and why not—both men probably knew every face within ten or twenty miles. But the pair of brothers was a disruption, their arrival like the stroke of a bell that made the farmer aware of time again, and all he had left to do in the day. He made his goodbye and his exit, out to an old workhorse of a pickup truck with a bed full of fifty-pound bags.

"Help you?" Already the old seed man sounded puzzled. They often sounded puzzled.

Smalltalk first. Sure is hot today. Sure is. Looks like you could use some rain. Sure could. Could always use more rain.

It was better when they were old. The elders were the ones with the longest memories, and a need to hang onto the stories of the things that had happened around them, especially the things that shouldn't have. They remembered events that younger people—Clarence's and Young Will's peers, especially—never knew, or never had time for.

Even Will Senior had known that, way back when.

"This may seem like a funny question," Young Will said. He was the one feeling talkative today. Just as well. He had the friendlier face, oval and open and guileless, and the taller stature that commanded attention. He looked as if he should still be in college, shooting hoops and resolute about never breaking the rules. "But have you ever heard anything about a man named Willard Chambers? This would go back quite a few years."

Then he produced the picture, the first one, black-and-white in a thousand grainy shades of gray. It had a vintage look, a vintage feel, showing a square-faced, wavy-haired man who cracked a grin both impish and wise as he gestured with a cigarette pinched between his thumb and forefinger. Did men in the prime of their lives even look like this anymore? Clarence had never seen one.

The old man dipped into memory's well and came up empty. "Can't say any of it rings a bell. Should it? What did he do?"

"He disappeared."

"Sorry to hear that." The old man's sympathy was genuine and matter-of-fact. You didn't get to be this old without a long acquaintance with loss. "When?"

"A little over fifty years ago."

"Mercy. That *is* a spell." From behind black-framed glasses sturdy enough to take a punch, the old man peered at the photo again, maybe looking for something familiar. "Did he come from around here? Have kin around here?"

"No sir, he didn't."

He took one more look at the photo, then gave them a fresh appraisal, seeing the connection in Clarence, maybe. He had inherited the square features, if not the freewheeling demeanor. He had the knitted eyebrows of a born worrier.

"Are *you* kin to him?"

"He was our grandfather," Clarence said.

The old man seemed to understand their need without having to know anything more. "A thing like that never does scab over, does it?"

Next came the second photo, along with a grainy enlargement of just its subject. "I know there's not much to go on with these, but is there anything here that looks familiar? The place, or who this might've been?"

This time the old man took the photos for himself. People did that a lot. They seemed unable to leave them on a counter. They had to pick them up, had to stare as if to prove to themselves they were real. Not that there was anything, on first inspection, that appeared false, or even out of the ordinary. Perception demanded time. People noticed the wrongness of it in subtle ways they couldn't identify, as if something fifty years behind this moment had left hidden hooks in the image, to hold their attention until they truly *saw*, and then forced their hand to thrust the photos back.

"No," the old man said. "But wherever this is, I think if I'd come across it once, I would've known to make sure I never went back."

Will nodded and slipped the photos into their folder again, the way he'd been conceding defeat for years.

"Did she have something to do with him disappearing?" the man asked. "That *is* a woman there, isn't it?"

No matter how many times they'd heard the question, there was still no easy answer.

"As far as we know," Will said, and left it at that.

Clarence stepped forward. "One last thing. Could we trouble you to listen to a recording? If you've ever heard anything like this, or about something like it?"

The old fellow was game, and slipped on the compact pair of foam-padded earphones Clarence gave him. They were downstream of an old Walkman cassette player, a clunky and outmoded thing to be toting around these days. But Will Senior had lived as an analog man in an analog world, and had made the original recording onto tape. For no reason Clarence could prove, it would've seemed wrong to digitize it for convenience; reducing it to a file would erase some ineffable quality in it that might be preserved by dubbing it to a newer tape.

He pressed PLAY.

The seed man listened privately in the baked stillness of the day, nothing but the chirring of insects outside and the chirping of birds that would eat them if they could. As went the photos, so went the tape, a slow-burn reaction that creased the old man's face with gradual repulsion. The recording went for a little over three minutes, but he had the earphones stripped away in two.

Clarence pressed STOP.

"Is that supposed to be a song?" the old man asked.

"I guess so. We don't know what else to call it."

"Call it quits, why don't you? Sounds like that aren't supposed to come out of folks' throats. No sir." The old man reached up to rub the back of his neck, bristly with gray stubble and as creased as a tortoise's skin. "The closest thing I ever heard to it . . . I come from a long line of Swedes. The women used to have a cattle call song they brung over. You don't hear it any more. It was an eerie-sounding thing, if you heard it at some distance. But you could still tell it was a woman's voice. But what you've got there . . ."

He shook his head, then regarded them with an uneasy fusion of suspicion and worry. "You seem like nice boys. Why would you want to go looking for anything to do with that?"

"You said it yourself," Young Will told him. "It's a scab thing."

◄◦►

They were both named for dead men, grandfathers they'd never met. Men who had died when their parents were still youngsters. For all Clarence knew, it was the first thing their mother and father discovered they had in common.

The carrying on of someone's name was apparently supposed to be an honor, and perhaps it was, but many were the times Clarence wondered if their parents had ever stopped to consider the obvious: the bigger the trophy, the heavier it was to lug around.

Clarence and Willard . . . neither quite felt like a twenty-first century name.

As Clarence was the firstborn, Dad had gotten first crack at him, saddling him with the moniker of a man who'd succumbed in his thirties to the black lung he'd carried up out of a West Virginia coal mine. His end had come hard and early, but at least it was certain. There was no room for doubt in it, only sorrow and blame.

Six years later, with their sister Dina in between, it was Mom's turn to christen her third child as if he were an avatar of the man who'd vanished around the time she'd been hitting puberty, and the recycled name an invitation for her father to return from whatever void had swallowed him.

The legacy of Willard Chambers was a more complicated thing for a namesake to live up to. He was restless, a roamer, but not without reason. Clarence was grown before he'd ever heard the term *songcatcher*, but that's exactly what the man was.

The inability of Will Senior to carry a tune was matched only by his reverence for those who could. He had an appreciation of history, and must have known by then that he'd lived it himself. He'd come through the Second World War, three years in the Pacific, fighting toward Japan one fierce island at a time, and seeing close-up the fragility of everything that lived and breathed.

Songs too. Songs were living things and could be killed by far less than bullets and fire. All it took was for them to stop being heard. He was a city dweller who had served alongside Okie farmboys and gangly fellows from Appalachian hollers. They brought with them songs he'd never heard on the radio. Obsessed as they were with life and death and the acts that bridged the two—murders and drownings and love gone wrong—they may have appealed to him for their stark understanding that he might not see tomorrow either.

But he had. Three years in the Pacific, and he suffered no worse than a case of paddy foot.

At some point, home again, he'd learned of the Lomaxes—John the father and Alan the son—and realized he'd found a calling. These were men who traveled the country in search of songs whose roots lay deep in the earth of crops and graves: rural blues, cowboy ballads, folk tunes from plains and mountains, prison work songs, and anything else that was a jubilant or despairing cry from the heart of a marginalized life. Will Senior bought the same tape recorder that Alan Lomax was using at the time—a compact, battery-powered reel-to-reel called a Nagra—and took it on the road whenever he could. Which amounted to as much as four or five months out of the year.

For reasons that likely went back to wartime, Willard had taken a special interest in the region known during the Great Depression as the Dust Bowl . . . an arid wasteland whose great dark eye overlapped western Kansas and eastern Colorado, a slice of New Mexico, and the panhandles of Texas and Oklahoma. He had it in his head that songs from there were most vulnerable, since so many who would've sung them had been scattered by the same winds that carried away the topsoil, leaving them mostly in the care of those who'd been too sick or old to move. He saw it as a race against time.

From everything Clarence and Will had heard about him, Willard Chambers wasn't a man you needed to worry about. He knew nearly everything there was to know about taking care of himself. His family just missed him, deeply, with the resentful ache that comes from being forced to share a man with an obsession, and counting the days until he and his '59 Chevy would be home again.

His eighth run west became his last. Neither he nor the Chevy made it back, or were ever seen again.

At least his gear—the Nagra and a Leica camera from his war years—had found its way home eventually.

Even that had taken months.

◂◦▸

They made it through five more towns north of Gilead, then it was the long ride south, back to the motel they'd been using for home base. Clarence took the wheel and Will took the map, looking over what tomorrow might bring. More of the same, that was obvious, only the route would change.

"One day," Clarence said, "every town in the western half of this map is going to have a red dot next to it. Have you ever thought about what then?"

"For you and me, you mean?"

"For Mom. If she even makes it to then. Except she probably won't."

"You mean just lie to her? Tell her we found something even though we didn't?"

"If it gives her some peace, finally, would that be so bad?"

"I see what you did there," Will said. "The next square you advance to after that is, okay, now that we've established lying as an acceptable option, why not lie to her now and save ourselves all that future trouble."

"I never said that."

"It was coming. Don't tell me it wasn't," Will said. "I keep telling you that you can bail any time you want. This doesn't have to be a two-man project. It never did."

Maybe not, but to Clarence it had always felt that way. No argument that he wasn't superstitious was as persuasive as the conviction that as soon as he let Will do this on his own, their mom would mourn a vanished son, too.

It had begun when his brother was nineteen, a college sophomore who'd enjoyed just one year of Daytona Beach debauchery before deciding he'd rather spend spring break in Kansas. Mothers Day was coming in a few weeks, and his idealistic kid brother could think of no better gift to give theirs than the answers she'd craved for decades.

Just like that, huh? Sure. Why not.

You didn't let an earnestly headstrong nineteen-year-old do something like this on his own. No telling who he might run into, and his 4.0 grade average didn't mean he couldn't be stupid when smart mattered most. Elderly Klansmen and their ilk still protected killings half a century old, and there was an uneasy sense they weren't dealing with anything quite so prosaic here.

That first year, Clarence had been counting on the enormity of the task to discourage him, and had never been so wrong about anything in his life. Spring breaks turned into career-era vacations, one year became six, and whatever happened to Will Senior remained as much a mystery as ever. And Clarence still couldn't shake the feeling that, without him, his brother would meet his own bad end.

More than once, he thought of the man in the photo, the grandfather who was two decades younger than their father was now, and wanted to hear it from the man's tobacco-seared lips: Would he even want this for them?

Go on, live your own lives and quit trying to reconstruct mine, he imagined Will Senior telling them. *Have that kid you keep telling your wife you'll get around to.*

Just like that, huh?

What is it, son, you think you've got to wait until after you get me figured out before you do it? You think you'll be doing the same thing to your kids that I did to mine by coming out here to the world's breadbasket?

Something like that.

In that case, maybe you need to get clearer on your priorities.

Easy for you to say, old man. I'm the one you left cleaning up your fifty-year-old mess.

Willard never had a comeback to that one. He never even tried.

As they drove, the sun sank low, lower, the plains and the gentle hills thickening with shadows that reached for their car from the west. Everywhere you looked, it was nothing but wheat and the road that ran through it like a path through a forest. He pointed to the last remnants of some lost homestead, an ancient barn whose bones had bent, the entire structure weathered to a silvery gray, sagging in on itself and leaning like a cripple as if to wait for the good strong breeze that would finally end its struggle.

"I keep thinking I'd like to come back here with a truck one day and tear one of these down," he said. "For the wood."

Back in his real life, he and his wife owned a frame shop. One of these wrecks could give birth to a lot of frames. It appealed, that whole life cycle thing about new life springing from decay.

"Rustic never goes out of style," he said.

Will looked up from the map, reoriented to where they were and what he was talking about, and shook his head. "I think they should stay standing."

"They're barely standing as it is. That's kind of the point."

His brother went dreamy, pensive. "They're like monuments to some other time. You just want to knock them down and rip them apart? For what, somebody's wall?"

"Is there any reason wood rot and fungus should get first dibs?"

"You recognize the irony, I hope. You tear down a perfectly picturesque *real* barn to saw it apart and nail it around a picture of one. That's always seemed like a special kind of hubris to me."

"Also known as recycling," Clarence said. "I thought you were big on that."

Will grumbled and went back to the map, and Clarence took the exchange as one for his win column. His brother's problem? It was as if the weight of his name had infected him with nostalgia for an era he'd never experienced and could never have tolerated. He didn't have the stomach for it. Farms, at a glance, may have looked as if they were bursting with life, but ultimately they all led to something's death.

And whatever rotted out here would rot alone.

-◦-

It was the same the next day, and the day after that, and it was easy to imagine that Kansas was Purgatory in disguise. They'd actually died in a car crash in Missouri, and their sins would keep them on an endless road for decades of penance, except Will was going to move on a lot sooner than Clarence would.

Shortly after dusk, they returned for their final night in the latest motel they'd been using as home base. The strategy had emerged during their first trip. Rather than checking into a new place to sleep each night, they opted to settle for a few days at some central crossroads, from which they could branch out in any of several directions.

Sometimes you had to cling to whatever illusion of stability you could.

As Clarence showered off the August road sweat, Will got on the phone with their mother to tell her of the day's journey—the places they'd stopped, the people they'd spoken to—and what tomorrow would bring. What made him the perfect son made him a perfectly terrible brother. It wasn't just from out here that he called home every day. He called home 365 days a year.

There was no keeping up with that. You'd think he would run out of new things to say, but he always found more.

He's the daughter they always hoped I'd be, Dina had whispered in Clarence's ear last Christmas, after just enough wine, and neither of them could stop snickering.

"Say hi to Mom," Will ordered, and pushed the phone at him while he was still toweling off from the shower.

Clarence took it and dug to find a few topics that Will wouldn't have covered already, and it was okay, it really was. He reminded himself there would come a day when he wouldn't have this chance and would regret every awkward moment he'd been less than enthusiastic about taking the phone. Myelofibrosis, it was called; a bone marrow defect. There was no coming back from it. She had two years left, if she was lucky, just long enough to trick himself into thinking it wasn't really going to happen, that grieving was still decades in the future.

Then they swapped places, and while Will took his turn in the shower, Clarence cracked open his laptop to see if their latest ads had drawn any responses. Craigslist, local classifieds, weekly shoppers . . . for years they'd been sprinkling such outlets with some variation of the following:

> *Family seeking information on the disappearance of amateur musicologist Willard Chambers, of Charleston, West Virginia. Vanished somewhere in western Kansas in July 1963. He is believed to have gone missing while trying to locate an old woman who was at that time living alone in a remote area, and reputed to have a unique style of singing regarded as "unearthly."*

They would accompany it with his picture when they could. Sometimes they'd run the other one, too, the last photo of Will Senior's life, but it was always too small and indistinct to reveal the details that, with a hardcopy print, made people stop and stare with a rising pall of dread. But at least it showed the oddities of the setting surrounding that strange, stark figure, and maybe that was all someone would need.

Responses? Mostly a lot of nothing. The little that did come in, he could weed through it quickly and flush it with impunity. They could always count on well-meaning people who wanted to help but didn't know anything, and trolls eager to waste everyone's time.

But then there was today. There was always the chance of something like today.

I'm not near old enough to have met your grandfather, so I can't help you there. But when I was little, I'd go visit my Nana Ingrid and she used to scare me into obeying her with talk of an old lady she knew about when she was young. Everybody used to keep away and just let her be. The old lady, I mean. This would've been around a place called Biggsby. I don't know if it's even on the maps anymore, or if it ever was. The nearest place of any size at all is Ulysses, and that's not much. I should know, that's where I am.

What made me think of this is the singing part. Gran said they'd hear her singing sometimes, nights mostly. She used to know this type of song called a cattle call and said it was kinda like that, only she couldn't imagine it bringing the cows in. She said a voice like that would be more like to scare them away.

There's more, but I don't know what's important to you and what's not, and I'm not much for long emails even to people I know. But I love to talk!

He dashed off a reply, then looked up Ulysses on the map and poked his head into the steam of the bathroom to tell Will that, come morning, they would be going south, instead.

—◦—

They met her at a barbecue place in Ulysses, her suggestion. It smelled of hickory smoke and fryer oil, and they got there first by twenty minutes because she was fifteen late. Clarence knew she was the one the moment she walked in. She wore boots with shorts, carried a handbag big enough to brain a horse, and moved with precisely the kind of energy he'd expect out of someone who says "*But I love to talk!*"

She sized them up instantly too. "Hi, I'm Paulette," she said. "Paulette, Johnetta, and Raylene . . . can you tell our dad had his heart set on boys instead of girls?" She slammed the handbag into one of the two vacant chairs at their table and herself in the other. "You're buying, right?"

She shot up then and went for the counter to order for all of them, insisting she knew what was best, and best avoided. Paulette was both stocky and shapely, like a six-foot woman squashed down to a compact five-four, and Clarence eyed his brother as he watched her go. Not again.

"Already?" Clarence said. "Not three dozen words out of her and you're already there?"

Will scowled as if he resented the interruption. Somewhere along the miles and years he'd picked up a fixation that he was going to meet the love of his life out here on the plains. Some Kansas farm girl, all about family, whose commitment would be as certain and uncomplicated as the sunrise over the wheat. Did they even exist anymore, if they ever had?

"You don't match. I've seen couples who match. They don't look a thing like you and her."

Will balled up a napkin in his fist. "Maybe I should handle this while you go back to the motel and take your anti-asshole pills."

As they waited for their food, Paulette wanted to know all about them. If they were still from West Virginia, and what it was like there, and when she found out Will was now living in Boston, wanted to know what that was like, too. When she learned he was a cloud architect, she made a joke about castles in the sky, and Clarence could see him turn that much more into putty. She wanted to know what their parents were like, and when she learned they had a sister, wanted to know which of them Dina was more alike, and what came out of that was a surprise, because each of them had always assumed he was the one, a revelation that made Paulette laugh.

"I figure you're safe," she finally said, "because that ad of yours, that's just not the kind of story someone would make up to draw somebody out on her own. So break 'em out, let's see these pictures of yours."

They laid out Will Senior's portrait first.

"That version you had on Craigslist doesn't do him justice," she said. "Grandpa was kind of a hunk, wasn't he?"

"And here's the one we don't know where it was taken," Clarence said. "But it was the final shot on his camera. It was a twenty-four-shot roll of film, and the last eighteen were never even exposed."

Paulette stared a long time, the way people always did. It slowed her down. She forgot her jittery habit of every few seconds pushing her sun-streaked hair back from her face, behind her ears.

"Well," she said at last, "this looks about like what I would've imagined from those old stories Nana Ingrid would tell to scare me into minding her."

Black and white in a thousand grainy shades of gray: The last photo on the roll of 35mm film in Willard's Leica appeared to have been shot up a slight incline, a wide dirt path bordered by two ragged rows of stout sticks, as long as spears and nearly as straight. They'd either been branches or saplings, cut and stripped, then jammed into the earth like a loose palisade wall. In all their searching, the purpose of this remained a mystery. Beyond these sticks, and through them, in the middle distance, was a glimpse of what he assumed was a farmhouse, and a pair of trees in summer bloom.

But in the foreground, she stood. She stood on a ladder of shadows that the low sun of morning or evening threw from one row of sticks across to the other, something strange in her stance, as if she had to lean back from her own wide hips. She wore an apron around her middle, ill-fitting, refusing to lie smoothly, and a scarf around her head, knotted at her throat.

"Here's the blow-up detail, just her," Clarence said.

Now her true wrongness began to emerge. Her face was mostly shadowed, just enough visible to make you wish you could see either more, and know what she really was, or less, so you didn't have to entertain doubts. The only features that caught the sidelight were a bulbous nose and a blocky chin that appeared to thrust forward from a lantern jaw. The rest was suggestion, and all the worse for it. Something about the way the features all fit together seemed . . . off. Like something carved from wood, and badly. The mouth looked grim and straight across, wider than wide. And given the scarf and direction of the sun, he could think of no reason her eyes should gleam with glints of light. Will Senior had been photographer enough to not bother using a flash outside like this, if he'd even possessed one.

Paulette was still shuffling from one print to the other. "Last shot on the roll, you said. What were the others?"

"Just landscapes. Nothing distinctive about them."

Paulette tapped the blow-up. "Well, Nana Ingrid used to say she wasn't really a woman at all. Or maybe not anymore, or maybe she told it both ways. Just something that dressed like one. To hide. Stories like that, you believe them when you're little. That's why they work, you don't want her to get you. Then you get a little older and you think it's just talk."

"What kind of stories?"

"Oh, you know, the usual threats. How if I didn't behave, she was going to come steal me, cook me. Or throw me down her well. Which of course was bottomless. Or use my bones to make a nest for her vulture. Nana could be creative sometimes."

"What did she call this woman?" Clarence asked. "She had to have a name."

"Old Daisy. Never just plain Daisy. Usually Old Daisy. Sometimes Crazy Daisy, if she was going for a laugh."

"Daisy? Seriously?"

"I know," Paulette said, and tapped the detail photo again. "That's the most undaisified woman I've ever seen."

Will leaned toward her from across the table, and she mirrored him right back, as if the two of them were already excluding him. "How old was your grandmother when she first knew about Daisy?"

"She grew up around her. So, from the time she was a little bitty thing until she was close to my age."

"What happened then?"

"She got hitched and moved a few miles away and squeezed out my mom." Paulette swept the photos together and shoved them at Clarence. "Better put these up for safe keeping. We're about to get nine kinds of messy here."

He slipped them into their folder as the food arrived, beef ribs and pulled pork and slaw and onion rings made with jumbo Vidalias. A couple bites in, he was willing to admit that, okay, Paulette knew her barbecue joints.

"How close did Ingrid live to her?" Will asked.

Paulette shrugged. "Down the road, is all she used to say."

"How far does that mean?" Clarence said.

"I have no idea. You know country people. 'Down the road a piece.' . . . That can mean just about anything."

"But your grandmother saw her, right? These weren't just stories to her, too?"

"Saw her all the time. Never up close, though. Nobody ever saw her up close. There's some people, you know, they're just not neighborly, so you let them be. Back then, I guess it was seen as more peculiar than it is now. Now it's just a way of life all over. But even then, there had to be people like that, and I guess they didn't push it. She did fine on her own, puttering around that old place." Paulette grinned, recalling more. "That didn't stop the area boys from trying to look. Nana Ingrid's brother was one of them. They'd dare each other to sneak up close to Old Daisy's property and try to get in a peek, and they'd get a good scare. Before they got too close, she'd spot them and screech at them and they'd scatter. In fact, that's what some people thought that crazy singing she did was all about. To keep people away. Same as a rattlesnake shaking its tail."

"A threat display."

"And I guess it worked," she said. "Have you got it? Can I hear it?"

She wiped her fingers with a wet-nap as they handed over the Walkman and the earphones. The tape was already cued up, and unlike many people, Paulette didn't shut it down early. She hung in there until the end.

"I gotta say, that's not what I was expecting," she said while stripping away the headphones. "That doesn't sound like a crazy person. It hardly sounds like a person at all."

Clarence had always thought the same thing, but never liked to lead people to the conclusion. It was always more validating to see them arrive at it on their own.

"Maybe I'm just dense, but there's one thing I'm not getting here," she said. "If nobody ever saw your grandfather again, then how do you happen to have his last pictures and recordings?"

"The greed and kindness of strangers," Will said.

"The camera was something he got while he was in the army. He epoxied a nameplate on it, so it wouldn't be as easy for someone to steal," Clarence said. "Three or four months after he went missing, our grandmother got a call from a pawn shop in Hays. The family had raised all the hell they could out here, her and our uncles . . . filing missing person reports, and they got it in some newspapers, and on the radio, a little TV. So the pawnbroker recognized the name when some vagrant brought in the camera and tape recorder in the same bag our grandfather used to carry them around. Oilskin, so it wouldn't soak through if he got caught in the rain. The story the pawnbroker got out of him, once he got him past the bullshit about how they were his, was that he found the bag on a junk heap along the side of the road someplace west. By that time, he'd been carrying them around a couple weeks or more, until he could find someplace to sell them, so he couldn't pin it down where he found them. Nobody got a chance to press him on it, because once he realized he wasn't going to get any money for them, and maybe there was a murder investigation in it too, he was out the door and gone."

Will cut in to finish as if he were feeling sidelined. "The pawnbroker wasn't a big fan of the cops either, so he got in touch with our family directly. Said he'd get our grandfather's things to them and let them decide what they wanted to do about that."

"Decent of him," she said. "What'd they do?"

"They had the film developed, had prints made, and copies of the tape. They sent them out to different departments. It didn't help. Since there was no body and no car, I don't think they were taking it seriously, once they understood that these trips of his weren't anything new. I think they just figured he liked it that way and decided to stay gone. Start over somewhere else. He wouldn't be the first."

Paulette narrowed her eyes. "Wait a second. Nobody ever found his car, either?"

"No."

"Doesn't that seem weird to you that both him and his car vanish, but his camera and tape recorder get found?"

Will appeared mystified she would even ask. "That's just what happened."

"Yeah, but . . ." She pecked at the folder holding the photos. "Say Old Daisy is responsible. Somehow, some way. Somebody is, so let's say it's her. She gets rid of him. Obviously. She knows enough to get rid of his car, too. That's pretty cunning. You can't drop a car down a well. But then this bag of other things that could be tied to him, she's so careless with it she just tosses it aside like it doesn't matter? Even though she stood right there facing him as he took her picture? Does that make sense to you?"

Clarence stepped in, locking ranks. "Like he said. That's how it happened."

But Paulette was right. Sometimes it took an outsider to point out the obvious. It had never gnawed at him until now. He'd known the story since childhood. Had grown up taking every detail for granted without appreciating what some might actually imply.

"Daisy didn't know what a camera was?" he mused. "She knew what cars were, she could see that, even if she didn't drive one herself. But the camera and tape recorder . . . no. She didn't know. In 1963, she didn't know. How is that possible?"

"Like *I* said. She kept to herself and they were glad to let her do it."

Clarence moved the decades around in his head like blocks. "How far back are we talking about with your grandmother, anyway? How old is she?"

Paulette did some quick calculating. "She'd be seventy-five, seventy-six now."

"So if she grew up around Old Daisy, that'd be as far back as twenty years before our grandfather disappeared. Give or take. And she was old then?"

"That was the story. It sounded like she was one of those people who'd always been around, as far back as anyone could remember. But you know, some people, they look and act older than they really are, so that's how it gets to seeming that way. And if you don't see them up close . . ."

"Did you ever see her?"

"God no. I never wanted to. Nana Ingrid talked like she was still around, but this was at her married home, miles from where she grew up. She must've been making it up. She'd step out on the porch sometimes and stare down the dirt road like she was watching for the old hag, like she might spot her passing by and call her over if I didn't behave. But that was just part of the threats. This was, what, thirty, forty years on from when she was living out there, so the woman had to be dead by then."

Had to. Yes.

"It's a hard old life, out like that."

Had to. Unless a woman wasn't what she was at all.

"You say Ingrid's still with you?" Clarence said.

"She's in a home now. Good days and bad days. But yeah."

"Could she tell you where Daisy's place was? Exactly? And how to find it?"

Paulette hesitated before answering, like someone who hated to let people down but would do it anyway. "Look, I was glad to help if I could, if it didn't take too long, but I'm not looking for a new project to take on. And that Wal-Mart produce aisle isn't going to run itself."

"We'll pay," Will blurted. "We'll make it worth your time."

Clarence wondered how obvious it would be if he kicked his brother under the table.

"'Worth your time' is like 'down the road a piece,'" Paulette said. "There's lots of wiggle room in what it means."

⟶⟨○⟩⟶

Two days later, on the word of Paulette's grandmother—on one of her good days, he hoped—they headed out into the prairie wastes again, deeper than they'd ever had reason enough to go. There had never been much point to going where people were so few and far between that the land hardly seemed lived in at all.

It had once, though. The rubble and residue lingered. Along roads that had crumbled mostly back to dirt, they passed the scattered, empty shells of lives long abandoned. Separated by minutes and miles, the remains of farmhouses and barns left for ruin seemed to sink into seas of prairie grass. The trees hung on, as tenacious loners or clustering into distant, ragged rows that betrayed the hidden vein of a creek.

"I think this might be it. Where Nana grew up," Paulette said from the back seat. "Can we stop?"

She'd been guiding them from a hand-drawn map that took over from where the printed map left off.

Clarence nosed the car toward the side of the road, sniffing for where the driveway used to be, and found it—a weedy landbridge between stretches of clogged ditch. He didn't go far past. Any debris could be in that grass. He killed the engine and they got out to stand in the simmering silence of the day as Paulette compared the place as it was now with a photo borrowed from an album at her parents' home.

"Is this it?" Will asked, and he sounded so tender.

"I think. I don't know. But it should be. It's just hard to tell."

Of course it was. The picture showed life. However hardscrabble, it was life: a troop of skinny children, boys in overalls and girls in plain dresses, clowning around a swing fashioned from two ropes and a slat of wood. That could be the same oak, right there, sixty-odd years bigger. The sun-blasted, two-story farmhouse looked as though it could be the corpse of the one behind the children. It seemed to be the same roof, even though half of it was now gone, exposing a framework of rotting rafters. Unseen in the photo was a windmill out back that must've pumped their well. It still stood, a rusted, skeletal tower as tall as the house and crowned with a giant fan. A few of its sixteen blades had fallen free, while the rest ignored the wind, the gears too corroded to turn.

He reconsidered. There was still plenty of life here. It was just nothing human.

"It would kill her to see the place like this," Paulette said. "Literally kill her."

Which could have been an act of mercy. Yesterday's trip to the nursing home had left him with a new appreciation for living out like this until the end. It had to hasten things, a swifter demise than being warehoused in a stinking building devoted to death by increments, surrounded by people whose bodies and minds raced to see which could deteriorate faster, and the cruelest thing was having enough of a mind left to realize you were one of them. Out like this, fall and break a hip? He'd take three days of dehydration on the floor over years of the other.

Paulette had wandered ahead of them in a daze, as if time had slowed, exploring the trunk of the oak, the front of the house, pieces of the past hidden in the weeds.

"I came from here. I came from this," she said, although whom she was speaking to wasn't clear. "And I never bothered to come see. Thirty miles, and I didn't even come out for a look."

"Nice we can pay her for the privilege," Clarence murmured, not because he begrudged her the opportunity, but because he knew it would get a rise out of Will.

"Shut up. Don't you say anything more about that," Will said. "Besides, *we* aren't paying her for anything. *I* am."

And he didn't know why it rankled him so. Years ago they'd vowed to never pay for information. It could only encourage people to lie. For that matter, why did it rankle him so much that his brother was now bankrolling each year's venture? Because he could afford to, that's why. Right now, at least, cloud architecture was some of the best money in IT, and this was the way Will wanted to spend it, and the worst part of it was that Will pulled in six figures doing something he excelled at but didn't even enjoy. All the money in the world couldn't buy him what he seemed to want most: to live in a simpler time.

"I'm sorry," Clarence said. "I just want to get this done."

"I know."

"Except I don't know what *done* is supposed to look like. Even if we find that old hag's house and it's still standing, we're not going to walk in and find a skeleton at the table wearing Grandpa's army dog tags. It's never going to be that neat and clean."

At their feet was a decayed shard of post snarled in a rusty length of galvanized fencing that twisted through the grasses and weeds like a wire snakeskin. Will stared at it, seeming to ponder how he might straighten it out, make it all better.

"I know," he said again.

"I won't ask you to promise today, but when we find it, at least start thinking that maybe it should be the end of the line." He put a hand on his brother's shoulder. "We'll find the place in the picture. We found out who the woman was. We got a name, and there might be some old records where we can find out a little more. That's a lot. Maybe it should be enough to get to the last place Grandpa got to, and admit that the two of them are the only ones who know what happened next, and we just can't know. But we got here. We closed that circle. Can you live with that?"

Will thought a moment, then nodded. "I guess I'll have to. I just hope it'll be enough for Mom."

"Come on, slackers, let's go!" Paulette called over to them from the car. He hadn't even seen her return to it. "We haven't got all day!"

-◦◦-

Under the vast and cloudless prairie sky, they prowled roads no one seemed to travel anymore. He recalled that the area had once been called Biggsby, and had been so inconsequential as to not even merit inclusion on modern maps. By now there was no indication this place had ever deserved being thought of as a town. Biggsby—it was the name of a hostile field sprawling between horizons, a forgotten savannah where animals burrowed and mated and devoured each other undisturbed.

Paulette's map seemed not quite right, maybe a casualty of faulty recollections: a curve in the road that shouldn't have been there, an expected crossroad that wasn't. They tracked and backtracked, futilely hoping to find things waiting just as they were in a photo shot fifty years ago. If only it could be as certain as spotting that inexplicable gauntlet of branches from Will Senior's last photo.

Even Nana Ingrid, who remembered it firsthand, hadn't had an explanation for that.

"She kept it in good repair, whatever it was for," Ingrid said from her wheelchair. *"We used to call it her cattle chute. Even though she didn't raise no cattle."*

They stopped to explore a series of ruined farmhouses that seemed like possible candidates, each little different from the others, all sagging roofs and disintegrating walls, collapsed chimneys and wood eaten to sponges and splinters by the onslaught of the seasons.

"Even if she did, you wouldn't want to bring the cattle straight to your door."

They found sofas reduced to shapeless masses erupting with rusty springs, and boxy old televisions whose tubes had shattered, and it was these castoffs that made him think no, none of these were the place, because as old and neglected as these features were, they were still too modern.

"What about there?" Will said, back on the hunt and pointing at a spot they'd passed twice already.

It was the gentle slope of the land that first made Clarence suspect they'd found it at last. The place was farther off the road than anywhere else they'd tried, and if these were the same trees in the background of Willard's photo, then they were willows with another fifty years of growth behind them, nearly sweeping the ground now to screen the house from sight from the road.

House? What they found was a slumping hovel, a single-story dwelling made of both durable stone and vulnerable timber. It seemed far older than the other ruins they'd inspected, something a pioneer might have built as a first outpost for taming a wild frontier. Behind the willows that bowed and bobbed in the wind, it sat in the midst of an immense stillness pregnant with the whispers of rustling leaves and insects whose chirring in the weeds sounded as sharp as a drill.

It felt right. This was the place. It felt right because something about it felt deeply wrong. This was a place poisoned by time.

And now that they knew, Young Will went back to the car, parked along the side of the road, to retrieve Will Senior's heirloom camera. The vintage Leica still worked. They'd been built to last decades, to survive wars. He brought it with him every year, but until this moment, Clarence had always assumed it was some sort of totem, the only physical connection he could have to the man whose name he'd been born to carry. He'd never mentioned an intention to actually use it.

His brother stationed himself down below, camera at his eye as he framed up the incline, until he was satisfied he'd found the vantage point from which Willard had shot his final photo. He then pointed at a spot on the ground that had once been striped by a ladder of shadows.

"Stand there," he told Paulette.

"What for?" She didn't sound happy about it.

"For scale."

She complied, but seemed to find the act physically repugnant, as if Daisy had left behind contaminants that would infect anyone who stood where she had. Good luck. If she'd lived here as long as legend suggested, there couldn't be a square inch of earth her gnarled feet hadn't cursed.

Clarence was more captivated by the thought of where Will Senior had hidden away, probably the night before, to make his recording. He'd gotten close, perhaps within twenty yards. There was a hint of distance in the sound, but not much; for comparison, they had the voice of Willard himself, the parts they never played for anyone else.

He pondered the ground he stood on. *From here.* Maybe the old man had hunkered low and listened to what he should never have heard and sealed his fate from right here.

They moved on, toward the remains of the house, finally ready to touch it. It was a shelter no longer, the outside world having invaded long ago, through the glassless windows and crumbling walls and the entrances whose doors had fallen off their hinges. Where the roof had drooped inward, it was open to the sun and moon alike. Weeds grew in every crack, and generations of predators had denned in the corners to gnaw the bones of their prey.

Yet even in its disintegration, traces of the life once lived here lingered: a chipped mug, a blue enamel coffee percolator, a salvageable spindle-back chair and the table it accompanied. A row of large cans, rusted almost to lace, remained on a cupboard shelf. In an alcove that might have been a closet sat a battered washtub whose accumulated filth couldn't quite hide the suggestion of ancient stains.

Gutbucket—the word came to him before he knew why, then he remembered it from his own digging into Willard's obsessions, as a folk term for a cheap upright bass made from a washtub.

He kept coming back to that improbable row of cans.

"Did she ever die, that anyone knew of?" Clarence asked.

"You got me," Paulette said. "If she did, Nana never heard about it."

"Wouldn't it have been news if she had?" He squatted in front of a block of iron, half hidden by weeds and tumbled rafters, and realized it was a wood-fired stove. "She kept to herself, okay, but one day, someone's got to realize nobody's seen her out for a year. Somebody's going to check eventually. They wouldn't let her rot in here forever."

"Maybe she just walked away," Will said.

"To go where? Where do you go from here?"

"You'd have to ask her," Paulette said, quieter now. "Maybe that's why Nana was always looking for her on the road."

They made their way around back, where the land rolled away into fields of nothing. A minute's walk in one direction led to a heap of fungus-eaten wood, the collapsed shell of an outhouse. It made his stomach roll to speculate what might turn up if they started scraping through the dried-out layers down in the trench. A minute's walk in another led to her well, the bucket and rope long gone, but the mortared stone wall around it remained intact. It was too dark down the well's gullet to see. He pried a rock from the grassy soil and lobbed it in, and seconds later heard a splat of thickest mud.

"How stupid are we, we didn't even bring a flashlight?" he said.

But there would be nothing to see, would there? He doubted she would poison her own well with a corpse. This was someone, something, resourceful enough to make a Chevrolet vanish, so surely she had better options for her dead. And it occurred to him that while he still thought of her as female, at some point he had ceased thinking of her as a woman.

"Clarence. Get over here."

He hadn't realized that Will and Paulette had drifted back to the house, where they both stood peering at the foundation.

⟨-o-⟩

He must have listened to the full recording a thousand times throughout his life.

It begins with the sound of clunks and fumbling, and spread atop the creamy hiss of tape is an ambience of crickets and tree frogs. If fireflies could make a sound, he imagined it would've captured them too.

"There we go. Missed it. Shoot. Not used to doing this in the dark." Willard's voice is close and hushed, the voice of a man hugging the ground. "Welp . . . if she's gonna do it again, she better do it while the batteries are still good." His disappointment is palpable. "Now that I've heard it, I don't know what to make of it. Nothing about it seems to point to any tradition I ever heard. That just might be my own gaps." He falls silent, musing as the night fills in around him. "The feeling I get from it . . . it . . . it's like some kind of lamentation. There's sorrow in it. Sorrow and rage." Then a miniscule break in the sound as Willard pauses the tape. When it resumes after an indeterminate recess, his whisper is taut with excitement. "Here she goes again."

He lets Old Daisy have the next three minutes to herself. Only once does he interject, not meaning to, but unable to halt the shaky sound of a sharply drawn breath as her voice peaks to a terrible warbling crescendo that could strip the trees of their leaves and claw scars across the cold white face of the moon.

Until the night is still again, and even the crickets and frogs seem cowed.

"Jesus, Mary, and Joseph," he whispers. "That poor woman. That poor soul. How does . . . is she deformed, is that how . . . ?"

He lets the tape roll awhile longer, with nothing more to add that the infinite night can't say better, and with a greater sense of awe.

◄◦►

Along the house's foundation, Will had cleared some of the rampant weeds and dirt and buildup of wind-tossed leaves, and still it wanted to not be seen: a rough-hewn door into the earth.

"Storm cellar. Where we're standing right now is smack dead center in the middle of Tornado Alley," Paulette said. "You ever see *The Wizard of Oz*? It's not like that."

They cleared away more, untangling the weeds from a heavy chain that held the entrance closed, lashed across the door in a sideways V whose point was threaded through a lock nearly the size of his fist, rusted but still sound. Even if they found a key, he doubted it would turn. The chain's ends were anchored into the door's hinge plates, and here was the weak spot. The wood along the edges had rotted enough that they were able to tug on the chain to rip up the hinge plates, bolts and all. They heaved the door open, opposite the way it was meant to swing, and the storm cellar exhaled a musty sigh of roots and earth, like the smell of a waiting grave.

"Watch those steps," Will warned him. "They may not be any sturdier."

But they held, a dozen of them sloping down to a floor of dry, hard-packed earth and walls so coarsely cut they looked like adobe.

With the door open, enough light spilled down inside for them to see. They barely had room to stand beneath the crude rafters, black with creosote, that kept the hovel above and the tons of soil between from falling through.

He wished it had all failed long ago. He wished they'd never found this place.

"Jesus, Mary, and Joseph," his brother whispered. One trepidatious step at a time, Will moved to where it dwelled along one wall—did it sit? or did it stand?—and when he was close, began to reach.

"Maybe you ought not touch it," Paulette said.

He stilled his hand. "Why not?"

"Because I wouldn't."

Again: "Why not?"

"Maybe I've just got more sense than that, I don't know."

Clarence was with her on this one. And Will withdrew his hand.

That it was some sort of sculpture was obvious, yet he couldn't even tell what it was made of, much less what it was meant to represent. It was as tall as he was, with features and symmetry, but far more bulky. To look at it was to understand it had to have come from someplace, been worked by sentient hands, and realize he could never know enough about the world and its shadowed quarters to fathom who or where or why.

Was it metal? Stone? It appeared to be a mixture of both, marbled into each other under the temperatures of a blast furnace. Aspects of it glinted in the light that the rest seemed to swallow.

"A meteorite, maybe?" Will said. "That's my guess."

As sculpture, it was pitted and rough, but that it had been shaped at all seemed miraculous. It must have been incomprehensibly hard to work with. Its weight had to be immense. It was contradictory, various parts suggesting man and animal, mammal and mollusk, demon and dragon, a creature fit to dominate anywhere, be it ocean, land, or sky. It was a nightmare rising from a slag heap left over from the formation of the galaxy.

"So nobody else is going to say it?" Will asked. "Okay: 'I don't think we're in Kansas anymore.'"

But Kansas wasn't any reference point here. For no reason he could defend, Clarence knew beyond a doubt that this grotesque effigy predated even the idea of Kansas. It predated the nation, maybe the continent, the mountains to the west and the great bisecting river to the east. For all he knew, it came from an epoch when the land was one mass, a single crucible of primal forces surrounded by one titanic sea, the globe like a turbulent eye staring back at the affront of creation.

Then how had it come to be here and now? Perhaps it was as simple as waiting out the eons, impervious to time, until it was unearthed in a field.

He sensed it all in the presence of this thing. The thoughts were in his head as if it had forced them. He couldn't have been the first.

"We should leave," he whispered.

"Guys? Check it out."

Paulette was pointing at the rafters. With their eyes better accustomed to the shadows, they were ready to see what hid in plain sight when the statue was all they were prepared to notice. It was everywhere, on the rafters and the upright timbers bracing the earthen walls and beneath the dust on the steps, a single message repeated over years and decades: COME BACK. Etched into the wood with the points of knives and awls, a thousand utterances of the same plaintive incantation: COME BACK COME BACK COME BACK.

"That thing?" Will jabbed his finger at the statue. "Did she mean that thing? It was real, it was here?"

"I don't think so." Paulette cut an impatient glance at him as if she pitied him for his misunderstanding. "I bet she meant her people. Family, friends, neighbors. Her people. Her . . . world."

Funny. He'd always considered her a loner, a freak who reveled in her isolation.

"Maybe Nana was right after all," Paulette said. "Maybe it really wasn't just Old Daisy out here once."

Will stared at her. "She said there were more like her?"

Paulette nodded. "Nana said there used to be a whole passel of them. This would've been way back. Kept their heads down, hid their faces, wore sacks, some of them. Didn't want to be seen, didn't want to have anything to do with newer neighbors, didn't want anyone else even coming close. People like that, they were like moonshiners used to be, and meth cooks now. You learned to steer clear if you didn't want a load of buckshot coming your way."

For the moment, Clarence quelled the urge to leave. "You didn't say anything about this before."

"Because it wasn't something I grew up with, all right? Nana never said a thing about it when I was little and she was telling her stories to keep me in line. And she only said it the once. This was after they put her in the home." Paulette sighed with exasperation. "It wasn't a serious talk. We were laughing about it, how scared of Daisy she had me. I thought it was just some notion that got in her head after she started to get dotty enough to finally believe her own stories."

"Maybe," Clarence said, "she was dotty enough to finally let it slip."

"If it was even true, they wouldn't have been people she'd ever seen. According to her, it was something she heard about from her own grandmother. So we're talking waaay back. Civil War times, or not long after. There's no way Old Daisy could've been around here since . . ."

She clammed up, not even wanting to say it. Maybe because she could no longer be certain of absolutes, and hated to lie.

Above him, behind him, and all around: COME BACK COME BACK COME BACK.

"Then what happened to the rest of them?"

"That's probably a dirty old secret that died out with somebody a long time ago." Paulette looked both solemn and sad. "What do you think? You come from West Virginia. If I've heard stories about what used to happen in your mountains there, then I know for sure you must have."

There was that. Yes. People who trekked up into the hollows to nose around where they didn't belong, and never came out again. Or one group taking such a dislike to another they decided they could no longer abide living side by side. The population had always been sparse out here, and he supposed there was a time when not a lot could come of rumor and a mass of unmarked graves.

Especially if the dead were . . . different.

And if there was a sole survivor, killers left them for all manner of reasons, by accident or as reminders or to soothe their consciences that what they'd done wasn't actually genocide.

God damn. Will Senior had sensed it simply from listening once in the dark. *It's like some kind of lamentation. There's sorrow in it. Sorrow and rage.*

Young Will trudged across the cellar and slumped onto the steps, heedless of the dust, then shot a baleful look at the statue. "A lifespan like that? The way she looks in the photo? This thing *did* that to them?"

Clarence couldn't bring himself to agree. Not out loud. Not to Will. Impressionable Young Will. "Do you hear yourself, what that sounds like?"

"Well, I've sure as shit spent my life hearing what *she* sounded like." He turned his gaze on Clarence, no less spiteful. "That thing's not natural, not one bit. There's something coming through it. Don't tell me you don't feel it. I can see it in your face. You're the worst liar I ever met."

Clarence approached the stairs while Paulette watched as if she suddenly feared both of them blocking the only way out. Nobody could fight like brothers.

"Come on. Let's go," Clarence said, as gently as he could. "We're not going to learn anything more here. We've already learned more than we ever wanted to."

Will fixed him with a look that nailed his feet to the floor. "He's not even dead. You realize that, don't you? I'll bet you anything he's not. He could still be alive even without that thing's influence. He'd be, what, around ninety? It's no big deal to hit that anymore. All this time we've taken it for granted he would've come home if he could, but what if family didn't mean as much to him as everyone assumed it did. We never even met him, you and I. But think about it. Doesn't it sound like home just turned into a place for him to plan the next trip? And songcatching, maybe that was only the surface of what he was really out looking for."

Clarence's first impulse was to argue, until he realized he had nothing to wield. He'd bought it all on faith. He'd never considered this alternative. Not seriously. He'd swallowed the easier story to accept and let it dictate his life.

Maybe it was Willard Chambers all along who had made sure his car was never found, and that his Nagra and his camera were. If he didn't need them anymore, maybe they'd prove more useful as circumstantial evidence of death.

"He loved Mom," Clarence whispered. "He loved Grandma. He loved Aunt Jane and Uncle Terry. He did."

"And then he found something that meant more."

Will stood up, finally, as around them, the storm cellar grew thick with the weight of eons.

"I was named for a deserter. Mom hung that on me." His face curled with the disgust of betrayal and a life of self-told lies. "He may have done his duty in war, but back home? He was a deserter." Will nodded, confirming it to himself. "But there's a side of me that can't totally blame him for it."

When he looked at the statue again, his anger was all but dissipated.

"It must've been worth it."

He shouldered past, and when Clarence hooked a hand around his arm, Will whirled. Next thing Clarence knew, he was sprawling across the hard-packed earth with a dull, throbbing ache in his cheek, as somewhere out in the blur, Paulette gave a startled cry of warning that plunged into sorrow.

When his vision cleared, he saw Will gripping the statue with splayed hands, tense as a cable but motionless, until his head tipped slowly, ecstatically, back and he made a reedy sound that seemed to come from a much older man. His bladder let go in a spreading dark stain.

Though sunk in the earth and surrounded by walls, the statue had brought its own climate. Clarence felt it deeper than skin, a gust of particles and waves, the solar wind from a black sun. Outside was August, but down here was a numbing gust of absolute zero, the point where every molecule froze, everything but thought, and the invitation beckoned: *Come . . . join with it . . . step outside the boundaries of time. It only burns for a little while.*

His instinct, still, was to intercede, the way he'd always done. It was what big brothers did, pulling their little brothers out of traffic when they stepped off the curb, and out of the deep water when they fell in over their head. Maybe he could do it without harm, and Will was not yet a conduit for whatever was coming through that timeless chunk of shrapnel from the cataclysm that birthed the worst among gods.

And maybe he couldn't. But it had always been expected of him to try.

Then Paulette was at his side, clutching his wrist, levering his arm down again. He'd never have dreamed he could let her do it so easily. He knew she was going to join Will before she seemed to realize it herself. As their eyes met, and from a place beyond words she urged him to let his brother go, he saw the conflict play itself out, then the resolution: that she preferred the vast unknown to a life she didn't want to go back to, as long as she didn't have to do it alone.

For all he knew, Will had even been counting on it.

⋅◦⋅

They stayed down in the cellar a long time, long after Clarence had made it up the steps. He sat with his back to the hole some twenty paces away and shivered in the August sun. He didn't want to look. He didn't want to listen. Yet he didn't want to drive away without knowing what, exactly, he would be driving away from. If there was a chance, the slightest chance, he still had a brother he recognized.

And when their shadows fell across him, long and distorted, he had time to wonder if he hadn't made the last mistake of his life.

It didn't seem particularly lucky that there would be time for many more.

"I don't think I'll be going home for a while," Will said. "You probably guessed that already."

He knew their names. *Will. Paulette.* He knew their faces. He knew their clothes and the sound of their voices and the smell of them after a long, hot day. He just didn't know who they were. To see them now was like looking with one eye off-center. The halves of the image didn't quite line up.

"What am I supposed to tell Mom?" he asked.

"You can tell her whatever it takes. I haven't lived at *home* home for years. How different will it be?"

"Except for the part where you call every day."

"I could still check in from time to time." He looked down at the dirt with a murky little smile, as if it had whispered a joke. "It won't matter that long, anyway."

This from a son who could barely be coaxed into admitting his mother had two years, at best, to live.

Then Will held out the camera, the well-traveled Leica that had led them here, full circle after half a century. Its last shot from earlier, around front—Clarence didn't know if he could ever bring himself to get it developed. Until Will took him by surprise, so he would have no choice.

"Go on, shoot one more. Both of us," he said. "Show Mom I'm okay. Show her that we're happy."

Clarence steadied himself and shot it, the camera alien in his hand, like someone else's heart. It had passed to him, but it wasn't his. It would never be his. Behind them, these imposters in familiar skins, the hovel sat as it always had, slumping into itself year by year, as patient as decay, and the land stretched empty for miles.

"Here," Clarence said. "You're staying . . . here."

To Paulette, nothing seemed more natural. "It's got everything we need."

And that was that. They turned their backs on him, returning to the cellar, and the last he saw of Young Will was his arm, reaching up from below to swing the rotting wooden door closed again. As Clarence remembered the other day, not without shame, telling Will that he and Paulette didn't match.

They would. One day, they would.

On the drive back to the motel, solitary and endless, the pain worse than if a piece of him had been amputated and burned before his eyes, he passed the same dead barns and farmhouse ruins but saw them differently now. Had that really been him, last week, talking of breaking one down for the wood?

It was inconceivable now. No telling what such a place might hold. They only looked dead from the road.

Maybe she just walked away.

To go where? Where do you go from here?

She had her pick, didn't she? There were so many, all waiting like carcasses for the flies to come and settle and breed.

His eyes started to play tricks, imagining he caught a glimpse of her in this one, that one, and the next. Peering out at him from between fungus-eaten boards, and then there were worse tricks to come, as he divined it wasn't just her. No, she had a companion, a man the likes of which they didn't make anymore. A changed man who wouldn't even know his own grandson if he watched him drive by.

Because there were so many more lasting things worth knowing.

◄◦►

The phone calls started three weeks later.

But the first came at nearly four o'clock in the morning, so Clarence missed it, and it went to voice mail.

I was right. He's out here. Somewhere. I can feel him. I can feel him passing by in the night. It's happened twice. Sure as god made little green apples. But I don't think he wants to be found. Maybe it's because I'm not worthy of finding him yet. You think so? Hello? Are you there?

After that, Clarence got a new phone for everyday use, and let the earlier one go straight to voice mail. Permanently. He wanted the connection. He just couldn't hold up his side of the conversation.

If you were dreaming the dreams of a mountain under the sea, how could you tell anyone what they were so it would all make sense? That's what this is like.

He went to Boston, where he shut down as much of Will's life as he could, and took over the phone bill, so the conduit would remain open. How Will was keeping a charge in the phone was anyone's guess.

We're getting closer. I can feel him. He's a mighty thing. I wonder if he'll be proud or angry. Paulette says hello. I think that's what she meant.

The months passed, and the calls came in when they came, infrequent and random, no pattern to it, other than the way every time he thought Will had finally stopped, *surely* by now he'd stopped, another message was waiting a day or two later.

I was wrong. This isn't what I thought it was going to be. I just don't know if it's better or worse. It's . . . it's the knowing that changes you. Like a download of information wakes up something that was always inside. I never could buy it that what they call junk DNA is just junk. Are you even there anymore? Why don't you ever answer?

And it was Will's voice—he would recognize it anywhere—yet something was different about it each time. It was more than how each call sounded a bit farther away, fighting past a little more static and noise than the previous time. It was in the resonance of his throat, and the tones it produced.

Mom's gone. Isn't she. I don't know how I know that, I just do. Don't be sorry for her. She's lucky. She's beyond what's coming. You should be too. I shouldn't be telling you this. You should kill yourself, though. Rochelle first, then yourself. You should be okay then. I know you, you won't want to do it because she's pregnant, but you'll be glad you did. That day will come. If you can't trust your baby brother, who can you trust?

A thousand times a day, he thought of cutting the connection. But never could.

I shouldn't tell you this. When they come, they'll look like meteors. But that won't be what they are at all. When the sky changes color, it'll be too late. Nothing will make any difference then. They'll already have you. That's when you'll wish you'd listened to me. Don't ask what color, I can't really describe it. But out here, I've seen the kind of green the sky turns before a tornado. That's a start.

We're really getting close now. I wonder if Daisy will let me call her "Mother."

And when it had gone nearly a year between calls, and so much had changed, and Clarence was a father now, with a father's fears, he knew better than to think the calls were done. They would never be done. Even when they no longer conveyed any words he could understand.

Since coming home from Kansas for the last time, alone, he hadn't listened to his grandfather's tape any more, the longest in his life he'd let it idle. There was no more to learn from it. He would rather forget.

But there was no forgetting such a song. He knew it, still, the moment he heard it begin, coming through miles and static and time. He would always know it.

Yet now there was a difference. He could no longer hear the lamentation in it. Just the rage. It was a song of endings and rebirths, a song for green skies and streaks like blue-white fire among the clouds. A song he would never be fit to join and sing.

And, finally, it was coming from more than one throat.

He counted two the first time.

He counted four the next.

In the end, he counted a choir of multitudes.

FURY

DB WATERS

He coded in, drove to the call-out's address, and soaked the tidy gravel driveway in blue light. Revolving half-moons flashed from his car in the black sky and picked out his boss, Lynn. She looked strange and maybe that was when he realised none of this was going to be routine. Automatically, he put on the whites. He pulled on his gloves.

It seemed to him he had arrived to find the scene already set. Lynn was curled up tight like a foetus, crouched down on the concrete step by the property's entrance, her arms wrapped around her knees as if locking her body into itself. Yet it all appeared very ordinary: newish, bright, clean. A modern estate. But it was gone three in the morning and, even now, cautious yellow slits of light had arranged themselves in the curtained windows opposite; enquiring eyes had begun to stir.

As he composed himself for the task ahead, he felt an attraction to the place take hold. He cleared his throat in the moist air and at once a dull weight acknowledged itself and squeezed down upon his chest. But its meaning, and possibilities, remained hidden.

He stared in silence at the property, as if in submission.

It seemed to him, as he gazed at the house, that he was simply revisiting a familiar place. A crazy thought. This was a new house. He had to remind himself of the fact. But immediately within him a voice countered: a new home, yes, but built on old soil. And he recalled the almost reckless haste that had brought him to this place tonight. As if he had sensed the evening would yield a vital, dense new experience he must give himself up to. Or get back in touch with.

Noting the hastily cordoned-off area around him, he tested his gloves, smoothing the thin rubber all the way down his fingertips as the chill air silenced his thoughts.

He made his way towards Lynn to report in, and approached the splintered remains of the front door. It presented to him a twisted mess, torn away from brass hinges that gleamed like curls of old butter. A uniform was already with Lynn and, as he approached, damp spirals from the polystyrene cup of coffee she was clutching were snatched by the black air and quickly erased. She'd managed to spill most of the drink anyway, he could see, and a pattern of sickles had indented the soft surface of the cup.

He started to speak, but stopped. Lynn looked up at him, exhausted. Her mouth was moving, and he saw the tight flesh of her jaw-line working up and down (lifting that familiar dark mole on her cheek, up and down, like it was some kind of tired optical illusion, he thought) and then realised she was repeating the same line over and over, murmuring to herself.

"I'm sorry . . . so sorry . . . this doesn't usually happen . . . I'm sorry . . . so sorry."

The uniform tried to offer comfort as Lynn shot him an odd look that was part wounded, part embarrassed. He didn't like it. That mangled, twisted-up door before him, the look from Lynn, and the too-tight closeness of the gloves he knew he must wear. Somehow events had started to coalesce into obscure patterns he found threatening. And he longed to be inside. He longed to connect to the night's work: the damage, the crime, his justified place in it all.

"Old soil, yes," he heard himself say, and immediately felt foolish. He forced himself to focus.

He noticed how Lynn—when she'd driven up to the call-out's property— hadn't bothered to keep her own lights flashing. It was a small thing but it told him that Lynn hadn't taken the call-out too seriously—not at first anyway. She'd probably suspected the usual, predictable domestic. Only it hadn't been that at all; and now, as he snatched a quick look down at her, he felt sorry for her, and it was then he realised how Lynn, sitting perfectly still, had carefully drawn her feet away from a messy circle that spread before her like syrup. She'd been sick, he observed.

"Do you need anything? I have spare gloves if—" she said.

"I have everything I need," he answered, reluctantly turning his hands away from the gaze of the house so Lynn could see them. She nodded.

He arched down and slid past her and what remained of the shattered front door, and bent his way inside. It was, he felt, an almost apologetic kind of welcome—the ruined entrance, the need to be on his guard against injury. Even so, he saw his fingers spread out to touch, and perhaps stroke, the walls that greeted him, and he appreciated how they granted their support to his unsteady movement. It occurred to him he was grateful and he didn't find that strange.

Without delay, and out of sight, he dispensed altogether with the gloves, peeling them off his fingertips, loosening their unreasonable grip until, finally, they dropped to the floor. He did not care. He was glad. He was glad because his fingers, freed and already reaching out to touch, would now be able to make contact with the real essence of the house.

He felt himself yield to it, wanted to.

And all the time the house, opening up generously before him, took him deeper within itself. The walls supported him, steadied and orientated him, and he took encouragement from their silent help. He dipped his head.

Around him, ribbons of POLICE DO NOT CROSS tape looped and fell like half-hearted birthday banners across the gaping entrances and exits; and he thought how they might remain exactly as they were until, like his gloves, they too would prove superfluous.

As he moved forward he reached inside his overall pocket for a handkerchief as the pungent press of something irretrievably decayed affronted his senses. Fresh white paint—how old was the place? One year? Two at the most?—had already turned grey in patches and he thought of mushrooms, mushrooms smudged against paintwork. But he could offer no explanation.

Taking in the entrance hall, with its mould-ridden walls, it seemed to him they had somehow become animated. He tried to concentrate, reason it out. Usually, crime scenes gradually became accounted for; he knew that. If not explained in full, at least hypothesised. And where a hypothesis could be put forward, a case could be built on, worked on, pushed to conclusion.

But *here* was different; *here* made him feel something was jammed hard in the machinery of logic, blocking progress.

He made himself focus. As he approached the kitchen he observed that all the lights throughout the property had been turned on. He hadn't needed to touch a single switch. The light immediately relaxed him, bathed him in its brightness, and again he felt the yearning to submit.

The kitchen took him in.

For a moment he flinched, had to turn away. But then a fizz of static erupted from his radio and distracted him for a moment; he bent to answer it. It was Lynn's voice. She was still outside. Her voice was all quiet and subdued and she told him:

"Two upstairs—main bedroom, turn right at top of staircase. The other two—"

"Yes?"

"Other two—one—a teenage girl—she's against the bathroom wall and—"

"Against?"

"Just listen. The boy—the little boy—he's—he must've been—moving across the landing because he's high up—he's close to the ceiling."

Lynn wasn't making much sense. Obviously she was still unwell. A sudden, nagging panic started to needle somewhere behind his eyes and he wanted to be gone. But he couldn't leave. He couldn't just wait outside, like Lynn. Instead, he came to understand what held him there, and what would inevitably follow. For he knew they waited for him upstairs. Lynn had told him so. But he had known it anyway. He was sure he had.

His attention turned back to the kitchen and the scene that, before Lynn's call, had defied his understanding. But what he had seen there wouldn't be unremembered, even though he had tried to immerse himself in his usual procedural duties. Everything hung in jagged strips. The kitchen cupboards, the doors and drawers, all smashed beyond recognition. Some pieces that remained of an old oak Victorian dresser had escaped, thrown out across the floor like lumps of giant broken biscuit. An old heirloom perhaps, he wondered, and gazed down at the thing, saw how it had been made to crumple in upon itself like sheets of crunched brown paper. Everything around him—the neat rows of matching units that hid away the utensils, the solid black lacquered door that led to the living-room close by—had been meticulously pulverised. Bare wood gaped, exposed and livid in its stark freshness; a reek of fresh pine perfumed the air from splintered remains that had been torn open.

The room had been attacked—even the fridge too, he noticed, stunned by what had unfurled before his eyes. Something had hit the room's contents from the outside, with immense force, as if punched, causing the kitchen units to shatter inwards.

Slowly it occurred to him: a deranged man, in possession of a hammer, might easily—

No. Not a person. He gazed harder and came to see why. Tins of food from ruined storage units had spilled out in a semi-circle across the shiny plastic kitchen floor, oozing like sea waste. A colourful tide of oils, vinegars, various smashed jars and twisted bottles of sauces—already congealed in places—reflected towards the ceiling the image of his own face.

Yet most of the ruined tins and cans had actually been forced further *back* into the dark recesses of their cupboards rather than spilt out into the room. He peered closer. Bits of mangled tin, glass, cutlery, plastic bottles had been driven through the backs of the cupboards; he drew himself down, eye level, and saw the gaping wounds in the flimsy pine panels, exposing the bare brickwork on the other side. And that was where the tangled objects had finished their journeys: embedded within the wall itself.

So he dipped a cautious hand inside one of the broken units and pushed his fingertips towards the back until he felt rough cool brickwork. There his fingers traced the outline of what was, he assumed, the irregular shape of a crumpled can so perfectly smooth against the wall that it was impossible to detect any protrusion at all. It appeared that the wall had simply taken the object into itself.

Once more the smell of something damp and decomposing chased him, breaking down the clean spaces of air around him, until he withdrew his hand from the shattered cupboard, coughed, and spluttered into the hankie. Soon he recovered. The smell was already less offensive to him. Perhaps the house had made him accept its scent?

The fridge caught his attention. Wrenched free, flung onto its side. He bent to examine its wide-open door and the plastic-coated wire shelves crushed somewhere at the back like bleached bones. The light remained on, shining a dim halo of cool blue around him. He gently tugged for a time at a bent white spoke of the shelving until he realised just how lost in thought he'd become. He was unable to pull it free. The spoke had been driven cleanly into the white flesh of the door. Like everything else he'd witnessed, it all lingered, deliberate and stubborn, on the other side of understanding.

Then he wiped his fingers clean with a small tremble. After a moment, he wiped them again. He assumed they'd become smeared with something from the fridge. But as he watched the red scratches darken and bleed, he simply smiled—grateful that he could move so freely over the surfaces of the house with his uncovered hands. He accepted that he must have contaminated the crime scene, but it wasn't important. What was important was protecting the house, being welcomed by it and part of it.

Soon the stairs were upon him.

He turned towards them and watched as they curled out of view like the sketch of a question-mark.

Half-way up he noticed the brightly coloured things dotted about at random against the wall; they followed him up as he climbed the stairs to the landing above. Bright things—plastic—and driven firmly into the wall like nails or screws. Then he ran a hand, shaky and oddly dissociated from the rest of himself, along the whites of his overall until he located the pocket, found the crumpled handkerchief within, and thrust his fingertips into its softness. A little blood soaked into it.

With his other hand he reached out and touched the coloured dots in the wall. Botched DIY. He nearly smiled. As he reached forward, and a part of him still wished to understand, he saw them for what they were: pieces of old toys from a children's playroom. He touched them, their tiny smooth protrusions, and noted their sheer unlikely reality. One piece immediately before him had grown into something not plastic at all as he carefully reached out. He teased a grip of sorts around it with his fingers. And instead of plastic, dusty fur revealed itself. He tugged at it a little harder; with his fingertips he scratched away, until slowly his excavation was complete.

Tiny loose nuggets of plaster fell away; the air around him shaded into delicate lemon columns that trickled down to the carpet.

Quickly, he forced the thing free. Hadn't Lynn mentioned something about a young lad in the house? So, then, he stood there, midway up the stairs, and in his hand a steady unblinking eye gazed up and met his own. It held him. He stared down into the palm of his cupped hand. And all around him it was quiet, the air as if holding its breath, as he looked down at the indelible softness resting in his palm. With a flood of tenderness that returned unwelcome layers of memory, he found himself regarding a nearly intact teddy bear.

He paused to study the bear, its staring eye, and could shape no better explanation: it had been pressed into the wall. Or drawn there, like so much else.

And he wondered: where on earth was Lynn? Why wasn't she back inside by now?

Things *couldn't* have happened, at least not the way he had seen them, and for the briefest instance he feared himself for tolerating whatever was here that had so thoroughly denied him the judgement and grasp he required. It seemed that the longer he spent within these walls the less sure of himself he became.

He ignored the rest of the bright dots embedded in the staircase wall, ignored their closed-off histories and private meanings—had the tiny objects once brought pleasure, how much had they been played with? Against his will, he stretched out an arm to straighten a wonky picture as a soft clump of light brown strands tumbled down from behind the frame. A twisted nest of dead hair, human and glossy, rested at his feet. And once more against his intentions, he bent down to it and touched the small greasy bundle . . . and cried out in disgust as he felt its recent warmth.

Bloody fingertips dug deep into the handkerchief he clenched in his pocket. After a moment, and ignoring the hair, he tried to re-insert the teddy bear back inside the hole in the wall. But it fell out and he didn't try again. He wiped his fingers against his handkerchief.

The stairs guided him further up.

At the top he turned right, and just as Lynn had warned him, the first thing he saw in the main bedroom ahead was a shape that had perhaps been the mother. The door was swung viciously back and he entered swiftly.

As he approached it, the shape drew him into the room and he was about to call it in (for Lynn would need more details, they'd need to arrange the photos) when he found himself transfixed by the image before him. The corpse of the woman—it rested about eighteen inches or so above the carpeted floor—had been hurled there, driven into the wall. The bones squeezed to strips of splinter and folded into the hard surface like lengths of damp paper pressed down and smoothed flat.

As he stood there, the sense of grim motive that dwelled within the walls shaped into clarity for him and he saw how everything had repeated itself in the house. Objects, toys, people. It was the same thing. He imagined the fury.

He didn't want to run his fingers against her, and resisted. The torn tissue of the skin, her flattened innards, still clung to the semblance of a recent human form. But the wall had taken her in, absorbed her, and it was not possible to detect where her human presence ended—and the grasp of the house began. Appalled, his fingers slowly reached out and touched it.

And he had to admit, it was wonderful, admirable.

He patted the wall with gentleness and the wall repaid him with a dribble of dark red from the woman.

The rich gag of blood overwhelmed him, and he had to move away. That was when he noticed the husband. He turned away. He certainly tried to turn away. A twisted knot of elbow suspended before his gaze gave one final, impossible twitch and then was gone. White plaster closed over it, and then there was nothing. He was no longer horrified.

The radio buzzed alive and a different reality intruded. It was Lynn.

"Something's not right. Get out fast!"

Then the line was broken up and she was lost.

But there was no danger. The family, he reasoned, were dead, after all. What could Lynn possibly mean? All was well. Yes, he answered himself, firmly. All was correct. He didn't call her back.

A moment passed before the radio, snatched from his grasp, slammed hard against the unclean carpet. He stood and watched the thing. Watched as his radio was swallowed into the bedroom's surroundings like some kind of jungle animal that had crept back into its jungle camouflage. He felt calm, ready. And then it came fast: an intense ache that first built somewhere near his shoulders; so that he collapsed to the floor, attempted to crawl out of the room, back towards the top of the stairs, though he didn't know why. Then an exquisite agony of brisk breaking inside him, of quick snapping. The forensic whites that had protected him became dark with maroon dots that seeped through the fabric. Yet the injuries, if injuries they were, failed to register any pain. In the house, an eager weight pressed down until his consciousness turned to a grey smudge.

◄○►

They released him some weeks later. Starched white sleeve of the concerned nurse, her sleeve had somehow got in the way of the swinging door as he turned to leave.

He tried to remember. Remembered someone's sharp voice when it had already been too late. The voice warning him that something had gone wrong, urging him. Get out fast, it had said. That woman's voice on his radio annoying him. Yes, that had been it. As if she hadn't any confidence in him to take control of the situation—or to take care of the house. But it'd been *him*, not her, who had borne witness within the property back then.

It all seemed long ago. For now he was walking away from that hospital, unreal and lost to himself, as he made his way to the house. The call-out's house. Summoned once, now summoned again.

Only there was no house.

He stood in an empty space instead.

After a moment he welcomed the old sensation. He sensed a sudden, clean reality as something began tearing, gnawing at his insides, and he knew he would never leave, not again. This time his connection to the place was fuller, stronger.

He couldn't explain it; he only knew it was somehow linked to this place, came from here. And still it grew: this eager biting away at something deep within himself. Soon the implosion would be complete.

But then his arms were flung forcefully across his chest, and made to press hard there as his limbs, hideously, continued an insane inward journey, thrusting ever deeper in a fatal contortion. Until they were completely drawn within his body, and he had folded into himself.

Sometime later, the neighbours exposed a tiny curled mass of dead and twisted limbs. The police were called. Close against the earth, they found him, his fingernails encrusted with dirt, and heavily soiled. As if he had been frantically fending something off—or embracing it.

GRAVE GOODS

GEMMA FILES

P ut the pieces back together, fit them against each other chip by chip and line by line, and they start to sing. There's a sort of tone a skeleton gives off; Aretha Howson can feel it more than hear it, like it's tuned to some frequency she can't quite register. It resonates through her in layers: skin, muscle, cartilage, bone; whispers in her ear at night, secret, liquid. Like blood through a shell.

The site they're working on is probably Early Archaic—6,500 B.P. or so, going strictly by contents, thus beating out the recent Bug River find by almost 2,000 years. Up above the water-line, too, which makes it *incredibly* unlikely; most people lived in lakeshore camps back then, right when the water levels were at their lowest after the remnant ice mass from the last glacial advance lying across the eastern outlet of Lake Superior finally wasted away, causing artificially high lake levels to drop over a hundred metres. Then isostatic rebound led to a gradual return, which is why most sites dating between the end of the Paleo-Indian and 4,000 years ago are largely under water.

Not this one, though: it's tucked up under a ridge of granite, surrounded by conifer old growth so dense they had to park the vehicles a mile away and cut their way in on foot, trying to disturb as little as possible. Almost a month later—a hideously cold, rainy October, heading straight for Hallowe'en—the air still stinks of sap, stumps bleeding like wounds. Dr. Anne-Marie Begg's people hauled the trunks out one by one, cross-cut the longest ones, then loaded them up and took them back to the Reserve, where they'll be planed in the traditional manner and used for rebuilding. Always a lot of home improvement projects on the go, over that way; that's what Anne-Marie—Dr. Begg—says.

Though Canadian ethics laws largely forbid excavations, once Begg brought Dr. Elyse Lewin in to consult, even the local elders had to agree this particular discovery merited looking into. They've been part of the same team practically since Begg was Lewin's favourite TA, operating together out of Lakehead University, Thunder Bay; Lewin's adept at handling funding and expedition planning, while Begg handles both tribal liaison duties and general PR, plus almost anything else to do with the media. It was Begg who sowed excitement about "Pandora's Box," as the pit's come to be called, on account of the flat slab of granite—lightly incised with what look like ancestral petroglyphs similar to those found on Qajartalik Island, in the Arctic—stoppering it like a bottle. Incised on top *and* below, as Aretha herself discovered when they pried it apart, opening a triangular gap large enough to let her jump in; shone the flashlight downwards first, just far enough to check her footing before she landed—down on one knee, a soggy crouch, too cramped to straighten fully—then automatically reversed it, revealing those square-cut, coldly eyeless faces set in silent judgement right above her head.

"How'd they get it here?" Morgan, the other intern, asks Lewin, who shrugs and glances at Begg before letting her answer.

"The slab itself, that's found, not made—shaped a little, probably. More than enough rockfall in this area for that, post-glacial shear. Then they'd have made an earthwork track like at Stonehenge, dug underneath—" Begg uses her hands to sketch the movements in midair. "—then piled in front, put down logs overtop, used them like rollers. Get enough people pushing and pulling, you're golden."

Lewin nods. "Yes, exactly. Once the grave was dug, there'd be no particular problem fitting it overtop; just increase the slope 'til they had a hill and push it up over the edge, down-angled so one side touched the opposite lip, before dismantling the hill to lay it flat again."

"Mmm." Morgan turns slightly, indicating: "What're the carvings for, though? Like . . . what do they mean?"

"Votive totems," Begg replies, with confidence.

The forensics expert—Dr. Tatiana Huculak—just shakes her head. "No way to know," she counters. "Told us yourself they don't look like any of the ritual marks you grew up with, remember? So it's like a sign in Chinese, for all of us—just as likely to say 'fuck you' as 'God bless,' unless you know Pinyin."

Begg's already opening her mouth to argue when Lewin sees Aretha's hand go up; she shushes them both. "Oh dear, you don't have to do *that*!" she exclaims. "Just sing out, if an idea's struck you."

Aretha hesitates, eyes flicking to Morgan, who nods. Courage in hand, she replies—

"Uh, maybe. I mean—even when you don't know the language, there's still a lot you can get from context, right? Well . . ." She hauls herself up, far enough past the slab to tap its top, nails grating slightly over rough-edged stone. "'Keep out,' that'd be my guess," she concludes. "'Cause it's up here."

Lewin nods, as Huculak and Begg exchange glances. "Logical. And down there? On the underside?"

Here Aretha shrugs, uncomfortably unanonymous for once, pinned beneath the full weight of all three professors' eyes.

". . . 'stay in?'" she suggests, finally.

◀◦▶

Working this dig with Lewin's team was supposed to be the best job placement ever, a giddy dream of an archaeological internship—government work with her way paid up front, hands-on experience, the chance to literally uncover something unseen since thousands of years BCE. By the end of the first week, however, Aretha was already beginning to dream about smothering almost everyone else in their sleep or hanging herself from the next convenient tree, and the only thing that's improved since then is that she's now far too exhausted to attempt either.

Doesn't help that the rain which greeted them on arrival still continues, cold and constant, everything covered in mud, reeking of pine needles. Sometimes it dims to a fine mist, penetrating skin-deep through Aretha's heaviest raincoat; always it chills, lighting her bone-marrow up with sharp threads of ache, air around her so cold it hurts to inhale through an open mouth. Kneeling here in the mud, she sees her breath boil up as cones fall down through the dripping, many-quilled branches, their sticky impacts signalled with rifle-shot cracks, and every day starts the same, ends the same:

wood mould burning in her eyes and sinuses like smoke, impossible to ward off, especially since the Benadryl ran out.

"Jesus," Morgan suddenly exclaims, like she just hasn't noticed it before, "that's one hell of a cold you've got there, Ree. Does Lewin know?"

Aretha shrugs, droplets scattering; hard to do much else, when she's up to her elbows in grave-gunk. And: "Uh, well . . . yeah, sure," she replies, vaguely. "Can't see how she wouldn't."

"Close quarters, and all? You're probably right. But who knows, huh? I mean . . ." Here Morgan trails off, eyes sliding back to the main tent—over which two very familiar voices are starting to rise, yet again—before returning to the task at hand. ". . . she's kinda—distracted, these days, with . . . everything. I guess."

"Guess so."

Inside the main tent, Begg and Huculak are going at each other like ideological hammer and tongs, as ever—same shit, different day, latest instalment in an infinite series. It's been a match made in hell, pretty much since the beginning; Huculak's specialization makes her view all human remains as an exploitable resource, while Begg's tribal band liaison status puts her in charge of making sure everything that could conceivably once have been a person gets put right back where it was found after cataloguing, with an absolute minimum of ancestral disrespect. Of course, Begg's participation is basically the only reason they're all here in the first place, as Lewin makes sure to keep reminding Huculak—but from Huculak's point of view, just because she knows it's true doesn't mean she has to pretend to like it.

"I'll point out, yet again," Huculak's saying right now, teeth audibly gritted, "that the *single easiest way* we could get a verifiable date on this site continues to be if we could take some of the bones back and carbon-date them, in an honest-to-Christ lab . . ."

Aretha can almost see Begg curtly shaking her head, braids swinging—the way she does about fifty times a day, on average—as she replies. "Carbon-date the grave goods, then, Tat, to your heart's content—carbon-date the *shit* out of them, okay? Grind them down to paste, you want to; burn them, smoke the fucking ashes. But the bones, themselves? *Those* stay here."

"Oh, 'cause one of 'em might share maybe point-one out of a hundred-thousandth part of their genetic material with yours? Bitch, please."

Lewin's voice here, smooth and placatory as ever: "Ladies! Let's be civil, shall we? We all have to work together, after all, for a good month more . . ."

"Unfortunately," Huculak snaps back, probably making Begg puff up like a porcupine. Hurling, back in her turn—

"Hey, don't denigrate my spirituality just because you don't share it, is that so hard? Say we were in Africa, digging up Rwandan massacre dumps—things'd be different *then*, right?"

"You know, funny thing about that, Anne-Marie: not really. They'd be the same way anyplace, for me, because I am a *scientist*, first and foremost. Full friggin' stop."

"And I'm not, is what you mean."

"Well . . . if the moccasin fits."

At that, Aretha whips her head around sharply, only to meet Morgan's equally-disbelieving gaze halfway. The both of them staring at each other, like: *seriously?* Holy cultural slap-fight with potential impending fisticuffs, Batman. *Wow.*

"Knock-down drag-out by six, seven at the latest," Morgan mutters, sidelong. "I'm callin' it now—fifty on Tat to win, unless Anne-Marie puts her down with the first punch. You in, or what?"

Aretha hisses out something that can't quite be called a laugh. "Pass, thanks."

Morgan shrugs, then turns back to her designated task, head shaking slightly. "Your loss."

Going by her initial pitch, Lewin genuinely seems to have thought hiring only female associates and students would guarantee this little trip going far more smoothly than most, as though removing all traces of testosterone from the equation would create some sort of paradisical meeting of hearts and minds: cycles synched, hands kept busy, no muss, no fuss. The principle, however, was flawed from its inception: *just 'cause they ain't no peckers don't mean ain't no peckin' order*, as Aretha's aunties have often been heard to remark, 'round the all-gal sewing circle they run after hours out of their equally all-girl cleaning service's head office. It frankly amazes Aretha how Lewin could ever have gotten the idea that women never bring such divisive qualities as ambition, wrath, or lust to the metaphorical table, when she's spent the bulk of her career teaching at all-girl facilities across the U.S., before finally ranging up over the border—

But whatever. Maybe Lewin's really one of those evo-psych nuts underneath the Second Wave feminist frosting, forever hell-bent on mistaking biology for destiny no matter the context. Just as well she's apparently never thought to wonder exactly what those pills Aretha keeps choking down each day are, if so.

On puberty blockers since relatively early diagnosis, thank Christ, so she never did reach the sort of giveaway heights her older brothers have, and her voice hasn't changed all that much, either; that, plus no Adam's apple, facial and body hair kept chemically downy as any natal female in her immediate family, even if the other team-members felt inclined to body-police. But the plain fact is, they've none of them seen each other in any sort of disarray since they left base-camp—it's too cold to strip for sleep, let alone to shower, assuming they even had one.

This is typical paranoia, though, and she knows it; the reason everyone here knows her as Aretha is because she *is*. That's the name under which she entered university, legally, and it'll be the name with which she graduates, just like from high school. She's a long damn way away from where she was born at this point, both literally and figuratively.

Looks back up to find Morgan still looking at her and blushes, sniffing liquid, with nothing handy even halfway clean enough to wipe the result away on. "Sorry," she manages, after a second. "*So* gross, I know, I really do. I just—sorry, *God*."

Morgan laughs. "Dude, it's fine. Who knew, right?"

"Yeah." A pause. "Think it would've been okay, probably, it just hadn't rained the whole fucking time."

"And yet."

". . . and yet."

Morgan has a great smile, really; Aretha'd love to see it closer up sometime, under different circumstances. But right now, little moment of connection under pressure already had, the only thing either of them can really think to do about it is just shrug a little and drift apart once more—Morgan back towards the generator array, which is starting to make those worrying pre-brownout noises yet again, while Aretha heaves herself up out of the pit and stamps sloshily towards the tent itself, planning to sluice her gloved hands under the tarp's overflowing gutter. This brings her so close to the ongoing argument she can finally see what the various players are actually doing, through that space where the tent's ill-laid side gapes open: Begg and Huculak squaring off, with Lewin playing referee. It's not quite at the cat-fight stage yet, but if Morgan's placing bets, Aretha's at least setting her watch.

"Look, Anne-Marie . . ." Huculak says, finally, "I know you want to think these are your people outside, in the grave—but I've been studying them hands-on for weeks now, and I just don't think they were, at all. I don't think these were *anybody's* 'people.'"

"Jesus, Tat! What the hell kind of Othering, colonialist bullshit—"

"No, but seriously. *Seriously.*" Huculak points to a pelvic arrangement, a crushed-flat skull, as much of the spinal column as they've been able to find. "Pelvis slung backwards, like a *bird*, not a mammal. Orbital sockets fully ten ml larger than usual, and side-positioned, not to the front; these people were barely binocular—probably had to cock their heads just to look at something in front of them. Twice as many teeth, half of them canines, back ones serrated: this is a meat-eater, exclusively. And that's not even getting into the number of vertebrae, projection processes to the front and rear of each, locking them together like a snake's . . ."

"You've got three bodies to look at, barely, and you're already pushing taxonomic boundaries? Phylogenetic analysis by traits is a slanted system, makes it too easy by far to mistake clades or haplogroups for whole separate species—"

Ooh, bad move, Dr. Begg, Aretha thinks, even as that last sentence starts, and indeed, by its end Huculak's eyes have widened so far her smile-lines disappear completely. "Oh really, *is* it?" she all but spits. "Golly gee, I didn't *know* that, please tell me more! Hottentot Venus what?"

"You know what I'm saying."

"I know *exactly* what you're saying, yes; do you know what *I'm* saying? Or did you just start shoving your fingers in your ears and singing *lalalala I can't HEEEEAR yooou* the minute I started talking, like usual?"

Begg snorts, explosively. "You've seen the dig, every damn day for a month—it's a *grave*, Tat, you just used the word yourself. Full of grave goods. Animals don't *do* that, if that's what you're implying."

"Of course I'm not saying what's in there is animals, for shit's sake; an offshoot of humanity, maybe—some evolutionary dead end. Like Australopithecus."

"You telling me Australopithecus had snake-spines?"

"*No.* But just because we haven't found something yet doesn't mean it never existed."

"Good line, Agent Mulder."

"Oh *fuck you*, you condescending, indigenocentrist *fuck*—"

Lewin raises her hands, goes to interpose between them, but they ignore her roundly—both wider as well as darker, more built for the long haul, able to shrug her off like a charley-horse. Huculak glares up as Begg stares down, hands on hips and braids still swinging, and demands: "Seriously, is that what we're down to, right now? The black girl and the Indian, calling each other out as racists?"

Huculak twitches like she's about to start throwing elbows, trying to divert the urge to punch first and answer questions later; the movement's actually violent enough to rock Begg back a micro-step, make her start to flinch involuntarily, right before she catches herself.

"You first," is all Huculak replies, finally, voice flat.

And: "*Ladies,*" Lewin puts in again, a tad more frantically. "We're scientists here, yes? Professionals. We can differ, even quarrel, but with *respect*—always respect. This is all simply theory, for now."

Now it's Huculak's turn to snort. "For*ever*, she gets her way," she replies. "And she will."

"Bet your ass," Begg agrees. "'Cause this is Kitchenuhmaykoosib Inninuwug First Nation land, and that's *not* a theory, so those bones go right on back in the ground where we found them, just like your government promised. No debate."

Lewin looks at Huculak. Huculak looks away.

"Never actually thought there would be," she mutters, under her breath.

·◦·

The grave goods Huculak finds so uninteresting are typical Early Archaic: a predominance of less extensively flaked stone tools with a distinct lack of pottery and smoking pipes, new-style lanceolate projectile points with corner notches and serration along the side of the blades suitable to a mixture of coniferous and deciduous forests, increased reliance on local chert sources. What's odd about it, however, is the sheer size of the overall deposit—far more end scrapers, side scrapers, crude celts, and polished stone *atl-atl* weight-tubes than seem necessary for a mere family burial, which is what the three bodies Begg talked about would indicate: one male, one female, one sexually indistinct adolescent (its pelvis missing, possibly scavenged by animals before the cap-stone was laid).

Folded beneath a blanketing layer of grave goods so large it almost appears to act as a secondary grounding weight, the three bodies nevertheless take pride of place, traces of red ochre still visible on and around all three rather than just the male skeleton, as would be customary. Weirder yet, on closer examination, the same sort of ochre appears to have been painstakingly applied not only to the flensed bones themselves but also to all the grave goods as well, before they were piled on top.

In burials from pre-dynastic Egypt to prehistoric Britain, Aretha knows, red ochre was used to symbolize blood; skeletons were flensed and decorated with it as both a sign of respect and of propitiation, a potential warding off of vampiric ghosts: *take this instead, leave us ours.* With no real sense of an afterlife, the prehistoric dead in general were thought to be eternally jealous, resentful of and predatory towards the living . . . but particularly so if they'd died young, or unjustly, and thus been cheated of everything more they might have accomplished while alive. Like the Lady of Cao, Aretha thinks, or the so-called "Scythian Princess," both of whom died in their twenties, both personages of unusual power (the former the first high-status woman found in Moché culture, the latter actually a Siberian priestess buried in silk and fur and gold), and both of whose tombs also contained the most precious grave good of all, startlingly common across cultures from Mesoamerican to Hindu to Egyptian to Asian: more corpses, often showing signs of recent, violent, *sacrificial* death.

Retainer sacrifice, that's what they call it, Aretha thinks, her head spinning slightly, skull gone hot and numb under its cold, constantly wet cap of skin. *Like slaughtering horses so they can draw the princess's chariot into the underworld, except with people: concubines, soldiers, servants, slaves—maybe chosen by lots, maybe volunteers. Killing for company on that final long day's journey into whatever night comes next. In Egypt, eventually, they started substituting* shawabti *figures instead, magic clay dolls incised with spells swapped in for actual corpses; an image of a thing, just as good as the thing itself. Unless it's not.*

Text taking shape behind her eyes, wavering: she can almost see it on her laptop's screen or maybe even a page somewhere, whatever reference-method she first encountered this information through. How in Mound

72 at Cahokia, largest site of the Mississippian culture (800 to 1600 CE, located near moden St. Louis, Missouri), pits were found filled with mass burials—53 young women, strangled and neatly arranged in two layers; 39 men, women and children, unceremoniously dumped, with several showing signs of not having been fully dead when buried, of having tried to claw their way back out. Another group of four individuals was neatly arranged on litters made of cedar poles and cane matting, arms interlocked, but heads and hands removed.

Most spectacular is the "Birdman," a tall man in his forties, thought to have been an important early Cahokian ruler. He was buried on an elevated platform, covered by a bed of more than 20,000 marine-shell disc beads arranged in the shape of a falcon with the bird's head appearing beneath the man's head, its wings and tail beneath his arms and legs. Below the Birdman another corpse was found, buried facing downward, while surrounding him were piles of elaborate grave goods . . . .

Cahokia was a trade centre, of course, the apex of an empire; makes sense they'd do things big, lay on the bling. This, meanwhile . . . this is different: smaller, meaner. The faces of the three prime skeletons have been smashed, deliberately, as if in an attempt to make them unrecognizable, a spasm of disgust or desecration; God knows, Aretha's spent more than enough time piecing them back together to know how effective that first attack was, how odd that it should be followed up with what reads as an almost equally violent avalanche of reverence. But then there's the cap-stone, the lid, the flensing and the ochre, plus the ochre-saturated grave goods pile itself—all added later, at what had to be great cost to the givers. Like a belated apology.

No retainers, though. Not here.

Not where anybody's thought to look, as yet.

This last thought jolts Aretha out of half-sleep at last, making her sit up so sharply she almost falls over, a blinding surge of pain stitching temple to temple; holds herself still on her sleeping bag, breathing slowly as possible to thwart nausea. She presses her fingers up against the edge of her eyesockets until white dots flicker behind her eyelids, forcing the pain back by pressure and sheer will, until—gradually—the agony recedes. The minute she's able, she slips her boots back on, grabs her excavation spade and trowel and ducks out of her tent.

The mist, cool on her flushed face, brings a moment's relief. Not sure if her giddiness is inspiration or fever, Aretha heads for the grave pit as fast as she can.

The light is dimming; she won't have long. Can't see anybody working, which suggests they're at dinner, in the chow tent. But no, not all of them, it turns out. Because as she pauses by the main tent, she can hear Dr. Begg arguing with someone yet again—over the sat-phone, this time. Who?

Curiosity gets the better of her. She edges up to the tent's outer wall, holding her breath.

". . . don't know *who* she knows, is my point, *Gammé*," Begg says. Aretha frowns, translating: *Gammé* for grandmother, the elder who helped swing the tribal council towards permitting this dig in the first place; Aretha's never heard Begg sound this uncomfortable with her. "But if it's somebody with enough clout, somebody who decides they don't want to honour the arrangement any more—" She stops; sighs. "Might be more money involved, sure. Maybe not. And maybe money's not what we should be thinking about, right now."

A longer pause. "Well, you saw the pictures, right? Yeah, they're the ones Tat already sent. So if people start agreeing with her—" A beat. "Okay, what? No, I'm not going to do that. *No.* Because this is *science,* not story-time, that's why, and by those standards, what Tat says makes *sense.* Muddying the waters with mythology isn't going to—hey, you there? Hello? *Hello?*"

No reply, obviously; the receiver slams down, *bang.* Sometimes the phone cuts out for no reason, even with satellite help—vagaries of location, technology, all that. So: "Oh, fuck *me,*" Begg mutters, and goes trudging away, still swearing at herself under her breath.

Mythology?

There was a moment, back in Week One . . . yes, she remembers it now. Sitting around the one smoking camp-fire they'd ever risked as the tarp above dipped and sloshed, Lewin asking Begg to fill in the tribal history of this particular area and Begg replying, slightly snappish, that there wasn't one, as such: *Lots of stories, that's all; heroes and monsters, that kind of shit.* "We don't go up there much, that place, 'cause of the—"

—and a word here, something Aretha'd never heard before, clipped and odd: *buack, paguk, baguck.* Something like that.

(*bakaak*)

Bakaak in *Ojibwe*, pakàk in *Algonquin*, a version of Begg's voice corrected, from somewhere deep inside. *It's an Anishinaabe* aadizookaan, *a fairytale. They split the difference, usually, and call it Baykok.*

Like the Windigo, Morgan suggested, but Begg shook her head. The point of the Windigo, she replied, was that a Windigo started out human, while the Baykok never was.

It's a bunch of puns stuck together. Bakaak *means "skeleton," "bones draped in skin";* thus bakaakadozo, *to be thin, skinny, poor. Or* bakaakadwengwe, *to have a thin face*—bekaakadwaabewizid, *an extremely thin being. Not to mention how it yells shrilly in the night,* bagakwewewin, *literally clear or distinct cries, and beats warriors to death with a club,* baagaakwaa'ige. *Flings its victim's chest open,* baakaakwaakiganezh, *to eat their liver . . . .*

Why the liver? Aretha asked, but Begg just shrugged.

Why any damn thing? It's a boogeyman, so it has to do something *gross. Like giants grinding bones to make their bread.*

You could do that, you know, as long as you added flour, Huculak put in, from the fire-pit's far side. *Just a flatbread, though. Bone-meal won't bond with yeast.*

Thank you, Martha Stewart.

Is that what Begg's grandmother just said, over the 'phone? That the skeletons look like Baykok—Baykoks? That Huculak's right, and also wrong? That Begg—

Oh, but Aretha's head is burning now, bright and hot, like the Windigo's legendary feet of fire. So hot the raindrops should sizzle on her skin, except they don't; just keep on falling, soft-sharp, solid points of cold pocking down through the sodden, pine-scented air. And the pit gaping open for her at her feet, a toothless, mud-filled mouth.

She drops to her knees, scrambles over the lip, slides down messily inside.

By the time Morgan comes by it's . . . well, later. Aretha doesn't know by how much, but the light's just about completely gone, and she's long since been reduced to scraping blindly away at the grave's interior walls with her gloved fingers. Looks up to see Morgan blinking down at her through a flashlight beam, and smiles—or thinks she does; her face is far too rigid-numb at this point for it to be any sort of certainty.

"'Lo, Morgan," she calls up, not stopping. "How was dinner?"

"Uh, okay. What . . . what're you *doing* down there, Ree? Exactly?"

"I have to dig."

"Yeah, I can see that. Are you okay? You don't look okay."

"I *feel* okay, though. Mainly. I mean—" Aretha takes a second to shake her head, almost pausing; the pit-walls blur on either side of her, heave dangerously, like they're breathing. Then: "It doesn't matter," she concludes, mainly to herself, and goes back to her appointed task.

"Um, all right." Morgan steps back, raising her voice incrementally with each new name: "Tat, Dr. Huculak, c'mon over here for a minute, will you . . . like, right now? Anne-*Marie*? Dr. *Lewin!*"

They cluster 'round the edge like flies on a wound, staring in as Aretha just keeps on keeping on, almost up to her wrists now in muck. "Aretha," Dr. Lewin begins, at last, "you do know we mapped out that area already, yes? Since a week ago."

"I remember, doctor."

"You took the measurements, as I recall."

"I remember."

"Okay, so *stop*, damnit," Huculak orders. "You hear me? Look at what you're *doing*, for Christ's sake! Anne-Marie—"

Begg, however, simply shakes her head, hunkering down. "Shut up, Tat," she says, without turning. To Aretha: "Howson, Ree . . . it's Aretha, right?" Aretha nods. "Aretha, did you maybe hear me, before? Up there, on the sat-phone?"

"Yes, Dr. Begg."

"Uh huh; shit. Look . . . the Baykok's just a story, Ree. It's folklore. You're not gonna find a, what—separate bunch of human bones in there, is that what you're thinking? Like a larder?"

Still scratching: "I'm not thinking that, no."

"Then what *are* you thinking?"

Aretha wipes mud off on her cheek, gets some in her mouth, spits brown. "Sacrifice," she answers, once her lips are clear again. "Like at Cahokia; slaves for the underworld, not food. But then again, who knows? Might've been both."

"Uh *huh*. How long you been down there, Ree?"

"I don't know. How long did they co-exist, Neanderthals and Homo habilis? 'Cause they did, right? I'm right about that. Lived long enough to share the same lands, even interbreed, enough so some people have Neanderthal DNA . . . ."

"That's the current theory," Lewin agrees, sharing a quick, dark look with Begg. But: "The hell's she saying?" Huculak demands of Lewin, at almost the same time. "Elyse, don't you *vet* your damn volunteers? We need to get her out, back to the Rez at least, get her airlifted somewhere—"

"Just shut *up,* Tat," Begg repeats, still not turning. "Morgan, you're her friend—on my count, okay? One . . . two . . . ."

But that, precisely, is when the wall of the grave-pit finally gives way. Releases a sudden avalanche of half-liquid earth that sweeps Aretha back, pins her under, crowns and crushes her alike on a swift, dark flood of roots and stones and bones, bones, bones.

Here they are, I was right, she barely has time to think, reeling delirious, her arms full of trophies, struggling to raise them high. *See? See? I was right, they're here, we're*

(*here*)

But who's that, back a little further beyond her team's shocked rim-ring, peering down on her as well? That tall, thin figure with its cocked head, its burning, side-set eyes? Its featureless face carved from jet-black stone?

She hears its scream in her mind, thin but distinct, a far-flung cry. The wail of every shattered skull-piece laid back together and set ringing, tuned to some distant tone: shell-bell, blood-hiss. Words made flesh, at long last.

(*here, yes*)

(*as we always have been*)

(*as we always will*)

⤙⤚

Aretha comes back to herself slowly, lying on a cot in the main tent, pain-paralyzed: hurt all over, inside and out. The out is mainly bruises, scrapes, a general wrenched ache, but the inside—that's something different. Like the world's worst yeast infection, a spike through her bladder, pithing her up the middle and watching her writhe; whole system clenched at once against her own core, a furled agony-seed, forever threatening to bloom.

She'd whimper, even weep, but she can barely bear to breathe. Which at least makes it easy—easi*er*—to keep quiet while the other talk around her, above her, about her.

"Baykok, huh?" Dr. Huculak's saying, while Dr. Begg makes a weird snorting noise. "Looks more like a damn prehistoric serial killer's dump-site, to me. And how'd she know where to dig, anyhow?"

Morgan: "She said she had a dream. Whispered it, when I was taking her vitals."

Dr. Lewin sounds worried; Aretha wishes she thought it was for the right reasons. "Yes, as to that. How bad's her damage?"

"That's one way to put it," Huculak mutters, as Morgan draws a breath, then replies: "Well . . . she's fine, I guess, believe it or not. Physically, anyway."

"What about the—"

Morgan's voice gets harder. "Those scars are old, not fresh. Surgical. And none of our business."

Lewin sighs. "If they mean what I think they mean, I'm not happy with . . . 'her' choice to misrepresent 'herself,' on the project application form."

"Can we not use bullshit scare-quotes, please?" Morgan asks. "I mean— check the University rules and regs, doc. Pronouns are up to the individual, these days."

"Is biology? Aretha is—is female, just because 'she' says 'she' is?"

"Uh, yeah, Dr. L, that's *exactly* what that means. Just like a multiracial person's black if they say they are, or anybody's a Christian if they say so, even if they don't go to church." The fierceness in Morgan's voice puts a lump in Aretha's throat. She cracks her eyes open, tries to find words to thank her with, but her lips won't work; all that comes out is a dry clicking, some insect clearing its throat from inside her mouth.

But Huculak's already moved into the pause anyhow, adding: "Like those things in the pit'd be human, if they could say so."

At this, Begg turns, confronting her. "Excuse me, *things*? We're back there again? What the fuck happened to parallel evolution?"

"Oh, I don't know—tell me again how your elders think of them as ances- tors, Anne-Marie. Tell me they *don't* call them monsters."

"Sure, okay: this is Baykok country, like I said that first week, which is why somebody non-tribal—some hiker from Toronto—literally had to stumble over the cap-stone for us to even know it was here, and why we had to cut our way in, after. But all that proves is that superstition's a powerful thing. My *Gammé*'s in her eighties, and frankly, when it comes to archaeology, she doesn't know what she's talking about."

Huculak scoffs. "Yeah, and Schliemann never found eight different versions of Troy by looking where Homer said to, either."

"Oh, so what—folktales are fact disguised, is that the song we're singing? Schliemann using *The Iliad* as a guidebook was the exception, not the rule; he got lucky, and what he found was *not* what he'd been looking for, either. Which is exactly what's happened here, all over."

"A pile of bones that don't look human, with a much larger pile of bones attached which do," says Huculak, voice heavy with sarcasm. "Yeah, sure, no big mystery *there*."

"Well, in point of fact, no. You heard Aretha: retainer sacrifice, like in a hundred other places, and do you really think we need monsters for that?" For once, Begg sounds more exhausted than angry. "It's classic Painted Bird syndrome, Tat. Whatever makes a person different enough from the herd to be rendered . . . pariah, alien, monstrous: this little family with their wide-spaced eyes and their snake-spines, or my *Gammé* when she came back from Residential School, hair cut and wearing white kid clothes, barely able to speak her own language anymore. Or Aretha here, for that matter, once Elyse got a look at her chest . . . ."

Lewin lifts her hands. "Don't bring me into this, please."

"But you're already *in* it. We all are." Now it's Huculak's turn to sound uncharacteristic, all her usual snark gone. With some difficulty, Aretha turns her head, sees the woman bent down over something long, greyish-brown and filthy: one of the fresh-dug bones, plucked from a teetery, cross-stacked pyramid of such, off the gurney she stands next to. "I mean, I'd need to do a full lab workup to verify, but some of these remains—they still have flesh on them, under the muck. Like, non-mummified flesh."

Dr. Lewin, blinking: "You mean they're—"

"Recent. Yeah."

"But they were buried. How—?"

"You tell me. Anne-Marie?"

Begg opens and closes her mouth. "Well," she starts, "that's obviously—um. Okay. I mean, that's . . ." She deflates, slumping. "I don't know what that is," she says at last, near-inaudibly.

You'd think Huculak would be proud to have thrown her chief rival off so thoroughly, but no; she looks equally taken aback, almost scared. Lewin just stands there, studying the tent's tarp floor, like she's misplaced something; above, rain drums the roof, incessant, a dull cold tide. Morgan's gaze flicks from one to the next as the silence stretches ever more thin, disbelieving, 'til it finally falls on Aretha, and her eyes widen. "Shit—Ree! You're awake!" She hurries over to the cot and kneels down, stroking Aretha's forehead. "How you feeling, babe?"

Babe. In Morgan's mouth, the word sounds good enough to make Aretha cry, or want to.

"Hurts," she husks instead, through chapped lips. "All through my groin, lower abdomen . . ." She tries to move and hisses, agony spiking her joints. "Elbows and knees, ankles, too."

Morgan puts the inside of one wrist to Aretha's forehead, then takes her pulse; Aretha's creeped out by how pale her own wrist looks when hefted slackly in the tent's lantern-light, its veins slightly distended and purpled. "Fever feels like it's gone down, at least," Morgan tells her, attempting an unconvincing smile. "But since that's as far as my Girl Guide first aid training goes, all I can tell you beyond that is you need a hospital, like *now*. Dr. Begg, is the sat-phone working again?"

"Um, no, not yet."

"Fine. You know what? It's half an hour back to the access road; give me that damn thing and I'll get it to where it can get a signal out, then call an airlift to get her down to Thunder Bay."

Lewin puts a hand to her mouth, Victorian as all hell. "Oh dear, not at night, in this rain! What if you get lost, slip and fall, or—?"

"Ma'am, I'll be fine, my boots are hiking-rated. Seriously."

But: "No, Morgan, trust me, bad *bad* idea," Huculak says, Begg nodding agreement. "Wait for daybreak, for the weather to clear, that'll free up the signal link—"

Both stop as Morgan, already bent to lace her boots tighter, slashes one hand across the air.

"I have a compass and a map," she tells them, not looking up, "a flashlight, a knife, and I'm not gonna melt. Plus it's safer on foot than trying to drive, when it's like this. Anybody wants to go instead of me, I'm amenable, but you better speak now or forever hold your peace: Ree's my friend, and I'm not putting her through one second more of this than we have to."

Straightening, she glares 'round, hands on hips, but no one objects. So she stuffs the blocky sat-phone away and ducks down with a shrug instead, planting a swift kiss on Aretha's forehead—too light to fully track, here and then gone, almost hallucinatory. Like a promise.

"See you soon," she murmurs, swinging her knapsack onto her back.

But: *no,* that same voice hisses, from inside Aretha's mind. *I—*

(*we*)

—*think not.*

⟨◦⟩

Aretha doesn't remember falling asleep. When she wakes, the pain has diminished astonishingly; not gone, still twinging through her hips and knees when she swings herself into a tentative sitting position, but so much less it's near-euphoric. She feels light-headed, insubstantial; even the forest's damp pine-reek doesn't burn the way it used to. For a few moments, she simply enjoys breathing with something like her normal ease.

Then she sees the light, or lack thereof. The similar lack of company. No sat-phone on the table, just dirt and bones. No Morgan.

Shit.

Wrapping the sleeping bag around her like a puffy cloak, she stumbles out into open air, for once blessedly free of rain; no visible sky between the trees, but there's less sinus-drag, cueing a possible shift in air pressure. Lewin, Begg and Huculak are huddled around a Coleman stove maybe ten feet away, clustered gnats and moths flying up like sparks; Lewin turns as Aretha nears, almost smiling as she recognizes her, which is . . . odd, but welcome. Things *must* be bad.

"Aretha!" she calls out, voice only a little strained on the up-note. "You look—better. Than you did."

Aretha clears her throat, even as the other two shoot Lewin looks whose subtext both clearly read *are you fucking kidding me?* ". . . thanks," she manages, finally. Then: "Morgan?"

Lewin sighs. "No, dear. Not yet."

"How—long?"

"Two hours, maybe three," Huculak replies. "Anne-Marie went out looking, but—"

"I didn't find her," Begg says, a bit too quickly, too flat. "Not her."

Aretha nods, swallows again. No spit.

"What *did* you find?" she asks.

Tracks, that's the answer; about five minutes' walk from the camp. They're narrow but deep, as if carved, each a slipper full of dark liquid, welling up from underground. The soil is saturated here, Aretha can only suppose, after a solid four and a half weeks of precipitation—but there's something about the marks, both familiar and un-. They look . . . wrong, somehow. Turned upside-down.

"They're backwards," she observes, at last. Bends closer, just a bit, and wavers, not trusting herself to be able to crouch; the water throws back light, Huculak's beam crossing Lewin's as Begg hovers next to them, holding back, waiting to see if Aretha can eventually identify that particular winey shade without prompting.

"Not water," Aretha says, throat clicking drier yet, and Begg shakes her head. "No," she confirms, and Aretha dips further, sniffing hard. Smells rust, and rot, and meat.

Blood.

Lewin recoils, almost tripping, but Huculak stands her ground, demanding: "And you didn't think to tell us? The *fuck*, Anne-Marie!"

Begg stays where she is, rooted fast, as though every ounce of protest in her has long since drained out through her heels. Doesn't even bother shrugging.

"Not much point," she says, simply. "You'd've found out eventually too, once either of you thought to ask. But Aretha here's been a whole lot better at that than most of us throughout, hasn't she? Which is sort of interesting, in context."

"How so?"

"Things my *Gammé* told me over the years, that's all, about this area. Stuff I discounted automatically, pretty much, because—well, *you* know why, Tat: because science. Empirical data vs. subjective belief, all that. Because I've tried so fucking hard to never be *that* sort of Indian, if I can help it." She pauses here, takes a ragged breath. "But what do you know, huh? Sometimes, a monster isn't a metaphor for prejudice at all, plus or minus power. Sometimes, it's just a monster."

Huculak stares at her, like she's grown another head. "What?" she asks, yet again.

"What I just said, Tat. We should probably get going, if we're going to."

"Going to—?" Lewin apparently can't help prompting, carefully.

Begg sighs, windily, as though about to deflate. "Try, that's what I mean," she says, after a long moment's pause. "To leave, I mean. Before they get here."

"'They,'" Lewin repeats. "They . . . who?"

Now it's Begg's turn to stare, even as Huculak—possibly just a tad swifter on the uptake, or simply paranoid enough to connect the dots without being asked—draws a sudden in-breath, a choked half-gasp; hugs herself haphazardly, grasping for comfort, but finding none. While Lewin just stands there, visibly baffled: it doesn't make sense to her, any of it, and *can't*, really. Not in any *scientific* way.

"They were here first, that's what *Gammé* always told me," Dr. Begg—Anne-Marie—remarks, softly, as if to herself. "Hunted us like animals when we came into their territory, because that's what we must have seemed like to them, the same way *they* did, to us; things with some qualities of people, not people who just happen to look like things. So we fought back, because that's what we do, but there were more of them, and they were—stronger, fought harder. Started out taking us for food, then for slaves, then for breeding stock. Changed so they could hide, everywhere. Hide inside of *us*."

"Neanderthals," Aretha says. "And *Homo habilis*."

Begg smiles, slightly. "The current theory," she replies, echoing Lewin. Not looking 'round as she does, even to watch how Lewin—her cognitive refusal suddenly punctured, sharp and clean and quick—begins, at last, to buckle under her own words' weight.

Behind them, the grave-site still gapes uncovered, rain-filled, ochre seeping. From above, Aretha muses, the unearthed cache of grave goods must look like a huge, slightly layered blood-blotch, all that remains of some unspeakably old crime. An apology made on literally bended knees, pot sweetened with a pile of tools and corpses, yet left forever unaccepted.

Huculak—Tat—clears her throat, knuckles still knit and paling on either elbow. Complains, voice weak: "But . . . we didn't know."

"I did."

"You never *said*, though."

"No, 'course not, because I didn't want to think it was true. I mean, c'mon, Tat; seriously, now. Would *you?*"

"Well . . ."

(No.)

Deep twilight, now, under the trees, overlaid with even deeper silence. Deep enough Aretha can finally start to hear it once more, rising the same way her pain does, threading itself through her system: the song of the bones, set shiver-thrumming in every last wet, cold part of her; that note, that tone, so thin and distinct, a faraway cry drawing ever nearer. Like blood through some fossilized shell.

And oh, oh: *Anne-Marie was right, not to want to,* she thinks, faintly, as she feels her knees start to give way—as she droops, drops, ends up on hands and knees in the mud, the blood-smelling earth. *I'm not even Native, and I don't like that story much, either. Not at all.*

Not at all.

"Who's that?" Aretha can hear Lewin—Elyse—call out, faintly, squinting past her, into the darkness. Adding, hopefully, as she does: "Morgan? I—is that you, dear?"

To which Anne-Marie just shakes her head, while Tat begins to sob. And Aretha, looking up—seeing those familiar features hanging flat against the thickening curtain of night, mouth slack-hung and eyes empty, set every-so-slightly askew—doesn't even have to wait to hear the bones' answer to know the trick of it already, to her sorrow: that skeletal shadow poised behind, head cocked, holding Morgan's skin up like an early Hallowe'en mask with the scent of fresh-eaten liver on its breath. That line of similar shadows fanned behind, making their stealthy, back-footed way towards them all, with claws outstretched.

Don't worry, the bones' song tells her, from the inside out, as the Baykok sweep in. *This darkness is yours as much as ours, after all: a legacy, passed down hand to hand, from our common ancestors. Where we are, and were, and have been. Where you are, now, and always.*

The only place any of us have left to be.

Not so different, then, after all: cold comfort at best, and none at all, at worst. Not that it really matters, either way.

Every grave is our own, that's the very last thing Aretha Howson has time to think, before the earth opens up beneath her. Before she falls headlong, wondering who will find her bones, and when—what tales they'll tell, when dug free . . . what songs they'll sing, when handled . . . .

How long it'll be, this time, before anyone stops to listen.

BETWEEN DRY RIBS

GREGORY NORMAN BOSSERT

I wipe the drop of sweat from my eyebrow, shift my stool so I can watch the American family in the mirror behind the bar. Most of the tourists who wander here from the Dutch side of the island choose to sit on the patio. Most tourists choose another place entirely; the Belle Vue caters to the folks who work in the tiny industrial park on the outskirts of Marigot, and its view is of a warehouse and the parking lot of the health clinic, with a few palm trees hanging limp and listless in the swelter.

But this family insists on sitting inside. "Out of the sun," the father says, tipping back a soggy golf cap. His paunch frames a ring of belly sweat on his pink polo shirt. The mother fans herself with one of those cap-less visors; the sunburnt skin between her shoulder blades creases, channeling a slow stream of perspiration under her halter top to pool in the small of her back. A boy, around ten I guess, slumps in a basketball jersey with arm holes that hang to bony hips. A girl, a few years older, perches in her chair prodding her phone, she and her brother both with the oblivious perfection of privileged children.

Or is their disregard too studied, too perfect? I fish the lighter from my pocket and set it on the bar.

"Voilà, Mademoiselle," the bartender says, startling me. "Nous avons enfin obtenu quelques glaçons." He slips a napkin across the bar, sets my rum and ginger ale on it. The sweat on his arm is an even sheen, the dark gloss of a lifelong resident.

My fingers are pale in comparison, despite my five years on Saint Martin, despite my Senegalese mother, despite my need to blend in. Too much Parisian grey in my skin, too much smog and concrete, too many long low-angled shadows and twilight on the snow I must not think of. My arms are unevenly burnt and flabby and sweat-streaked and wholly beautiful.

At least the bartender is speaking to me in French. Behind me, the American family is getting drinks, the waiter explaining in patient English that ice cubes are coming. I am sure I look native to their eyes, a slow local in this slow local bar that is far too busy for my peace of mind. All of Marigot is too busy for me, sleepy though it is compared to the Dutch side. Too many strange faces, too many odd accents. But the bartender's French, the unmistakable island lilt, the distant hint of my mother's creole on his tongue, is reassurance.

In the mirror, the parents are studying the menu in a sort of baffled dread. "What are we doing here," those looks said, so far from the pastel-painted markets by the cruise ship landing, manned by Dutch students on their year-off adventure, always within safe range of a McDonald's or Pizza Hut or Starbucks. Their confusion, the way their eyes twitch as the bartender hacks at the ice with a pick, the way their sweat-slick shoulders hunch forward. All that, too, is reassurance.

The boy has twisted in his chair, has pinned a gecko's tail to the wall with one finger; as I watch in the mirror the tail pulls free and the gecko drops to safety. The girl has set her phone down. Her reflection gives me a look too dry and flat, and a fresh layer of sweat breaks out across my scalp, under my bra. I smell my own fear. The girl is rolling her can of Coke across her forehead, and her reflection is too distorted, the mirror too dank and corroded for me to tell if the glints are sweat or just the can's condensation.

The humidity, which finds everything, can make my lighter unreliable. I fight the urge to try it, imagine the lure of the flame. Instead I pull out my little pocketknife, open it so the blade faces upward, rest the last joint of my forefinger upon it.

The clatter from the other end of the bar, ice rattling in glasses, the waiter and the bartender laughing over something small. The bartender brings it over, with a wide smile and low chuckle. "Pour la femme cool, pas comme certains . . ." he says, with a tilt of his beautifully scarred cheekbones toward the American family. He slips another napkin next to my glass, sets the thing on it. It's a little snowman chunked from the ice, toothpick arms and eyes scraped hollow. It is insulated from the hot planks of the bar by the napkin, like a little beach towel—not the pastel prints they sell in the market here but a bright Nordic white—and its fresh-carved curves and wooden limbs are smooth, dry, perfect. Everything I cannot, not with the girl still watching, *must* not think about.

◄◦►

The snow hotel was a full day's trip north of Helsinki. It was mid-afternoon by the time I got off the train, and the sun was already on the horizon. Two other women headed to the hotel came off the train—a tiny Texan named Casey and broad-shouldered Kate from Australia—and we shared a taxi out to the hotel, trading stories of our travels in our variously accented English and French.

The hotel was disappointingly mundane at first. The cab dropped us off at a low wooden building that could just as well have been a storage unit but proved to be the office, dining room, and common lounge. But then we took the tour: the guest "cabins" not just built of snow and ice but carved into snow spirits and ice queens, yetis and yokai, all connected by paths that wandered labyrinth-like between head-high snowbanks and widened here and there into gardens of frost flowers and ice pools filled with grimacing snow-molded monkeys. The more we saw of the place, the stranger it got.

The same could be said of our guide, who proved to be the owner, chef, bellhop, and chief sculptor. He was Finnish, but spoke English with a heavy Australian accent. Every individual part of him was massive: barrel-body and hands like mittens, but all assembled onto a normal sized frame, like a doll pieced together from mismatched parts, with a tiny mustache that looked glued on as an afterthought. His name was Matti Kokko, and something about the way he announced that, tapping his huge fist against his hat, gave Casey such a case of the giggles that she had to stop in a grove of snow cacti and pretend to blow her nose for a good minute.

The last stop on the tour was the sauna, built of unstained planks in the same simple style as the main building. Matti was the architect, of course, and clearly proud of the details: the beech-trimmed shower in the small changing room in front, the propane heater for the surprisingly spacious sauna itself. A porch looked out over the lake, with steps down to a hole in the ice "if you want to be traditional," Matti said. And speaking of tradition, he was firm on the rules of the sauna: no changing the thermostat, not too little or too much water on the stones, and absolutely no clothes, not even a bathing suit. "Not healthy, dangerous even," he said. "The steam must touch the skin, the skin must be free to sweat. Tonight I will show you, right," that last said so matter-of-factly that it wasn't *entirely* creepy, though it did set Casey giggling again.

↤◇↦

I lasted about twenty minutes in my cabin. The charm of its yawning Green Man entrance and forest-nook interior, complete with vaulted ice branches and snow squirrels, couldn't distract me longer than that from the fact that it was literally freezing. I pulled on a second pair of tights over the first, dug a book out of my bag, and set off back to the main building.

I stopped on the way to take a picture of the snow snow monkeys. Matti might be somewhere on the spectrum from madcap to plain mad, but he was without doubt talented; the monkeys lounged in swirls of ice, arms around each other's backs, heads back in bliss. I was kneeling on the ice of their pond trying to get a good angle when a voice said, "Isn't it so funny, the way they try to act like human? It makes you laugh, how they try and fail. Are you headed to the lounge?"

She was on the path in just slippers and a white terrycloth robe, straight blond hair still wet and slipping from a turban of towel. She stood there with a small smile, head at an inquisitive angle, until I realized that she had asked a question. I admitted I was, dusted snow from my hands and knees, and joined her on the path.

"I am Anna," she said, slipping her arm through mine. "And you?" I stared—flustered by the casual familiarity and by her elusive accent, every word precise, equal in stress and slightly lilted so that the end of a sentence or a question came unexpectedly—for a few seconds before stammering, "Chloé." And because her patient regard seemed to require more, added, "Chloé Martin, from France."

"Ah, the French are so perfectly fashionable," she said. I stared again at that, seeing as I was a walking mound of layered wool and wind-proofing. If she was being sarcastic, though, there was no visible sign, just that somehow solemn smile, that inviting tilt to her head.

"Are you coming from the sauna?" I guessed.

"I have been swimming in the lake. Matti Kokko tells me that the people do this, here."

So not a local, then. There were no goose-pimples or raised hairs on the arm under mine, though, where her sleeve rode up, and her skin was neither flushed nor pale, but a perfect tan.

"You must be from somewhere north," I said. "Or south," I added, thinking of hearty Australian Kate.

"I must," she said. Again I couldn't tell if it was a question or not, and before I could think of a response that wasn't awkward, we'd arrived at the main building.

-◦-

"I think she's a cop," Casey said, around a mouthful of breakfast. "The way everything she says sounds like she's questioning you? The mysterious accent?"

"She isn't Finnish?" Kate said, pouring equal parts coffee and sugar into her cup.

"I don't think so," I said. "Icelandic, maybe?"

"Russian. A Russian spy," Casey said.

"You Americans with your cops and spies," Kate said. "Anyway, she doesn't sound Russian."

"She's buff enough to be one. A cop, I mean. In the sauna last night—"

"You used the sauna?" Kate laughed. "Good, you can show me how it works. I'm not sure I could make it through Matti's sauna lessons without cracking up."

Casey made a quick hushing gesture, turned into a wave. "Hey, Matti, awesome breakfast."

"Breakfast is a serious meal here," he said, as he topped off coffee cups.

"Coffee is a serious meal here," Kate said, approvingly.

"The Finns drink more coffee per capita than any other nation," Matti said. "It's good for the health, keeps the bodily fluids flowing." He slapped his belly.

Kate's face turned a delicate pink. As soon as Matti had stumped back into the kitchen she splurted her mouthful of coffee onto the tablecloth and sniggered. "Matti is just flowing with healthy fluids."

"The man is a *barrel* of health," Casey said.

"So you *did* take a sauna with him!" Kate said.

"Not really," Casey said. "I went down to check it out last night. Well, I went down to warm up, honestly. It's closer to my cabin than the lounge here. Anyway, Anna was already there, and she had the sauna going, so I stayed a while. It was pretty great, actually. Made sleeping in an igloo a lot more pleasant. Matti showed up just as we were leaving. He did look a bit put out that we hadn't waited for him. "Stay and I show you our sauna traditions." But I was cooked through, and Anna was already dressed. Not that she wears much, yeah? Even though it's like negative a hundred degrees out. It's that spy training."

"And she's spying on . . . what?" I asked. "Matti's snow snow monkeys, perhaps?"

"Reindeer smugglers," Kate suggested. "Reindeer who are smugglers."

Casey looked around, leaned in. "On Matti! She asked a lot of questions about him. Well, sort of half-questions. Did you know he used to have a wife in Australia?"

Kate got an odd look on her face.

I shrugged. "Maybe she is interested in him," I said. "As a man, I mean."

Casey shook her head doubtfully.

"Just because he is, ah, broad and she is thin doesn't mean there cannot be an attraction," I said, a little crankily. "To be honest, the shape she has, it's so . . ." I waved a hand in something like frustration. "So perfect, it is more unnatural than his."

"No fat shaming here, sister," Casey said, and blushed. "It's just that, well, Anna was very friendly in the sauna."

"Ah," I said.

"I think Matti could tell, too. 'The sauna, it is not a place for the erotic, it is a place of safety,' he said. As he was stripping down, mind you."

"So international womanizing woman of mystery versus Matti the sculpting criminal," I said. "Who knew snow hotels were so exciting?"

"Keeps the bodily fluids flowing," Casey said.

◄o►

A day later, and I had visited a reindeer farm, hiked through some beautiful forest, and taken a snowmobile ride to see the northern lights, but I still hadn't taken a sauna.

I had come close, the evening before. I'd walked down to the lake after the snowmobile ride, to get one more look at the aurora, and found Matti sitting on the porch of the sauna with a pipe and a lantern, like a ship's captain keeping watch. He had just finished, he said, and offered to go another round and show me what to do. The thought of taking off even a single layer of warm clothing, in front of him or not, was just too daunting. I shivered for a few minutes beside him on the porch, and the lantern light and the smell of his pipe and his quiet comments on the shimmering colors over the lake were enough to leave me optimistically sleepy.

I did not get much sleep, though. Despite leaving my layers on, and the hides and blankets and down sleeping bag, my snow-carved forest nook was just too cold. Kate was in the same boat; we commiserated over pre-breakfast coffee in the lounge. Anna was there as well, in a thin pullover and jeans, hair slicked back as if she'd been for a pre-dawn swim.

"Your friend Casey, she is around," she said, or asked.

Kate waggled her eyebrows at me, out of Anna's sight. "Casey seems to have figured out the secret of sleeping well here," she said.

Anna looked from Kate to me, one eyebrow raised.

"Saunas, I guess," I said.

"Keeps the bodily—" Kate said, and lost the rest in a giggle. She bit her lip and poked at her phone.

"Your friend checked out," Matti said, coming from the kitchen with a basket of bread and the coffee pot. "Yesterday afternoon. She left a note, said she had learned that Finland was not for her, and was traveling to Spain."

Anna said, "You did not know."

I shrugged. "We only met her on the train here."

"Texans," Kate said. "They walk alone." She frowned at her phone.

"Walk," Anna said. "Yes, that is what I am doing now." She got up, in her gracefully abrupt way, and left without looking back.

"Well now," I said, when Matti had had returned to the kitchen. "Do you think that perhaps Anna got a little *too* friendly with Casey?"

Kate was still grimacing at her phone. She took a breath, and a quick peek toward the kitchen.

"Chloé, you know how Casey said that Anna said that Matti had had a wife in Australia?"

Once I had parsed the English, I nodded.

"Well, that rang a bell, or rather, the name Kokko did, in context. So I texted my mum. She's a big one for the local news back home. And yeah, I was right. Claire Kokko, how could you forget a name like that? Matti's wife, yeah? And dig this. Around ten years ago, she disappeared. Went for a coffee, some dull dull suburb of Melbourne, and never came back. Big manhunt, womanhunt, whatever, Matti on the TV asking for help. I *thought* he looked familiar. Anyway, not a trace. And then a year later, they found her body. Taken *apart*."

"You have animals in Australia, yes?" I said. "Dingos and, er . . ."

"She was found in a condo downtown. An *expensive* condo. It had been sublet, and the tenant's identity turned out to be stolen. Stolen from a couple who had gone missing three years before."

"So you think Anna *is* a policewoman, investigating Matti's wife's death?" I put my hand over my mouth. "My God, you don't think *Matti* . . ."

Kate slumped back in her chair, shook her head. "Nah, my mum says he was cleared by the investigation, no doubts. She even remembered that he'd returned to Finland. But that doesn't mean Anna isn't here because of that."

"Casey was right, then."

Kate shrugged, and yawned. "If so, I hope she was right about the sauna helping her sleep. I am dead tired."

◄◦►

By dusk, which came mid-afternoon, I was giddy with exhaustion. I walked down to the sauna, hoping to find Matti on the porch with his pipe and lantern, but found Anna instead, stepping up from the lake, with nothing at all but her own perfect skin, glowing green and blue by the aurora.

"Beautiful," she said, it could have been a statement or a question, but she followed it with, "You have come just in time to join me," as if it had been an address, as if she'd meant me.

She brushed past me, held the door open, as if there was no choice but to follow her. I did.

"You must leave your clothes here," she said, in the small front changing room. "It is dangerous, otherwise."

"So Matti says," I said.

"There is much to learn from him, such extraordinary things," Anna said, and went into the sauna, leaving me to undress in the dim glow coming through the little round window in the sauna door, leaving me to ponder her, and Matti, and Kate's story. What extraordinary thing would Anna, supercop Anna, perfect Anna, think to learn from madcap Matti? "Taken *apart*," Kate had said.

There were towels by the sauna door, too small to wrap around me but I took one anyway, clutched it in front of me and opened the door.

The heat was breathtaking. I blinked against the steam, for a second convinced that Anna had disappeared. She was sitting on the upper rank of benches, leaning into the corner, almost invisible. Her skin was the same warm brown as the wood.

"You will find it cooler up here," she said, patting the bench beside her. "Casey found it more comfortable."

"I'm sure she did," I said, and then regretted my tone, but Anna seemed oblivious. And then I'd waited too long and there was no choice but to sit where she'd offered or be obviously rude. Anyway, her gesture had been too careful, too mannered to seem erotic. Maybe I had Casey's cop theory too much in my mind, but I felt like I was being sat down to an interrogation. *Good cop or bad cop?* I thought, and sat.

"Good," Anna said, which might have sent a chill down my spine if I hadn't already been half-melted. The wood of the bench was like a stove beneath me.

Sitting skewed in the corner like that, either my legs were going to jam up against her or my shoulder would. I tried to split the difference and ended up pretty much plastered to her. I was slick, and somehow also gluey, with sweat. But where I touched her, all down my side and thigh, felt cool and dry.

"Ah, no, the steam must touch the skin, the skin must be free to sweat, remember?" Anna said, and slipped the towel from my lap. "Now, I have so much to ask you."

So then, bad cop, I thought.

"No, no, you must not think I am bad," she said.

I stopped breathing.

She put her hand on my thigh, slid it higher, and where her hand passed, the sweat disappeared, leaving the dry traces of her slender fingers. Her other hand slid behind my neck. It was neither warm nor cool, dry with a textured smoothness like the pages of a good book between your fingers. She pulled our faces together with a slow strength I could not have fought, had I tried. Her head tilted, not like a kiss but like a question. I shut my eyes, not in surrender but in despair.

The door flew open behind me. Something cold and wet grabbed my upper arm, pulled me around and off the upper bench. I landed on the lower bench with a thud.

Matti stood over me. He scraped a forefinger up my cheek like a razor, shook the sweat off it with a grunt. He let go of my arm and I slid back against Anna's legs. My arm felt bruised; I cupped it and my palm came away bloody. Not my blood, though, this was dark and half-frozen.

"Casey," Matti said, and I thought he was confusing me with her, but he continued and my own blood went half-frozen. "You missed a piece."

He leaned over me, crushing me into Anna, his belly pushing my head back into her lap. He grabbed her by the forearm and pulled, and the skin of her arm came away, crumpled in his fist like paper.

I pulled my legs up and kicked him away, crawled down the bench and rolled to my feet. Anna was ahead of me, stepping over me with those long legs to the center of the sauna.

"Oh, you've torn it," she said, lifting her arm, tendons sliding in the light.

Matti turned, fumbled in his pocket with his free hand, pulled out a lighter. He flicked it, a shaky arrhythmic scratching until it lit. Anna's eyes caught the flame, a confused flashing as her head snapped around and her hand swung down, a ripping sound as she tore the lighter from Matti's hand, along with his thumb and three fingers.

A beat of silence and stillness, then, as the blood blossomed from Matti's hand.

As if reluctant to end that silence, Matti did not cry out. He gave a small sigh that sounded more of resignation than it did of pain. I had no breath to scream, no will to move.

And Anna, Anna gasped as if in wonder or delight. "Look how it is inside," she said. "Is it not beautiful? Are you all not filled with wonder?"

She looked up at me, head at that inquisitive angle, and reached toward me with her left arm, that had had the flesh torn away.

Matti sighed again. "Look," he said, echoing her with an extraordinary gentleness, and raised his hand in front of her face, cupping blood. Anna held my gaze me a second or two longer, but the lure of his voice, his wound, seemed too great. She leaned over his hand, a drop here and there splattering her cheek, and raised a hand to the frayed edges of his flesh.

Matti, his voice so calm and matter of fact now, said, "Ms. Martin. The lighter. Please. While she is distracted."

The urge to look along with Anna was hard to resist, or maybe it was the fear of looking away. I cupped my hand over my eyes and looked down. The lighter had landed under Anna's feet, up against her heel. Matti's thumb still clung to it.

"I can't," I said. "I'm sorry. I can't." I did not look up.

Matti sighed again. "The stove, then," he said. "The burner, under the rocks."

Still looking down, I stepped backward until my calf hit the bench, edged sideways until I felt the burn of the stove against my side. I fumbled at a rock, thinking of throwing it, got it loose but the heat was too great. I dropped it clattering onto the floor, and froze as Anna made a curious "huh" in response.

The rocks were in a steel basket, under which flickered a blue propane glow. Heart pounding—*oh god how my blood will fountain if she . . .* I thought—I slowly took my towel from the bench and dipped it in the water bucket and grabbed the edges of the steel basket and lifted.

The water steamed out of the towel in seconds and the steel seared through the cloth and almost, almost I said again, "I'm sorry. I can't." The door to the sauna was just three steps to my left. But the basket was rising, inch by inch, from its brackets. I groaned, and behind me Matti finally cried out, if faintly.

There was a wet splat, and Anna cooed, "Oh, see how it almost makes sense underneath. We are finding out so much."

"Ta gueule!" I screamed and pulled the basket loose. It was too heavy to throw, or even to hold; it tumbled onto the bench spilling rocks. I shoved the towel into the flames of the burner, a puff as the last of the water steamed off and then smoke and finally flame and I whipped the towel around behind me.

I hit nothing, of course, and the towel spluttered and smoked in that too moist air, so I turned with a sob, straight into Anna's even gaze. She was looking over her right shoulder, hair swept back to trace the long curve of her back, one foot behind the other heel, hip cocked at the ideal angle of a sculpted Greek youth, her lips pressed lightly to Matti's ruined hand.

I flicked the towel against that perfect shape and she went up in flame.

And then she went out.

Her skin had burnt away like paper in a poorly set fire, leaving the logs untouched. No logs here, though, just muscle, bone, sinew, nerve.

"Oh," Anna said, looking down at herself. She ran bony fingertips over the starfish ducts of her breasts, the ridged muscles of her abdomen, the protruding angle of her hipbone. Her exposed flesh was dry; her fingers made a sound like pages turning.

"It was an old skin," she said. "We thought it looked good, but see, I don't think it works right." She prodded the smoldering remains of her skin with a toe bone. "Would yours do this?" she asked in her half-question voice. Her eyes were intact, their porcelain and china blue stare all more curious without the lids.

Matti's knees wobbled, but she was holding him up with no apparent effort with one hand. "Go," he said, "or she will take you apart. Like a child takes apart a toy. My wife Claire . . ."

"We learned so much from her," Anna said. "Look!" She slipped her fingerbones between her belly muscles and under her ribs, rummaged around inside herself with a rustle like autumn leaves. She pulled out something dark and oblong, I think it was her spleen, and held it out to me. "I feel that we are very close. This looks like Claire, Matti Kokko, does it not?"

Matti was still looking at me. "Go," he said.

"But see." Anna rolled the thing with her thumb against the white joints of her fingerbones and it crumbled like a clod of earth. "That's not quite right," she explained. "I'll show you."

She wiped the crumbs against her ribs, then shoved the tips of her fingers through Matti's shirt, his skin, the cartilage under his sternum, and deep into his belly. "Mmm," she said, and then "Ah!" She let Matti go and he folded down, with a sound like beach ball deflating. She held out his spleen, flexed it bulging between her fingers. "You are all so rich. Filled with such beauty," she said. "We want so much to be like you. Will you help?"

I ran. Backward at first, through the sauna door and into the changing room, but the outside door was latched and I had to turn my back on Anna to find the handle.

It should have been a shock, going naked from the sauna to the arctic air, but I was already deep in a greater shock. I thought of diving into the lake, hiding under the ice, except I was now certain that I'd find Casey there, disassembled. I took the path, instead, winding toward the office, bare feet slipping on the ice, snow drifting from the branches to catch in my hair.

A shape protruded from the ice at my feet: a chest, splayed arms, head back and staring at the stars. I had taken a wrong turn; it was one of Matti's snow snow monkeys. He'd carved them with such patience, such skill, for what? A remembrance? A lure? The monkeys were *almost* perfect. "It makes you laugh, how they try and fail to be human," Anna had said, when I first met her here.

I did not laugh, but I did turn around.

There was a woodpile by the side of the sauna under the overhanging roof, and an axe on brackets above it. I took it and walked around the front of the building. The front door was still open and steam billowed out. There was something obscene about that exposure of the inside to the out, something in the steam coming through the door that was too much like the way the blood had bubbled up from Matti's hand. The axe was not enough. I put it down and lifted the tank of propane from its frame, walked until the hose ripped loose with a hiss, kept walking through the front door and the changing room and into the sauna.

Anna was crouched over Matti's body. Even as exposed muscle and ridged bone, the curve of her back was perfect. She was singing softly, I thought to herself, but then she asked something I couldn't quite catch and I realized that she did not understand that Matti was dead.

The propane tank was heavy, so I set it on the floor. Gas still hissed from the disconnected hose. I waited for it to reach the burner and ignite.

Anna stopped her rummaging and cocked her head. Then she rose, hands and knees dripping, and turned.

"Chloé," she said. "I am finding such wonderful things. Shall I show you?" She took a step toward me, and with that I realized that, of course, the burner in the stove could not light the propane because it had been burning that same propane until I ripped the tank loose.

Now I laughed.

Anna laughed with me, and clasped the bones of her hands together. "It is such a mystery to us!" she said. "What will you do next?"

That was a mystery to me as well. It was all a mystery: saunas and snow monkeys, Australians and Texans, Finns and Parisiennes, Matti fleeing that mystery, that insatiable curiosity from one side of the world to the other, then luring it back again, waiting in his sauna for that one guest too perfect to sweat. Sitting on the porch in this darkest coldest place with just the light of his lantern, keeping watch for all of us.

I turned my back on Anna. I walked back into the cold and found the lantern. It was dark, but a tiny flicker still clung to the wick. I felt about for matches, but of course, Matti had used a lighter. It would still be on the floor at Anna's feet, and she did, it seemed, understand lighters.

I walked back in and tossed the lantern into the sauna. It hit Anna's shin with a dull clunk, and then there was a *woosh* as the gas spilling from the hose ignited.

If the tank had blown right away, I would have gone with it. At that point I honestly did not care one way or another, as long as Anna went with me. But the gas burnt steadily for a while, the hose writhing like a thing alive. I held the door shut, and watched through the little round window.

That door, that Matti had made of good local wood, would save me when the tank did blow, would shelter me until the emergency crew came out from town and pulled me from the wreckage: one French tourist injured, one American missing—blown into the lake, the reports would be amended come the spring thaw—one local dead in the explosion of a sauna not built to safety codes. Nothing in the reports would indicate that there had been one other there. But I know she burned, because I held the door and watched through the window. I held and watched until the handle seared into my hand and the glass cracked and splintered in my face.

If she had tried to leave, I doubt I could have stopped her. The speed and strength she'd shown when she took Matti's fingers was far beyond us.

But she just stood there over the tallow flame of Matti's body, as her organs swirled up like leaves in a bonfire and her bones came loose, joint by joint, to drift like ash, watching me with endless fascination.

❧

The American family is watching me in the mirror. The boy is standing over the parents, his arms slack and dry over their sweat-slimed shoulders. He's twirling a toothpick in his mouth, but it's not a toothpick, is it? It's the gecko's tail, and the couple, not parents, no, the couple don't see because they don't look, won't look. Their faces are turned away from his, and their expressions of dread are not for the Belle Vue or its menu or its inhabitants, but for something that they brought with them that was far more foreign.

The girl is not with them in the mirror. She standing beside me. She has put a hand on my thigh, as if to wake me from my remembrance. I know if she were to lift her fingers from my skin she would leave a dry cool impression of her perfect fingers, like Anna's. If I were to look into her eyes, I would see her wonder, her desire, her need to fit in, like Anna's. Like mine.

But she does not lift her hand, and I do not look up. I watch those cool dry perfect fingers slide higher, where the flesh is soft, and start to tighten. I feel my own fingers, damp and swollen with the heat, against the edge of the blade on the bar. Did Matti feel this sense of resolution? Did he think, heart pounding, "How my blood will fountain?"

The bartender, with his scarred cheeks, his wide smile, his icepick, seems to me the sort to stop, despite his fear, and turn around.

"We learned so much from you there," the girl says. "I feel we are close to understanding. We are so looking forward to what you'll do next."

Are we all not filled with wonder?

THE DAYS OF OUR LIVES

ADAM L. G. NEVILL

The ticking was much louder on the first floor and soon after the ticking began I heard Lois moving upstairs. Floorboards groaned as she made unsteady progress through areas made murky by curtains not opened for a week. She must have come up inside our bedroom and staggered into the hall, passing herself along the walls with her thin hands. I hadn't seen her for six days but could easily imagine her aspect and mood: the sinewy neck, the fierce grey eyes, a mouth already downcast, and the lips atremble at grievances revived upon the very moment of her return. But I also wondered if her eyes and nails were painted. She had beautiful eyelashes. I went and stood at the foot of the stairs and looked up.

Even on the unlit walls of the stairwell a long and spiky shadow was cast by her antics above. Though I could not see Lois, the air was moving violently, as were parts of her shadow, and I knew she was already batting the side of her face with her hands and then throwing her arms into the air above her scruffy grey head. As expected, she'd woken furious.

The muttering began and was too quiet for me to clearly hear all of what she was saying, but the voice was sharp, the words sibilant and near spat out, so I could only assume she had woken thinking of me. "I told you . . . how many times! . . . and you wouldn't listen . . . for God's sake . . . what is wrong with you? . . . why must you be so difficult? . . . all the time . . . you have been told . . . time after time . . ."

I'd hoped for a better mood. I had cleaned the house over two days, thoroughly but hurriedly for when she next arose. I'd even washed the walls and ceilings, had moved all of the furniture to sweep, dust and vacuum. I had brought no food indoors but loaves of cheap white bread, eggs, plain biscuits, and baking materials that would never be used. I had scalded and boiled the house of dirt and rid the building of its pleasures, with the exception of the television that she enjoyed and the little ceramic radio in the kitchen that only picked up Radio Two from 1983. Ultimately, I had bleached our rented home of any overt signifier of joy, as well as those things she was not interested in, or anything that remained of myself that I forgot about as soon as it was gone.

The last handful of books that intrigued me, anything of any colour or imagination that enabled me to pass this great expanse of time, that burned my chest and internal organs as if my body was pressed against a hot radiator, I finally removed from the shelves yesterday and donated to charity shops along the seafront. Only the ancient knitting patterns, gardening books, antique baking encyclopaedias, religious pamphlets, old socialist diatribes, completely out-of-date versions of imperial history, and indigestible things of that nature, remained now. Faded spines, heavy paper smelling of unventilated rooms, leprous-spotted, migraine-inducing reminders of what, her time? Though Lois never looked at them, I'm pretty sure those books never had anything to do with me.

I retreated from the stairs and moved to the window of the living room. I opened the curtains for the first time in a week. Without any interest in the flowers, I looked down at the artificial iris in the green glass vase to distract my eyes from the small, square garden. Others had also come up since the ticking began, and I didn't want to look at them. A mere glance out back had been sufficient and had revealed the presence of a mostly rotten, brownish snake; one still writhing and showing its paler underbelly on the lawn beneath the washing line. Two wooden birds with ferocious eyes pecked at the snake. Inside the sideboard beside me, the ornaments of the little black warriors that we bought from a charity shop began to beat their leather drums with their wooden hands. On the patio and inside the old kennel, that had not seen a dog in years, I glimpsed the pale back of a young woman. I knew it was the girl with the bespectacled face that suited newsprint and a garish headline above a picture of a dismal, wet field beside an A road. I'd seen this young woman last week from a bus window and looked away from her quickly to feign interest in the plastic banner strung across the front of a pub. Too late, though, because Lois had been sat beside me and had noticed my leering. She angrily ripped away the foil from a tube of Polo mints and I knew that girl by the side of the road was in trouble deep.

"I saw you," was all that Lois said. She'd not even turned her head.

I wanted to say, "Saw what?" but it would do me no good and I couldn't speak for the terrible, cold remorse that seemed to fill my throat like a potato swallowed whole. But I could now see that the girl had been strangled with her own ivory-toned tights and stuffed inside the kennel in our garden. The incident must have been the cause of Lois's distress and the reason why she'd withdrawn from me to lie down for a week.

But Lois was coming down the stairs now, on her front, and making the sound of a large cat coughing out fur because she was eager to confront me with those displeasures lingering from the last time she was around.

The ticking filled the living room, slipping inside my ears and inducing the smell of a linoleum floor in a preschool that I had attended in the nineteen seventies. In my memory, a lollipop lady smiled as I crossed a road with a leather satchel banging against my side. I saw the faces of four children I'd not thought of in decades. For a moment, I remembered all of their names before forgetting them again.

Reflected upon the glass of the window, Lois's tall, thin silhouette with the messy head swayed from side to side as she entered the living room. When Lois saw me she stopped moving and said, "You," in a voice exhausted by despair and panted out with disgust. And then she rushed in quickly and flared up behind me.

I flinched.

◂◦▸

In the café on the pier I cut a small dry cake in half, a morsel that would have failed to satisfy a child. I carefully placed half of the cake on a saucer before Lois. One of her eyelids flickered as if in acknowledgement, but more from displeasure, as if I was trying to win her over and make her grateful.

What I could see of her eyes still expressed detachment, anger and a morbid loathing. Tense and uncomfortable, I continued to mess with the tea things.

We were the only customers. The sea beyond the windows was grey and the wind flapped the pennants and the plastic coverings on idle bumper cars. Our mugs held watery, unsweetened tea. I made sure that I did not enjoy mine.

Inside her vinyl, crab-coloured handbag the ticking was near idle, not so persistent, but far below the pier, in the water, I was distracted by a large, dark shape that might have been a cloud shadow. It appeared to flow beneath the water before disappearing under the pier, and for a moment I could smell the briny wet wood under the café and hear the slop of thick waves against the uprights. A swift episode of vertigo followed and I remembered a Christmas tree on red and green carpet that reminded me of chameleons, and a lace cloth on a wooden coffee table with pointy legs similar to the fins on old American cars, and a wooden bowl of nuts and raisins, a glass of sherry, and a babysitter's long shins in sheer, dark tights that had a wet sheen by the light of a gas fire. Legs that I couldn't stop peeking at, even at that age, and I must have been around four years old. I'd tried to use the babysitter's shiny legs as a bridge for a Matchbox car to pass under, so that I could get my face closer. The babysitter's pale skin was freckled under her tights. And right up close her legs smelled of a woman's underwear drawer and the material of her tights was just lots of little fabric squares that transformed into a smooth, second skin as I moved my face away again. One thing then another thing. So many ways to see everything. One skin and then another skin. It had made me squirm and squirt.

Across the table, in the café on the pier, Lois smiled and her eyes glittered with amusement. "You'll never learn," she said, and I knew that she wanted to hit me hard. I shivered in the draught that came under the door from off the windswept pier, and my old hands looked so veiny and bluish upon the laminate table top.

Slipping the gauzy scarf around her head, she indicated that she wanted to leave. As she rose her spectacles caught the light from the fluorescent strip, a shimmer of fire above sharp ice.

There was no one outside the café, or on the pier, or the grassy area behind the esplanade, so she hit me full in the face with a closed fist and left me dazed and leaning against a closed ice-cream concession. Blood came into my mouth.

I followed her for ten minutes, sulking, then pulled up alongside her and we trudged up and down the near-empty grey streets of the town and looked in shop windows. We bought some Christmas cards, a pound of potatoes we'd boil fluffy and eat later with tasteless fish, and carrots from a tin. From the pound shop we picked up a small box of Scottish shortbread. In a charity shop she bought a pencil skirt without trying it on, and two satin blouses. "I have no idea when I'll be able to wear anything nice again."

As we passed Bay Electrics I saw a girl's face on two big television screens. Local news too, showing a pretty girl with black-framed glasses who never made it to work one morning just over a week ago. It was the girl inside the kennel.

"Is that what you like?" Lois whispered in a breathless voice beside me. "Is that what you fancy?"

Increasing her pace, she walked in front of me, head down, all the way back to the car, and she never spoke during the drive home. At our place, she sat and watched a television quiz show that I hadn't seen since the seventies. It could not have been scheduled, possibly never even recorded by ITV either, but it's what she wanted and so it appeared and she watched it.

She couldn't bear the sight of me, I could tell, and she didn't want me watching her quiz show either, so I removed my clothes and went and lay in the basket under the kitchen table. I tried to remember if we'd ever had a dog, or if it was my teeth that had made those marks on the rubber bone.

An hour after I lay down and curled up, Lois began screaming in the lounge. I think she was on the telephone and had called a number she'd recalled from years, or even decades, long gone. "Is Mr. Price there? What do you mean I have the wrong number? Put him on immediately!" God knows what they made of the call at the other end of the line. I just stayed very still and kept my eyes clenched shut until she hung up and began to sob.

Inside the kitchen the ticking lulled me to sleep amongst vague odours of lemon disinfectant, the dog blanket and cooker gas.

⤙⊙⤚

Lois was doing a one-thousand-piece jigsaw puzzle; the one with the painting of a mill beside a pond. The puzzle was spread across a card table and her legs passed beneath the table. I sat before her, naked, and stayed quiet. Her toes were no more than a few inches from my knees and I dared not shuffle any closer. She was wearing her black brassiere, a nylon slip, and very fine tights. She had painted her toenails red and her legs whisked when she rubbed them together. The rollers had come out of her hair now too and her silver hair shimmered beside the fairy lights. Her eye makeup was pink and gloriously alluring around her cold iron-coloured eyes. When she wore makeup she looked younger. A thin gold bracelet circled her slender wrist and the watch attached to the metal strap ticked quietly. The watch face was so tiny I could not see what the time was. Gone midnight, I guessed.

Until she'd finished the puzzle she only spoke to me once, in a quiet, hard voice. "If you touch it, I'll have it straight off."

I let my limp hands fall back to the floor. My whole body was aching from sitting still for so long.

She mostly remained calm and disinterested for the remainder of the time it took her to finish her puzzle, so I didn't have many memories. I only recall things when she is agitated and I forget them when she calms down. When she is enraged I am flooded.

Lois began to drink sherry from a long glass and to share unflattering reminiscences and observations about our courtship. Things like, "I don't know what I was thinking back then? And now I'm stuck. Ha! Look at me now, ha! Hardly The Ritz. Promises, promises. I'd have been much better off with that American chappy. That one you were friendly with . . ." Increasingly roused, she padded back and forth through the living room, so long, thin and silky with her thighs susurrating together. I could smell her lipstick, perfume and hairspray, which usually excited me, particularly as her mood changed to something ugly and volatile. And as I sensed the vinegar of spite rising up through her I began to remember . . . I think . . . a package that arrived in a small room where I had lived, years before. Yes, I've remembered this before, and many times, I think.

The padded envelope had once been addressed to a doctor, but someone had written NO LONGER AT THIS ADDRESS on the front, and then written my address as the correct postal address. Only it wasn't addressed to me, or anyone specifically, but was instead addressed to "You," and then "A Man," and "Him," and all on the same line above my postal address. There were no details of the sender, so I'd opened the parcel. And it had contained an old watch, a ladies wristwatch, with a thin, scuffed bracelet that smelled of perfume, and so strongly that I received an impression of slim white wrists when I held the watch. Within the cotton wool was a mass-produced paper flier advertising a "literary walk," organised by something called "The Movement."

I went along to this walk, but only, I think, to return the watch to the sender. It was a themed walk on a wet Sunday: something to do with three gruesome paintings in a tiny church. The triptych of paintings featured an ugly antique wooden cabinet as their subject. There was some kind of connection between the cabinet and a local poet who had gone mad. I think. There were drinks after the tedious walk too, I am sure, in a community centre. I'd asked around the group on the walk, trying to establish to whom the watch belonged. Everyone I asked had said, "Ask Lois. That looks like one of hers." Or, "Speak to Lois. That's a Lois." Maybe even, "Lois, she's looking. She's due."

I'd eventually identified and approached this Lois, spoken to her, and complemented her on her fabulous eye makeup. She'd looked wary, but appreciated the remark with a nod and tight smile that never extended to her eyes. She said, "You're from that building where the down-and-outs live? I was hoping you were going to be that other chap that I've seen going inside." And she'd taken the watch from me, and sighed resignedly. "But all right then," as if accepting an invitation from me. "At least you returned it. But it's not going to be what you think, I'm afraid." I remember being confused.

That afternoon I'd not been able to stop staring at her beautiful hands either, or the idea of her wearing nothing but the tight leather boots she'd worn on the walk. So I was glad that the watch had a connection to this woman called Lois. I think my attentions made her feel special but also irritable, as if I were a pest. I wasn't sure how old she was, but she had clearly tried to look older with the grey coat and headscarf and A-line tweed skirts.

From a first sighting she had made me feel uncomfortable, but intrigued and aroused also, and at the time I had been lonely and unable to get the cold, unfriendly woman out of my mind, so I had gone to the community centre again knowing that is where the strange group of people, The Movement, met monthly. This dowdy, plain and depressing building was the centre of their organisation, and had pictures painted by children covering the walls. On my second visit plastic chairs had been set out in rows. They were red. There was a silver urn with tea and biscuits on a paper plate too: Garibaldis, Lemon Puffs, and stale Iced Gems. I was nervous and didn't really know anyone well, and those that I thought might recognise me from the walk seemed unwilling to converse.

When something was about to occur on the stage, I sat in the row behind Lois. She was wearing a grey coat that she didn't take off indoors. Her head was covered by a scarf again, but her eyes were concealed by red-tinted glasses. She'd worn those boots again too, but had seemed indifferent to me, even after I'd returned the watch and she'd suggested some kind of enigmatic agreement had been made between us the first time we met. I did suspect that she was unstable, but I was lonely and desperate. I found it all very bewildering too, but my bafflement was only destined to increase.

To replicate the image in one of the hideous paintings that I had seen on the literary walk, a picture responsible for sending a local poet mad, a motionless elderly woman had sat in a chair on the low stage. She was draped in black and wore a veil. One of her legs was contained inside a large wooden boot. Beside her chair was a curtained cabinet, the size of a wardrobe but deeper, the sort of thing budget magicians used. On the other side of her was a piece of navigational equipment; naval, I had assumed, and all made from brass with what looked like a clock face on the front. A loud ticking had issued from the brass device.

Another woman with curly black hair, who was overweight and dressed like a little girl, came onto the stage too . . . I think she wore very high heels that were red. When the woman in the red shoes read poems from a book, I felt uneasy and thought that I should go; just get up and leave the hall quickly. But I lingered for fear of drawing attention to myself by scraping a chair leg across the floor, while everyone else at the meeting was so enraptured by the performance on the stage.

After the reading, the woman dressed like a little girl withdrew from the stage and the hall darkened until the building was solely lit by two red stage lights.

Something inside the cupboard on the stage began to croak and the sound made me think of a bullfrog. It must have been a recording, or so I had thought at the time. The ticking from the brass clock grew louder and louder too. Some people stood up and shouted things at the box. I felt horrified, embarrassed for the shouters, uncomfortable, and eventually I panicked and made to leave.

Lois had turned round then and said, "Sit back down!" It was the first time she'd even acknowledged me that evening and I returned to my seat, though I wasn't sure why I obeyed her. And the others near me in the hall had looked at me too, expectantly. I had shrugged and cleared my throat and asked, "What?"

Lois had said, "It's not what, it's who and when?"

I didn't understand.

On the stage, the elderly woman with the false leg spoke for the first time. "One can go," she'd said, her frail voice amplified through some old plastic speakers above the stage.

Chairs were knocked aside or even upturned in the undignified scrabble toward the stage that was made by at least four female members of the group. They'd all held pocket watches in the air too, as they stumbled to the stage. Lois got there first, her posture tense with a childlike excitement, and had looked up at the elderly woman expectantly.

The old veiled head above her had nodded and Lois had risen up the stairs to the stage. On her hands and knees, with her head bowed, she then crawled inside the curtained cabinet. As she moved inside, kind of giggling, or maybe it was whimpering, the elderly woman in the chair had beaten Lois on the back, buttocks and legs, quite mercilessly, with a walking stick.

The stage lights went out, or failed, and the congregation fell silent in the darkness. All I could hear was the clock ticking loudly until a sound like a melon being split apart came wetly from the direction of the stage.

"That time is over," the amplified voice of the elderly woman announced.

The lights came on and the people in the hall started to talk to each other in quiet voices. I couldn't see Lois and wondered if she was still inside the cabinet. But I'd seen enough of a nonsensical and unpleasant tradition, or ritual, connected to those paintings, and some kind of deeper belief system that I cannot remember much about, and couldn't even grasp back then, and so I left hurriedly. No one tried to stop me.

I think . . . that's what might have happened. It might have been a dream, though. I never really know if I can trust what appears in my head like memories. But I've recalled that scene before, I am sure, on another evening like this one as Lois bemoaned our coming together. Maybe this was as recent as last month? I don't know, but all of this feels so familiar.

Lois began calling me after the night she entered the cabinet on the stage of the community hall. On the telephone she would be abusive. I remember standing by the communal phone, to receive the calls in the hallway of the building in which I had rented a bedsit. Her voice had sounded as if it were many miles away and struggling to be heard in a high wind. I then told the other residents of the lodging to tell all callers that I was not home and the phone calls soon stopped.

I met someone else not long after my brush with Lois and The Movement . . . Yes, a very sweet woman with red hair. But I didn't know her for long because she was murdered; she was found strangled and her remains had been put inside a rubbish skip.

Not long after that Lois came for me in person.

I think . . .

Yes, and there was a brief ceremony soon after, in the back of a charity shop. I remember wearing a suit that was too small for me. It had smelled of someone else's sweat. And I was on my knees beside a pile of old clothes that needed sorting, while Lois stood beside me in a smart suit and her lovely boots, with her fabulous eye makeup, and her silver hair freshly permed.

We had been positioned before the wooden cabinet that I had seen at the community centre, and in the odd paintings inside the chapel on the literary walk. And someone had been struggling to breathe inside the box, like they were asthmatic. We could all hear them on the other side of the purple curtain.

A man, and I think he was the postman in that town, held a pair of dress-maker's scissors under my chin, to make sure I said the words that were asked of me. But there had been no need of the scissors because even though our courtship was short, by that time I was so involved with Lois that I was actually beside myself with excitement whenever I saw her, or heard her voice on the phone. At the charity shop wedding service, as we all recited a poem from the poet that went mad, Lois held up the ladies wristwatch with the very loud tick that had once been sent to my address, though intended for someone else.

We were married.

She was given a garish bouquet of artificial flowers, and I had a long wooden rule broken over my shoulders. The pain had been withering.

There was a wedding breakfast too, with Babycham and cheese footballs, salmon sandwiches, round lettuces, sausage rolls. And there was a lot of sex on the wedding night too; the kind of thing I had never imagined possible.

At least I think it was sex, but I can only remember a lot of screaming in the darkness around a bed, while someone kind of coughed and hiccupped in between lowing like a bullock. I know I was beaten severely with a belt by the witnesses, who were also in the bedroom at a Travelodge that had been rented for the occasion.

Or was that Christmas?

I'm not sure she's ever allowed me to touch her since, though she takes her pleasures upstairs with what I can only assume was inside that box in the community centre and at our wedding. I may be her spouse, but I believe she is wedded to another who barks with a throat full of catarrh, and she cries out with pleasure, or grunts, and finally she weeps.

The betrayals used to upset me and I would cry in the dog basket downstairs, but in time you can get used to anything.

—◦—

On Thursday Lois killed another young woman, this time with a house brick, and I knew we'd have to move on again.

The disagreement culminated in a lot of hair pulling and kicking behind some beach huts because I had said hello to the attractive woman who'd been walking her dogs past our picnic blanket. Lois went after the dogs too and I had to look away and out to sea when she caught up with the spaniel.

I got Lois home, up through the trees when it was dark, wrapped in our picnic blanket. Shivering, all stained down the front, she talked to herself the whole way home, and she had to lie down the following day with a mask over her face. The episode had been building for days and Lois detested younger women.

While she convalesced I read Ceefax alone—I had no idea that channel was still on the telly—and I thought about where we should go next.

When Lois came downstairs two days later, she wore lots of eye makeup and her tight, shiny boots and was nice to me, but I remained subdued. I was unable to get the sound of the frightened dog on the beach out of my mind; the yelp and the coconut sound and then the splashing.

"We'll have to move again. That's two in one place," I'd said wearily.

"I never liked this house," was her only response.

She relieved me into a thick bath towel, using both of her hands, kissed me and then spat in my face.

I didn't see her again for three weeks. By then I had found a terraced house two hundred miles away from where she'd done the killing of two fine girls. And in the new place I'd begun to hope that she'd never return to me. Vain and futile to wish for such a thing, I know, because before Lois vanished at the seaside, she'd slowly and provocatively wound up her golden wristwatch while staring into my eyes, so that my hopes for a separation would be wishful thinking and nothing else. The only possible severance between me and Lois would involve my throat being placed over an ordinary washbasin in a terraced house and her getting busy with the dressmaker's scissors as I masturbated. That's how she rid herself of the last two: some painter in Soho in the sixties and a surgeon she'd been with for years. Either a quick divorce with the scissors over vintage porcelain, or I could be slaughtered communally in a charity shop on a Sunday afternoon. Neither option particularly appealed to me.

In the new town there is evidence of The Movement. They've set themselves up in two rival organisations: a migratory bird society that meets above a legal high shop only open on a Wednesday, and an M. L. Hazzard study group that meets in an old Methodist church. No one in their right mind would want an involvement in either group, and I suspected each would convulse with schisms until they faded away. There are a few weddings, though, and far too many young people are already missing in the town. But I hoped the proximity of the others of Lois's faith would calm her down or distract her.

Lois eventually came up in the spare bedroom of the new house, naked save for the gold watch, bald and pinching her thin arms. It took me hours with the help of a hot bath and lots of watery tea to bring her round and to make the ticking in the house slow down and quieten, and for the leathery snakes with dog faces to melt into shitty stains on the carpet. She'd been through torments while away from me, I could see that, and she just wanted to hurt herself on arrival. But across several days I brought Lois back to a semblance of what we could recall of her, and she began to use a bit of lippy and do her hair and wear underwear beneath her housecoat.

Eventually we went out, just to the end of the road, then to the local shops to treat her to new clothes, then down and along the seafront, where we'd eat child-size vanilla ice creams and sit on the benches to watch the misty grey horizon. We'd not been down to the sea much before a drunken, unkempt man asked her to do something rude and frightened her, and then another dirty youth in a grimy tracksuit on a bike followed us for half a mile and tried to tug her hair from behind.

That second time, while I pumped two-pence pieces into an arcade machine to win some Swan Vesta matches and Super King cigarettes tied up in a five-pound note, Lois got away from me. I ran the length of the pier and shore looking for her and only found her after following the sound of what I thought was someone stamping in a puddle in the public toilets. And then I saw the bicycle outside.

She'd lured the lad who'd yanked her hair on the promenade inside the ladies toilets and been thorough with him in the end cubicle. When I finally dragged her out of there, little was left of his face, that I could see, and the top of his head had come off like pie crust. When I got her home I had to put her best boots in a dustbin and her tights were ruined.

Two people from The Movement came and saw us at home after the incident and told me not to worry because hardly anything like that was investigated anymore, and besides the police had already charged two men. Apparently, the smashed-up lad was always knocking about with them and they had form for stamping on people in the grimy streets. The visitors from The Movement also invited us to be witnesses at a wedding, which I instantly dreaded despite hungering to see Lois all dressed up again.

The wedding was held in the storeroom of a Sea Scout hut that smelled of bilge and in there, within minutes, Lois met someone else: a fat, bald man who did little but leer at her and sneer at me. She also did her best to lose me in the crowd, and there were a lot of people there to whip the bridegroom with leather belts, but I kept my eyes on her. At the wedding breakfast I saw the fat man feeding her the crisps that come with a sachet of salt inside the bag. He wasn't married and wasn't in The Movement either, so I was appalled by the fact that they let single men attend an event like that. At one point, as I hid below Lois's eyeline, I even caught her slipping the fat man our telephone number. All of the other women felt sorry for me.

I barely recognised Lois after the wedding in the Sea Scout hut. For days she was euphoric and acted as if I wasn't even there, and then she was enraged because I was there and clearly preventing her from pursuing another opportunity.

The fat man even approached me in the street when I was out shopping and spoke down to me and said that I may as well give up on Lois, as our relationship was dead, and that he intended to marry her within weeks.

"Is that what you think?" I said, and he slapped my face.

I writhed beneath the kitchen table for three days after the incident with the fat man, before getting up and dressing in Lois's clothes, which made me giddy. When I got the eye-shadow just right, my knees nearly gave way. But I still managed to leave the house in the early hours to pay a visit to the fat man. Lois ran into the street after me, shouting, "Don't you touch him! Don't you touch my Richey!" When some of the neighbours started looking out of windows, she retreated indoors, sobbing.

Well aware that Lois was absolutely forbidden from making such an overture to a new partner, without my voluntary participation in a divorce, Richey hadn't been able to restrain himself from making a move on her. Through the spyhole in the door of his flat he saw me with my face all made up and he thought that I was Lois. He couldn't get the door open fast enough. Then he stood in the doorway smiling, with his gut pushing out his dressing gown like a big shiny pouch, and I went into that bulb of guts with a pair of sharp scissors, my arm going really fast. He didn't even have a chance to get his hairy hands up, and into his tubes and tripes I cut deep.

We cannot have oafs in The Movement. Everyone knows that. I found out later that he'd only been let in because the woman in the bird migrating group, the one who always wore her raincoat hood up indoors, had her eye on "Richey" and had believed that she was in with a chance. She was only one week from crossing over too, but I think I saved her a few decades of grief. Later, for sorting out Richey, she even sent me a packet of Viscount biscuits and a card meant for a nine-year-old boy with a racing car on the front.

Anyway, right along the length of the hall of his flat, I went through Richey like a sewing machine and I made him bleat. I'd worn rubber washing-up gloves because I knew my hands would get all slippery on the plastic handles of the scissors. In and out, in and out, in and out! And as he slowed and half collapsed down the wall of the hall, before falling into his modest living room, I put the scissors deep into his neck from the side, and then closed the door of the lounge until he stopped coughing and wheezing.

Heavy, stinky bastard, covered in coarse black hair on the back like a goat, with a big, plastic, bully face that had once bobbed and grinned, but I took him apart to get him out of his flat piecemeal. Unbelievably, as I de-jointed his carcase in the bath, he came alive for a bit and scared me half to death. He didn't last for long, though, and I finished up with some secateurs that were good on meat. I found them under the sink in the kitchen.

Took me three trips: one to the old zoo that should have been closed years ago where I threw bits into the overgrown cassowary enclosure (they had three birds); one trip to where the sea gulls fight by the drainage pipe; and one trip to the Sea Scout hall with the head, which I buried beside the war memorial so that Richey could always look upon the place where he got the ball rolling.

When I got home, I shut Lois in the loft and took down the smoke alarms and burned all of her clothes, except for the best party tights, in the kitchen sink with the windows open. I went through the house and collected up all of her things and what I didn't dump in the council rubbish bins I gave to charity.

Before I left her growling like a cat, up in the loft amongst our old Christmas decorations, I told Lois that I might see her in our new place when I found it. I went downstairs and put her ladies' watch on my wrist and listened to it tick rapidly, like a heart fit to burst. Inside the sideboard, the little black warriors began to beat their leather drums with their wooden hands.

Lois was still clawing at the plywood loft hatch when I left the house with only one suitcase.

THE HOUSE OF WONDERS

C.E. WARD

An acrid waft of blue tobacco smoke woke me from an early evening doze in my comfortable chair in the garden. I started suddenly and sat up rather disorientated, glancing across at Stevenson who reclined in the wicker chair on the porch of the summerhouse, the local newspaper open untidily on his knees, having paused in his perusal to light his gnarled old briar. He returned my look with a smile, and puffed his pipe as though his life depended on it, overpowering the pleasant scents of the flowers with the pervasive fumes of his Navy flake.

"Did I wake you?" he asked facetiously. "I've just been looking through the obituaries, and I see that Jack Froston has died. Aged 67—no great age."

"Wasn't he a friend of yours? I had no idea that he'd been ill. It must have been quite sudden."

Stevenson tamped the glowing ashes in his briar with a forefinger so apparently unfeeling I'd often suspected the stained brown digit was made of the same material as his pipe. "Well, the last time I saw him he wasn't wonderful—which could hardly be expected after that odd business with his last book. He was a changed man after that. Lost a lot of weight and got quite apathetic and short tempered. None of the boundless enthusiasm he'd once had, and his writing suffered; no more books but just the odd piece for a magazine or journal. Obviously Janice's death was a blow to him too, and it was after her funeral that Jack and I got talking over a few drinks at her wake. That was when he told me a few strange things about the last book he'd researched and written, and that he believed his problems had originated from there. *Showmen of England,* do you recall it?"

I sat up in my chair intrigued. "Yes, I have a copy of it on my shelves somewhere. Quite interesting and quirky if I recall correctly and full of obscure photographs as all his books were. It wasn't quite his usual territory was it? Country houses, old customs and folklore were more in his line. His research was as thorough as always of course—I knew nothing about the Buffalo Bill Wild West Show appearing locally in the early 1900s until I read about it there. Every interesting travelling show, fair, place of amusement and exhibition from the 1830s to the early 1970s must have been included."

"Not quite everything," Stevenson replied in that low and mysterious tone I was used to between draws on his briar. "He told me that he'd omitted a full chapter of the manuscript which he'd intended his publisher to have. The odd thing I remember him saying about that was that he'd researched it *too* well. He was very drunk at the time and I didn't take that much notice, and it's sad to say he was very much on a downward slide with all his very heavy drinking and smoking. I only saw Jack a couple of times after that, and he was becoming very reclusive and cutting himself off from the few friends who'd still put up with his moods and manner. It was after his friend Wildman died that he really put up the shutters. But not before he'd told me some very strange things at our last meeting."

"You mentioned a missing chapter? Did he tell you much about its content?"

Stevenson refilled his pipe and lit it, thick, choking swirls of smoke drifting off above his head into the clear June sky.

◂◦▸

I was coming to that. Tell me, have you ever heard of Spangler's House of Wonders? I thought not. It was a place of amusement, if that's the right description, back in the late nineteenth century up until 1969. It lasted around a hundred years I believe, and was originally a cheap and lurid place of amusement in the East End of London, nestled among the poorer music halls and gin palaces. Eventually it moved to be housed in a Georgian property just off the front of a seaside town on the East Coast—the place isn't important so I won't mention it. You must recall the sort of establishment I'm talking about; crudely garish, slightly tawdry and certainly down at heel in the last few decades of its existence. A place where Victorian and Edwardian holiday makers, tourists and bored thrill seekers would flock, tired of ice-cream, sandy beaches, bathing huts and the vagaries of our uncertain English summer weather. A place to idle away an hour or so, was Spangler's, and it was really no different to similar establishments at other resorts dotted around our coastline. A man by the name of Hawkins was its proprietor, and after him, his son. Mr. Spangler, whoever he was, appeared to have relinquished any original rights to the business late in the 1880s—and only his name remained on the brightly illuminated sign above the doors and ticket booth, which promised "Thrills, Curiosities, Magic, History, Antiquities and Relics of the Ages for the price of a Shilling!" Beneath this extravagant promise were lurid paintings on boards—Pharoah's army and chariots being engulfed by the Red Sea, its huge and sweeping waves more reminiscent of Noah's flood than the hand of God of Moses's time, as the turbulent waters covered both a background of pyramids and the sphinx; a storm-wracked whaling schooner hunting a huge green serpent of unknown but grotesquely monstrous species in the turmoil of crashing waves in a boiling expanse of sea, and a curious and statuesquely feminine Pandora opening her richly decorated box, which emitted a bright glow illuminating the crude beauty of her startled face. These, and more, to tempt and draw the curious clientele. Inside, beyond a heavy green fringed velvet curtain and a dimly lit corridor, one entered various apartments. One, full of glass display cases containing natural and decidedly unnatural phenomena; a "dead and preserved mermaid," the only existing unicorn horn and skull, skeletal remains of "the Little People" who apparently once roamed these isles so freely, that sort of thing. Another held historical memorabilia—locks of dead monarchs' hair, the campaign desk and snuff box of Napoleon as well as his famous cocked hat and death mask, the "missing" colour of the 44th Regiment taken from the slain at Gandamack following the infamous Retreat from Kabul, nestling among other "lost" Roman Eagles from the massacre of the Teutoberg Forest—all of highly suspect and dubious provenance of course. Religious relics featured as well; a nail and splinter of wood from the Cross of Calvary, a shard of timber from the Ark—even a Roman denaria from the reign of Tiberius alleged to have been one of the thirty paid to Judas Iscariot for his betrayal of Christ. All viewed in rooms and grimy glass cases where the light was dim to add to the reverent atmosphere, not of course to impede a too searching examination and scrutiny! A gallery of waxworks followed, mostly in a Penny Dreadful Chamber of Horrors fashion, depicting crime and punishment with scenes of quite horrific and barbaric torture. And at the end, in more prosaic manner, some rows of mechanical amusement machines, where by dropping pennies in slots, one could see what the butler had, or watch executions by axe and rope outside castle walls and prison gates; or ghostly goings on in haunted bedrooms and cellars performed by tiny clockwork figures in miniature rooms and diorama type vignettes in glass fronted boxes—"Working Models," as they were called.

I myself saw the place twice, though in very different ways and circumstances. The first time was when I was very young, on holiday with my parents. What I've just described springs from my memory of that visit. This was just before the War, in 1939, and I think we went in more to get some relief from what was a very hot and sunny day as much as anything—of course I was keen and initially entranced by the air of circus and brash theatricality of the place. As I said, once inside you were struck by the gloom, the only light coming from a few multi-coloured electric bulbs—I suppose it had originally been gaslight in its earlier years—but what really arrested you was the cold. Of course we were all wearing light summer clothes, but there was a chill about that place I've never experienced elsewhere in my life on such a hot day outside; and you know just how many churches, cathedrals and abbeys I've visited over the course of long years. There were very few other people in there, and most of them didn't seem to want to linger for very long. There was an air of long neglect, dust, disrepair and a certain tarnished and faded grandeur overshadowing the whole exhibition—not uncommon in such places of course—but even the old man who sat perched in the ticket booth outside had been aloof and unfriendly. We wandered from one dimly lit room to the next, gazing at indistinct objects and dust enshrouded relics in their dirty glass cabinets, not so much with an air of wonder but rather an uncomfortable and uneasy scrutiny; and I think we were all quite glad, after I'd been allowed to drop a penny or two into the amusement machines and working models in the final gallery, to take our leave and get out into the sunlight and fresh air once more.

I still have unpleasant memories of the waxwork figures. Most, as I've said, were of the most awful executions and tortures. The rack and the headsman's block were accompanied by such horrible foreign refinements of man's cruelty as the Chinese Water Torture, which showed a poor wretch with horribly distended stomach being forced to drink from a tube by two inscrutable looking Boxer soldiers, while the Algerian Hooks portrayed a writhing and slowly dying sufferer impaled upon the same. One would have sought consolation by the knowledge that the torn flesh was but wax, and the freely flowing blood and entrails just red paint and packing straw; and yet there was something in the attitude and expressions of the frozen in time mannequins that suggested a most disturbing realism and a firsthand eyewitness knowledge. The working models were equally unsettling—one, "The Haunted Bedroom," gave me nightmares for weeks. It was just as well that one intriguing machine, entitled "Our Secret Past" and also stating "The Fright of your Life! View at your Peril!" was roped off under a low archway, with an "Out of Order" sign propped up against its booth.

I need to fast forward nearly twenty years now. I'd been back to that same seaside town around 1958 while on a short holiday in the area, and remembering my childhood visit to the House of Wonders, was curious to see if it was still there. Of course, a lot had changed since the war and my distant memories of the place, and I was disappointed but not surprised to find that the establishment had gone, and not just boarded up and derelict but the whole edifice a vacant lot strewn with bricks and rubble. I made a few enquiries, and learnt that a bomb from Nazi Germany's Luftwaffe had put paid to it—as well as the pier pavilion and a couple of other municipal buildings—in 1941, a group of Dorniers having mistaken the place for Lowestoft. What I hadn't expected to be told was that Spangler's House of Wonders had shut up shop and vacated the area just a week before the bomb from the air raid had destroyed the entire building.

"You might call that fortuitous," Mr. Donovan, the gentleman in the local museum where I made my enquiries informed me. "But the truth is that the building was required for the war effort, being used as an air-raid warden's post rather ironically as things turned out. The fact is that Spangler's had outworn its welcome here. There'd been some complaints about the nature of the business and some of the people it seemed to attract. There was talk of black market trading, war profiteering, Nazi spies and fifth columnists, even German paratroops and storm-troopers; you name it, sir, but these were anxious and suspicious times. Well, there had been reports that there were some strange comings and goings there—always late at night and under cover of darkness. A couple of 'spivs' as they were called, had already been arrested selling black market tobacco and petrol coupons in the place during its opening hours—so the police began keeping quite a close surveillance on Spangler's day and night. It wasn't long before one of the duty constables, from his concealed position in a shop doorway across the street, noticed a small, hunched figure, very muffled up, make its way into the old exhibition hall by way of a door next to the main entrance. The constable was under strict orders to observe and just make notes in his pocket book, and this is what he, and his relief and other officers did for the better part of a month. During that time the same strange person was seen on various other occasions, always in the small hours between midnight and before dawn, sometimes alone but at other times accompanied by either a man or woman. The odd thing was that none of these people appeared to leave. Of course, the building was both old and large and rambling; and the police train of thought was that these late night visitors, whoever they were, were leaving by some concealed exit through the cellars, roof, or an adjoining party wall into one of the next door premises. Naturally, by now they were very suspicious; not least by the constant short person who appeared to lead the others to Spangler's, gain admittance, and answered no description to either old Hawkins the proprietor, or his son, who were the only people known to live in an upstairs apartment on the premises.

"The Chief Constable was both concerned and curious as more and more of his officers' reports landed on his desk every morning. He'd been naturally cautious, not wanting his men to accost anyone before he had a clearer picture and something more substantial to go on—but four weeks on he was no further forward. None of his men could provide anything more than the scantiest descriptions of any of the persons they'd observed, due to the distance of their concealed position and the darkness; but one detail was recurrent—the ones who accompanied the short figure were invariably unsteady on their feet and appeared either enfeebled or inebriated. It was time for a more daring strategy, and as undercover officers posing as tourists had already been successful in the two former arrests, this plan was repeated, with certain subtle refinements. Four plain clothes men were to visit Spangler's shortly before closing time, and by causing a diversion two of them were to remain inside the premises while the other pair left to return and keep watch on the outside later that evening.

"The way things turned out, it wasn't anything like as difficult as they'd imagined. Old Mr. Hawkins took their admission fee from his ticket booth and, as his son wasn't around at the time and he employed no other staff, all the officers had to do was find somewhere quiet to hide in the dark nooks and corners of the waxworks exhibition. As most of the attractions in the town bore "Closed for the Duration" signs and the beach was entangled with barbed wire and off limits, this exercise went unnoticed by the few other visitors around. A Sergeant Fargill and DC Newcombe were left inside, good, steady and experienced officers who'd been in the force for years, and when the last few visitors filtered out and Mr. Hawkins sauntered feebly through the exhibition, turning off the dim lights and making a very cursory short-sighted inspection, they obviously went unnoticed as the doors were locked and the proprietor ambled off to his living quarters upstairs. All that Fargill and Newcomb had to do now was lie in wait, observe whatever might occur, and take any necessary appropriate action.

"PC's Hicks and Stanley returned from their mugs of tea and sandwiches at the station just after dusk, and took up their positions some sixty or so yards away from the House of Wonders. As it was September with double daylight hours in force, they sympathised with the plight of their two colleagues inside, who were no doubt craving some tea and a smoke. Sometime after midnight, Hicks grabbed Stanley's arm—he'd seen the approach of the familiar short figure, swathed in its usual dark coloured long coat—but this time apparently alone. There was something horrible in the way the figure kept ducking its head at what in the darkness looked like a small pile of white table linen clutched close to its chest; and the hungry, sucking noises which it made as it did so made both men feel distinctly nauseous, uneasy and apprehensive. Within moments the almost dwarf-like man—for all observers had agreed its gait and appearance to be male—had opened and swept through the side door; not on this occasion as smoothly as others for the bundle it was carrying in its stunted arms, which looked in the uncertain light to be a large child's rag-doll with limp white arms dangling loosely, hampered its movements. It wasn't the time or place for discussion of course, and within the next two minutes something else alerted them to a new course of action and thinking.

"It was the shrill blast of a police whistle, quickly followed by another. One stopped after a long continuous burst—the other blew harder and at short intervals—until it became as silent as the first. By this time both Hicks and Stanley were at the doors by the ticket booth, hammering at the wood and glass with their truncheons, and demanding entrance at the tops of their voices. Wood splinters flew from the bruised timber and chunks of broken glass fell from the panes above—and then most horribly a pair of flexing, veined hands shot through the shattered windows—clutching with white knuckles at the mullions and pulling at them desperately, impervious it seemed of the cuts and tears the jagged, broken shards were inflicting on the scrabbling white flesh. Lights came on within, and as the door was unlocked a wild figure burst out between the two horrified policemen, its hair flying and outstretched hands dripping copious black, wet runnels in the moonlight. Mr. Hawkins stood in the open doorway, frail, bewildered and incongruous in his dressing gown, and in a very short time he'd been arrested and other policemen, the Chief Constable among them, was at the scene.

"The proprietor, and his son when found, were of course taken in for questioning, and Spangler's House of Wonders was most thoroughly searched. It was all to no avail as despite the rumours, no German spies, paratroops or fifth columnists were found, or anything else remotely suspicious. Mr. Hawkins and his son maintained an aloof and difficult silence, though their reclusivity and eccentricity hardly marked them as either Nazi sympathisers or black marketeers; and their utter denial of any knowledge of nocturnal visitors to their establishment could not be shaken, even against the officers' oral and written statements. A window at the rear of the premises, in the amusement arcade, was found to be open; this looked onto a small yard which could only be accessed by a gate in a high brick wall which led into an alley back out onto the main thoroughfare. The Chief Constable and his detectives were both embarrassed and mystified by a mass of loose ends— which included a missing police officer, for DC Newcomb had vanished without trace. Sergeant Fargill, for it was he who had fled from the House of Wonders with bubbling moans of terror and severely lacerated hands, was of no help either. After having been found struggling frantically in a coil of barbed wire on the seafront, he'd been rushed to hospital with his injuries, later discharging himself, returning home and shooting himself through the mouth and brains with a Webley .38 service revolver he kept in a bureau.

"It doesn't need me to explain how Spangler's House of Wonders was forced to close down and move out shortly after this. What the police hadn't achieved the council soon did, and Hawkins and Son and all their impedimenta were evicted and taken away, destination unknown, in a small fleet of Pickford lorries. I don't think Hawkins made any real fuss about it. His takings and custom evaporated after the business with Fargill and Newcomb, and the place had attracted a more unpleasant reputation and darker stories and suspicions than the ones which had preceded them. You must remember that this was wartime and people could disappear without anyone taking too much notice, what with call ups and war work, to say nothing of those with less honourable motives. Well, DC Newcomb was obviously immediately missed—and before morning a frantic and distressed woman was in the police station reporting that her two-year-old daughter had similarly vanished from their Anderson shelter in the back garden. And that was when a few other reports started to filter in, of three different people who were strangers to the locality and had only been missed by their relatives at home after a protracted silence, and four more local women of, shall we say, dubious morals?

"To cut a long story short, these people simply weren't found. Not one of them, ever again. You can imagine of course the problems the poor, harassed Chief Constable found himself dealing with. One of his own men ending his life so unexpectedly and horribly and another one vanishing without trace was bad enough, but when the rest of his officers' statements and reports of their surveillances had been examined and analysed, the count of people seen entering the House of Wonders rose to ten, rather than the eight who had been definitely reported missing. It goes without saying that the Chief Constable and others made a very unpleasant but convincing assumption that it hadn't been a doll which PC's Hicks and Stanley had glimpsed clasped tightly in the short suspect's arms."

And that was pretty much all Mr. Donovan could tell me. Not something you expect to hear of a seaside town's history, and certainly not something they're ever likely to broadcast. An attraction that would be exactly the opposite should it still have been standing there! I remember pausing to look at the piles of rubble, bricks and rotting timber after I'd been told this; a scene of utter devastation and a blasted eyesore. I've since heard it was never actually rebuilt on, but turned into a bland if functional car park.

So what became of Spangler's House of Wonders after the second move in its strange and chequered history? It appears that Hawkins moved inland, and rented a farmhouse in Leicestershire, where for the next few years his exhibits were mothballed and put into storage in the farm's large outbuildings and barns. He'd intended to re-open after the war somewhere else on the coast, miles from where he'd been originally of course, but he was taken ill in early 1945 and died a few weeks before VE Day. It was his son who finally resurrected the exhibition; only it never found a permanent home again but rather became a Travelling Show. Hawkins junior bought some vehicles, carts and tents—of which there was a large stock of ex-military surplus going at very reasonable prices at that time—and right up until his death in 1959 he was on the road with his exhibition up and down the country, throughout the summer and winter months, often working alongside and collaborating with and setting up next to the itinerant circuses and travelling fairgrounds who toured the British Isles in such profusion then. Naturally, an operation like this couldn't run on the father and son routine of the past, not that the younger Hawkins had a son or any family to help him; so there were a few drivers and labourers hired, mostly men of a wandering and transient nature of course. It seems that most were more footloose and of a vagabond leaning than was usual with Spangler's as their employer however, for none seemed to stay for more than a few months and many left within just weeks—some without even claiming their rightful wages it was said.

It seems that the bad odour and dark reputation of Spangler's followed it from both its early years in the stews and slums of London, where admittedly, little was known of the nature of its departure and transfer, and the seaside resort on the Norfolk coast the details of which I've described. Of course, the nomadic and roving nature of the business naturally earned it the kind of mystique not to be totally unexpected—what perhaps was more disturbing were the stories of dead farm livestock in remote areas where the show had been in the vicinity—cattle, sheep, goats, even indeed the foxes and predators blamed for the deaths, found torn and bloodied in fields and woodland, the subjects of sustained and frenzied attacks. Worse than this were the actual people; of whom six women and two men were found in various rural areas between the years 1947 and 1958, similarly attacked but with no common motive or thread running through them other than the presence of the travelling show in the area at the times of their deaths. There were various investigations by the police of course, but with nothing firm to go on they invariably came to nothing. Human post-mortems are of course more thoroughly conducted than animal ones, and one common factor did emerge from these; all the unfortunate victims had suffered quite horrible injuries and their blood loss was acute, notwithstanding the severity of their wounds.

Mr. Hawkins Junior was taken ill during early 1959, and as his condition worsened the travelling show made its progress back to the farm from where it had been stored, and there its casual employees were paid off and Spangler's mothballed once more. Hawkins died later that year, intestate and reclusive, taking any knowledge he might have had about the business and its history to the grave with him. The collection of curiosities which had been Spangler's stock in trade were sold off at an auction held on the premises by the agents and trustees of the estate, some to private collectors, a few to museums, and all of the amusement arcade machines to John Wildman, the friend of Jack who I mentioned earlier—and this is where the story I'm telling you gets really curious.

◄◦►

Stevenson paused to repack his battered briar pipe bowl with his noisome flake tobacco, taking his time and lighting it up in the considered, leisurely way he always adopts having aroused my interest fully. The pipe lit to his satisfaction and blowing out blue-grey smoke rings, he continued.

◄◦►

Wildman attended the auction when it was held in 1961. Believe it or not there wasn't a great deal of interest in coin operated amusement machines back then, and he bid and purchased every last one of them, some twenty-four in number. More than half of them were early but run of the mill one-arm bandits and the spring bagatelle type machines, as well as a more recent automated fortune teller and "Laughing Sailor" in a glass booth. There were also eight of the more interesting and elaborate "Working Models," all turn of the century stuff and quite quaint, but in various states of repair and poor maintenance and rather unfashionable at that time. The last machine was the rather curious "What the Butler Saw" booth which I remembered seeing on my visit to the House of Wonders as a child. Whether the machine had ever received a repair during the long interval when I saw it there and by the time it stood as a multiple lot at the auction I can't say; all I do know is that when Wildman bought it, it still wasn't working and a faded "Out of Order" sign was still attached to it by some rusty drawing pins in its shabby, varnish peeling wood frame. This didn't worry Wildman at all, as he was very hands on, experienced in both clock-making, and engineering, being a very skilled craftsman and mechanic. He'd made a good living repairing motor cars, clocks and watches, owning as he did both a garage and a small jeweller's shop in Stafford. His spare time was devoted to collecting and repairing old fairground and amusement machines, so the job lot bought from the auction for less than a hundred pounds would you believe, was grist to the mill for him.

Over the course of the next few years Wildman painstakingly restored and repaired those amusement machines. He was of course a busy man, what with the running of his two businesses, and time was often at a premium and he wasn't a man to cut corners. His labour of love eventually restored all the fruit machines and working models back to their former glory, and he was always happy to show interested visitors his collection whenever the opportunity arose. It was in this way that Jack Froston came to know John Wildman, through a chance encounter at a vintage car rally; Jack had a couple of early MG's he used to show of course. Well, the two of them got chatting and Jack happened to mention he was writing *Showmen of England*—and that was how a short while after he was being shown around Wildman's private collection, and making a few notes and taking some photographs for his intended chapter on Spangler's House of Wonders.

Jack never made it very clear to me how much he already knew about Spangler's, but I got the impression he'd probably heard as much, if not more than I had. We never really discussed its past history in any detail, and as by the time I heard what I'm telling you now Jack was in a very bad way, I thought it best not to. One thing's certain; John Wildman was pretty ignorant of the whole affair, and as Jack hardly intended writing about dark and unsubstantiated rumours and lurid unpleasantness in what was basically going to be a "coffee-table book," he didn't feel any need or reason to enlighten his new friend. Jack told me he'd actually made a pretty disturbing and startling discovery about Spangler's elsewhere before his visit to Wildman—but I'll come to that in its proper place; if I'm truthful I'm not sure any of it makes any real sense.

Well, there the two of them were, on a Sunday afternoon: Jack was enthusing in all the right ways to Wildman, making notes, taking pictures, and dropping coins in slots to watch *An English Execution* and *The Castle of Phantoms* when he came to the dismantled casing and internal workings of *The Secrets of our Past* lying in confusion on a bench in one untidy corner.

"Work in progress," Wildman smiled in explanation. "I've left it till last as it won't take that long to put right. Yes, it does look a mess, but it's an orderly one I can assure you. The photograph drums seem to be undamaged and it's really just in need of a thorough clean—not been working for many a long year." He laughed again at Jack's keen curiosity and questions. "Yes, it sounds very intriguing and frightening doesn't it? No—that's not what's put me off! Typical showman's patter and rhetoric: I'm sure it will be pretty tame and hardly live up to its spine-chilling billing and warning. We'll know soon enough. I should have it up and running in about a month and when I have, I'll let you know and you can have the honour of dropping the first old penny in the slot and taking a look. How's that?"

For some reason Jack couldn't explain at the time he actually wasn't keen on Wildman's well intentioned and generous offer at all. He didn't say so of course, and he left shortly after. He continued writing his new book, but his usual zest and enthusiasm seemed to have waned somewhat, notwithstanding the copious notes and photographs he'd made and taken of Wildman's collection; and it was with a sense of relief that he eventually put the manuscript of the chapter about Spangler's with the rest of the finished book, his only task to amend it before sending it off to his publisher. The very next day Wildman telephoned him, and informed him that he'd got the amusement machine back in working order and would he like the first look at it?

Which was how Froston found himself back over in the large outhouse which Wildman used as his private museum and workshop, as his friend, with a touch of the theatrical, unveiled his latest restoration by tugging off the large white dustsheet which shrouded it.

"It looks different to what it did the last time you saw it, eh?" Wildman beamed, hoping for a positive response from Jack. "It's quite an early machine—I actually found the maker's label inside dated 1892. I've not actually seen anything quite like this before; yes, that's the viewing aperture and you push that pointer-lever device across to which show you want to see. I think they're in the right order but it was very difficult because the plate drums aren't identified anywhere and the poor state of the photographic images discouraged me from trying to take them apart. They're very tightly packed to produce the illusion of a moving picture, you see. Ingenious stuff, and it's all clockwork, ratchet and pinion power. Want to try *The Death of Thomas a'Beckett*? or *Murder in the Red Barn*? There's ten to choose from but they're all Penny Dreadful stuff I'm afraid."

Jack smiled and looked at the choice illustrated by a small series of garish and crudely drawn plates under the viewing aperture. He moved the pointer to *Spring Heeled Jack at Large* but then, intrigued by the final plate which was more badly scratched and damaged than the rest, he moved the pointer to that and dropped in his penny, stepping up close to view the show. There was a click and a slight whirring sound as the coin activated the old mechanism, and for a few moments nothing but an impenetrable blackness could be seen yet the machine was turning the photographic drum reel from its low racketing noise. Jack was just beginning to think that either whatever illuminated the photographs had failed or there was some other technical problem his friend had overlooked, when slowly the blackness began to lighten into dim and indistinct shapes; a grey and dismal row of tenement rooftops and chimney stacks came into flickering view as with the sudden pale light of an early dawn morning, and the panorama lowered and widened, disclosing a grimy uncared for terrace of brick built dwellings in a shabby and unidentified street, the pavements damp with early morning rain. Someone, a woman in long skirts and bonnet it appeared, hurried in the jerky, stop motion effect of the crude cinematography along this slum thoroughfare, pausing with frequent regularity to look behind her. Jack told me he was actually smiling at the quaint crudeness and unengaging naivety of the vignette at this moment—but what followed made him smile no longer. Another figure had appeared in the frame from the direction the woman had first taken; short of stature and muffled in an enveloping cloth hood and cape which reached to its ankles. Those ankles could be vaguely discerned at the ragged raw hem of the cloak as they almost skipped and hopped in the most disturbing fashion, and both ankles and feet which appeared naked had a thin and wasted look to them as they pattered horribly along the wet pavement. The woman, now having noticed what was behind her, began to run—not with the theatrical angst and exaggerated histrionics one might have expected from an early staged melodrama—but with a look of sheer terror upon her face. Whatever pursued her moved swiftly, closing the gap between them in short moments, its hood bobbing over a head mercifully obscured but with straggling white wisps of hair escaping from it and a suggestion of long white sharp teeth in the lower portion of a face momentarily exposed. A hand, as thin as the ankles and feet, emerged from the folds of the cloak as it sped along, raising a sharp and cruel looking knife of unusual design. The vignette darkened again, and Jack stepped away from the antique viewfinder, a cold sweat on his brow and actually finding himself shaking.

"It's got a bit longer to run," Wildman said, listening to the drum still turning in the machine and oblivious to his friend's discomposure.

"I've seen enough, thanks," Jack replied. "John, I don't like your new toy very much if I'm honest. What I've just watched there is really creepy, not to say disturbing. I can't believe all the drums are like that one. If they are, I would get rid of the thing or destroy the photographs in the drums and find something to replace them with. If you don't, you'll be having nightmares for the rest of your natural."

Wildman laughed off Jack's remarks. "The Fright of your Life! View at your Peril!" he chuckled making his voice eerily hollow. "Does what it says on the tin, then? I thought you were made of sterner stuff than our Edwardian forebears, Jack?"

Jack was annoyed at Wildman's good natured ribbing as well as still frightened by what he'd witnessed. "I'm quite serious John. There's something not right about that thing. You be very careful with it and I'd think of moving it on if I were you."

The vintage arcade machine stopped whirring and fell silent once more as he finished his sentence. Wildman saw his friend off with the remark—"You probably missed the best bit"—which didn't amuse Jack at all. When he recounted all this to me at our last meeting, he reckoned that for almost a fortnight afterwards he had recurring and unpleasant dreams about that old arcade machine and what he'd seen.

"That figure was truly the stuff of nightmares," I remember him saying between copious mouthfuls of neat Scotch. "And believe me when I say I'll never get its foul image out of my mind." Of course I tried to make light of the matter, suggesting overwork and stress, but Jack wasn't having any of it. "You didn't see it, thank God," he told me lighting another cigarette from the burnt down butt of the one he'd been nervously smoking. "But this I know.

That series of horrible photographs, however they were done, weren't acted out or carefully stage managed—they were a record of some awful event in real life, something that actually happened—of that I'm certain."

It was impossible to get Jack to see it any other way, and of course I had to tread carefully as his wife had died suddenly in a car accident a few weeks after the visit to John Wildman's. That had been a tragic and odd business in itself. Janice had always been a careful driver and she'd swerved off the road late one evening returning from dropping some chapters of *Showmen of England* to Jack's publisher in Stafford. A couple following in their car behind witnessed what happened and thought she'd tried to avoid what looked like a smallish child who appeared to be standing in the road and which they themselves caught a fleeting glimpse of in their headlights. Janice's car hit a hedge and then a tree and she was killed outright. The couple stopped of course and tried to help her but there was nothing they could do. There was no sign of any child and an odd thing emerged at the post-mortem. Janice's injuries, though serious, hadn't been the cause of her death; sudden heart failure was recorded, and the coroner put that down to major and traumatic shock arising from the accident. Perhaps odder were the manuscript pages scattered on the passenger seat. They were the pages dealing with Spangler's, and that was when Jack made the decision to withdraw that chapter of the book.

"Janice was both reliable and totally thorough," he'd told me. "She wouldn't have left part of the manuscript in the car and brought it back with her so what was it doing in there? No one's going to explain that."

Jack was devoted to Janice of course, and he really started on a downhill trend after her death. As I've said, I was one of the few he'd really open up to, and at our last meeting he also told me about John Wildman, who died about two months after Janice. Wildman had viewed all the drums in the arcade machine except the final one he understood from telephone conversations, and his friend had been reassuring him that they were all pretty tame period melodramas with poor sets and poorer actors.

"I'm saving the shocker until last," he'd tell Jack humorously. "I'm going to savour that one—on my own at night to add to the atmosphere of course," he joked, despite Jack's protestations.

About a week later Jack answered his door late at night to an unexpected and visibly frightened visitor who was none other than John Wildman himself. He almost collapsed into Jack's arms, he told me, and it was some time before he could collect himself to speak.

"I was a fool—a bloody fool—I should have listened to you," he said finally, his face drained of all colour and his eyes darting about him in a frantic and searching manner. "I don't know what to do now—what have I done? I watched that last drum of pictures earlier; like you I didn't get to the end, but I saw more than you did. Worse than that, what I saw didn't appear the same as what you described to me. It started in a similar way—but that figure you described—it turned and seemed to be looking at the viewing aperture, directly into my eyes . . . It came towards where I was standing looking at it. My God, I saw its face, its eyes and its teeth . . . and the long knife it carried. I jumped back, something was moving inside the machine and it started scratching the panels in there. The glass broke in the viewing box. I ran then, and how I've driven here I don't know. Whatever it is, it's in the machine or God help me, it was. You've locked the front door? Are all the other doors and windows secured? I daren't leave here until morning."

Jack swore that the two of them spent a long and uncomfortable night drinking whisky in front of his living room fire, starting at every nocturnal noise that they heard through the long small hours. Whether the snuffling and scraping sounds around the curtained windows they heard around an hour after John Wildman's arrival were a collective symptom of overwrought imaginations he couldn't say, only that they were real enough to them to preclude any further investigation to their reality or otherwise. The following morning, Wildman left in his car without a word while Jack was making some tea for them; and it was later that same day that he heard that his friend was dead, having been found drowned and floating in the local reservoir close to his abandoned vehicle. Coroner's verdict—Death by suicide while of unsound mind.

—◦—

Stevenson refilled and lit his scarred old pipe once again. He looked down at the newspaper lying on his lap as though deep in thought and past memories. "Well, and now poor old Jack has died," he said finally. "I just hope that his passing at least was peaceful. Strange story, don't you think?"

"Very strange," I replied, lighting a cigarette to combat the foul smell of my friend's tobacco. "And more loose ends than an old piece of frayed rope.

Are you deliberately holding something back in that annoying way of yours, or is there a rational explanation to all that you've told me?"

Stevenson grimaced and blew a series of smoke rings which eddied and dispersed on the summer breeze. "True stories often have loose ends," he said. "So why should this be different? I can tell you a few more facts that I discovered after what Jack had told me and one of them was this. You know the carpark I mentioned earlier that was put on the site of Spangler's in that East Coast resort? A portion of it collapsed earlier this year—I read the newspapers unlike you—and what do you think they found underneath? Long forgotten cellars, that's what, dating back to well before the Georgian house that had stood there. A lot of unidentified human remains and bones too; mostly adults but one of a small child. Of course, that stirred up a lot of the old stories and a museum in Oxford got in touch with the paper, mentioning some exhibits that it had purchased from the Hawkins estate sale back in the '60s. They'd recently been recovered from long storage, and one of them was of a very shrivelled and almost black dwarf-like corpse in a dusty glass case, with sparse white hair, unusually long incisor teeth, and the remnants of a woollen shroud or cloak about it. Apparently it wasn't labelled but appeared to have had a wooden stave or post driven through its chest at some time for an unknown reason. Well, some clumsy idiot cracked the glass leaning on it, and the whole thing crumbled to dust within minutes of the air getting to it. It begs the question of what exactly the pygmy-like corpse was and when and who rammed a stake through it and for what rational reason? Jack reckoned that Spangler collected some very odd items for his exhibition and this was something obviously passed on to Hawkins and Son."

Stevenson tapped out his pipe on his garden chair. "You're quite right about my own sense of the dramatic of course," he said, "Which is why I didn't mention the title of that peepshow Jack and Wildman witnessed. It was *The Whitechapel Horrors and Murders Exposed!* Is that why Spangler handed over his House of Wonders to Hawkins at the end of 1888? Was he implicated in the Ripper murders even if just as an accessory to one of his more exotic exhibits? You talk of loose ends. Speaking personally I have no wish to delve further. For all I know I could have said more than I should have about the matter for my own safety already—something dreadful lurked in Spangler's House of Wonders for sure—and I feel it was something living, or at least half living and keeping an existence both furtive and horrible until someone decided to end its privations. Hawkins Junior shortly before his death would be my guess. After that . . . can vampires become ghosts? Ghosts who still want to remain in darkness and keep their dreadful secrets? . . ."

Stevenson gave me a searching stare and then a grim smile before leaning back in his chair and draping the newspaper over his face to snooze. I left him to it, going for a stiff drink in the house, for the sun had clouded over in the last few minutes and the air had turned distinctly chillier.

THE NUMBERS

CHRISTOPHER BURNS

A sun the colour of paper edged above the farm and the wooded hill. He walked quickly because he understood that if he slowed he would become thoughtful, too nervous, and then lose confidence and turn back. Crows, shiny and black as blotches of spilled ink, strutted and clacked in the misty field, and at its far perimeter a low shape slid through the greyness and then vanished. He immediately recognised the russet brush and purposeful slink.

Mud webbed the dark farmyard and a heavy reek of cattle layered the still air. Near the farmhouse door a dark green Land Rover was partly illuminated by a light from the kitchen window. Two dogs, Border collies, ran up with vigorously wagging tails and dirty paws. Danny scratched their ears contentedly: they had made no judgement on him. Quite suddenly the door opened and his brother stood there, his back against the light.

"For God's sake," Martin said. "Danny, what are you doing here?"

"I saw a fox," he answered quickly, as though that alone were the reason for his presence. "It was in this field just now."

"You didn't come all this way to tell me that," Martin said, settling a cap on his head and closing the door behind him. Danny noticed that he had lowered his voice, as though he did not wish his wife to overhear. "And where's your car? You haven't walked all this way, have you?" After a pause he added, with a touch of resignation: "I can see that you have. It's just like you."

"I couldn't sleep."

"Listen, it's not right that you show up unexpectedly at this hour. It's not the kind of thing that rational people do. Understand?"

Danny looked at the ground and traced an arc across a cobblestone with the toe of his shoe. "It could go for your chickens," he explained. "Take the Browning; we could find its earth and dig it out."

"What are you here for? Forget the bloody fox and just tell me why you're here."

"I try to help. You know I do."

After a few seconds Martin sighed and pulled his cap further down on his forehead. Eager to be at work, the collies circled round the brothers' feet, nostrils raised, their breath condensing in the chill air.

"I know it's early," Danny said, and the words resembled a plea. "And I should have thought harder about things. But I didn't want to wake you up." He paused, and added: "Both of you, I mean."

Even as he spoke, the details of his last visit shifted uneasily in Danny's memory and he felt his confidence begin to fail. But Martin hadn't yet mentioned the gaffe, the perceived insult, so it was possible that Sarah had never told her husband about what she had been asked.

"We still have to get up at the same time as you and I used to get up," Martin said. "Farming hours never change. Ten, fifteen minutes earlier and we'd have been eating breakfast. But I don't suppose you've eaten breakfast, have you?"

Danny did not answer. His brother could easily make him feel ashamed.

Martin walked past him and unlocked the Land Rover's back door. As soon as it was open the collies jumped inside. Danny could hear the gritty brush of their paws on the floor as they turned round and round before settling down.

"There must be something I can do," Danny said. "Give me some animal feed, or a spade, or a hammer and nails—anything. Just tell me what needs done."

Martin unlocked the driver's door, opened it a fraction, and paused. "I can't think of anything that I'd want you to do," he said flatly.

"Don't you trust me?"

"As I said, I can't think of anything," Martin repeated without varying his tone. He climbed into the driver's seat but kept the door open.

"I tried to get office work but no one will take me," Danny said.

"That's because of the mess you got into; didn't that occur to you?" There was a pause, and Martin added: "No, I don't suppose it did. You're not the brightest with numbers, are you? Not the world's best planner. Figures don't mean much." He closed the door and wound down the window. "I'm going to check the flock in the west field. They'll be lambing soon. I'll be back in twenty or thirty minutes."

"I'll come with you," Danny said eagerly, and added; "we should look for that fox."

Martin did not answer, but instead shook his head like a man confronted once again by a problem he had never been able to solve. And then he started the car engine and banged on the horn several times. In response an upstairs window opened fractionally and yellowish light glanced down into the farmyard. Danny did not dare raise his eyes.

"I've got my brother here," Martin called, his voice like a herald's.

Danny could not hear an answer, but he saw the light withdraw and heard the click of the closing window.

"Sarah will fix you something to eat," Martin told him. "After that, it's best that you go back home. Understand?"

"Is she all right?" Danny asked, a little hesitantly.

"Of course: why shouldn't she be?"

"No reason. I was just asking."

"She's fine," Martin answered, and closed the door.

Danny watched the vehicle bump down the road, its tail lights fading into a mist whose upper layers were melting beneath the angled sunlight. And then he opened the farmhouse door.

He stood in a small whitewashed room that had once been an outhouse. It had double hooks with working clothes and hats, shelves stacked with tins and opened boxes, waterproof jackets and footwear, a gun and shells, a small dismantled engine thick with oil, gardening tools, bags of what he assumed must be some kind of grain, and a flagstone floor spotted with dried mud. A spider hung in a web across the bulb in the ceiling. It annoyed Danny that he should be accused of a lack of discipline by a brother who had such a disorganised room. The next door led to the modern kitchen and it had been left open so that he could smell hot food and feel the warmth. He pushed his hands through his hair, which was damp and which he had allowed to grow too long. His shoes were muddy and he wondered about taking them off and leaving them on the floor next to Martin and Sarah's boots and wellingtons, but decided against it. It was possible Sarah would not be pleased to see him; she could even demand that he leave.

He called her name, at first quietly and then loudly when there was no response. He heard her shout a hello from somewhere upstairs; he was not sure where—maybe the bathroom.

"It's me—Danny," he shouted, although he knew it was not necessary to announce his presence.

There was a pause of six seconds—he timed it—before she called back that she would come down in a few minutes. He unlaced his shoes in readiness but did not take them off.

When Sarah appeared in the kitchen he could see that her hair was still damp from the shower, and that the strands were curled up at their ends; she had dyed it blonde again since they had last met. She wore an old thin sweater and jeans that were ripped across one knee, but the sweater appeared to sit awkwardly on her body, as though parts were sticking to damp patches on her skin. Once again, he could see why his brother had married her.

"Don't tell me, you'd like something to eat," she said drily.

"I don't expect you to make me anything," he replied, trying to be considerate.

"You wouldn't be here if you didn't want to eat," she answered, opening the fridge. "I can do eggs, bacon, fried tomatoes, and toast. I'm sorry but Martin has just finished the last of the sausages. And I can make more coffee."

Danny kept his coat on but took off his shoes and walked into the kitchen. The tiled floor was pleasantly smooth. There was a hole in one sock that his big toe poked through: until that moment he had not noticed it, but now he realised how incongruous it must look.

"Martin didn't say he was expecting you," Sarah said. She had switched the cooker on and was arranging food in a frying pan.

"He wasn't. I couldn't sleep."

"Something on your conscience?"

Danny thought it best not to answer, not just yet, anyway. "I offered to help but he didn't seem to want any," he said. "It's not like it was when we were kids together."

"That was a long time ago. We're all different people now."

He was not sure how to answer, and rather than leave a silence, Danny thought of the food he was about to eat and said, "You're very kind."

Her response was so quick he was not even sure that he had finished speaking.

"Yes," she said, "I am. In view of what you said to me last time."

Danny looked down at the tiled floor. "I picked things up wrong," he murmured, although he was certain that other men would have responded in a similar way to Sarah's careless teasing.

"You needn't hint that it was somehow *my* fault," she told him, as though she had read his thoughts. "What I said was normal conversation: you're the one who took it to be something else. You get carried away by your imagination, don't you? It's not the first time it's got you into trouble."

"Sorry," he said weakly.

"Danny, let's get it straight. I'm married to your *brother*. We're very happy together. We intend to stay that way. So let that be an end to things."

He looked up, ready to defend himself. "It was when you suggested—"

"I said *an end*. We'll forget that it happened and never speak of it again. All right?"

"All right," he agreed, and bowed his head so that she would not see his discomfort.

It was obvious now that Sarah must have remained silent and told Martin nothing. Danny felt both pathetically grateful and at the same time angry that he was morally in her debt.

"Sit down," she instructed. Her voice had not softened.

Danny sat on the far side of a polished wooden table that stretched between them like a barrier, and he tucked his feet under the chair so that his bare big toe was out of Sarah's sight. He searched for something neutral to say.

"How's my nephew?" he asked after a short pause.

"Andrew takes his finals in a couple of months. Everything's going well. He's confident. And when he comes back home he'll be going into partnership with us." Sarah went on as if making a company announcement. "He has a really good business brain and lots of ideas about taking the farm in a new direction."

"A family business, then," Danny said, but she did not react to the edge in his voice.

"You should have let Andrew advise you," Sarah told him. "If you were too proud to listen to your brother you should have listened to your nephew."

But Danny believed it would have been absurd to take advice from a twenty-two-year-old. And besides, he felt nothing but contempt for academic theory, especially when it was concerned with the practical skills of accountancy, management, and farm practice.

Food sizzled and spat in the frying-pan and when the smell hit Danny his nose began to run. He had not eaten a cooked breakfast since the last time he was at the farm. He searched in a pocket for a handkerchief, realising as he did that the only one he had was dirty. Sarah pushed a box of tissues towards him.

"Sorry," he said after blowing his nose noisily and then searching for a container to drop the tissue in. "It's a cold," he lied.

"There's a bin over there," Sarah said, pointing, and once again he felt inadequate for not noticing. "Mist never helps a cold," she continued. "And the farm has been built in the shadow of a hill. As soon as Andrew gets here we'll take a holiday to anywhere that's hot."

"Martin and I always played on top of that hill when we were kids. The trees weren't as tall then, of course. We could climb the lower branches together. And I used to swear to Martin that I could see the sea."

"I hope he didn't believe you. The sea's ten miles away. It must have been your imagination."

"It seemed real to me." Danny paused, and could not help but continue. "In those days I thought we'd own this farm together for the rest of our lives."

Sharpness returned to her voice. "Don't bring that up again; Martin gave you a good price for your share. If you'd taken advice you'd still have most of that money."

The kettle began to boil.

"Sarah," he said with a kind of mild insistence, "these buildings and those fields used to be my property."

"Yours? Only half of them were, and you couldn't manage your share anyway. You don't have the sort of brain that Martin and Andrew have. The partnership would have been bankrupt if we hadn't bought you out."

Sarah lifted the breakfast onto a large plate and put it in front of him along with a knife and fork.

"Danny," she told him firmly, "farming's not an occupation for lazy people or daydreamers or people who can't understand elementary accountancy."

The comment hit him like a slap. For a few moments he held the cutlery in an upright position, like a character in an animated film, and then he pressed the point of his knife into the fried egg so that bright yellow yolk spilled from it.

Once the food was in his mouth it was evident to Danny that he was generating too much saliva, so he reached across for another tissue. He felt foolish because he had become so clumsy. Maybe being misunderstood was a natural consequence of being gauche. And it was demeaning and unjust that all the valuable work he had done on the farm had never been given its true value, either morally or financially. Not only that, but his contributions were habitually dismissed with a guiltless ease.

"I could help," he said, like a supplicant repeating an appeal.

"Martin doesn't want you to help. Not any more."

"I'm good at practical work. You and Martin don't think so, but I am. I've fixed guttering and fed the animals and dug ditches and delivered lambs." He was not sure if he sounded eager or desperate. And then he added: "It would help if I could earn some money."

"Yes, Danny, if the task is simple then your work is acceptable. But you nearly lost us some of those lambs. And you're no good at all if the work involves thinking ahead or seeing consequences. Deep inside, you know you're not."

He nodded weakly as though he agreed to the wisdom of such an arrangement. This was how it was, Danny thought as he sank into self-pity: he had never been appreciated. Instead he was exploited, unrewarded, and often unable to make himself understood.

Sarah put a mug of coffee down in front of him. On its side there was a picture of a Victorian strongman lifting a gigantic weight. And then she spoke with an artificial brightness, as if she needed to close off any further discussion of the future.

"You look as if you're enjoying that breakfast," she said, walking to the sink. "You're nearly finished."

It took a few seconds for Danny to answer.

"Yes," he said, "yes, I am. Thanks."

"I have things to do," she said briskly, turning to the kitchen sink. "When you're finished, maybe you could make your way back home."

It was not a question, but Danny answered with a justification.

"I think it was just as well that I came here. I saw a fox outside. He was very close to the buildings. Something needs to be done about him."

Sarah did not answer but he noticed the momentary despairing shake of her head. She was standing at the sink and facing away from the table. Danny studied her back for a moment and noticed how her clothing was still sticking to it. He fantasised idly about peeling it from her skin. And then, unexpectedly, overwhelmingly, he was seized with a kind of desperate clarity.

He stood up and pushed back the chair so that its legs grated harshly on the floor. "I'll be back in a second," he said.

Everything was different. From this moment on both past and future dissolve and Danny lives only in the present, and when he acts he feels as pure and as faultless as a rainwashed stone.

He goes to the outer room, picks the Browning shotgun from the wall, loads it, walks into the kitchen and discharges one barrel into Sarah's back. She is catapulted forward across the sink, her sweater punched with holes, and then she slides backward and sprawls on the floor in a clatter of falling dishes. The room is still shuddering with the noise and smoky reek of the blast and her eyes swivel helplessly towards the ceiling. Danny walks across the tiled floor and looks down. Sarah's lips are moving but he doesn't know if she is actually saying something or if he has been momentarily deafened. He uses his free hand to stick a finger into each ear and waits until his hearing returns. Her words are distant, muted, like whispers from beyond a wall. He shoots the second barrel and her face disintegrates.

Danny goes back to his seat, finishes eating his breakfast and drinking his coffee, and then returns to the outer room and puts his shoes back on. He is still annoyed that there is a hole in one sock. For a short while he rotates the shell cylinders in his hands, and then he breaks and reloads the Browning. Its metallic clicks are as reassuringly engineered as the tumblers of a safe. Then he puts two extra shells in his pocket and goes back outside to wait in the chill of the farmyard with the shotgun held in both hands and level across his hips. In the barn the cattle are lowing, but the mist is clearing and the rising sun is the colour of a communion wafer.

He cannot tell how long he waits, but as he is growing cold he never stops hoping that his brother will return soon. Eventually the Land Rover bounces back up the track and stops at the very spot where it had been parked. Martin opens the door. He looks puzzled and annoyed and unforgiving.

"I don't want you to shoot that fox," he says firmly. "This is *my* farm. *I* make the decisions. So you can put the gun back where you found it."

Danny fires one barrel and his brother is flung across the seat so that his body is bent backwards and half in, half out of the cab. The engine is still running and crows are rising in a racketing wave from their roosts. In the back of the Land Rover the terrified collies yelp and whirl in circles trying to escape. Martin slides forward, moving in a heavy, ungainly yet unstoppable manner as though his centre of gravity has shifted downwards. He comes to rest on the muddy cobblestones with one leg crooked beneath him and the other held straight out. His hands flutter ineffectually and he makes a strange noise, part exaggerated sigh and part bubbling hiss. Danny aims at his brother's chest, fires again, and Martin's clothing is torn into shreds. Then Danny takes the spares from his pocket, reloads, shoots the dogs, and pulls them out of the back. Their bodies smell of blood and wet fur.

He returns to the outer room, picks up a box of shells, and loads two. He does not check their specification and he does not count how many are in the box. Then Danny walks to the Land Rover, steps over his brother, props the shotgun against the passenger seat, and closes the door. When he sets off he hears a dragging thud as Martin's body slips to the cobblestones. He can still smell the dogs so he opens the window. Chill air courses like a balm into the interior. As he drives away he does not look for the fox.

For the next half-hour Danny fires at any figure that he considers a target. At first there is a car that he waves down as if asking for help before shooting its astonished driver through the side window. Next he kills two men waiting at a bus stop: one sprawls inert on the pavement with outstretched arms, the other sits with his head bowed and hands clasped to his chest, as if in prayer, while a third man runs away with a curious loping gait and is out of range by the time Danny has reloaded. He drives on and sees a young nurse coming out of a shop with a newspaper in her hands. He knows her face but not her name, and when he fires he watches her body collapse as if somehow it has deflated and become smaller. Another man is shot in a doorway, his glasses knocked from his face by the blast, but Danny drives away before he can tell how badly the man has been hit. Next there is a woman walking her spaniel on a lead: she seems to understand what is about to happen and she raises one hand as if that might offer protection. It does not, but this time he spares the dog. Suddenly freed, the spaniel runs away, stops, and then slowly returns, dragging its lead along the pavement behind it. Minutes later Danny halts opposite a mailbox. A postman is scooping letters into a bag and has left the engine of his van running. Danny calls across to him. The postman looks up and is shot full in the face. Mail scatters around him like pages from a destroyed book. And lastly Danny murders a young girl with a child in a pushchair. She lies on the pavement as still as a butchered animal while he broods about killing the terrified child, but when he checks his ammunition he finds that there are only two shells left so he decides that he must drive away.

Danny does not know how many shots he has fired or how many people he has slaughtered. Numbers mean nothing to him, and neither do names or personalities. And only when he has reached the coast does he understand that this has always been his destination.

He leaves the Land Rover at the roadside with the door open. A path leads through grassy dunes to the shore and he follows it with the Browning still in his hand. In the weak sunlight his shadow is just visible as it passes like a ghost across trodden sand and scattered litter. From the road far behind him comes the distant penetrating wail of police sirens.

Danny reaches a broad pebbled beach that leads to a cloudy sea. The grey and brown stones crunch and grate under his weight and he sits down heavily above a contour left by the last high tide. The air has a thin vinegary smell, and he can see tiny flies covering a dead gull that has been washed up on a nearby strand of blackened seaweed.

He takes off his shoes and his socks, placing a sock into each shoe. One sock has to be folded carefully so that its hole is hidden on the inside. Then he reverses the Browning and pushes it into the shingle with its barrels pointing upwards. He looks ahead to an unclear horizon. The sea has retreated across dark sand and the distant water has the dulled sheen of corroding metal.

Danny crooks his right leg so that his toe is near the trigger, but his movements are restricted and clumsy and unreliable so he rolls up his trouser leg and tries again. This time the clothing is tight against his flesh, like the inflated cuff on a blood-pressure monitor, and he has to force his toe inwards before it can touch the guard. But the toe slips and the shotgun fires.

The blast flings him backwards and for several deafened whirling seconds he does not understand that he is stretched out on the shingle like a castaway. For a while he stares at the grey indifferent retreating sky and then he struggles to sit up. There is a pain along the right side of his head like the touch of a hot iron and a clotting ferrous taste in his mouth that he thinks could be both blood and explosive.

His fingers are quivering and there are garbled shouts from somewhere behind him but he cannot tell what the words mean or how near are the people who are yelling them.

Danny lifts the shotgun, breaks it open, transfers the remaining shell to the barrel alongside his right leg, and closes it again. Then he pushes the stock back into the pebbles. The stones click against each other like celebratory ice in a glass. He forces the stock deeper until it is lodged securely. A sudden breeze from the sea blows across him and ruffles his hair and he remembers that he had intended to have it cut.

He puts his mouth close to the muzzle, flinches, and wonders if his lips will blister with the heat. Then he takes his mouth away and tilts his head to check how close his right leg is to the guard. He bends the leg so that the toe is near to the trigger. It will be difficult to get it right but this time he is confident he will succeed.

After all, Danny thinks, everyone deserves a second chance.

BRIGHT CROWN OF JOY

LIVIA LLEWELLYN

[::AFTER::]

Once upon a time, when I was a little girl, there were birds. Thin delicate arrows of bone and feather, crossing the dry horizons of the earth like the needles of the universe, stitching the planet together with their call. Billions of them, spiraling in coils like wind-swept dragons kissing the baby blue vault of the sky. Settling into the trees during cold nights like clusters of fluttering dark leaves, and bursting into high bright song every morning as the unstoppable sun breached the horizon like a volcanic god. Once upon a time, I was a girl and there were birds.

But those days have been gone for many long millennia. All warm-blooded life, all land once bone dry, all seasons once cold—all have been long banished from this warm water realm; and all the birds have died, along with most of the animals we few remaining half-humans remember, those magnificent amber-eyed creatures of feather and fur. Like childhood, they exist solely as memories, outdated maps to a country we can never return to. In the wake of His passage, all has been transformed.

When I sleep, I dream deep and hard, as we all do. Sleeping, I drink in and drown in memories, the last memories of the last survivor of a long-dead race. I awake still dreaming, the smell of pine pitch and rustlings of birds and trees lingering in the tendrils of those long-lost territories.

Gradually, always, the sounds disappear into the soft song of stone chimes hanging from the arches of my roofless chamber, sounding out the passage of tiny cnidarians as they float and swim through the hot damp air. I rise up from my bed and watch their pulsing bodies push through the ceramic domes, tentacles trailing like strands of winking lights. Outside, larger beings, capillatas and medusas and creatures I have no names for, catch in the overgrown vegetation then burst free in silent explosions of gelatinous flight, disappearing into the pale sunless mists that have muted day and lightened night. These are the birds of the world now. And they are stupendous. They are beautiful.

The boy, hardly a boy anymore but something caught between boy and alien wonder, lingers in the crumbling remains of the other room, waiting for me to rise, his soft lips always in a slight smile that hides a mouth of teeth that ages ago fused together into a single ridged wall of bone. His reluctance at leaving me behind on the evolutionary ladder touches me. Sometimes I catch him slumbering, and I press my unclothed body against his, eyelids lowering as I join him in reverie. More and more, we remain like that for immeasurable passages of time, flickering images of past lives washing through our conjoining flesh and minds, breaking apart only when some mysterious creature brushes past us in its accidental perambulations through our home. No such lingering coupling for us this wan morning, though. Outside and far away, on the last and highest mountaintop in the world, our youngest children patiently await us, and as if in a dream I have realized that the time has come to meet them.

⊷

[::MEMORY #2724869.1::]
July 17, 24—, 11:38.52 PM
Roman Wall City, Mount Baker
PrionTech TemporalCortexDiary #74543.01

[::WAKE::]
[::WAKE::]
[::WAKE::]
[::REMINDER: 12:15.00 AM CAR PICK-UP, 1:00.00 AM DESTINATION SUMMIT CRATER ESTATES::]

He is coming. He is coming. He is coming. The alarm is going off, but it's this nightmare that's really ripping the sleep from me, again. I'm waking up as I always do, trembling and panting, sheets all twisted around my body, the mattress and my t-shirt are so wet and slick that—no, I didn't wet the bed. Huh. Well, that was a horrifying moment. God, it's so hot. I bet the AC has gone out again. Let me check.

I was whispering when I woke up. *He is coming.* Repeating it, chanting, like a prayer. How long have I been saying those words? My mind keeps going over the dream. The horizon, the Pacific bulging up and out like a bowl until the waters break.

No, it's working, barely. Going through the motions. *[::REC OFF::]*

[::REC ON::] I went to the bathroom, and now I'm in front of the open food locker, letting this feeble chill wash over me as I drink the last of the filtered water—though I'd specifically saved it for my morning tea, and my grocery appointment isn't until the 19th. Oh well. I needed it. I probably shed five pounds of sweat onto my poor bed.

It's pitch black outside, so I'm rolling both the blinds and the UV shades up. I hope the video for all of this is uploading. No lights in the apartment, no reflection in the window except for a faint purple wink of the wireless implant at my left temple. I'm pressing my nose against the glass, I can see all the way across and down the southwest slopes to the edges. Autumn comes earlier every year, and already great swathes of gold and red run through the forests, needles and leaves falling faster than rain. People are saying this is the final die-off, that this is the start of the end. They say that every year, though. There are little pockets of light all the way down the mountain into the foothills and valleys, pockets of those like me who can afford 24-hour electricity and avoid the brownouts. The rest of the slope is dark as a tomb. Occasional flashes of light, though—probably fires. Sometimes police cars or ambulances.

Sometimes, though I don't know why I think this, the lights look like something else. Organic, almost bioluminescent, like the flashing of giant anglerfish, luring we few night owls outside, into our benthic doom. There they go, again.

[::M-FLASH::]
seven years ago, after the Pan-Pacific tsunami waters receded
valleys and rivers of green fire.
[::/M-FLASH::]

I don't know if this is even uploading to my online diary or if I'm the only one who will ever read this, when I'm old and bored and out of memories to make. The aurora borealis—bands of bright orange and cold blue flickering high above the horizon. Unfolding and spiraling upwards in thin streams, like twisters of wildfire, like the ocean is unraveling. It's the wrong time of year for the lights. How odd.

Beyond the valley, beyond the peaks of the Olympic Mountain Archipelago and the Vancouver Island Ranges, is the Pacific. I can't see it from here, even as high up as I am and as much as the ocean has risen, but those even higher and far richer than me, those with homes at the summit with their high-powered telescopes, they can see the coast grow closer with every passing year, filling up valleys, sliding over low foot hills, filling in all the spaces of the world. In less than two hours I'll be in one of those summit homes, one of those guests of a guest affairs where I'll be granted access to the gated stronghold of one of the few remaining mega rich families via the arm of my handsome silver-haired date, a banking acquaintance further down the ridge at Colfax Peak, who's probably looking for a companion higher up the mountain he can move in with when the waves start knocking at his door. I'm not judging: tonight I'll be doing the same thing. We all spend our lives looking up now, much more than looking down. There's so much less to look up to anymore. I should get ready.

[::REMINDER!::] Pack my collapsible water bottle, in case there's no timer on their bathroom faucets.

Oh, the nightmare. I never got around to having that DreamCatcher app installed in my wetware, way back before internet access got so slow and spotty you can't upgrade anything anymore, and so I was going to think all the images into this diary when I woke up—that was the whole point of this entry. And of course, I've forgotten most of the details. All I remember now are bells, gigantic church bells or gongs, a constant thunderous ringing as all the oceans of the world pour up into the sky, and everything sinks below.

[::/MEMORY::]

◄◦►

[::AFTER::]
We take the long way, as always, across the great delta to the watery marshes that lap against the chain of ancient mountain peaks we and the other remaining elders have made our final home. I never need to remind or insist, the boy knows my every routine as if it is his own. Roads and trails have been reduced to shadows and suggestions of themselves, spectral threads of our previous passage that are only slightly less overgrown than the surrounding jungle. Our feet know the way only by instinct anymore. You could call it mere, but instinct seems more and more to be the wondrous order of our endless day. We sleep and dream and eat and breathe in the super-saturated air; and decades and centuries and perhaps even millennia go by before we stop and think, *I am doing this, I am picking up that, I remember that place and that time, I am here, right here, and it is now*. And we no longer remember the terrible, human limit of finite days and years, all that weight of decay and mortality. Time simply is, it stretches out like this wilderness, like the waters, like the river of stars that spirals across the sky, drawing ever closer with every phase of the moons. There is so much of it now. Sometimes the boy and I weep at the thought, the thought of us being within it and a part of it, of becoming vast and endless and, and. And.

So much endless becoming. We lap at the edges, daring to taste, to wonder: what will it be like, when we finally succumb, are subsumed? And then, like tiny fish, we dart away. For now.

Through jungles of gold and green ferns, high as trees, across warm rivers and wetlands, draped in brown hanging moss and blood red flowers. All the colors of a crisp northern fall, erupting out of an endlessly sub-tropic world. Masses of giant starfish-headed worms cling to boulders, their rows of bead-black eyes noting our progress as their suckered arms grind the smooth surfaces away. We find the skiff, an ancient hardwood beauty, tied to the tree that has grown higher and thicker in the long stretches of time between each journey, and slip into the currents. Skeletal vestiges of the tips of skyscrapers glide past, covered in green, followed by slender tree trunks and vines mimicking the angular shapes of the towers they once latched onto and fed off of, towers that collapsed ages ago as the trees grew on. Our public spaces, our thoroughfares and byways are lush carpets of sea grass in shallow waters, waving us through the serene backwaters of what were once our last cities, our last homes.

Above the roof of the wilderness, three pale spires float into view. The fourth barely rises above the tree line, looking like the broken stub of a finger bone. And then: a column-lined stone road leading to an arched gateway that devours it like a mouth; and beyond the gate, the high stone and granite walls of the crumbling former holy palace that has become through all our ages and evolutions so many different kinds of schools, the crown that rests on the highest summit of the last remaining land mass in the world. Next to the water's edge, a figure sits at the broken base of a cyclopean Buddha, worn back down into the featureless aerolith from which it was born. The man. He spends all his time now with the children, watching them grow, teaching them and learning from them, embracing change almost as quickly as they do. I wonder which of the youngest I will no longer recognize. I wonder which of them will no longer recognize me. Someday, the boy and I will join them, as will the few remaining humans like us, the elders who still live alone in the lands; and then it will be all of us together, a colony of one, pulsing and expanding as one, drawing up all the waters of this world as our body becomes a sail with which to catch and ride the sonic songs of distant stars.

The skiff catches the shore, and the boy leaps out. The man moves forward, offering to me his graceful, fingerless hand. He sees and speaks and breathes solely through his limbs and soft skin now, his features long subsumed into the smooth brown of a hairless head that even now the ghost of a welcoming smile lingers within. He pulls me up with ease, and we stand together in the shadows of the leaves, arms encircling, foreheads touching. He still knows us, but he no longer knows who we are. A familiar fading purple light at the side of his head winks once, like a candle that sputtered out only to immediately die. He is trying to commit our faces to permanent memory again, his brain and the technology going through the motions without understanding that it is nothing more than a death rattle. Like the boy, and all the other Elders, whose cerebral hardware and ports died out at the start of the After, their past lives have vanished. There is only the present for them, a memory-free, streamlined evolution into the future. Only I still remember that even these moments will be wiped away clean. I have no choice. I cannot forget.

[::M-FLASH::]
his beautiful silver hair
[::/M-FLASH::]

◄◦►

[::MEMORY #2724869.3::]
July 18, 24—, 02:05.07am
Ballad House, Summit Crater Estates, Mount Baker
PrionTech TemporalCortexDiary #74543.04

[::FILE CORRUPTION::]
—by the standards of today, I'm rich and jaded and cruel, but even for me it's a bit grotesque. I could never eat that. I politely decline and the waiter gracefully moves away into the crowd with their silver tray. The first group is back from their tour, moving through the double doors into the living room, most of them excited and flushed, a few somber and quiet. People forget their drinks and their important conversations, crowd around them, touch their bright red cheeks and gasp and laugh. What they've just seen, few people in the world have seen for hundreds of years—and even the most powerful people on the planet, scientists and politicians and queens, they have not seen, will never see this thing. Perhaps they don't remember it exists anymore. We're all so busy running from the ocean and cowering under the sun, there's no time for anything else anymore. A shiver is running through me, despite the almost suffocating heat in the room. I'm in group twelve. I don't mind waiting. I've found out that when you're the last, it means you can find out little things the ones who went before you didn't know, secrets and cheats. Sometimes you learn how to stay as long as you want.

I'm walking over to the side of the room, now, to the bar. Except for my date, I don't know any of these people here tonight. Not the usual crowd that attends these events.

No more unlimited ice—they started rationing before the first half-hour was up. Our hosts have been gracious and apologetic, explaining the lack of usual amenities to the unusual temperature spikes, to the diverting of resources to other areas of the estate. Money can buy anything, but we've long been coming to the end of how much there is in the world to buy.

Another drink, with a single shard of ice, no larger than one of my nails. Gone. It's disappeared so quickly, I might have imagined it. I'm walking out into the square outdoor courtyard that sits in the middle of the house, and look up past the slashing lines of concrete and steel to the faint twinkle of stars pushing through the humidity and haze. God, what an ugly-looking building. Uglier than most. Certainly not a mansion, barely a house. More like some giant reached into the mountain, grabbed the top of a nuclear bunker and pulled it halfway out of the rock. It's been built to survive anything, I've heard—all of the buildings at Summit Crater have. Our hosts insist that they designed every last detail of their home, as well as all the other homes on the gated estate, but over the decades, rumors have flown.

[::M-FLASH::]
weapons testing facility
center for disease control
torture and detention center
?astro-archaeology?
[::/M-FLASH::] [::REC OFF::]

[::REC ON::] Boring conversation over with. It's almost my group's time to go. People are pointing up. The lights again, the aurora borealis, stream-ers of thick blue and white lights overhead like comet showers. What was the name of that famous one, that crossed the planet's path every century? *[::SEARCHING. . .SEARCHING. . ./SEARCH::]* No internet. Never mind. I'm standing in the middle of the courtyard with everyone else, staring up at the moving sky. All the constellations, spiraling, circling. All of us, drifting like torn sea grass, falling up—

In the next room people are laughing, like waves over breaking glass. I'm stumbling over to a bench, my evening companion suddenly at my side, his hand around my bare arm. My head bent down. *It's okay, I'm not drunk*, I hear myself saying as I'm rubbing my eyes. *It's just the stars. It's just the bells.*

[::/MEMORY::]

◄◦►

[::AFTER::]
All schools look the same, smell the same, sound the same as we walk through their echoing halls. Even after so many eons, even in air so thick with water that most days now the boy's and my too-slowly-evolving antediluvian lungs struggle to breath. Those elders who are further down that starry road than the rest of us agree. They remember, too. The tiny purple and blue lights that still spark and wink at the sides of our glabrous heads, they remember for us. They let us forget nothing. The colors of curled crayoned papers fluttering against cream and lime walls. The speckled linoleum, yellowed and cracked with blooms of algae and moss bursting between each square. The long hallways, silent and high and wide, lined with rusting lockers and dusty windows and open classroom doors. The miniature size of each round-edged wooden desk and rickety chair. All as familiar as if we were human children again. The only thing missing is the soft smell of chalk in the air.

I reach out with the tip of one long sticky digit, and touch the faded remains of a drawing of tall green plants. The paper is so delicate that it dissolves at my slightest touch, bursting into thousands of particles that hang in the air like insects. Had it been the work of one of my thousands of children, back in the early centuries of the post-transformation of the world, when we were still more human than not? The implant in the dissolving remnants of my brain comes up with no memories. As we move down the cracked stone floors, past pale branches with snapping flowers and clusters of tall sea grass erupting from lockers and doorways, a single bell peals gently from one of the towers. Wind, perhaps, or a school of floating polyps. The boy and I smile in unison.

Hallways and stairways converge, pouring into a roofless, multi-leveled atrium. Tiny lizards sleep on the balustrades and warm floors. The man heads off in another direction, down wide steps of graying marble that lead to underground rivers, bioluminescent rooms, and glittering nocturnal pools, where those children and elders reside as a single entity that is so far beyond and above us that the boy and I hear its song only as a faint impulse, a tug of the heart that catches only to release and melt away before we can join in.

Not yet. It's not my time just yet.

The boy and I continue down the steps toward the masses of supine bodies that cover the floor, drape across balustrades and up stairwells, hang over balcony railings like glistening tapestries. Toward the center of the room they begin to merge, bodies conjoining and melding together, forming a singular living mass that flows down through a wide, round fissure in the middle of the space. Beneath the collective breath and shifting of their bodies, the constant low roar of the ocean works its way up through the remains of the mountain, through the funnel of pulsing flesh that endlessly descends toward their brothers and sisters in the watery chambers below. Plumes of brine and sweet decay fill my lungs, the scents of my children and the elders as they begin their final journey into the ever-increasing being that shall someday span the ocean, that shall someday consume the entire planet, that shall someday take its place once again as a traveler of the dark river of stars, that shall someday find some other bright blue world in which to sink and shrink and settle and dream until the time is right once again for the cycle of life to repeat.

We make our way through ropes of softening bone, columns of vibrating limbs, our hands running over humming flesh as we pass through the room to the other side. I feel their thoughts vibrate into me like electrical currents, welcomes and salutations and declarations of familial love, equations and astral projections and all the cosmic revelations that come with pending godhood. The air becomes easier to breathe, and the myriad needle pains of my ageless body fade. These children of mine do not understand me, but they love me and they heal me, because I have shown each of them the wondrous and mind-altering glimpse of what is to come, of what we will all become. I alone contain the glimpse of our future-self.

◦

[::MEMORY #2724869.4::]
July 18, 24—, 04:12.08am
[::SEARCHING::]
PrionTech TemporalCortexDiary #74543.07

Dammit dammit I forgot to turn the diary back on until now. Much better now—it was just the heat, that's all. And now I'm standing at the end of a long underground hallway with one of my hosts, and the six other people in my group, my silver-haired date included. I'm looking back down the hallway, and I can't quite make out the door we entered through. That's how long it is. There's a steep slant to the floor. We went down.

My date is next to me, holding my hand, we're watching in silence as our host and their security team unlock the door. We're all looking away, respectfully, although they're not entering codes. The entire door is covered in locks and cogs and tumblers. It was built for a world without electricity—that's why there are small shell-shaped recesses in the walls. For candles or lamps, maybe. I bet this used to be a shelter. The higher the oceans drive us, the lower we sink. I can't help but feel we deserve this, that we brought this all on ourselves.

Enough of that. My date's hand is at the small of my back. He's smiling, and I'm returning it. This, right here and now, is an incredible, singular moment I'll remember for the rest of my life. This will shape and define me in ways I have yet to understand. It's only a few degrees cooler within the mountain, but I'm so unused to the difference, I'm almost high—and this is just the start. The vertigo and confusion of earlier in the night is gone—I was overheated, dehydrated, the alcohol didn't help. Guests always faint at these things, we don't know how to pace ourselves anymore. Now I'm practically levitating with excitement.

The door is clicking, our host—he's saying something . . . it was once one of only three in the Northern Hemisphere, but he has it on good authority that the other two are long gone, and there are no more in the south . . .

something about quadruple-insulated glass walls, twenty-four-hour security, blast doors and walls . . . slow down, I missed a date. It's very old, the oldest thing you could imagine, created even before the Ice Age, whenever that was. One of the guards is ushering us through into a small antechamber, where we're being instructed to slip on long fur-lined coats with hoods, face masks, gloves, heavy booties that look like tree stumps. The room is growing cool, very cool, very quickly. We're crowding together, there's just enough room for all of us with all this fabric swaddling our fancy outfits. I'm pressed between my date and a young man, maybe fourteen or fifteen, with long blonde hair and a baby-soft face. Familiar—the host's son, or a donor clone? So hard to tell anymore. The door behind is clanking shut, and the door in front of us is now opening. *He is coming,* I whisper. Shaking my head, laughing like I told a stupid joke. I meant to say, *this is it.*

The woman in front of me is passing out as the door slowly opens—
—super-cold—
—murky heat of th—
—opens into the snow—

[::FILE CORRUPTION::]
—*she cannot remember this image*
—*yes we agree*
[::FILE LOCK::]
—son-clone, is speaking to my date, I'm catching the end of their conversation, his amazing offer we're both now saying yes to in unison, as we're directed back through the two-foot-thick doors into the hall. It seems our night of wonders has yet to end.

⊶

[::AFTER::]
Past the oculus of ocean-saturated flesh we wander, through the crumbling arch of a doorway and up wide stairs. More hallways, lined with worn stone doors. Rough bands of dead coral and the tiny bones of antediluvian sea creatures are embedded in the surface of the walls, creatures completely unfamiliar to me. After the After, there were waves of tsunamis that circled the surface of the world again and again, remaking it entirely new, there

were epochs of monstrous and amazing creatures that thrived and died off in mass extinctions as the planet recalibrated again and again, as we who survived realized that we too had recalibrated, and were part of the chain of change. To our right, light pours in through rows of windows, the glass panes long cracked and worn away. Fog sifts over the sills in flowing bands of soft pure white, and our thin bodies turn it into coiling serpents that wilt and fade in our wake. That color is a rarity now, it reminds me of a moment so thoroughly buried in my past, that to access it takes lengths of time that spans the cycles of the moons. Only with the help of my children can I melt the eons away. But it is more than that. I want them all to know what it was to be awake, alive.

The boy stops before one partially open door. I follow him in. In this place, more than any other, sometimes the old thoughts and emotions reemerge, and curiosity comes to life again within us. This is the room with the globes, row after row of round, almost weightless planets and moons, perched on stands that allow them to spin and gyre in place. I don't know if the boy remembers what they represent anymore, but it is clear he remembers his pleasure in spinning them, in staring at the continents and islands and rivers and seas whirling with the touch of his hands. Most of the map features have vanished, some globes have rotted away into half-shells, others are simply dust. All are static snapshots of a planet whose surface has shifted countless times. Faint traces of maps cover the classroom walls, painted on the stone and plaster. Long ago, when they were legible, I could make out trails and calculations, the plans of routes and journeys, cuneiform scratches that spelled out destinations. There was a time we thought we could reverse the process, escape our fate. But from this place, the highest mountaintop in the world, there was no where else to run.

An elder appears before us in the doorway, its featureless head nodding as multiple arms beckon us forward. I don't recognize it. Are they someone I once knew, in our human life before the After? They have no mouth. Their port, if they ever had one, is dead, and their mind is already becoming attuned to the writhing confluence below, their body soon to follow. No urgency drives its movements, only instinct, and so we continue our circuit around the room, taking as much time as we need and desire, our fingers entwined, mesmerized by the thick layers of pasts crowding the space like ghosts. We let them wash over and through us until we are sated, until some restless primal human emotion or urge in each of us has subsided. I let the boy leave the room first, and I follow, both of us letting the elder lead us to the end of the hall and into a small classroom covered in soft rugs and lined with chains of bright prayer flags.

Multiple heads and eyes turn toward me. It always takes me by such surprise, it's a jolt to my heart I never can steel myself against. Multiple human heads, human faces. Is this what I looked like when I was a child, or when their father, the boy, was a newly-formed child clone? Small mouths and noses, rows of even teeth, pupils of blue and hazel and green that dilate beneath lids lined with delicate lashes of hair, but that's where any resemblance ends. Their bodies are tall and thin like reeds, they tower over me. Some of the children have no ears, a few have thinning hair, most have no genitals. They have arrived at that moment in their lives when puberty once would have taken over and shaped them into adult human beings, but they are about to take a far different path to adulthood, if it can be called that anymore. They will shift and morph, and there will be ages of wandering and discovery of each other and what lies beyond the horizons of these waterlogged peaks. They shall dream, dream of an existence in which they never awaken. And eventually they shall return, and become part of the whole, become what I saw rising from the waves and its dreams so many, many countless ages ago.

The boy stands at the side of the room as I make my way to the middle. As I lay down, hands reach out and touch my naked skin. I settle in, relaxing as my children form a cocoon around me, bodies draped over me, each touching the other so that none of them are not in some way connected to the others. This is how they communicate, how they learn. I close my eyes. Eventually, I feel the delicate touch of fingers at my left temple. They are about to merge with my wetware, enter the vast network of memories and files. There is only a moment of unease, and th—

[::REC INTERRUPTED::]
[::REC OVERRIDE::]
[::ACCESS TRANSFER COMPLETE::]

⟶

[::MEMORY #2724869.5::]
July 18, 24—, 05:32.08am

Ballad House, Summit Crater Estates, Mount Baker
PrionTech TemporalCortexDiary #74543.08

[::FILE CORRUPTION::]
—ver seen such lightning in the sky. Great bolts of it split the dark apart, each
one so bright that we gasp in shock and clutch our eyes every time the sky lights
up around us. And yet no thunder—this storm is completely silent. The aurora
borealis has vanished, pushed away by whatever system is moving through the
night. The boy is guiding the hands and face of my silver-haired date to the massive telescope that rests on the edge of the expansive covered terrace that crowns
the house. Their fingers move together and apart, the boy's hand rests against
the back of the man's head as he adjusts the lens until the man nods slightly.
They work well together. *[::DELETION::]* He's got the hang of it now, and the
boy is moving away, letting the man aim the massive column of bright metal
in a slow arc back and forth across the slopes of the mountain. He's exclaiming
how he can see into people's apartments, halfway down Mount Baker, watching
TV, arguing, having sex. He's looking for his apartment now—not his current
home, the one he grew up in, that's long been subsumed by the Pacific. The boy
is smiling. Everyone does this, apparently. They all want to see remnants of the
places they once lived in, the towns their parents and grandparents came from,
the waterlogged vestiges of Bellingham, Everett, Seattle, the cloudy peaks of the
Olympic archipelago. Everyone wants to see their past.

Despite the eerie weather, a few other people have joined us, close friends and
family of the hosts only, the most private of parties within the most private of
parties. Everyone has a drink in one hand, is ranting about the strange room
half a mile below our feet, the odd lights in the southern sky, the restlessness
and unease that none of us can seem to escape. I'm sitting down in a cushy
chair, clutching the arms and staring up at the tiny votive candles that flicker
on cocktail tables scattered across the space. I'm squeezing my eyes shut until
all I see are orange flickerings of hot life that wink in and out of view.

Someone is talking softly about the bells.

The boy is tapping me on the shoulder, it's my turn now. The man is stepping
aside, placing one hand on my back again as I take his place. I'm following

his instructions, moving the levers around as I adjust the lens. *You won't see the old cities*, he's telling me, *except for the skyscrapers, most of them are gone. Further out*, I'm telling him. The boy is helping me turn the telescope—it moves easily but I'm surprised at the weight of it beneath my hands. Together we aim it south and east, just beyond the remaining mountain peaks. I'm looking for our enemy ocean. I want to see exactly what's coming for me.

Long slivers of silver. The light of the full moon, reflecting in the silky rippling dark. That's it. The ocean. A continent of water, nothing more. From here, it's so benign. I sense no malice in the horizon before me, no intent. Above it sits a night sky hazily studded with stars, stretching out forever. Everywhere, so much neutral, quiet water and space. I'm blinking, staring at the crest of the horizon again. The silver light quivers slightly—is it curving? Are the waters moving? *Whales*, I'm saying, *are there still whales out there because it looks like something's swimming across the surface*, and the man replies *no one's seen a whale in two hundred years* while the boy is reminding us of the floating cities, multitudes of ships sailing in unison from one land mass to the next and now it's hitting me oh god I know I know what's happening. *He is coming I'm so cold I'm so cold I'm saying this out loud oh it's a wave it's a wave the light at the top of the wave tsunami it's a tsunami* and thunder, so loud it stops my hear—

[::FILE INTERRUPTION::]

—ailing of the tsunami sirens begins, echoing all up and down the mountainside. Behind me, screaming, crashing of chairs, the sounds of panicked people scattering like flies. *I'm going, are you coming because I'm not waiting*, the man is shouting at me, but I shrug his hand off my arm, *just go already*, I start to yell but he's already gone, I can hear his voice from far off telling people to get the fuck out of his way and the boy is placing his hands around my trembling tight fingers telling me *it's okay it's okay just let go I won't leave you I'll make sure you're safe* and silence now except for distant commotion from other parts of the house the squeal of car wheels and horns a single gun shot, and my breath sounds like some panting anim—

[::FILE INTERRUPTION::]

—oor beneath my feet, traveling up through my bones, as fast as those deep white lightning strikes ripping up through the night. A vast, heavy, steady roll of the earth, so powerful my heart is matching it beat for beat, as if there is no other way to survive. My head is slamming against the telescope, I'm bouncing back against the boy. The building is moaning along with the earth, cracks ripping through the walls and sending dust and pebbles of concrete showering through the air, the glass terrace doors shattering. I *[::UNINTELLIGIBLE::]* and the boy and I start toward the doors, and freeze again. Blast plates are lowering. The building is a watertight box, impenetrable, it's how they've survived so many other waves. But we have to be on the ins—

[::FILE INTERRUPTION::]

—other massive strike rolls through the air, almost tugging us behind in its wake as it travels up through the mountain but lesser than the one before, and I grab the boy and he holds me tight. Lights and engines, shutting down all around us. I'm squinting in the dark, looking for any sign of life looking for any way out but I can't see it. We're standing at the top of a world that doesn't exist anymore. No wind. No quakes. No sirens. It's so quiet. So quiet.

We're going to die, I'm saying, and the boy is replying *I know. He is coming*, I say. *Yes*, says the boy. We hold each other in the dark, listening for the coming wave, but it's still so far away. The aurora borealis is back, or whatever that light is, a deep and relentless green that I now see rises up out of the ocean. I have to, I can do this, I can move, I'm walking stiff choppy steps, the boy beside me always, I'm grasping the telescope handles again and he's helping me move it. *Is this what you want*, he's asking, I'm saying *yes I need to do this, I can't just stand here and wait. Tell me what you see*, he's saying, *don't stop talking, just keep telling me what you see*, and I'm telling him:

Great ribbons of fire dancing along the edges of the water, the edge of the water, a wall moving continually without breaking, green and blue, deep colors like a crown.

So beautiful.

Stars moving behind, or comets, little sparkles of white light like glass in the sun like glass on tar roads when the sun hits it you remember how that looks.

The water is lighting up now, can you see it? All the blues and greens are, it's like a wall of stained glass, liquid fire.

So fast. So fast. Sorry, I can hardly breathe, I didn't think it would be this fast.

Put your arms around, yes, tighter. Tighter.

This is it.

I can feel it now, yes, that, rumble, that roaring, louder, everything's trembling, OH MY GOD the wave is passing over the edges of the Olympics it's coming so fast now there's something in the water. Something in the—

OH GOD OH MY GOD IT'S NOT WATER THIS [::UNINTELLIGIBLE::] NOT WATER THAT ISN'T LIGHT there are so many parts so much movement coming NONE OF THIS IS WATER it's so wide it so wide oh my god oh my god it's almost HE'S HE'S HE'S—

[::UNINTELLIGIBLE::]

EVERYWHERE EVERYWHERE EYES EYES EYES I SEE YOU I SEE YOU INSIDE INSIDE INSIDE I SEEEEEEEEEEEEEEEE—

-o-

[::AFTER::]
The air is choked with green wisps of gossamer webbing, thread-thin streamers that catch against our bodies, collide and collect against the vines that have made their way up to the rooftop of the school. The boy and I pull them gently from our naked skin. There is no repulsion in our act, no curiosity. We only wish to set them free. Like us, they are a part of this world, they are our dreaming god set free to cover and transform this planet, a component of our communal body whose purpose we cannot yet fathom, an integral

part of the great After, of the great god, and in fact ourselves. The threads drift away in the slow breeze.

Downstairs, our children sleep in the classroom, dream in each other's arms, their last afternoon surrounded by the ghost ruins of a human childhood they never experienced. Tomorrow they will be moved lower, closer to their conjoined siblings. Already their minds have processed the unimaginable, and it's sparked the beginnings of a physical transformation into the very thing they uncovered in my mind. Or so we believe. We will not know for certain until it is finished, until we join them. Three floors above them, the boy and I spread out on the rooftop at the base of the broken spire, our bodies warming under the heat of a surprisingly strong sun that dares to occasionally break from behind an oddly cool haze. The man sits somewhat apart from us, his head nodding back and forth slightly. More and more he does this, his earlier greeting already slipping from his mind as his thoughts become attuned to all our children below, those at the beginning of their journey and those nearing the end. By the time we leave the school, he'll remember little of our time together, if anything at all. The boy has these moments as well. There are long periods where he sits in our home, his thoughts adrift, his body trembling and shifting as he fights and accepts the biological call. What I feel inside, perhaps it was something I once called sorrow. I still remember everything that has happened in my life, before and After, except for one insignificant event that the loss of plagues my every waking thought, and I do not know why. Is it that moment when I dared to look upon the face of an ancient elder being? Is it that moment I became the first and only human who looked in his infinite eyes and did not go insane? Is it his face my children need to discover within my mind, or some other elusive memory that is hidden to me, some incident in my life that prevents me from becoming a part of the whole?

I'll probably never know.

Below, the jungle spreads out before us in a thick carpet, down to the river that winds in and out of the edges of the ocean, an ocean smoothed out and dampened with patches of bright and dark greens, bubbles and slicks of primordial flesh that crest the surface and slide back down silently to the nurturing depths. Where the river and ocean and vast marshes all come together in a torrent of untamed life, I can make out the remains of the low, flat fields where I and the other elder humans who had once been female lay on our backs in countless rows, where we watched the seasons pass and the moons circle the skies a million times over as eggs poured out of us, a torrent of latent life, the only way our newly-transformed bodies could give birth. Those birthing fields once spread to the horizon. Every remaining human female from every corner of the world traveled here, like spawning fish, trapped in a biological drive our transforming bodies were helpless to ignore. Countless times I've sat on this roof with the boy, watching sexless elders like the man tend our future children, moving our brood into the school as they hatched into life. Countless times I've walked into those school rooms, opened my mind to their probing thoughts, and given them access to the image of what we once were and are once again becoming. A great elder being, reborn.

There are so few unhatched eggs now, and the fields are being subsumed into the wide maw of the encroaching marshes and swamps. This part of the cycle is ending. Birthing has ended. There are no more females or males in the world, and most of the human elders are gone. Melancholy—is that the word? Perhaps, but also anticipation. Curiosity. Wonder and joy. All the things that oceans and mountains cannot hold, that nature cannot impart or receive, that universes cannot feel.

I stretch my arms high into the air. Who is to say what will happen when I am received into the oculus below, when my body and mind and that tiny bit of circuitry that will not die join everyone I have ever loved and birthed and known. Perhaps this time we will become a being that rejects nothing and accepts all. Perhaps this time no one will be forgotten, and everyone remembered. Perhaps there will be no more dreaming.

◄◦►

[::MEMORY #2724869.4::]
July 18, 24—, 04:12.08am
[::LOCATION UNKNOWN::]
PrionTech TemporalCortexDiary #74543.07

[::/FILE CORRUPTION::]
[::FILE UNLOCKED::]
—is this it? is this the memory of the dreaming goddess?

—yes this is what mother saw
—yes this is what we must find
—yes below the water, below
—yes this is what we will become
[::PLAY FILE::]
—passing out as the door slowly opens—she's the first to feel the super-cold air slashing through what now feels like the murky heat of the antechamber. She's falling against me, one of the guards is catching and moving her to the side as the door opens into the snow vault. Stupid, I'm crying a little, I never ever thought I'd feel cold air again, the cruel cold air that squeezes your lungs and stings your eyes, not the sad semi-efforts of the food locker or the AC. Rows of dim track lighting illuminate the chamber, most of them pointed at the center of the room. I'm staring at the very last remaining pack of snow from Everest. This is it. The heart of a glacier that once crowned the highest peak of the planet, that carved deep canyons in the earth that remain to this day. This is the last piece of glacier anywhere in the world. The great goddess Chomolungma lies naked and bare. All the mountains are naked and bare. We killed them all.

I'm stepping forward, slowly, one of the guards watching my every move. Someone is exclaiming as they walk to the other side, the host explaining how they moved it here thirty years ago from another facility—two more people are asking to leave the chamber, the sub-zero temperature is just too much for them. It's not what I imagined it would look like. Parts of it are dirty and gray and hard, pocked with thousands of tiny holes. I don't know what I was expecting—a mile-wide river of brilliant white and blue ribbons that glowed like a pearl, like in an old movie or book? It sort of looks like a chunk of cement the size of a delivery van. The man has pulled his face mask down, and he's sniffing the air. I do the same, even though our host advises against it. The air is so dry and crisp it hurts to breathe. I don't have any words for what it smells like. We smile and laugh and clouds of white jet out of our nostrils and mouths, hanging in the air like insects.

We're walking around it in a circle now, the host rattling off a number of statistics and facts, I don't care about those. No, he laughs, they won't chip off bits for the drinks. The guards never take their eyes off us—they're all armed. There's a small round spot on one side of the rectangle, shiny as glass, no longer grey but pure brilliant white from years of supplicating hands wearing it away. So beautiful I almost gasp. One after another, we're removing a glove and placing our hand briefly in the hollow. It's my turn. Biting. Needle-pricks against my skin, wet-smooth ice, numbing, gelid. Life, ancient and incomprehensible, connected to all, to me. This *is* me.

Walking away, slipping the glove back on even though we'll be back in the antechamber and undressing in seconds. Feeling the warmth soak through the layers of freezing skin and stiffening muscle, burning through me in delicious pain as if I've dipped my hand in fire. My heart, racing. I'll never not be cold again. I've touched the heart of the world. I am this world. I'm not insignificant anymore.

[::LOCK::]

THE BEAUTIFUL THING WE WILL BECOME

KRISTI DEMEESTER

Katrina's father started taking her skin when she was thirteen.

"Research," she told me when I poked at the gauze wrapped around her forearm and then took another bite of her sandwich. Mrs. Papillo shot a look our way and frowned, a witchy finger pointing to the red card at the head of our lunch table that meant we were supposed to be silent.

I waited for Mrs. Papillo to turn away before I nudged Katrina between the ribs. "For what?" I mouthed to her, but she shook her head, turned a small tangerine over and over in her hands.

I did not eat the carrot sticks my mother had packed for me but spent the rest of lunch watching Katrina. Waiting for her to stretch her arm across the table or move in such a way that the gauze would ride up, if only for a second or two, so that I could see that patch of skin her father had taken from her, how he had marked her as different. As something special.

When the lunch period ended, Mrs. Papillo passed a hand over each of our shoulders, her voice a harsh, violent thing when she paused next to me. "Mary Anne, you didn't eat your lunch."

"My stomach hurts," I said, and she stared, those pale eyes passing through me, like I was nothing, like I was a ghost, and then she nodded her head, and

I stood with the rest of the class and filed past the trash cans. When it was my turn, I buried the carrots, the veggie wrap, and a sugar-free pudding beneath a stack of napkins. Pressed what I would not put inside of my body into plastic and tried not to think about how my stomach pooched over my jeans.

For the rest of the day, Katrina tugged at her sleeves, covered that strip of gauze so that only the edge of the tape peeked out.

On the bus ride home, she didn't sit next to me, and I tried to ignore her ponytail, the silver butterfly clip she always wore refracting the sunlight into a thousand pieces. Devor Birmingham sat next to me instead, spent the entire ride scribbling a single dark line in his notebook, a sweet, sour smell of sweat all around him.

When our stop came, I scrambled past Devor, but Katrina did not wait. Ahead of me, she walked quickly, her face trained on the ground, her legs flashing white under her dark skirt as they carried her further and further away.

"Katrina!" I called, but she did not slow, and I would not run after her, I would not, and she stumbled, the notebook she clasped to her chest tumbling to the ground, and then she was running up her driveway, the door opening for her as if by magic, and then the darkness swallowed her, all of that blackness reaching out and then there was nothing left in the space where she had once been.

There, on the browning grass, I knelt, her notebook clutched to my chest, and I watched the curtains, waited for my best friend to appear, her hand pressed to the glass, a smile playing at the edges of her lips, but she did not. I counted to fifteen, and then I went home, Katrina's notebook burning against my skin.

In my bedroom, I flipped through the pages, but every one was blank, all of that white space waiting to devour the fingers hovering over it, and I shoved the notebook under my bed.

The next day and the day after that, Katrina did not come to school. Both days, I pretended to eat my lunch, balled up bite after bite before dropping it onto the cold linoleum, and Mrs. Papillo smiled to see my empty lunch bag, and everything inside of me felt light. Like air. Like clouds.

During art, I cut a piece of printer paper until it fit against my forearm and taped it down. I hoped that I would bleed, that maybe Katrina's father would somehow know that my skin was beautiful, too, but nothing happened and so I crumpled up the paper and left it next to my desk.

The next day, Katrina was back at school, and a puke yellow bruise snaked along her collarbone and up her neck, and she looked at me from eyes too dark for her pale face.

I passed her a note during math. "What's wrong with you?" it said, but she folded it up and put it in the little white pleather purse that she carried and did not look at me for the rest of the day.

That night, my mother placed celery on my dinner plate, a square of soggy lettuce, a baby carrot, and I cut them into smaller and smaller pieces until there was nothing left, and my stomach felt like a small, shriveled thing.

"You really do look better. Thinner," my mother said, and I curled my palm against my stomach, thought of what it would be like for Katrina's father to slice away the flesh just under my belly button; what it would be like for him to place me inside of his mouth.

On Monday, gauze streaked across Katrina's upper arm, and I tried to catch her eye throughout Social Studies, but Katrina focused on Mrs. Papillo and her stupid maps, and I spent the rest of the period wondering what it would feel like for a knife to trace out pieces of me, lift me out and into the air so that there was somehow the same and less of me.

My stomach cramped throughout lunch, and I watched Katrina. She stared at something I could not see, and Mrs. Papillo didn't notice that neither of us had eaten. When I got back to my desk, there was a note with the loop-ing, curved letters that betrayed Katrina's handwriting. It was addressed to me, and I cupped it against my palm, waited for something to happen, for something to change, but there was Mrs. Papillo at the front of the classroom, and everything identical to every other day, so I opened the note.

"Under the tree. When it gets dark," it said, and I held those words inside of my mouth for the rest of the day. Like honey. Like a jewel.

After I pretended to eat the dinner my mother made me—a spoonful of brown rice, steamed snowpeas, and a sad, rubbery slice of chicken—I locked myself in the bathroom and stripped down to my underwear—a stretch of baby pink cotton cutting against pale flesh, and I pinched and pulled my skin until it was something that I didn't recognize, and I wished for something sharp.

Dark was a long while coming, and I stayed in the bathroom, listened as my mother washed our plates, tried not to listen when she closed her bedroom door behind her, the lock echoing through the empty house. I tried not to listen to her cry, and when she called out my father's name into that nothingness, I covered my ears with my hands.

I didn't see Katrina at first, but my eyes had not yet adjusted to the dark, and she stood behind the tree—our tree—a large maple whose leaves painted the dark with brilliant fire. Deep orange and russet burned against the night air, and there was the heavy scent of smoke all around me, and I swallowed, my throat suddenly dry.

It technically didn't belong to either Katrina or me, but stood between our houses and marked the halfway point between us. For five years, we'd stood under those branches, whispered back and forth, and the leaves were heavy with our secrets.

"Up here." Katrina's voice came from above me, and I looked up. A pair of dark eyes stared down, and I squinted, tried to make out the rest of her, but she shrank backward. "Come up."

One foot over the other, hands scrabbling against bark, and I was up, the ground falling away from us, and the stars burning large and bright. Katrina sat beside me, her hand guiding mine beneath the gauze, her fingers showing me all of the holes that her father had left.

"Does it hurt?"

"I don't know. I can never remember if it does or it doesn't."

If it was me, I would remember. I brought my fingertips to my mouth, but I could not taste Katrina.

"You've lost weight. So small. You'll shrivel up and drift away." Katrina wound a strand of my hair around her fist. "He thought I was asleep last night, and when he came in my room, I didn't make a sound, pretended like I was a mouse."

I held my breath and the branch swayed beneath us. I wondered if we fell, which of us would remain in the dirt.

"Will you come with me?" she said, and her hands were my hands, and she was squeezing and squeezing, and her eyes were pools of inky blackness as if the pupil had swallowed up everything else, and I felt all of the lightness in my stomach, all of the food I had not eaten and how it filled me up. I thought of my mother sitting alone in her bedroom and swallowing her tears, and my father who found another woman more beautiful, and I told Katrina yes, yes, I would go with her.

When she smiled at me, it was like sunshine, warm and soft against my skin, and we slipped out of the tree, ignoring the rough bark tearing at our legs, and we moved through the night. Katrina laughed, high and bright, and it was almost like nothing had changed, like there had never been a thin, white piece of gauze to come between us, and I matched my pace to hers, and we moved faster and faster through the shadow world.

Katrina's house was dark, the shutters like old blood against white wood, and she led me around back, pressed her fingers to her lips, and then opened the back door. A deep smell, like earth, like rainwater gathered into an ancient pool, came flooding out, and I coughed into my hand, but the smell was also somehow right. Something that had always been.

Katrina led me through the kitchen where we had spent afternoons baking cookies, eating batter off of wooden spoons; where we huddled over bowls of Frosted Flakes on Saturday mornings while her father slept on in his bedroom. In all of those years, Katrina's father would hover just behind us, and if I glanced over at him, he would smile, his brown eyes crinkling at the edges. Sometimes, when I woke before Katrina, he would pour a bowl of cereal for me, ask me about school or about what T.V. shows I liked. He would push the sugar bowl toward me and laugh in all of the right places. Nothing at all like my own father who glared when I helped myself to a second bowl of bran flakes and mumbled under his breath that if I wasn't careful, I would end up like my mother.

Far away from my mother, from my father and the tight, sharp words between them, away in the world that Katrina and I created, there were no mothers, no fathers, no careful eyes watching every bite of food that went scraping past my lips, no clipped phrases measuring out the weight of me, no mirror image of my mother's shame, her own body reflected in mine.

Before me, Katrina stopped short, and I slammed into her, my belly curving into the hollow of her back, and I did not move away but leaned into her hair. I never wanted to move again, wanted our skins fused together, a single beating heart that moved through the world like a wondrous thing. A thing that had no beginning and no end, our bodies indistinguishable from the other, and no one would look at the thin casing of skin that covered my hulking form and then look away. Because we—because I—would be more beautiful and strange than anything they had ever seen.

She brought a finger to her lips and then extended her arm, pointed down the hallway to a thin strip of light that spilled from beneath a closed door.

It was not a bedroom I remembered seeing before. In my memory, the kitchen jutted like a broken tooth off of a small living room stuffed with uncomfortable furniture and a television too large for the space; at the opposite end of the kitchen, a cased opening led to a narrow hallway, Katrina's bedroom on the left, her father's and a single bathroom on the right. The door I saw now was at the end of the hallway in a place where there had never been a door.

A shadow passed into the space between the wood and the floor, and Katrina held her breath, her back still against my chest, and I did the same. Together, we waited for the door to open, but the shadow moved on. There are times that I think we never breathed again.

"He's working," Katrina said.

"On what?"

"I hear him talking to it. Late at night. He says that it's so beautiful. That it saved him. Then there are noises, like an animal. I cover my ears then. This way," Katrina said, and I followed her into her bedroom, the door opening and closing quietly. She did not turn on the light and walked to the center of the room where a patch of silver moonlight streamed in from the window behind her. Her fingers caught on the bottom of her shirt and tugged upwards, the skin on her back pale and smooth. On her right shoulder, a large patch of gauze marred the smooth flesh, and she stood perfectly still.

I went to her, and she bowed her head when I peeled away the cloth, her voice low. "He whispers when he opens me up."

Katrina shifted, and I watched raw skin ripple, held my hand over the spot as if I could contain her, as if I could keep all of her inside, but she was pouring out, bright blood against that pale skin, and I thought again of how it would feel to be sliced apart and stitched back together as something better.

"You're so lucky," I said, and Katrina turned to face me.

"I didn't like it when he would come in to tell me goodnight. He would wait until he thought that I was asleep and then sit next to me for the longest time. Sometimes, he laid down next to me and asked if he could kiss me, and it was always too long, but he would get up and go away and the next morning he wouldn't look at me." Her breath came hard and fast, and I wound my hand through hers. "The first time he cut me, I fought him. Screamed until my throat went bloody, but he didn't stop, and he cried and cried and cried. Said that it was better this way. After, he didn't come to kiss me goodnight. He was right. It was better this way. Each time he took more and more, but I locked everything inside. Learned how not to scream."

From the hallway came the sound of something moving and then the sound of a door creaking shut.

"Hide," Katrina said, but I shook my head, and she grasped my arms and pushed me toward her closet.

She shut the door on me but not all the way, so I could see a corner of the window, the edge of her dresser, a wooden music box open and a tulle-skirted ballerina gone still. Her clothes smelled like lavender.

I couldn't see Katrina's father, but I could hear him: could hear his breathing gone jagged as he shuffled into the room; could hear him whispering, his voice sliding over me like oil, and I hated Katrina. Hated her for her smooth, flat stomach and her beautiful mouth. Hated her for having a father who loved her. Hated her for being so lovely that her father wanted to take her apart, to carry those small pieces of her with him like a treasure.

The hard, sharp sound of scissors echoed through the room, and I opened the door a bit more and listened for Katrina's silence.

I could see her now, and her father knelt before her, a pair of heavy handled scissors clutched in his right hand, his left wrapped in her hair. She looked back at me, across all of that empty space, and opened her mouth. "Please." Her lips formed around the words, but there was no sound.

Rising, Katrina's father stumbled backward, his hands thick with his daughter's hair. "Thank you. Thank you," he said, and he closed the door quietly behind him.

Katrina turned from me when I left the darkness of her closet, and I went to her, touched her on the thigh, and she tucked herself tight, tight, tight against the wall.

I went out the window as I had so many other times, letting my weight fall against the ground and then rolling with the momentum. Katrina did not shut the window behind me, and I ran all the way back to my house, my lungs and muscles burning.

In the morning, my mother sliced half a grapefruit and placed it before me with a pink packet of sweetener. She watched as I took my spoon and mashed the fruit until the juice threatened to overflow and brought the rind to my lips. She smiled and patted my hair. "Good girl," she said and didn't eat any breakfast of her own. The blouse she'd put on that morning, a deep blue the color of ocean water, was too big, and she plucked at it as she watched me, uncomfortable in this new, thinner body that she inhabited. It hadn't been enough for my father to stay. We hadn't been enough for him to stay.

When the bus came, I didn't get on. My head hurt and there were small pinpricks of light when I moved too quickly. Instead, I waited at the tree—our tree—and when my mother's car glided past, all I could see of her face was a smear of frosted pink lipstick.

I plucked a leaf from the branches and folded it until it was nothing more than a bite and then placed it between my teeth. Chewed and swallowed. I wondered if it would take root there, unfurl delicate little tendrils into soft dirt and fix me in this spot forever. It was nice to think of things like that, but my legs moved, and I carried that green inside of me as I ran to Katrina's house.

At some point in the night Katrina must have closed the window because the curtains covered the glass, but I didn't want her to see me there. She would tell me to leave, would rob me of the only thing that I wanted, and so I crept low to the ground, my chin scraping against grass, and I opened my mouth to it and took another bite.

Katrina didn't understand what it was like to empty herself, to waste and waste away until everything inside was hollow. A vast thing covered in dull skin that needed cutting away.

The back door was still open, and I slipped inside. Once, when my father still came home every night, still told my mother and me that he loved us, I would not have been able to fit through a space so small, but I was so much thinner, my bones and skin withered to almost nothing, and I moved through the kitchen like water.

The doors to the bedrooms stood open. At the end of the hallway, the extra door, the door that shouldn't be there, stood closed, and I pushed myself toward it. Katrina did not rise when I went past her door but watched me from underneath her blanket, a jagged line of dark hair falling across her cheeks, and turned away from me. It didn't matter what Katrina thought. Not anymore.

The handle was hot against my palm as if someone had touched it only moments before, and I leaned into it, the door swinging open without a sound.

The room was empty except for a large table. Katrina's father had draped a white sheet over the exposed wood and here and there were dark red stains that twisted outward like bulbous eyes and elongated necks, and I thought I could see myself trapped inside those stains. Beneath the sheet, a small form lay still, and I could make out a nose, the slight concave curve where eyes should be.

The floor creaked beneath my feet, but I didn't care who heard me. Katrina was still in her bed. I would have heard her if she rose, felt her moving through the empty space I'd left behind, but there was only the cold whisper of air moving against my legs as the door closed.

"You shouldn't be here," Katrina's father said. He sat in the far corner of the room, and his body bent and stooped toward something on the floor, his hands rising and falling, something metallic glinting from between his fingers. Sewing. He was sewing.

"No," I said, and he looked up at me, his hands pausing in their work, and my skin sang for him, sang for those hands to slip beneath my own flesh and strip it away. Make it beautiful. Make it whole.

He pointed to the table, to that still form, and he looked at me, eyes like an animal, glittering and bright. "I had to. My own daughter, and all I could think of was the way she would feel beneath me, the taste of her breath in my mouth. It made me sick to think," he said, and there were tears on his cheeks and blood on his hands.

"I had to," he said, and his hands pulled back, and I saw the crooked stitches, the skin pieced and pulled together like a quilt.

"A doll," I said and placed a hand on his shoulder. He didn't shrug it away, didn't grimace the same way my father had in those last months when my mother touched him or when I came into the room.

My stomach curved inward, my hip bones protruded like the way they do in magazines when I lifted my shirt, and he watched me pull it over my head, his breath hitching as I did.

"I'm enough. Please. I'm enough."

When he lifted his knife, I leaned into him, and my body was all air, all lightness, and there was only the movement of his hands against my skin and my blood like lace against the floor. "Father," I said, and he lifted the pieces of me and placed them on the table. Beneath the white sheet, the form moved, the chest rising with breath, and I reached for it, reached for the beautiful thing I would become.

When he was finished, he draped the white gauze against my skin like a bridal veil, and he kissed my forehead, his lips feather light and dry like a moth's wing.

I closed the door behind me, left him to his work, placed one foot in front of the other until I stood in Katrina's bedroom. She did not speak but pulled the covers back, and I climbed in next to her.

She curled into me, her arms tight around my abdomen, the raw, exposed meat burning and raw, and brought her lips to my ear. "Sister," she said.

Together, we slept.

In the next room, something new, something beautiful, woke and gasped into the gathering dark.

WISH YOU WERE HERE

NADIA BULKIN

ell us a ghost story," said one of the women, the pouty one, the one named Melissa. She was the nice, friendly one for now, the one asking questions, the one who wanted to stop at every little roadside fruit stall and pose next to every possibly rabid monkey, but Dimas knew this kind of tourist. Eventually, she was going to exhaust herself, and then—fueled by a high metabolism and the vengeance of unmet expectations—she was going to become his worst enemy. That was why he was counting on the other woman, Rose, to keep the group stable when they reached their breaking point, which was probably going to be on Day 3. He could already tell that both Melissa's and Rose's men would be useless.

For now, however, the tour was still in its "honeymoon" phase. Melissa was still excited, leaning out of the seatbelt that Dimas had forced her to buckle; Rose's man Ben's cellphone was still fully charged, and Melissa's man Josh was still full from breakfast, too. Rose was—well, it was hard to tell how she was, sitting in the back row and not having spoken the whole morning except to say that she and her husband had slept "fine." So, Rose was fine.

"A ghost story, eh?" Dimas glanced over at his driver, Nyoman, who shrugged. "Well . . . here's a story. An army unit is sent to a remote village in the middle of the jungle in order to move the villagers to a new settlement that's, uh, less remote. They need the land for an army base. But the villagers have lived there for a hundred years, and even though the government offered to buy the land, many times, they always refused to go. So the army drives up to the village in the middle of the night. They go to the first house on the main road—nobody home. They go to the second house—nobody home there, either. Third house—"

"Nobody home," said Ben.

"Right, nobody home. So the soldiers look at each other and say, where is everyone? Did they evacuate? Why did they leave all their belongings? Then suddenly, they realize one of their men is missing. All that's left . . . is his head. The soldiers panic. They're shooting at shadows, but it doesn't help. One by one, they're all killed by something they can't quite see, until finally, there's only one soldier left, and he's out of bullets. He squats down by a chicken coop, closes his eyes, and prays to Allah as he hears something come out of the darkness. He breaks open the chicken coop and throws a chicken, screaming, 'Take it!' There's a big crunch and so he looks and . . . it's a woman. Except she's got claws on her hands and feet, and her eyes are yellow. She's a tiger-woman. Of course, the soldier starts running back toward the trucks. Except this time, all the houses are full. The villagers are home. And they're eating his comrades."

Dimas laughed uncomfortably. Nyoman shot him an odd look. It was indeed an odd story to tell, one he would never have told two months ago—it involved soldiers dying. But in this new, rapidly-reforming world—this spinning, twisting lump of mud—nothing was off-limits. Or so he'd gathered from the drivers who blasted through Jakarta's red lights, yelling "Reformasi!"

For at least thirty seconds, the tourists said nothing. And then Josh, who had wasted no time telling everyone that he had already been to the island twice and he knew all its "ins" and "outs," said, "That's not really a ghost story, is it?"

Dimas stared over his shoulder at Josh, his plastic work-smile stretched across his mouth like the surgical masks the Japanese tourists liked to wear. "You're right," he said. "It's not."

Josh, clearly uncomfortable, smiled back almost in spite of himself.

Then Rose spoke. "So what happened?" Her voice was flat as the banana leaves slapping the windows of the van. "Did the government leave them alone?"

"Oh, no. The army came back with helicopters and sprayed the village with napalm until everyone left. It's an army base now—"

Without warning, Nyoman swerved violently to the right, unleashing a barrage of screams from the Americans. Dimas jammed his fingers against the window to protect his head. Josh spilled his iced coffee and Ben became very upset about what this traumatic maneuver might have done to the apparently breakable Rose. "Sorry!" Nyoman said, in exaggerated English, and then added, staring meaningfully at Dimas, "Animal ran into the road."

◄◦►

They paid the security guard eighty thousand rupiah each to enter the historic broken temple complex. Last month, it would have been seventy thousand, and four months before, it would have been forty thousand. The security guard kept it close to triple the cost of a bowl of noodles—one for each of his children. The Americans had no idea, and didn't complain. The dollar was monstrously in their favor, after all.

As the five of them trudged toward the ruins—Nyoman stayed in the van, partly to keep it from being stolen and partly because he would rather read the sports page and fantasize about the World Cup—Rose hung back with Dimas and asked, "Do you know a way to contact the dead?"

Dimas tried not to cringe as he squinted at her. She was hard to read behind those giant sunglasses. "Why, ma'am?"

"My son died in a . . . car accident," she whispered. "I just want to know he's all right."

Gatot, who ran the travel agency from a tiny office in Kuta, said that he had never before seen so many fever-dreaming grief tourists as were sleep-walking through Bali today. Most had lost parents or siblings, through plane crashes or cancer. They were good for business, because even the ones that didn't buy extensive reality-delaying package tours, like Rose's group, bought souvenirs and memorabilia and other *things* that they could wrap up and keep safe and take home with them, unlike the people they had lost. *It's because they think we're dying too,* Gatot said, and then defiantly snuffed out his cigarette on his own desk. *We'll just see who dies first.*

"He's all right, ma'am. For sure, he's all right."

"But how do you know?" A mosquito landed on her arm and deliberately sucked her blood. "I read about something that you have here. Jelangkung. Am I saying that right?"

He shook his head, watching her blood travel from flesh to insect belly. He had played with jelangkung. Ani's grandmother had showed them how, tying half a coconut shell to a pair of criss-crossed, rag-draped wooden sticks. *Give the ghost some respect*, her grandmother explained. *At least give it a head.* He also knew that a tourist would not have found that game unless actively searching for "ways to contact the dead." "Bad idea, ma'am."

"I thought we were supposed to get the full experience," Rose said. She had stopped walking, forcing him to pause as well, and by the way she was throwing out her arms, jangling her wooden bracelets, she was frustrated. "I thought anything was on the menu. That's what we paid for, isn't it? No-holds-barred, all-inclusive, complete-access bullshit. Right?"

He suddenly became conscious of a pain in his palms where his nails were digging. "Ma'am, jelangkung isn't like a person-to-person telephone call. It's like taking a megaphone and yelling, *hey, spirits, come find me.* Maybe your son answers. Maybe someone else. Maybe it's not like this in America, but over here, it's very, very crowded on the other side."

Rose took a deep breath in preparation for another rant, then apparently changed her mind and went hurrying up the hill with a new and soldierly determination. Dimas followed, trying to stop himself from shaking his head. At the crest, they looked out upon the broken temple complex, scattered across the bright green like a giant child's failed attempt to build a block tower. Dimas searched his pockets for his notes, because he didn't know anything about any of this. As a Javanese, all he knew about this island and its people was how good they were at cultivating an exoticism—just wild enough without being savage, *the rest of us can handle savage*—for Australians to fawn over. At the bottom, Melissa was waving enthusiastically.

Ben shouted something at Rose. He was pointing at one of the little half-fallen candi stupas. He was no bigger than a hand. On the hill, his wife was looking elsewhere, at the line of enormous trees that had been continuously beaten back by skidders and diggers, and before that, fires and saws. With his pulse pounding after the hike up the hill and Rose's demand and the thought of Ani's grandmother and the jelangkung, the trees seemed to be trembling. Ben didn't know that his wife wasn't watching, and he moved toward the stupa in large, grandiose steps, like an astronaut walking on the moon. Dimas was about to yell at him not to walk carelessly on the stupa when Ben suddenly slipped from view with a yelp that roused birds from the trees.

◄◦►

"Tell me a ghost story." Ben hadn't spoken since he was told that he'd be bedridden with a broken leg for the next two months, and Melissa and Josh had to leave because they started arguing over the merits of alternative medicine, and Rose announced that she was taking a walk to get some sweet polluted air. "Ghosts this time, no monsters."

The quiet, pretty nurse adjusting Ben's IV widened her eyes and smiled. In the next bed over, behind a thick green curtain, a wheezing patient stirred in their bed.

"All right," said Dimas, who tried to focus on summoning his pity for Ben. "A boy moves to a new city to go to university. He thinks he's very lucky because he rents a room in a house that's quite close-by, just two street blocks away. The most direct route to his house is down a wide stretch of street that—for some reason—never seems to be very crowded. The buildings on either side are either abandoned or under construction. Taxis and becak don't use the road. It's very strange, he thinks. He walks down the path a couple times, in daytime, and doesn't see anything peculiar. But most of the time, he tries to avoid it just like everyone else.

"So one night he's at the university very late, because he has exams and he's trying to study and the electricity goes on and off at his house. Finally, he packs his things when he can't stay awake anymore and as he leaves campus, decides that he can't be bothered to take the long way around to his house. He takes the direct route. The first thing he notices is that a strange fog is just sitting in the street, like a landed cloud. The second thing he notices is that there's a figure in the fog ahead of him: a crying bloody man, in rags. The boy has enough sense to know this isn't good, so he tries to swerve around the man, except the man then appears again, right in front of him, weeping *Help Me*. The boy doesn't say anything and picks up his pace and feels someone grab him from behind—it's a woman this time, with her eye gouged out, saying, *It Hurts*. The boy pushes her off and runs straight into a body that doesn't even have a head, just arms reaching out to take hold of him. Eventually he just begins to pray as he runs and eventually the ghosts stop coming so close and he's able to run the rest of the way home. When he gets home he asks his old landlord, who's smoking a cigarette on the porch, what that street is. The landlord says, 'Oh, that's where they killed communists in this city, in

1965. They dumped the bodies in the gutter. Tell me, boy, what did they say to you?' And the boy says, 'Well, I think they were asking me for help.' And so the landlord leans forward and says, 'They'll need it in hell.'"

It wasn't a very good story, but Dimas didn't know how else to finish it. He had heard iterations of the story from several friends of friends over the years, always about a neighborhood that no one seemed to know of, and that cold razor-wire line had always been the ending.

Ben didn't care because he was asleep from all the pain medication he'd requested, but the nurse was staring at Dimas incredulously. "There's a road like that where I'm from too," she whispered. "But why would you go and tell *him*? *He* doesn't understand what it was like."

Neither she nor Dimas would have been old enough to have any real memory of 1965, but she wasn't talking about that. She was talking about institutional, *genetic* knowledge—the amorphous plasma that stitched acquired data together into one cohesive, rational narrative. "He wanted a ghost story," Dimas said with a shrug. "That one has a lot of them."

Half an hour later, the Americans reconvened for a team meeting in Ben's room. Ben was still unconscious, and they didn't want to disturb him, they said, but apparently they needed his body to be their non-voting witness. Rose sat down near the bed and silently held Ben's hand, and Dimas started to excuse himself. But she stopped him, with a set of cool fingers pressed persistently to the spot where his pulse hit his wrist. "We've decided to go on with the tour," she said. Her voice was utterly without affect. Behind her, Melissa and Josh were uncomfortably squirming, sucking mango soda from straws. "Where do you think we should go next?"

◄◦►

Dimas purposefully sat at the end of a row of folding chairs—provided a quick exit, if needed, and allowed the three Americans to hopefully talk amongst themselves—and thanked God that Melissa, not Rose, demanded to sit next to him so she could ask him as many questions as possible about a dance he knew nothing about. But he had his notes, so he tried to explain to her the story of the stolen princess, her avenging husband, and the demon-king. Oh, and the warrior monkeys, which made Melissa's eyes gleam. Every so often Josh would interject, mostly to show that he could. Meanwhile, he could feel Rose staring coldly at him through both of her friends.

"Take a picture of us," Melissa said, slipping her little black camera into Dimas's hands and then leaning back into Josh. "Rose! Are you in the picture?"

Rose had to lean forward to get into view. Her look, naked in its resentment, was so awful that Dimas didn't even wait for Melissa to say *Bali Hai* before snapping the picture. He gave Melissa a thumbs up. His plastic smile was starting to ache.

After the kecak performance started, the audience of foreigners and wealthy natives—all from Jakarta, of course, no locals—prepared their cameras. As one chanticleer led a call-and-response around a fiery torch, the hundred male performers sitting in concentric rings on the ground shook as if inhabited by the splintered spirit of a cackling gecko god, arms outstretched and fingers frantically twitching. Dimas wondered how it felt, pretending to be possessed every sundown. He imagined them on their smoking break, sneering at tourists while they argued over where to buy shabu.

The fire leapt as Australian winds brought the night in, and the heavily made-up princess, legs wrapped so tightly that she seemed to have the lower body of a goldfish, began to skulk amongst the men. Ani had died in a fire. At least he assumed so, based on the charred remains of her family's convenience store. He told her to leave. He'd even told her to leave the city, the day after the students were shot in the street. But she dawdled. Froze. As if she wanted it to end this way. Ani did talk fatalistically about the fate of the nation, after the IMF deal was made and parliament re-elected the general for the seventh time. "Nothing ever changes," she said, but then they suddenly, violently did. Fiery beams fell between them and smoke filled his lungs and he couldn't wait any longer. What was he supposed to do? And why did she have to raise her eyes and look at him just before he turned his face toward his jacket, as if finally waking up from a deep sleep? Down in his gullet, amidst the muddy guilt and the true deep sadness that Allah knew he felt for the loss of Ani's life, lived the deep-seated fear that Ani's last moments on earth were drowned in the sort of bitterness that left a permanent stain.

Something was shaking beside him. He looked first at the dancers—the demon-king had emerged from behind a brick wall and caught sight of the princess, eyes on fire—and then at Melissa, who was the source of the tremors. Dimas thought at first that she was shivering, but when he saw her chin warbling and her eyes rolling back into the gulf of her skull and a small trail of saliva running down her chin, he knew this was worse. Then she slipped off her chair, falling onto a group of French tourists in the next row.

For a spare second in the desperate, dark moment that followed—Josh trying to control his seizing wife, Rose screaming at everyone to give the woman space, and the other tourists and all the dancers paying them no mind at all, *cak-kecak-kecak-kecak*, creating the unnerving sensation that the four of them had somehow fallen through a trap door past their waking world and into the next—Melissa's blue eyes focused. Those eyes looked at Dimas, and Rose, and maybe Josh as well, and it was not Melissa looking out. No, it was not. Their ears plugged, like passengers of a falling airplane, and then they were alone with it.

But ten seconds later, her eyes had rolled back again. The world righted itself, and now there was a German doctor on holiday holding up two fingers, and a woman in a hijab offering a dripping bottle of water with an unbroken seal, and a possum-eyed kecak dancer leaning down and asking, "She's on drugs, yeah?"

◂◦▸

"Tell another ghost story," said Josh. "The scariest one you know."

Melissa put her head in her hands and whined, "I'm tired of ghost stories." But Josh didn't even look at her, and Rose just pushed a glass of ice water in her direction, telling her she should stay hydrated. Melissa pushed it back so forcefully that Dimas reached his hand out to catch it. "Jesus Christ, Rose," she snapped. "I'm not your kid."

Rose looked at her sourly.

Josh took another tortured sip of Bintang beer and raised his eyebrows at Dimas. "Well? You got one that'll make me shit my pants or what?"

"I have a story," said Dimas. Melissa started making a strange animal noise, between a growl and a whinny. Before Ani died, she used to say that she would haunt him if one of his stupid adventures got her killed—they were never all that dangerous, just rope bridges and speeding motorbikes and haunted hallways, but they liked to play pretend. And Ani would lean in and say *"If I don't make it, I'll come back to get you."* Melissa, who was supposedly all better now, sat like a limp doll on the bench beside him, her jaw slightly slack as she stared ahead into the street, at the humming mass of travelers moving slowly in the half-light.

"A pregnant woman," Dimas started, then took a deep breath and began again. "A pregnant woman is tossing and turning in her bedroom in the middle of the night. She's been sick. She doesn't know what time it is, just that it's dark and she should be sleeping. But the lights to the living room are still on, and her mother-in-law asks her through the door if she's hungry. 'No thank you,' she says. What about some water? No, she doesn't want water either. How is she feeling, is she cold? And the pregnant woman finally says, loudly this time, 'I don't need anything!' So then her husband comes in the room, and wants to know who she's shouting at. Because his mother's not due to arrive until the next morning. So now the woman knows that she's being chased by a kuntilanak. That's the name of the ghost. Everyone here knows what it is. She's the ghost of a woman who died in childbirth and is searching for babies and blood in the afterlife."

A group of sunburned, middle-aged Australians burst out laughing, or crying, next to them—hard to tell which. They had their own tragedies. Their own demons to run from. Dimas looked back at his own cohort, but only Rose met his gaze. Melissa was humming along to "Hotel California," which had started playing over the Club Lizard speaker system for the sixth time that night. Josh was finally looking at Melissa, scorn mixed with longing.

"So the woman gets a pair of scissors from the bathroom and goes back to bed with the scissors clenched in her hand. She goes to sleep. It's still dark when she wakes up again, and there's a shape leaning down over her. And because she's a brave woman, she stabs it, right where she's supposed to—in the back of the head. The creature falls and she turns on the light and realizes it's her husband. And not only has she killed him . . . her beloved, the father of her child . . . but now she's alone with the kuntilanak."

Rose stared at him in hurt and shock. Out of the corner of his eye, he saw that Melissa had struck up a conversation with a man in snakeskin sitting next to her—he didn't seem to be part of the Australian group. "I'm sorry," Dimas whispered. "I don't know why I picked that story."

"I have an idea for a scary story," said Josh, "How about if you talk about what's going to happen to this country once it splits into twenty-seven pieces? How about that? What happens when all these fucking people . . ." He waved his beer around, even though two-thirds of the people in Club Lizard were tourists, ". . . realize that they don't have to worry about the military reining them in anymore? Why don't you give us a prediction for how fast things are going to burn down once the inmates are running the asylum?"

Dimas wondered if Josh had perhaps forgotten that he could speak English. He thought of Gatot's defiance—*We'll just see who dies first*—and forced himself to smile at Josh. He could see Melissa getting up and walking away with her new friend. Rose sitting in the dark, slowly opening and closing a pair of scissors. Ben eaten alive by mosquitoes in the hospital. And he saw himself in his sordid and bloody hometown, running through empty streets toward what used to be Chinatown, toward the burning building where he knew Ani would be waiting.

"Hopefully, by the time the world ends, you'll be gone," he told Josh, who didn't respond because he'd just now realized that the woman he'd walked through customs with, walked down the aisle with, was slipping quietly away into slippery anonymity. Fallen down a crevasse in the known world. It happens all the time.

⟨∘⟩

No one knew what dim, damp alley Melissa had disappeared into, and Josh was too angry to care. "Fuck her," he said, "She does this all the time. Remember Rio? She'll come back when she runs out of cash, the bitch." He kicked at a stop sign, covered in missing persons flyers for tourists who had largely lost themselves at will. *We Love You We Miss You Please Come Home.*

As they ambled back to the hotel, Rose tried again. "Please help me talk to my son," she begged. "I know you can. I know you know how."

Dimas glanced at her, and thought he saw something scuttle in the gutter behind her, something that cast an uneven, shuddering shadow on the heavily graffitied wall. "Bad idea, ma'am," he said again, staring at the glittering sidewalk—coated with dew and vomit. "I told you."

"He died so fast," Rose said. "Ben was driving. County road. We were coming back from a baseball game. Something happened, I don't . . ." She stared at a glowing red sun sign ahead of them for Bounty Discotheque. "There was something in the road. They said he didn't suffer, but . . . I didn't have a chance to say goodbye. I'm sure he's scared. He was such a little scaredy-cat."

Dimas spun around, cutting her off. "Mr. Josh!" His voice came out sounding very weak, very raw. The one thing Gatot always pressed, beyond comfort and satisfaction and legality, was liability: *keep your group together.*

He had been thoroughly scarred by a recent incident in which an Australian dive boat had left two divers behind to be eaten by sharks at the Great Barrier Reef. And here Dimas had already lost Melissa. "Mr. Josh, I think we should hurry back to the hotel!"

But Josh had stopped near a clump of skinny teenagers huddled on the stoop of a shuttered scuba store. He had his wallet out and was very conspicuously taking out stacks of weathered rupiah. "Blo'on," Dimas whispered, but didn't step in. Why risk it? He wasn't going to end up in Hotel Kerobokan for anyone, especially not a fucking tourist. He counted to ten, trying to still his nerves and the sense that something besides motorcycle exhaust and patchouli was swirling around them, until Josh stuffed a little plastic baggie into his back pocket and sullenly resumed walking.

"He could never sleep in the dark," said Rose. "But neither can I. Shapes look different . . ."

A local call girl in garish theater make-up stumbled out of Bounty, followed by an anxious-looking man three times her age. "Melissa!" Josh screamed at the call girl, who looked over her shoulder at him and sneered. "*Go home you wanker,*" her companion shouted. Josh slapped his hand on the hood of a nearby car—thank God, no alarm—and shouted back, "Come make me!"

It was a bad idea from the start. Cops were never very far from Bounty, and these days they—like everyone else in the country—were teetering on a knife's edge. Too many stories about docile village mobs decapitating bus drivers who ran over small children could make a policeman twitchy. Even the Dayaks, supposedly beaten into submission decades ago, had come out of the jungle and set logging equipment on fire. *Ya Allah!* What's a cop to do? Couldn't trust anybody anymore—not even two drunk Westerners who would have been sent home to their hotels in the good old days. The British man and the call girl eventually teetered away down Jalan Legian, but when the cops found ecstasy in Josh's pocket, that was it. Some chlorine-stained kids in sporty beachwear came out of Bounty to point and laugh, but Dimas hurried Rose away to the growling sound of what Dimas could only hope was thunder rolling down from the highlands.

◄•►

"Tell me a ghost story. A real one, this time."

He wanted to tell her that they had all been real, or might as well have been. He could have told a thousand other anecdotes, about mysterious lights and strange coincidences and unexplained illnesses and visions of dead passengers seen by only half the bus—but they had wanted *stories*, hadn't they? Stories with a set-up and an escalation and a terrible, brutal denouement.

"This is the last one," he said, and meant that, because there was a more than decent possibility that he would not make it to the final Day 5. He had seen another humanoid shadow while brushing his teeth the night before, and then found the window to his third-floor apartment open and the drapes dancing, and he knew they were being hunted. Correction: *he* was being hunted, and Allah had sent ghost-seeker Rose to Gatot's Tropical Adventure Tours in order to let him know that it was time for him to buck up and stop running from his fate, soldier.

Dimas was driving this time. He'd told Nyoman where they were going— the huge, unfinished Bali Grand Hotel—and Nyoman had laughed in his face and demanded double a day's pay to make the drive, which Dimas didn't feel like asking Rose about. Rose was cradling the hodgepodge shopping bag of a jelangkung's component parts—two broomsticks, half-a-coconut, permanent marker, incense, twine, a Superman shirt because her son's favorite character was Superman, paper stolen from the hotel room—on her lap as if they were the very bones of her child.

"My friend, my best friend, died in a fire. Along with her father and grandmother. Some people . . ." He shook his head. What to call them? Psychopaths, murderers? He'd run the streets alongside them, silent while they yelled. "Some very angry people set fire to their store. I was in there with them, trying to convince them to leave the city because I could see it coming—not the fire, of course, or the riots. But once the fires started, I knew what would be burned." His lip quivered. "I got out. Because I didn't wait. I was scared, you know. I thought I was going to die. I convinced myself that she'd follow, if she saw me running. I thought she'd make it out. I stood outside the building for ten minutes, I think, waiting for her. And . . ."

"And she didn't make it."

He glanced back at Rose through the rear view mirror. "She didn't make it. And ever since, I've been afraid of seeing her. Around campus. On the street. Even in a room full of people, I can't look at faces too closely. Because I left her, you see. Because that sort of betrayal leaves a . . . a *mark* in the world. Like a cigarette burn. I got so scared that I couldn't leave my house, but even then, I could feel *someone* sitting on the couch and just looking at me. That's why I decided to leave Jakarta. Just being near those buildings, I couldn't . . . I could feel her spirit. Her energy."

There was a small white mass in the road ahead that he realized in a few moments was a goat. He slowed to a stop, hoping the engine roar would scare it into moving, but its milky eyes barely registered the vehicle. Sighing, he kept his foot on the brake. He contemplated telling her that after a few lonely months, Ani had apparently found him again—bringing with her the shadows, the whispers, the cold sensation of being under someone's eye, the hazy cloud of a spirit's hug, the sick-in-the-gut *feeling* of hovering by a bungee cord over the gaping maw of the great unseen world—but when he opened his mouth, he was too afraid to say the words out loud.

Rose's voice had softened when she spoke next. "I know what that's like."

"After your son died?"

"Even before that. It got stronger after Connor died, but . . . I'd felt it for a long time. A *presence*. That feeling like even when you're alone in a locked room, you're never alone." Then she chuckled and wiped a tear out of the corner of her eye. "Ben always called it my guardian angel. I think he was just trying to make me feel better. But I've been thinking that maybe he's right. Who's to say it's not a guardian angel? Who's to say your friend's angry at you? Maybe she's just watching over you."

The goat's minder, an old man with a long beard, came out of the bushes and pushed the goat along with a few swats of a small stick. The old man flashed a black-toothed smile at their van—no, not quite at the guilt-eaten man at the wheel nor the mournful woman in the backseat, but at something just behind them, something that must have been beautiful.

"*I'd* be angry," was all Dimas said.

◄◦►

The Bali Grand would have been horrific, had it been allowed to live. It was gaudy, too heavy and too white and far too marbled for the gentle green hills it was nestled in. The general's son had signed off on the final design after an extended stay at the casino-hotels of Las Vegas. Thankfully, the project ran out of money during the financial crisis, leaving the hotel unfinished with its very bones exposed, like the broken-open jaws of a long-dead giant. Rumor was that the general's son still lurked somewhere amongst the pillars and arches, but that was bullshit. Everyone knew he was hiding in Europe, in a premium suite of a hotel he hadn't designed.

The Bali Grand was still horrific now, but for different reasons—under the flapping tarps and abandoned construction equipment it was undoubtedly haunted, if not by dead workers then by the ghosts of offshore private loans and weakly-regulated banks.

Dimas and Rose went to the partially-constructed lobby, where tile floors had been laid and a patchwork roof had been erected, to build their conduit. The jelangkung. Then they leaned the doll against the wall to watch them eat their martabak and wait for night to fall.

Nothing happened the last time Dimas played this game, with Ani and a couple other jokers at school. No one had been expecting anything, of course—they were just bored and trying to take their minds off exams. They gave the coconut-shell a googly face and asked the oxygen molecules and cigarette smoke whether they would pass their tests. Nothing tuned into their antenna. But this time, as Dimas led Rose in a shaky overture to the spirit world—*we're having a little party*—he felt that he was practically inviting Ani—whatever was left of Ani—to come forward.

Dimas saw Rose holding the wooden creature, turning the broomstick body gently in her hands like one of those hunchbacked beach-women who traverse the littered coastline hawking umbrellas and massages and temporary tattoos, and closed his eyes. Imagined the peace of the sea. He only opened them after he felt the pressure in the room plummet, as if an anchor had dragged him and Rose and the Bali Grand Hotel ten meters below the surface. With tensed muscles and an aching top row of teeth, he expected to see Ani levitating above the jelangkung, with peeling skin and denouncing eyes. But though the darkness had grown touchably thick beyond their struggling candlelight, he saw nothing. Just Rose . . . gagging on something lodged in her throat.

"Miss Rose? Are you all right?"

Rose was not fine. At that moment Rose was a broken vase, and someone—something—that wasn't Rose came spilling out of her like a gush of tar and slithered across the floor. No, not Rose. Also not Ani. And he was willing to bet the value of Rose's all-inclusive tour package that no matter how badly Rose wanted it to be, that it wasn't Rose's little boy Connor either.

The oily shadow crawled across the floor, wrapped itself around the jelangkung, and held it upright when Rose's grasp failed. It drenched the Superman shirt and twirled the permanent marker dangling from one broomstick arm. Rose whispered, "Connor? Sweetie, is that you?"

The jelangkung was supposed to tip and use the pen to mark a Yes or a No on the paper. It did lean in, at first—and then it started shaking. Violently. It was almost like a headshake, *NO NO NO*, but then with a terrifying bang and a howl from the ends of the earth, the wooden body flew apart. One broomstick nearly hit Dimas in the temple, and a shredded piece of the Superman shirt landed in Rose's lap. Like a taunt. Meanwhile, the shadow spread. Covered the ceiling beams and dripped down the unpainted walls. Occasionally, its edges would curl together and form the shape of a man or a cow or a tiger—*shapes look different*, wasn't that what Rose said?—and then it would flatten out and seep to another corner of the room. Though it had hitched a ride with Rose, this shadow didn't know sadness. It was more primitive than that: it was just hungry. It lay so oppressive on their fragile human souls simply because it wasn't human, and never had been.

By then, Dimas had slid over to Rose so he could quietly urge her to say goodbye, to end the ritual. She was feverishly muttering something—about Connor, and a number of other things Dimas couldn't identify—and he had to lean in close: "Miss Rose, you have to close the door."

This only made her whisper more frantically, clenching the Superman rag to her chest.

"Miss Rose, close the door so we can drive away. We can go to Kuta. See your husband . . ."

"Can't leave it . . ." Did she mean *the presence*? "I can't leave."

Every human cell in his body wanted to leave, because it knew this feeling and wanted to survive. This thing had come to this country wrapped around Rose's skeleton—it wouldn't have chased him. He'd have gotten away. Yet he helplessly sank to his knees as if his feet were lodged in mud. Ani's legacy, he supposed. Because that was when he finally felt her outside of her normal Jakartan habitat: the same electric seizure he'd feel when pedaling past her blackened building or the empty, tortured malls where they used to fantasize about a Someday Life of large televisions and luxury brands. He imagined her putting her arms around him, pulling him down, saying, *Stay.* Not meanly, not hatefully. But honestly. *Keep your eyes open this time, scaredy-cat. Here it comes.*

‹o›

A red-and-black centipede crawled across Dimas's hand, down into the dark concrete valley, and then onto the denim of Rose's jeans. Dimas, who'd woken up to the sound of rain, nudged her; Rose didn't react. He could feel the chill emanating from her body. He shifted to get a better look at her and confirmed the sick feeling in his stomach. She was dead. Eyes open, jaw slightly slack. Heart attack? Theft of the soul? He didn't want to touch her, but knew if he didn't close her eyes now then she would definitely roam the earth forever.

Very cautiously, he crossed the empty expanse of the hotel lobby, watching for shadows or drops in atmospheric pressure or noises of any kind. Nothing but the rain gave him goosebumps. He ran to the van, not bothering to shield his head.

He told the first cops he could find, two boys who probably should have been guarding a mall in Denpasar. For some reason—conditioning?—they believed his story, and promised to go up to the Bali Grand just as soon as the rain cleared up. Then Dimas drove back to Kuta. He thought about checking on Ben at the hospital, or Josh at the prison, but decided not to do either, not yet. He didn't even know where he'd find Melissa, if he'd find Melissa—probably in the Crime & Punishment section of the Bali Post. So instead he went to see Freddy, a tattoo artist who specialized in painting visions of the bug-eyed, toothy Barong, the good spirit-king.

Freddy welcomed him in and sat him down in front of the television. On the table were video cases of Freddy's favorite horror movies: a plastic mess of red eyes and long black hair and frightened, stupid teens. Dimas thought of *The Forgotten*—the legendary ghost story that the censorship board locked up years ago on account of being cursed. Rumor had it that a real ghost had been caught on camera during filming, and that a critic had died of a heart attack during an early screening at Pondok Indah Mall. He didn't remember what it was about anymore—something about a dead witch, and a secret room. *Tell me a ghost story.*

"Hey, did you ever track down *The Forgotten*? You know, the cursed movie?"

Freddy laughed. "Why? You want to watch it? I did find it, my friend. But it was nothing special. Turns out it was banned because the movie didn't have any kiai come in to beat up the evil spirit by the grace of Allah." He handed

Dimas a bowl of cup noodles. "Can you believe it? So stupid. But at least we can watch all the shitty movies we want now, after Reformasi."

Dimas wasn't convinced that the little vice president currently on television would change the rules of the censorship board, but he had been wrong before. Right now, the little vice president was forbidding the sort of language that had gotten Ani killed for being Chinese, for not being a true daughter of the land—so there was that. Freddy sat down on the couch with his own cup noodles and switched to the jittery black of channel 4, where a movie was already playing. A lady-ghost in a white shift was moving without weight through a foggy cemetery. If it started with her, it would end with her. She'd been terribly wronged. She'd be avenged.

"I think I did something terrible," Dimas said.

Freddy sighed. "You need to forgive yourself, 'Mas. She's not going to come all the way back here just to forgive you. She has better things to do now, right? She's at peace. Let her go."

A stray memory flickered, of Ani snorting iced tea out her nose at something he'd said about a teacher. "I don't mean that . . ."

"So what now? You left a tourist somewhere?"

"I think I let something loose. Something they were carrying with them."

"What, like heroin?"

"No, something worse." He imagined the shadow loping through the forest, flying among the bodiless leyak, feasting upon the grievers and the guilty and the human guides who so delicately threaded the needle-eye balance—a spirit-monster out of its ecosystem, devouring all in its path like a bulldozer on autopilot. "I'm so sorry. I never should have come to Bali."

He felt Freddy slowly turn to look at him as an uncomfortable, unmistakable tension started to clog up the room. On television, the ghost swept aside her long black hair to reveal a gaping, pulsing wound. Rotten and squirming and infested and yet, somehow, very much alive.

RAGMAN

REBECCA LLOYD

D ad left sometime in the early morning before the rest of us had woken up. We all knew it'd have to be me who tried to make him come home again. He'd done it before a few years back; stayed in The Rec. Yard office for the good part of two months before it got so cold he was forced to leave. But this time, it was May and the air was warm and scented, with new grasses and nettles coming up along the edges of the roads, and the dandelions brilliant yellow.

"So what if he holes up for months? He can't do any harm and he'll come home when he's had enough like he did last time," Rob told us slowly, as if we were children.

"You don't know what he's been like recently," Mum said, "you don't have to watch him wandering about and whispering to himself all the time. He's got kerosene in that office, Rob, and the place is heaving with old ledger books. I'm scared he'll burn himself to death. See if you can persuade him to start throwing some of the old paperwork away, Katherine. He might just do it if you talk to him carefully."

My plan was to sleep on one of the canvas army beds in the War Shed. Besides watching over Dad, I reckoned I could keep myself busy during the day putting prices on all the unmarked bric-a-brac, and trying to create some sense of order in the place. When we were kids, Rob and I played all day at

The Yard in the summer holidays; everything there was exciting and exotic, but Dad's objects had their special places then. He had a room for Victorian front doors, an area for cast iron drain pipes and heavy duty angle iron, a shed for baths with clawed feet—there was a great jumble of taps in there, and some fancy sinks, some of which looked like giant shells. Right at the back of the plot he'd made a sign for the dark green corrugated shed with the dented roof. It read "Salvage and Dreams from the Sea." He had anchors and ships' figureheads in there, ancient iron lobster pots, and a wooden mermaid with a startled face that Rob and I used to call Harriet. That was one of the sheds I could stay in for hours when I was little. I loved to go through the old postcards Dad kept in a wicker basket next to Harriet, and try to imagine the people who wrote them so neatly and formally, and what their lives must have been like in that old world of carpet beaters and moths. I remember one in particular, a postcard of a country cottage in a garden full of flowers, and someone had written, "My Darling Rosina, I have come to the end; this will be the last time I write. Do not think about me more, for I am gone." That used to make me shiver, but I didn't know why.

In the best of the outhouses, the one that never leaked when it rained, Dad kept Victorian bric-a-brac—toby jugs, tea sets, porcelain ballerinas, and all manner of china dogs and horses, and early over-eager souvenirs from creepy seaside towns. And we had a kitchen shed where we could find all sizes of copper and brass saucepans, and beautiful cutlery with yellowing bone handles, and high up on a top shelf out of our reach, rows of elegant dusty wine glasses. As the years went by, The Yard became more and more disordered and chaotic. Dad swore he'd never leave the garden ornaments out to go rusty, that he'd tuck them in behind the stained glass where they'd stay dry. But these days the herds of miniature iron cows are uniformly rust-coloured, and close by, the old watering cans and pitch forks from Blethick House are corroding in the weather.

There were a couple of places in The Yard I did not like to go at all when I was a kid because they filled me with a strange mixture of bewilderment and dread, and when I grew older, I felt exactly the same way. "It's all the eyes," Rob used to whisper when he knew I was feeling vulnerable, "you never know which of those toys is watching you."

I hate my brother.

Of all the weird objects my father collected in the early days, the things in the Toy House—the china dolls with glistening black eyes and fancy dresses, the ancient faded teddy bears, the mechanical tin soldiers—made me uneasy. My mother had once taken me to a small and stinking flat whose occupants took care of stray cats and there must have been upwards of forty of them living there. It was where we got Bluey from when the mice at The Rec. Yard started eating through the upholstery in the Chair Room. As we walked into the flat, everything was silent; I could just about still hear traffic on the road outside, and the whinging song of an ice cream van somewhere in the distance, but as Mum and I tried to choose the cat we wanted, the foetid atmosphere got to me until I was close to fainting. I can remember the cats gazing at us relentlessly, and the unbearable stench of the place. After that, I never could stand the thought of watching eyes.

When we got back with Bluey, I made the mistake of telling my brother how horrible the flat had been. "You can't even walk to school without finding something that frightens you, so it's not surprising, Katie," he remarked.

"Leave her be," Mum said, but in a way that made me suspect she agreed with him, "there's nothing wrong with being sensitive."

"There is when you think a dead leaf is a mouse, or a piece of tangled thread is a spider, or a sheet on the washing line is a ghost."

"Bloody liar," I shouted, "I never said I thought it was a ghost, I said it looked like one."

"You said it was writhing about in a weird way, and the wind couldn't possibly make it do that," Rob reminded me.

The other place I felt uncomfortable in was just beyond the wrought iron gate section, in a funny Tudor building that had probably been the first thing built on the land. It looked to us like a little schoolhouse or a teahouse, but the local library had no information about it, so we never have found out what it was for originally. It's big inside and it's where Dad keeps all his mirrors, hundreds of them. He claims that some of the more ornate ones with fruit and angels carved into the frames came from a hotel in Albania that had once been a castle belonging to King Zog the first. He used to say that the royal family fled into exile in 1939 when the Italians invaded Albania, but a curse was put on the huge stone castle so that anyone who occupied it after the royal family left would suffer bad luck. Rob and I asked Dad what did happen to the people who went to live there, but he only laughed and waved us away. Rob used to say that King Zog was an obviously made up name. One of the things about Dad in those days was that he was good at telling tales that seemed to exactly fit the mood you were in and because I was a funny morbid child, he told me some really strange stories as we sat in his office on rainy days.

⊷

Dad wasn't pleased to see me pull up in front of the Rec. Yard office; I could see him scowling at me even through the smeared dust on the window. He'd become so irascible lately that I knew I had to stay in my car for a good ten minutes before walking in to see him, otherwise there was every chance he'd shout at me. "It's his dementia," Mum mouthed at me, when I asked her why her arm was bruised. "He picks things up, stares at them for a while, and then throws them at me," she explained. "I've learnt to duck."

I could see him sitting perfectly still in his tiny office, almost as if he'd turned into one of the weird 1930s manikins he collected, and when I did finally walk in, the place stank of kerosene because, as Mum said he would, he'd set up and lit his latest Beatrice 33. He had a kettle on top of it, and some milk and tea on his desk, and against one wall he'd arranged a camp bed with an old duvet and a dusty cushion.

"I knew it would be you that got sent to spy on me," he said, "and I'm glad. You're the least aggravating. But you've got to keep busy otherwise I don't want you here."

"Yes, Dad."

"And don't go shifting things about so I don't know where they are."

"I wasn't going to move anything, just put prices on some things. Have we had any visitors today?"

"One tramp and his dog, the tramp spat and the dog piddled, but they've gone now. And don't go shifting things about so I don't know where they are. If I put a mermaid in one of the baths, it's because I want it there."

"I know that, I won't interfere with your stuff, I promise."

"What are you going to do here then?"

"Put some prices on the bric-a-brac, I thought."

"You camping out, or going home at night?"

"Staying here with you, Dad."

"Where—in the Mirror Hall?" He laughed of course, but I didn't rise to it.

"In the War Shed with Fred the Dead."

"And what are you going to do in the daytime?"

"Price up the bric-a-brac, Dad. It'd be easier to sell if people can see a price."

"Tell you what you can do before you start that, find the old hunting rifles and muskets and bring them in here."

"You want to clean them?"

"I want to use them, Katie. On trespassers like your mother."

"Look, Dad, all Mum said was that she thought it was time to give The Yard up. Have you any idea how much this land must worth now?"

"All the tea in China, I expect. And by the way, there are some tea chests behind the stained glass with old linen and lace in them, tablecloths and so on. Could you sort through that lot for me? Take anything that's disintegrating and give it to Ragman if it's good enough for him. Don't ask him what he thinks though; he's getting fussy these days."

"After that, do you want me to help you tidy up in here, Dad; there's paper everywhere."

Dad stared up at me and I watched the new slyness Mum had warned me about ripple across his features. "Then when you've sorted through the tea chests, go with Ragman to the Mirror Hall and dust all the mirrors, I haven't sold one for years and I'm wondering if dust puts people off."

I know my face changed rapidly and that Dad saw my alarm. "Surely there are more useful things I can do than that, aren't there?" I asked him.

"And while you're in the Mirror Hall can you wax some of the wooden frames. It'd make a nice smell in there. It's always been fusty-smelling, like mice had died in the corners with their tongues out." I shivered, and Dad noticed that too. "Come closer to Beatrice, you look perished," he said.

"When I was a child, that hall . . ."

"I remember; you didn't like the stories I told you in there."

"I didn't like the place itself and I still don't. I thought you knew that."

Dad laughed. "Yes I do know, but remember how you hated the Force Flakes Cloth Man because his feet looked weird, and you kept dropping him out of your bedroom window, until Mum took him away and burnt him. That was the kind of kid you were, very particular. And didn't you get spooked by sheets on the washing line; that was you, wasn't it?"

"I love you Dad. Why don't you come home this evening?" I asked. "I could get Mum to cook one of her fish pies. I could phone her now."

"Ah, and could you sort through all those coloured 1960s telephones, Katie, and put some on display? People have taken a fancy them lately. But don't go shifting things about so I don't know where they are."

Outside it had begun to rain. I clenched my fists in my coat pockets, and stared hard at my father. For the past forty years, he'd collected what he called "stuff." I think in some way he felt like the guardian of the passing of time. In fact, it was as if he was confronting the idea of time itself; as if he felt compelled to preserve all the physical trappings of history so they did not disappear from our sight.

—◦—

My first night in The Yard was pretty good. I'd gone out in my car to bring Dad and me fish and chips in the early evening, and he began to be less suspicious and gloomy after he'd eaten. We spent some time talking about Sheela-na-gigs and the three stone ones he'd picked up years ago.

"I haven't seen those for a while; did you sell them, Dad?"

"Of course not. They're in the Bathroom Shed, under some tarp with their faces to the wall. They shouldn't be seen, especially not by children."

"I know you think that, but this is not the nineteenth century."

"They're rude, Katie, and that's all there is to it. It wouldn't be so bad if their legs weren't splayed quite so far apart. They're vulgar in the extreme."

"They're not the only objects you're funny about, though, Dad. I used to watch you hiding things behind other things, or putting them in cupboards where visitors wouldn't ever see them."

"I don't deny it, Katie, but I can't exactly tell you why. Some objects have a peculiar charge about them, that's all I know." I could see he was beginning to regret he'd said it. He turned away from me and gazed into the darkness outside so I couldn't see his face properly, except when I also looked outwards and caught his reflection in the window—his eyes brighter than normal, his mouth open and slightly quivering.

"I bet you've never talked to Rob or Mum about things with peculiar charges, have you?"

He laughed, and I was relieved. "Of course I haven't because then they'd realise who you got your fanciful turn of mind from, and I'd be in trouble too."

"So why don't you ever stick up for me when Rob teases me?"

"What you don't realise about Rob is that he might not be as imaginative as you are Katie, but he's very easily frightened, and that's something you're not, are you?"

I shrugged, and thought of the Toy House and the eyes in there, some coldly blue and dead-looking, others currant black and gleaming, and the sad hanging button eyes of the teddy bears. But I didn't want to gainsay what my father had decided about me. "No, I don't get scared a lot," I said—and that much was true enough. "Are the outside lights still working, Dad, it's time I went to bed."

"The Yard lights have been off for at least two years now. I thought you knew that."

"Do you have a torch then?"

"Maybe somewhere, but I'd never find it. Where are you sleeping anyway?"

"I told you, in the War Shed with Fred, and I won't move anything about, so don't worry."

"Amongst all those boxes of ammo and great coats? Spooky, I'd have thought. Don't touch anything in there please."

I felt a small surge of adrenaline fizzle through my body, but it was quickly gone. "Have you got one of those old whale oil lamps or a Tilley lamp, Dad?"

"There are some in the bric-a-brac outhouse as far as I can remember, but none with fuel."

"Then why mention them when you know I need some light?"

He crunched up our old fish and chip wrappers and threw them in the bin. "Well, buy a torch tomorrow, Katie, or if you're incapable of doing that, why not just go home where you belong?"

"See you in the morning," I said, and stooped to kiss him.

I walked slowly down the dark path towards the War Shed, trying to recall where the potholes were along the way. It was cold. I heard a fox bark and my body tensed up even though I knew what it was—but in certain states of mind, otherwise innocent noises seem like harbingers for unknowable things. At the corner of the War Shed my ankle brushed against some nettles and the pain of it made me shudder. When I reached the open entrance, I coughed loudly so that any rodents had time to scarper before I went forward. Although I was tense in the darkness, I wasn't truly afraid; I'd known this place all my life.

It was an uncomfortable night though, and in the morning, my nose was freezing. I waited as long as I could in the camp bed and listened to the morning blackbirds and they, at least, made me feel all was possible.

⊸◦⊱

"Ragman is by the bookcases," my father said. He was already up and dressed and warming his hands on the Beatrice. "When you've finished with him, make sure you take him back there."

"Which bookcases?"

"Your nose is purple."

"I know that Dad. It was cold in the War Shed."

"There are big rats in there."

"Yes, Dad, big as greyhounds, I'm sure. Which bookcases is he next to?"

"The ones in the small outhouse. I left him there on a rocking chair, and that's where I want him to live now, so remember to return him please. If you're doing the mirror frames today, use the softest rags you can find, but do the dusting first, Katie."

I shrugged. "When was the last time anyone even asked if you had mirrors here, Dad?"

"In 1956. It was a couple and they wanted a beautiful oval mirror I had at the time with inlaid mother-of-pearl ivy leaves on the frame." I waited for him to think about the uselessness of me dusting the mirrors and waxing the frames, but it seemed he missed the point entirely. "I was hoping they'd buy that Venetian one from the sixteenth century. They were excited by it for a while, and then suddenly didn't want it, and it's still here to this day."

I knew the one he meant, it had a lot of those peculiar diseased-looking spots that mirrors get when the silver mercury is tarnished.

"It's a beautiful one," I said, "but too damaged, I expect."

"As you say, Katie. As you say. I have thought of destroying it from time to time."

"I can't imagine you destroying anything, Dad. You're the great preserver."

He laughed. "Well, let's not dwell on it anyway."

"Look, I think it'd help you a lot more if I just worked with the bric-a-brac. I'm sure if things had prices on them, people would be more willing to buy them. Don't forget that if a customer wants something, they have to pick it up and take it to you in the office to find out the price, then, if it turns out to be too expensive, they'd have to take it back where they found it, and the whole thing would be an embarrassing event. See what I mean?"

Dad gave me one of his sideways looks, but didn't respond. "If you're prepared to work in the Mirror Hall, Katie, I will consider coming home with you afterwards. I won't promise, but I will at least think about it."

"Deal!" I replied.

I took the wax and left the office to pick up Ragman. I was surprised to find him exactly where Dad said he would be, given his forgetfulness. When Rob and I were kids, we turned Ragman into a bogeyman and invented some frightening games with him; made him jump out at us, or lay in wait in improbable places. He's a long bag made of rope netting and full of old rags for dusting and cleaning. Dad was always very precise about which type of rag we should use for the different jobs we had to do when he used to make us help him. I picked the thing up from the stool and threw one end of it over my shoulder as if it was a body, and walked to the Mirror Hall.

I took a deep and slow breath before I went in. It certainly was dusty; I could feel myself wanting to sneeze, yet the idea of making a sudden noise in there seemed oddly ill-advised, so, laying Ragman on the ground, I pulled a length of cloth through his netting and wrapped it round my nose and mouth, and for a few minutes I squatted next to him and stared at the woodworm holes in the flooring. "Bit of a long time since you've seen any action," I whispered to him. "No, don't say anything; I don't want to get into a long conversation about how Dad doesn't feed you properly."

Some years ago, Dad had made low wooden partitions in the Mirror Hall, against which, and on either side, he propped his mirrors up so that they became long avenues of mirrors stretching from the entrance doors down to the small alcove at the bottom of the hall.

I estimated it would take me some time, a few weeks even, to dust and wax all the mirrors I could see stacked next to each other—and sometimes, two or three deep. As I thought about the job I had to do, sunlight came through the row of small windows high up on one of the walls and made columns of bright light that hit the floor along the central avenue and formed dazzling patches all the way down to the dark end of the room.

I was grateful the sun was out.

Each time I pulled one mirror away from its stack I expected to come across the putrefying body of a rat or mouse, but at least by lunchtime, the queer odour in the place was half disguised behind the homey smell of beeswax. I worked on into the afternoon, not bothering with lunch, as my throat had seized up and I could scarcely have eaten anything anyway. But the light had shifted and played now directly onto some of the mirrors and was so blinding that I couldn't look straight at them for more than a second. I needed a pair of dark glasses if this weather was going to hold, but I'd rather have been working in difficult light than in the inky gloom that cloudy weather would've given me. By the time I left, I didn't feel I had the patience to talk to Dad. I passed the office and could see he was in there, but instead of stopping by, I headed straight for the War Shed and my camp bed.

The first few days were awful. I felt crabby and resentful of my whole family, particularly of Rob who could've been helping me, especially as he was so defensive of our father. At the weekend, Dad came into the Mirror Hall with some tea and an old squashed cake. "It's only me," he called out from the doorway.

"Why did you say that?" I asked.

"I didn't want to startle you, Katherine."

"But who else could it have been?"

"A customer, of course."

"Like the place has been flooded with customers; I've only seen three people in The Yard this week, Dad."

"One of them bought a cream jug; a nice little piece. Country violets on it."

I shrugged, and took the tea he handed me. "What's Stallway's Reclamation Yard worth, a few million?" I asked.

"It's beginning to look beautiful in here," he said, "and everything's been all right, hasn't it?"

"Is that a question, Dad, or a statement?"

"Well, you look fine, a bit peaky maybe. No disturbances?"

"What do you mean?" I whispered. I wasn't expecting an answer from him, but I was curious to know if he had the slightest sense of what it was like spending time in the Mirror Hall. Over all the hours I'd worked in there so far, I'd never once dropped my guard. At the slightest sound or change in light or air current, I rose up and searched in all the dark recesses of that vast room. "What are you supposing would disturb me?"

Dad frowned. "Where's Ragman?"

"Over there, lying across that gold frame. And Ragman hasn't been disturbing me, no, Dad. He's good company; we have some very philosophical conversations."

"Good, I'm glad you're entertaining each other. That smell has almost gone, Katie."

"Until the wax dries out and fades," I answered. "Exactly what is it, do you think? I haven't come across anything decaying between the mirrors."

Because Dad didn't answer me instantly I turned to look at him, and for a second, I saw his expression unguarded and unintended; he had the look of someone deep in a state of confusion. But as quickly as I supposed I'd seen that, it was gone and the curious effect of sunlight and the mirror surfaces, now gleaming and dust-free, made me doubt what I had seen.

"Try not to look directly into the mirrors when the sun hits them, Katie. Not good for your eyes," he murmured. "In fact just think of them as objects and try not to look into them at all." He placed his hand on my shoulder for a minute and I knew he was pleased with what I'd done.

"Why, Dad?"

"Well, it's obvious isn't it?" His voice hardened and he moved a step or two away from me and glanced at the mirrors on our left. "It'll slow you down, that's why. And there are plenty of other things for you and Ragman to be getting on with in The Yard. You could be pricing up the bric-a-brac, a much more useful job, if you ask me."

He stood cross-armed in front of me, and I realised something for the first time as I stared up at him. "You don't like it in here either, do you, Dad?"

"What're you talking about?"

"You don't like being in here any more than I do," I repeated.

He shrugged, but it wasn't casual and dismissive as he'd meant me to think it. "It's a funny old building," he began. "Just one of those kinds of places."

"You used to tell me awful stories in here."

"That was just during the summer of 1999. A few short weeks only. I shouldn't have done that to an imaginative kid like you. I've always felt guilty about it. There's hardly any point in saying sorry now though is there?"

"Then what happened?"

"What do you mean?"

"After those few short weeks, Dad?"

"Life went on, Katie. What else is there to say? We had a lot of stuff coming and going in those days. If I'm right it was in the autumn of 1999 that we salvaged Blethick House with all those magnificent fireplace surrounds. Bring your cup back to the office this evening, Katie, and don't forget to put Ragman back on his chair," he said, turning to leave.

"What I remember is that quite suddenly you told us we couldn't play in the Mirror Hall anymore."

"Well, I didn't want you two breaking anything in here; you were really rowdy when you were kids, Katie."

"You told us you were afraid we'd stare too long at our own faces in the mirrors and get self-hypnotised and turn into zombies."

Dad bit his lip suddenly. "Did I really?" he asked. "Well that was just to keep you out of here. Mirrors could make us a lot of money, if only people would buy the damned things."

◄•►

Perhaps that jumpy conversation I'd had with Dad invaded my imagination more deeply than I'd thought, because the next morning as I waxed two baby angels on the frame of a huge mirror, I did not see and I did not feel—but a curious mixture of the two—a movement in one of the lower, older mirrors close by. I stopped what I was doing, and looked, not into it, but beyond to where a rat or leaf might have scuttled, and a waft of the same lingering odour, but now raucous and pungent, came to me. It was not the smell of a dead thing; that much I knew.

The mirror itself was in a terrible state, and I realised it was that same Venetian mirror Dad was so proud of, the one he supposed was worth a great deal of money. The mirror surface is an elegant oval within an ornate etched glass frame with a pattern of branching leaves and flowers surrounded by scroll work. It had been tarnished when Dad first brought it to The Yard, and now the black areas had increased, particularly between the mirror and the frame. I knelt down and stared at my face within it briefly. I looked tired and jowly, and dusting the mirror made me look worse still.

Although I was tempted to gaze down the long central avenue of mirrors to estimate how many more of the damned things I had to dust or polish, I resisted, as I knew it would worsen my mood and make it difficult for me to speak to Dad when we met to eat something in the evening. He'd cleaned up two more of his Beatrices, so that the office was fuggy with moist warmth but he could cook decent food for us, using all three. On that evening—and I remember it in particular because we had a short and sudden storm that seemed to be right overhead with frighteningly loud thunder—Dad was cooking sausages.

"How is it going in the Hall?" he asked.

"How long do you think it will be before all those mirrors are covered in dust again, Dad, one day, two days?"

"You know that Rob is building a website for The Yard? Well, he's going to take photos in the Mirror Hall to use on it, and so what you're doing is not useless, Katie. It might bring us in a lot more custom. Maybe even people from London, those with tan-coloured coats and real throwaway money." I didn't answer him, but I could see he was beginning to slough off the belligerent mood that had made him seek refuge away from Mum in the first place. "Please stop staring at me in that soppy way, Katie. Did you put Ragman back on his chair? Ah! I can see by your face you haven't. Still time before it gets dark, nip back to the Hall and rescue him would you and then we can eat."

I don't know how I'd forgotten Ragman, and I swore at myself for doing so. I'd left him hanging over a square-framed Victorian mirror, close to the Venetian one. I considered leaving him where he was for the night, but there was every chance Dad would wander into the small outhouse early the next morning and notice he was not in his chair. So I did return, and there were dense shadows gathering in the Mirror Hall when I arrived. If I'd been wearing noisy shoes, I don't know if it would've made a difference or not, because at that stage I had no knowledge about what later I came to know so intimately and horribly.

My shoes were soft and made no sound, and I stopped abruptly several metres from where I'd left Ragman because beyond him there was activity. I've never been able to find a better way to describe it than that. It was in the Venetian mirror, and the curious thing is that the mirror had all the appearance of being three dimensional as I gazed at it. I thought I saw the slow assembling—the suggestion only—of limbs and features, coal black, shiny, and then, as I drew a noisy breath . . . gone instantly. I walked forward a couple of paces, reached sideways for Ragman without taking my eyes off the blank oval mirror surface where this had happened. Where this had happened in my tired brain, I told myself as I clutched Ragman tightly to my body and walked fast to the small outhouse in the fading light.

I didn't speak much to Dad that night, nor he to me. We talked briefly about the woodworm in one of the oak tables and whether we should treat it again. From time to time Dad seemed to cast his eyes upon me, there is no better way to say it than that, but I didn't know what he was thinking exactly. "Would you like to bring your camp bed into the office," he said, finally.

"What, now?"

"I found a working lamp this morning; we could go over together and get it, Katie."

"What?"

"Your camp bed."

"Now why on earth would I want to do that, Dad?"

He shifted and stared out into the darkness. "Because I can see that something has got to you," he whispered so faintly that I almost didn't hear him. "You might be better off with me in here."

"I don't know what you're talking about."

"I'm not sure I do, either. It's a bit like your mum says; I'm obviously confused."

"Then why say it?"

Dad shrugged, and turned to gaze at me. "Funny old place, Stallway's Yard," he murmured. "I love it though, and I won't leave it."

"We could be home in an hour if we go now, Dad."

"Would you want to return to someone who thinks you're incapable of doing anything useful anymore?"

"She says you throw things at her."

He shrugged. "I won't sell this place Katie. It's like the inside of my own head."

"Rotting and rusty, then?"

"If you say so, and full of woodworm and darkness. Shall we get your stuff?"

"No. I'm fine in the War Shed. Fred is on guard in there."

Nothing he'd said was strange in itself; he was right, The Yard at night was creepy and I'd chosen to camp down in one of the sheds on the perimeter of the land, while he was a long way away in the warm office. But it wasn't those facts that now agitated me, but the beginnings of a stronger sense that he wasn't telling me something.

"How do you mean, it's a funny old place—funny how?" I asked.

Again, he shrugged and looked down at the palms of his hands. "All this stuff from so many different places and times . . . you know? Different people, all ghosts now." He laughed then.

"Are you deliberately trying to give me the creeps, Dad, like when I was a kid? I've got to walk across The Yard in the dark in a while, or had you forgotten that?"

"Look, that's why I went searching for a working lamp today," he said, and reaching into his pocket, he took out a lighter and drew a little Victorian brass lamp towards him that was standing amongst the clutter on his desk.

I was grateful.

"You need to tidy up all that paperwork, Dad. Maybe we should just stay in here tomorrow and go through the books. What do you think?"

"You don't want to work in the Mirror Hall anymore?" he said as he lit the lamp for me.

"Are you asking or telling me?"

"I won't make you go back in there if you don't want to, Katie. I shouldn't have insisted; you can do whatever jobs take your fancy in The Yard, or go home if you get too fed up."

"Why don't we both go home?"

"I should've seen that one coming. No, I'm not going back until your mother apologises."

I stood up and held my hand out for the lamp. "I've started that work with the mirrors, and now I'm going to finish it. Lend me your radio, Dad, for company. I think it's only difficult in the Hall because the light throws itself around in a distracting way."

"Is that why you're so tense, Katie?"

"Am I?"

"Because of the light?"

"It stinks in there, you know. You can never forget it."

"Still?"

"Even worse in the last day or so. Weirdly pungent; like a mixture between oil and human skin, and rotting fruit and garbage." Dad stood up, and for a moment looked more bewildered and vulnerable than I'd seen him for a while. I hugged him, something I told myself I should do more often, and I left for the shivery journey across Stallway's Reclamation Yard in the dark.

◄◦►

Even though it would mean trouble with Dad, as I lay in my camp bed the next morning, I decided to shift some of the mirrors about. Should he challenge me on it, I'd tell him I was trying to create more interesting effects so that Rob could take some good shots for the website. There was an alcove at one end of the Mirror Hall, it too was full of mirrors, some of them hanging and others leaning along its curving wall.

By mid-morning, I had exchanged three mirrors in the alcove for three others close to where I'd been working the previous day. The Venetian mirror was the last one I moved; I tucked it away in the alcove next to an Art Deco mirror and left the area. "Out of sight," I murmured, "and out of God damn mind."

Several times during the day, as I worked in the hall, I repeated those same words to myself as if they were a spell that once uttered, would take effect. But they became like the refrain from a song that lodges in the brain and refuses to leave; the more I said them, the more I realised that it was far, far too late for anything to change. I had seen what I had seen, and now a compulsion to gaze at that mirror again was growing in me with intensity as the sunlight faded and an afternoon of misty rain began.

Sometime later, Dad was suddenly behind me, and he'd come in so quietly that I felt as if my heart had roared into furious beating, and then stopped dead. I cried out—I think—and he stepped back, surprised. If I'd been so preoccupied that I hadn't noticed his coming, it was not because of the oak framed mirror I was oiling. "It's not . . ." I began, confusing myself with the sound of my own voice.

"What?"

I put my fist over my heart and held it there pressed into my rib. "You made me jump, Dad."

"So I saw," he replied. "What were you going to say—it's not what?"

"I was lost in my own thoughts; that's all."

Dad glanced away from me and I could see he was searching along the bottom line of mirrors. "You've shifted things," he whispered fiercely.

"I suppose I knew you'd notice, but look . . ."

"How many times do you have to be told, Katie?"

"For Rob's photos, I thought . . ."

"I hate it when you do things without asking me. What photos?"

"You said Rob was going to take photos for the website."

"And so he is. Where did you put it?"

"Where did I put what Dad?"

"Come on, Katie. Where is it?" He'd gone the colour of pale clay, and as if unconsciously mirroring me, he put his fist against his own chest. "Where is it?" he whispered again.

"In the alcove," I replied, "where I don't have to look at it."

"Show me."

"It's over there, Dad. Go by yourself."

Now I knew for certain that my father had an awareness of some kind. I thought he was going to find the Venetian mirror and bring it back, but instead he gazed at me for a long time from across the hall and I could not determine what his expression meant in the slightest degree. Shortly after that, he left, and some while later I heard the office door bang shut.

I decided to work in a different part of the Hall for the rest of the day; to take my mind off it. I pulled Ragman and all my oils and waxes over to the left-hand side wall where the air was less dusty and slightly warmer. I worked fast and well there, and felt comforted by the sounds of human voices and snatches of music on Dad's radio. Then, for no detectable reason—no sound, or shift in atmosphere or light, no thought of mine—I walked to the radio and turned it off.

The Yard could not have been more silent, I could hear no bird song, no sound of Dad whistling in The Yard, and even the distant noise of trucks on the main road was absent. I wondered how I had become so alert, so tense and so drawn to look. It was as if I was made of wood and strings and in the hands of a puppeteer. I made my way slowly towards the alcove. I half-hid at the edge of the curving wall, but in a position that allowed me see enough of the surface of the mirror. I waited there for several minutes aware of dust motes moving sluggishly in the light, and as I did, a thought came slowly into my mind that I was behaving like a mad woman, hovering around in one corner of a vast room waiting to see something I'd conjured—as my family agreed I was good at doing—out of thin air. At the very moment I turned to go, a curious change in texture or perhaps tint took place in the mirror until I could just detect the beginnings of depth in it. What silver the mirror still had seemed to roil subtly as if it was the surface of a still and sludgy pond.

Then I saw something that I could never have called a face. Perhaps it was no more than the suggestion of a mouth, open and richly dark inside, and sticky.

Somewhere in the background I could now hear Dad whistling and a series of mundane thoughts pushed their way into my mind like a school of little fish pursued by a hunting pike. Did he have a cake, had he made some tea, did we have any milk left, where had I left Ragman, was it time to phone Mum again, was Dad on his way to me, was he coming now—now? When my mind was clear again, I found that I was seeing nothing but the flat surface of the diseased old mirror once again, and that my left hand was clutching my neck hard. I left the Mirror Hall and went to the War Shed where I sat on my bed for a longish time in the gloom watched over by Fred the Dead, the manikin soldier with a child-like face.

By knowing how to distract my father, I managed to hide my sick fear from him that evening, although he was very aware that I was in a really dark mood. I made sure I didn't talk about anything in The Yard at all, but instead tried to lead him into memories of going on holiday to the seaside years before.

"And you always hated jellyfish," he said. "I remember when a great number of them got washed up on the beach, giant ones they were, and you refused to go near the water for ages after they'd gone."

"I still don't like them," I said. "It's the see-throughness that gets me. It doesn't seem natural for something in nature to be transparent."

"You were very squeamish at that age, Katie. Mum and I had a lot of trouble with you sometimes."

"Can we change the subject, Dad? I was trying to think of good memories, not horrible things."

"Well, thinking of horrible things; did you put Ragman back on his chair this evening?"

"Yes, and he sends his best regards."

◄○►

When I woke up, my mouth tasted sour, and it felt as if I'd bitten my tongue. I had the feeling I'd been involved in a savage nightmare, yet I had no memory of any such thing. I got up quickly and dressed, but not finding my shoes immediately I went to the Mirror Hall barefooted. I moved quickly to the alcove and positioned myself—I could've got a better view if I'd moved my head slightly, but I didn't need to, as what I saw was what I saw. Now with the beginnings of a face appearing, although smudgy and crudely wrought, then with sinewy limbs shifting and stretching, and a coal black chest, vigorous and protruding, something moved in that mirror as though, once again, it had the depth of a murky pond, and I was witnessing the emergence of its creature. This thing which lives there and stinks, I thought to myself. Whatever compulsion made me stand there gazing, did not lessen as the watery surface of the mirror appeared to bulge, and the head, now formed in its entirety, poked outwards into the same world I thought I inhabited. Then a limb followed, small handed and oily black, and dragged at the floorboards for purchase. I began to shift backwards, using a slight breeze that was playing on the backs of my legs to guide me to the wide open door behind, without my eyes ever leaving the mirror and its contents. But at the striking up of birdsong outside the hall, the thing seemed to shudder briefly before it withdrew sharply back into the confines of the ancient mirror. I'd learnt not only that the repulsive thing existed, but that it was cognisant—and that last fact, more than anything, revolted me in the extreme.

I went straight back to the War Shed and climbing into my cot, pulled my duvet tightly around me. I felt throttled with a terrible coldness and as I lay there waves of nausea overcame me so that I drew my knees up to my chest, and a curious deep loneliness, wretched and perplexing began to absorb me until I felt the huge solemnity of how each of us is alone on Earth. If I knew nothing else, I knew that having witnessed the filthy creeping thing come into being in front of my human eyes, I could never again be myself, and that thought filled me with a terrible rage. Had my life once been ordinary and simple, it was no longer true, but all gone now, like frail grass strands stripped from the carefully made nest of a small and cheerful bird. I stayed in my cot until late that morning, when I got up shakily and moved across The Yard to join Dad in the office.

"Where on earth have you been?" he roared at me. "I went to look for you in the Mirror Hall and you weren't there Katherine. Your car was still in The Yard. Where were you? Not moving my stuff about, I hope?"

"I'm not feeling too good; I stayed in the War Shed."

"You should've said."

"I just did, Dad. You should move the Beatrices a bit away from the desk, you've got so much paperwork on it that if you're not careful, you'll burn the office down."

"You sound like your mother."

"She misses you."

"How do you know that?"

"I just do. Why don't we go home?"

"I can't stand the way she's always trying to herd me about, always watching to see when I do the next stupid thing, or forget something. I'm never allowed to get on with my own disease uninterrupted."

"I never thought about it from your angle, Dad."

"Well, you've never asked me what it's like to have a rotting brain, have you? Anyway, never mind about me. You should go home, Katie. You look awful."

I leant against the edge of his desk. "I'm not leaving, but I'm done with the Mirror Hall now. I'm moving into the bric-a-brac outhouse."

"I won't have you shifting my things around. The Mirror Hall looked different when I went in there this morning. I don't just mean cleaner. What have you moved? Where is Ragman?"

"On his bloody chair, Dad!" I straightened up; the office felt cramped and stuffy and Dad's face had begun to harden.

"What have you moved?"

"I've moved the Venetian mirror into the alcove. You know that, I did it yesterday. You made a huge fuss about it."

"Yes, I remember, so you did—as if that could change anything." Dad stared at me in a manner that was more direct than I'd have thought possible for him, and I was certain that he did know about that black crawling thing. I knew also with a terrible clarity, that I couldn't ever talk about it to him, because—I intuited—he believed our recognition of its existence would nurture it further, and to some extent, I shared that thought.

"Where's Ragman," he asked again, as if to fill in the silence that had come between us.

"I just told you; he's on his chair. Asleep I expect. So where are the labels, Dad?"

"What? What do you want now?"

"The labels," I shouted, "to do the bric-a-brac!"

Throughout the rest of the day, a murderous dark feeling of hatred and revulsion was growing in me until I felt as if I needed to scream out loud. I was constantly distracted; the impulse to return to the Mirror Hall, to see the thing again, was close to overwhelming. But I worked on steadily putting prices on objects, twisting them around on the shelves to try to make them look more attractive—to the piddling tramp and his spitting dog—I thought grimly. I was glad of the cheerful burbling of the radio as I worked and the presence of Ragman propped up against a chest of drawers. "And a hard time you have of it, too," I told him, "sitting there watching me all day, and not lifting a finger to help."

Towards dusk, a black cat crossed The Yard and seeing it out of the corner of my eye, blurred and slinking, I shouted something out and stumbled hard against one of the Welsh dressers, giving the bone in my elbow a smarting blow. Perhaps it was that sudden jolting physical pain that broke through my reserve. I grabbed hold of Ragman and left the bric-a-brac outhouse instantly. When I reached the entrance of the Mirror Hall, I held my breath as if the air itself was contaminated. I could smell the rank, oily odour of the thing even from that distance. I picked up one of the bricks Dad used to prop the doors open, and went on towards the alcove with Ragman draped over my shoulder and banging softly against my knee.

I was frightened.

It felt as if my heart had migrated upwards and lodged somewhere in my throat, and a kind of strange pulsing had started in my head. The hatred I felt for that thing I'd seen was deep and steady in me by the time I reached the curved wall and gazed down at the old mirror.

I knew I had to wait. I lowered Ragman to the ground.

I could've smashed the mirror into tiny fragments then and there, but I needed to see, if only one more time, that awful thing as it crept out. Perhaps an hour went past, maybe less when the mirror's cloudy silver stirred and a shape began to poke out from the surface, as a snail might from a shell. Much the same as before, with a leisurely slowness that sickened me, the thing unfurled its spindly black limbs and pushed onwards as if feeling for the way out. I gripped the brick tightly and was on the verge of moving forward and destroying what I could see of the mirror and its inhabitant. Before I could find the courage, the creature was all of a sudden, like a fast birth, out and on the wooden floor, covered in a sticky slime, but moving with confidence down the line of mirrors away from me. As I came forward, it seemed to shrink into itself slightly and half turn its black ball of a head to see what was behind it. I could not tell if it had eyes. Then, for something so sticky, it shot with alarming speed into the Art Deco mirror and a mere second later there was no ripple on its surface; no evidence of what I'd witnessed. It had been not bat-like, or toad-like, but in some ways resembling both if only in the creeping and lingering gait with which it had begun its outward journey before it shifted its awkward head and became aware of me.

My plan had been to destroy the Venetian mirror before the thing had fully emerged, but I was not quick enough. Now though, I did not hesitate; I threw myself forward into the alcove and smashed the brick downwards onto the Art Deco mirror, but at the exact second I felt the impact and before the mirror could even crack, I saw, in a jumble of glutinous limbs and joints, the creature come out, close to my feet, and squirm away, as if it guessed my intention to attack it. I reeled backwards from the stench of it, and glimpsed it once, and then twice, moving at speed up the avenue of mirrors in the main part of the hall and I was left in helpless rage, clutching the brick.

◄◦►

Dad came to the War Shed early the following morning and sat on the box of ammo I'd been using as a bedside table. "I want you to leave today," he said. "Go home. You look ill."

"Will you come with me?"

He seemed to hesitate for a second. He stretched his shaking hand out and brushed a piece of my hair away from my face. "No, Katherine. Not yet. I have to stay here now until everything has become calm again."

"At home, or here?"

"You know what I mean, Katie."

"Do I?" I asked, sitting up.

"Let's not have this conversation. Why not just do what I want you to do?"

He was close to beseeching me, if not in his tone, in his look. I wondered again if I could talk to him properly, but no sooner had I thought it, than it seemed impossible.

"I want to stay one more day, Dad. I'll leave tomorrow. I promise you."

"Why must you stay?"

"I've already planned out the day's work," I lied.

"Working with the bric-a-brac, you mean?"

"Yes, working with the bric-a-brac," I repeated, looking straight ahead of me.

"So, if I come over there today, that's where I'll find you?"

"Why would you need to find me, Dad?"

He laughed slightly, but it brought me no relief. "To be sure you're not putting things where they shouldn't be. To make sure you're leaving things alone."

"Leaving things alone?"

"Yes. That's clear, isn't it?" his face looked yellow in the light, ". . . touching things!" he exclaimed, "interfering with it all."

"I'll see if Rob will come and stay with you," I said.

Dad stood up. "Oh God, no Kate. Don't do that please. It's you or nobody." I felt a sudden foolish surge of love for him, and getting off the army cot, I hugged him tightly. "Look," he whispered in my ear, "just leave things alone. Promise me? They are how they are; you shouldn't try to change anything."

I nodded, and he'd have felt me doing so against his cheek, but I had a new plan.

I sent him off at lunch time to buy us a last evening meal together and some beer. His face lit up at the thought of beer and he set off happily enough. He'd be gone for a couple of hours, of that I was sure as he was bound to call into the Ropewalk Arms for a drink. I walked over to the Mirror Hall with one of the old pitch forks from Blethick House, and a folding stool.

At first I could not bring myself to look for the thing; it could have been in any of the mirrors; that much I now understood. But I returned to the alcove and positioned the stool close to the curving edge so that I was as much out of sight as was possible, and waited.

My hand never left the pitchfork.

There were times when the emotions the thing stirred in me were so raw and powerful that my body began to twitch and I'd have done anything to be able to stand up and move around, or to scream. But I dared not. I'd first become aware of its existence in strong sunlight and you'd think, wouldn't you, that something which caused such revulsion, would arise from darkness not from light? I recognised that my fear was still strongly with me, but hidden behind the dense loathing that had driven me to lie in wait for it.

I've no idea how long I did wait before I saw it again. It began to poke itself tentatively out of the Venetian mirror. Its head was about the size of a coconut, it was hairless, and my mind interpreted its four spindly, sticky limbs as insect-like, yet belonging more surely to the animal kingdom, sloth, bat, toad—I could not pin it down and the confusion the sight of it brought to me increased my hatred of it. I could now see that its back was prune-coloured, and its skin, beneath a slimy layer, had a leathery wrinkled look to it. It seemed naked and unprotected as it made its way cautiously across the bare boards between mirrors as I stared at it. Some wild images came to me, as I stood up slowly. I thought of the day when I was eight, and we were on the beach, and I witnessed a hermit crab attempting to change shells, and noticed the hopeless soft curved body of the thing. I thought then how ridiculous it was. I pitied it and despised it at the same time.

But this thing filled me with . . . .

I'm sure I made not a single sound, yet something alerted it to me. It stopped and attempted to look around its own body, a thing about the size of one of those large Moroccan plates that people put on their walls sometimes. I saw its eye briefly then; revolving, indistinct and dark like the body, and as it turned to face me, its mouth, like that of the beak of a nightjar, became clearer.

I froze for a second.

It came on towards me, at first in a determined creep, and then as got closer, it began to rush. Bitter fluid rose in my throat and made my lips twist sharply downward as I lifted the pitchfork into the air. My aim was bad; I caught the sticky edge of its body with only two of the prongs, and the creature seemed to tear away, as it stared up at me. It was as if it was made of brown fibrous jelly, and it was on its way past me when I kicked Ragman right into its path, and as it disappeared beneath, I raised the pitchfork and stabbed it hard through Ragman, and saw both ends of him bend upwards as I did so.

◄◦►

The café in the village is always full of steam and noise, and it was where I headed on foot. The walk calmed me, but the image of the creature still came at me with each breath. It did not look into my face I told myself over and over again until it became a mantra I could cling onto. I sat in a recess in the café counting the faded swallows on the wallpaper and trying to listen to the noise of cutlery and plates, and the sharp chattering of women. The noise women can make when they're in groups has always made me recoil, the way it escalates harshly, becomes louder and squeakier until it reaches a pitch and a hum that tears your nerves to shreds. But now I was grateful to be able to hear it, as it helped distract me from what I had seen and what I had done. I stayed in the café until my body and brain knew each other once more.

Then, I headed back to The Yard.

Ragman lay as I had left him in the central avenue of mirrors. I picked up the pitchfork again, and inch by inch turned him over with the prongs. The body of the thing was not there, but the odour was powerful, and as I inspected the jumble of tightly packed rags in the rope netting, I realised there was a large wet stain spread across them. I heard Dad's Cortina coming back into The Yard, and so I lunged at Ragman again with the pitchfork, and spiking him securely, I picked him up and flipped him some metres across the Hall where he disappeared into another avenue of mirrors. I was back in the office before Dad had had time to open the boot and take out the groceries.

"Looks like I should've brought some whiskey back for you, never mind beer, Katie," he said.

I nodded and bent to unpack the food. "Good, easy to cook," I mumbled. "I'll make dinner."

"What's the matter with you?"

"You know you said you'd come home if I worked in the Mirror Hall?"

"I said I'd think about it."

"Well, have you?"

"Not much, Katie, I have to confess."

"I'm leaving tomorrow, and I want you to come with me. What's really going on with you and Mum?"

"Why do you ask that?"

"Because you're not as demented as you pretend to be, Dad."

"Oh, it shows, does it?"

"Yes, to me it does. Why are you trying to fool Mum?"

Dad shrugged. "She can believe what she likes—it's not my place to stop her."

"Did you really throw things at her?"

"Once or twice. Better than killing her outright, don't you think?"

"Don't make jokes, Dad. What's going on?"

Dad moved around his desk and sat down heavily on his creaky chair. When he gazed up at me, his cheeks were red and his eyes bright. "Have you ever considered how ridiculous it is that two people are expected to spend their entire adult life together, that the whole of society is based on that one idea alone?"

"Not really. What d'you mean?"

"I mean that I'm not going home to Mum, Katie. I can't live with her anymore, she's suffocating me slowly."

"So what the Hell are you going to do?"

He stood up, and then sat down again quickly. "What I am doing right now, Katie. I'm going to live in The Yard."

"By yourself?"

"How can I be by myself? I've got Fred the Dead, the startled mermaid, and best of all Ragman."

"Ragman?"

"Ah, I can see by your expression, you haven't put him back on his chair this evening, Katie."

At that point in the conversation, I was frying some chicken pieces. The greens and potatoes were boiling on the other two Beatrices. Dad was drinking another beer. "No. You're right there, Dad," I whispered. "I forgot about him."

"So where did you leave him?"

"In that place."

"In the Mirror Hall?" I nodded. "Well, he's going to live in the office with me from now on. He's always been with us and he deserves to relax in his old age."

I looked up at my father only to find him smiling happily and staring into our pot of potatoes.

✦

I left Dad in his office the morning after our last meal together and swore I'd never return. Rob never goes to see him and Mum is coping, but I do go back. I go back every month and spend an hour or so with him. I've never seen any customers in The Yard when I've been there, but Dad claims that hordes of people come. "Coach-loads, Katie, since Rob put up the website. The place has never been so busy."

"They just don't come when I visit?"

"That's right."

"So what have you sold lately?"

That question always sends him into a fluster, and he moves things about on his desk, and then puts them back where he'd taken them from. He doesn't answer the question, but glowers at me instead.

Dad's increasing neglect of The Yard had never done it any harm, in fact it lent the place charm and atmosphere, I loved to stare into the noble faces of the stone angels lined up along the paths, or to sit amongst the algae-covered mermaids and sea serpents, or to run my fingers over the vivid orange spots of lichen growing across much of the older stone work he collected.

But Stallway's Reclamation Yard is different now. A savage kind of rust has found every piece of metal or iron and caused flaky holes wherever it can, in milk pails, in watering cans, in tin baths in a way which seems curiously exaggerated. The water in the stone horse troughs, that I once used to gaze into on the lookout for the little newts that lived in them, has turned dark and stagnant and is full of abnormally large and energetic mosquito larvae with bulbous heads and sharp flicking tails.

The nettles growing around the edges of the outhouses are more vigorous than they used to be and the narcotic scent they put out on warm days is powerful. I sense more dust and mud, more rank weeds and thicker and dirtier cobwebs across the shelves and on the window sills. The effects of time and nature on The Yard had once been romantic and softening, but it seems to me now, that this place I have known all my life, has become mockingly grotesque.

But there is something more and something worse.

A small detail I have not mentioned, yet. When on that day, I turned Ragman over with the prongs of the pitchfork, to discover the floorboards beneath dry and Ragman's back stained with a sticky mess, I knew instantly that the thing had sought sanctuary within the rags and that was why I pitched Ragman as far away from me as I could and left him there.

Dad found him, and took him into the office, where he has given him the other chair.

When I talked to him about the stench in the office he said: "These days, my sense of smell has gone, Katie, so, no, I can't smell anything weird in here. It's probably because I keep the door closed and fresh air doesn't get in much. But then Ragman and I don't much care for fresh air, do we old codger?"

WHAT'S OUT THERE?

GARY McMAHON

Just after midnight. The interior lights reflect off the black window glass; too few stars punctuate the dark sky; clouds hide the moon. John walks across the kitchen, needing a drink of water. The tap makes a grinding sound as he turns it, and the water splutters as it starts to flow. He fills the glass, raises it to his lips, and drinks deeply of the cold liquid.

The lane outside is quiet and empty. He stares at the old, scarred stone wall opposite his window, the paved patio, the old potting shed that needs replacing because part of the roof blew off in a storm. Shadows stir, but that's all they are: formless shadows. He rinses the glass and puts it on the draining board.

As he is walking away from the sink, something bursts at speed through the cat flap. The noise is loud, fast, and full of panic. He stops moving, turns to watch the furred streak of his cat as she skids uncontrollably across the tiled floor.

"Whoa . . . what is it, Slinky?"

The cat slides into the far wall, coming to rest with her front legs apart, the claws unsheathed and splayed across the floor. The animal doesn't make a sound, just watches the now-silent cat flap.

John walks slowly and calmly towards the animal. As he gets near, he bends over so that he is closer to the ground. "Come here, baby. It's okay." He puts out a hand, opens his fingers, and moves them, waggling them in the air.

The cat stares past him, her eyes big and scared-looking. The fur on the back of her neck stands on end: a cliché come to life.

The cat doesn't move as he picks her up, but her body tenses against him.

"Don't worry. There's nothing to be scared of. Was it a dog?" He rubs the cat's forehead with his thumb; she likes that. As he strokes her, he turns to face the door. The cat flap is getting old; the clear plastic hinged visor is grubby so he can't see much of what lies beyond. But is that a small, misshapen shadow moving—or slouching—across his view on the other side of the door? He takes a few steps towards the door. The cat hisses. Her jaws begin to click in that way cats have when they're ready to attack. The specific sound—along with the jittery motion of the cat's jaws—has always unnerved him. He stops walking, but he continues to stroke the cat's head.

He only puts down the cat when he thinks she's calmed down. Once her fur has returned to normal and she doesn't look so panicked. She sits down on the floor under the dining table and starts to clean her paws. John switches off the lights, climbs the stairs, and goes into the bathroom. He leaves the bathroom light off and opens the window, looking down into the lane below. It is quiet. There is nobody there. The lights on the main street don't do much to illuminate the private lane, but he is pretty sure there is nobody hiding behind the shed, or sitting silently in the branches of the tree opposite the house next door.

He remembers one time when he heard strange noises outside late at night. This was back when Alice was ill. Tired, grumpy, he went downstairs and opened the door. On the patio, bravely standing its ground against four large house cats, was a fox. There was blood on its fur. The fox's eyes shone in the darkness, catching the light from his kitchen. The fox hissed; the cats slowly circled it. He noticed that one of the cats had a hunk of fur missing from its flank. Another of the cats was moving awkwardly, as if it had something wrong with one of its front paws.

He stood there fixated as in a single movement all four cats attacked the fox. By the time he'd come to his senses and ran at them, chasing them off, the fox had been torn to pieces.

Picking up the bloodied pieces of fox, he'd put what remained into a black plastic bin bag. He tied the top of the bag and dumped it into his wheelie bin, deciding not to tell Alice about what had happened. In her state, she would overreact, seeing signs and omens where there were none. He had not slept much that night. He kept hearing those strange sounds in his head: sounds that he knew had been the screams of the fox.

He pulls his head back inside and closes the window. After cleaning his teeth, he walks across the landing to his bedroom. The curtains are already closed; the lamp is on. Slinky is lying on top of the bed, her eyelids flickering.

"Shoo, cat." He waves a hand near her face and she hops down off the bed, saunters over to the window, and pushes her way through the curtains to sit on her usual spot on the window sill.

John is tired but he can't sleep. He checks his phone for missed calls or text messages, but finds evidence of neither. He resets his alarm to five minutes earlier than it has already been set for, switches off the lamp, and stares at the moving darkness. The fox screams inside his skull. He has not thought about that fox since it happened, but now he can't get it out of his head.

He turns over onto his side. The glowing digits on the bedside clock tell him it is 12:35 a.m.

John closes his eyes, sleeps but does not dream.

◂◦▸

The next morning John is too busy to even think about his cat's panicked entrance from the night before. He has to drive across town to inspect a property. There has been some kind of structural movement to a party wall. The owner is concerned that their house might fall down.

Driving through the morning traffic, he covers inches instead of miles. It takes him over an hour to do a fifteen-minute journey.

The house he is here to inspect is old; a Victorian detached property with a massive walled garden. An old woman answers the door. She is tall and thin, and still wears her white hair long, draped over her shoulders like a lace shawl.

"I'm John Trafford, from the building surveyors."

She smiles. "Please, do come in."

It doesn't take him long to realise that there is evidence of minor subsidence. The rear garden is on a slope; there is a history of mine workings in the area. But the cracks in the wall are cosmetic, so he doesn't have any bad news for the old lady.

"I'm so relieved," she says. "This house has been in my family for a long time."

She makes him tea, gives him biscuits, and tells him about her ancestry. He's heard it all before, in different forms on different visits to other people, but still he nods in all the right places, makes all the correct gestures. Despite the temptation, he doesn't check the time on his watch even once.

She waves at him from the doorstep as he pulls away. Right then, he suspects that she'd known all along what is wrong with the house wall. He found old repairs in the plaster. It is clearly an ongoing problem. Perhaps she simply wanted reassurance, or some company. He'd noticed there were photographs of her dead husband all over the house.

He finishes work early that afternoon. He doesn't have another appointment, and there is little paperwork to be done—and what there is can be filled in at home on his computer.

He feeds the cat, changes her water, and sits down to watch a football match he recorded a few days ago. He can't recall when. The days have blended into one; he no longer feels the passage of time. When Alice was still around, every day was different. Every smile was a variation on the last, like parts of an ongoing project. Each touch of her hand had thrilled him in a way that was subtly different from the time before. Unlike the old woman in the house with the moving walls, John does not have photographs of his dead spouse on display. He can't bear to see her face, not unless it is real. A photo isn't enough; it makes the pain more intense, reminds him that all he has is a series of carbon copies of the moments they shared.

The cat sidles up to him and begins to rub her face against his leg.

"Hey, Slinky . . ." He picks her up in his arms. She nuzzles his cheek, purring.

The cat had belonged to Alice. It was all she left him.

Realising that it is getting late, he prepares a light dinner: pasta, with an olive oil and rocket salad. Simple fare; it was once Alice's go-to dish whenever she was in a hurry. The football match is over so he listens to music as he eats, barely even tasting the food. He watches the cat as she chases a plastic ball across the room, her small paws slashing.

Later that night, as he sits in his dressing gown reading *A Tale of Two Cities*, John feels his attention shifting from the page. He closes the book and puts it down, stands, and goes into the kitchen. He stares at the cat flap, but it doesn't move. Glancing out of the kitchen window, he sees that the lane is empty. He kneels down beside the cat flap, shuffles closer, and waits, not quite sure what he is doing here.

Nothing stirs.

He pushes the flap with his finger. Chilly air wafts inside, but nothing else comes with it. He stands and opens the door, steps out into the darkness.

"Slinky . . ." Is that why he was compelled to come out here, because the cat isn't home? Jesus, what is he turning into, some sad bastard who worries more about a cat than he does about himself?

The night is still. There isn't even the sound of traffic on the road.

"Slinky . . . are you out here? Come on, girl."

The air moves and brushes against his cheek. He twitches, and turns. There is something dangling from the low branches of the tree opposite the house next door. He crosses the lane, barely even feeling his bare feet against the uneven ground, and approaches the spot. As he gets closer, it begins to take shape. There is what looks like a bundle of rags hanging from a V formed by a meeting of two branches. Someone has slashed to ribbons a shirt or a coat and thrown it into the tree.

He moves closer. The rags become something familiar. Slinky's crushed little face stares at him from the mess of tattered meat. There is no blood, no bones, just her fur, with her head still attached. He wants to cry but he can't. Knows that he should scream, but no sound will come. He is choked up with something—some emotion that he cannot understand.

Numb, he reaches out and disentangles her from the branches. She is floppy, empty; the cat she was is no longer there. He carries the dried carcass inside and sets it down on a dirty sheet, examining the remains. The cat has been flayed, but messily. The pelt is slit and slashed, but has for some reason been washed—or licked—clean.

What kind of predator is capable of this—or have some local kids decided to turn nasty? Turning towards the main road, he stares at the park railings, and pictures the housing estate on the other side of the park. This isn't a bad area, but sometimes he hears stories about gangs of youths straying from the estate to cause mischief. He thinks again of the fox; and of the four cats circling it. He imagines four people doing that to Slinky, his cat—Alice's cat, which she had loved so very, very much.

Then, gradually, the events of the previous night begin to come back to him. Slinky bolting scared into the house, her initial state of terror. The low, squat shape he'd glimpsed moving past the cat flap.

What kind of predator?

This wasn't done by children.

He wraps up Slinky's remains and puts them into a plastic bag, seals the top in a tight knot. He'll call the vet in the morning to have her properly disposed of. The vet might even be able to take a guess at what kind of animal has done this to a usually street-wise cat that is certainly no stranger to late-night alley fights.

-◦-

"To be honest, I have no idea." The vet, Sally, straightens from her table and walks to the sink, where she washes her hands. She was an acquaintance of Alice's. That's how they ended up with the cat: it was a rescue animal and Sally had helped them adopt it. She drifted away when Alice died. Now, whenever he sees her, she acts as if they are strangers. "My gut reaction would be that somebody used a knife on her, but there are a few things that cause me to doubt that was the case."

John turns and walks to the window. It is raining; a light drizzle turns the world grey. The sun is trying to come out, but the dark, smeary clouds are doing their best to hold it back. The quality of the light is weird, imperfect, like an unfinished matte painting in a cheap film. He turns back to face the room. "What do you mean?"

"For a start, there are tooth marks. If a knife was used, whoever used it also bit into your cat." Her face is pale, serious. She is beautiful, but her features are hazy, as if he is unable to fix them completely in his field of vision.

"I'm still not sure what you mean."

"Neither am I, I'm afraid. Bottom line: whoever or whatever did this, it's weird. I have no frame of reference for what's been done to your cat. I'd suggest calling the police. That's all I can think of. I'm sorry . . . she was a gorgeous creature." A smile flickers across her lips, parting them to expose her tiny white teeth. John imagines them biting through flesh. "I know how much you cared for your animal. It's always . . . difficult when you have to say goodbye."

"Yes," says John, opening the door to leave. "Yes, it is."

After settling the bill with the receptionist, he heads straight home. Work can wait; they'll understand when he explains what has happened. He drives through the streets and looks carefully at the faces of the people he passes, wondering if one of them killed his cat. But who in their right mind would bite, skin, and then clean the remains of a simple house cat?

Back home, he thinks about preparing some food, but decides that he has no appetite. He does a little work, answers some emails, and then waits for the night to come.

Lately he does a lot of this: waiting, just waiting, for one thing or another. His life seems to have become a sequence of periods during which he is sitting or standing around, awaiting the arrival of something that never comes. Since Alice's death nothing seems solid. It is all shifting, the edges blurring as he tries to stand his ground and prepare for the arrival of something that will change everything.

He thinks about the hospital waiting room and how much time he'd spent there. The endless appointments with specialists and consultants, none of whom could tell him what was wrong with the woman he loved. Alice had been calm and patient, but he had felt himself crumble. Instead of being the one to help her fight whatever illness had decided to take her, he was the one who cried every night, needing her to hold him and tell him everything was going to be fine.

In Alice's time of need, he had failed her. He had not been there when she needed him most. He can try to justify it all he wants, but the truth is that he was weak, and she had slipped into the darkness without him being there to hold her hand as the light dimmed from her eyes.

-◦-

That night he awakes long after midnight with the sense that a sound has disturbed him. It does not come again, but his skin bristles. Slipping out of bed, he puts on his clothes and pads downstairs. He leaves the lights off and sits down at the kitchen table. There are no sounds; the house is almost unbearably quiet.

"What's out there?" he whispers. "What is it?"

He glances at the cat flap and sees a small, blurred shape slipping past the grubby little plastic window. Gritting his teeth and clenching his fists, he stands and moves over to the door. He pauses there for a moment, taking deep breaths, and then opens the door to let in the still, northern night.

The lane is the same as always: dark, quiet, empty. But something is different, a detail that it takes him a few seconds to discern. On the patio opposite his house, there is a strange, yet familiar tableau: four scraggy cats standing in a circle around a fox. The fox has blood on its snout and its mouth is open. The cats are all injured; their fur is matted with blood; thin strips of flesh hang down from their sides, eyes and ears have been gouged by claws.

The strangest thing, though, is the absolute stillness. None of the animals are moving. They all stand there rigid, as if they have been stuffed, mounted and posed by an expert taxidermist with a taste for the macabre. Not a whisker twitches, not an eyelid droops, and not a claw flicks against the concrete paving stones.

John tries to move, but he isn't sure which way. In the end, he finds that he cannot move at all. Like the animals, he is frozen in place, waiting, waiting for something to develop. He senses that his presence is not important here; he is simply part of the background. Whatever is happening, he is peripheral, his role that of an extra. The main performance is yet to be played out.

The darkness in the alley seems to expand, and then to contract. There is the sound of something snapping—an elastic band, a tendon, perhaps even a small bone. Then, in that exact moment, the animals begin to move. The fox hisses. The cats walk in ever decreasing circles around their prey, their movements jerky and awkward—puppet-like. John looks on, unable to intervene. Clumsily, the cats pounce, taking down the fox, and all he sees is the splash of blood, the rending of flesh and fur. All he hears is the fox's familiar screams, as if they are an echo of that other night so long ago.

When he looks up from the carnage and turns to his right, she is standing there, at the bottom of the lane, with the empty road behind her. She raises a hand, steps forward into a patch of illumination formed by one of the streetlamps. Her face is as white as paper, but the features sketched there undoubtedly belong to Alice. She is wearing a long white dress, ripped down the sides, seams tattered, torn hem trailing in the dirt at her bare feet. He cannot help but see her as a battered reminder of his cowardice.

"No . . ." A scream builds in his sternum, rising to his throat, and then peters out to a weak exhaled breath.

But this feels like part of the same performance as the killing of the fox. There is a ritualistic quality, as if each of these events is a separate movement in a preordained routine.

She starts to walk up the lane, towards him, dragging her filthy feet. Her hair is matted with filth, with patches torn out to reveal the bare scalp beneath. During her funeral, there was a closed casket. She didn't look good at the end. One of her eyes is shut; the other one bulges obscenely from its socket. Her lips are moving, her teeth working at something inside her mouth. One hand keeps waving; the other is rigid at her side, as if she is unable to move it.

John backs away, his feet going out from under him as his heels catch on the step behind him. He falls down onto his backside, scrabbling in the dirt. Alice keeps coming; she keeps moving; she bears down upon him like a lion upon a felled wildebeest.

John raises his arms, shakes his head, and cries out something that might have been a word or just a muted scream.

She smiles, and when she opens her mouth he can see what it is she has been chewing. No, not chewing. Not exactly. Because chewed food is meant to be swallowed and this is moving the other way. Fingers, a small hand is trying to force its way up from inside her throat. Her neck bulges, swelling like a horrific pregnancy. Her mouth keeps opening, yawning beyond any natural limit. The sounds coming from her are like strangled sobs. Another hand squirms alongside the first one, and as he watches, a miniature and incomplete version of himself forces its way up and out between her distended jaws. Alice's head snaps in two due to the enormous pressure, and her legs buckle, sending her down to the ground. She lands on her knees and stays there, swaying, as the small being climbs out of her, naked and dripping in some kind of red-tinted fluid.

John sits up, wondering if he can still get away if he moves quickly enough. Then he wonders if he really wants to get away, or if he'd rather stay here, with her, the woman he still loves.

Finally, her body crumples, going down in a bloodless, boneless heap, leaving John with an insight. What is left on the ground reminds him of Slinky: an entirely unsuitable vessel. This time it has chosen more wisely.

The small, moist form does not attack. It moves slowly, sinuously, as if the muscles and bones are still forming, and climbs into his lap. John strokes its soft, yielding head, feels the blood as it pumps slowly and hotly though its veins. Tenderly he kisses the top of its skull. The inchoate entity raises its face and looks up at him, its fathomless eyes filled with love, with compassion and understanding beyond measure. He gazes at features both ancient and ageless: sunken cheeks, a toothless mouth, a nub of a nose with only rudimentary nostrils through which to draw in air.

John smiles and holds the soft warm body close, ignoring the tightening grip around his chest, the way it causes him to catch his breath. Whatever it is—whatever he was waiting for—he has finally found it.

Thin bones knit together to form a solid framework, loose skin tightens across a rapidly developing frame.

They hold each other tight. Tighter still.

NO MATTER WHICH WAY WE TURNED

BRIAN EVENSON

No matter which way we turned the girl, she didn't have a face. There was hair in front and hair in the back—only saying which was the front and which was the back was impossible. I got Jim Slip to look on one side and I looked from the other and the other members of the lodge just tried to hold her gently or not so gently in place, but no matter how we looked or held her the face just wasn't there. Her mother was screaming, blaming us, but what could we do about it? We were not to blame. There was nothing we could have done.

It was Verl Kramm who got the idea of calling out to the sky, calling out after the lights as they receded, to tell them to come and take her. *You've taken half of her*, he shouted. *You've taken the same half of her twice. Now goddam have the decency to take the rest of her.*

Some of the others joined in, but *they* didn't come back, none of them. They left and left us with a girl who, no matter how you looked at her, you saw her from the back. She didn't eat or if she did, did so in a way we couldn't see. She just kept turning in circles, walking backwards and knocking into things, trying to grab things with the backs of her hands. She was a whole girl made of two half girls, but wrongly made, of two of the same halves.

After a while we couldn't hardly bear to look at her. In the end we couldn't think what to do with her except leave her. At first her mother protested and bit and clawed, but in the end she didn't want to take her either—she just wanted to feel better about letting her go, to have the blame rest on us.

We nailed planks across the door and boarded up the windows. At Verl's request, we left the hole in the roof in the hopes they would come back for her. For a while we posted a sentry outside the door, who reported to the lodge on the sound of her scrabbling within, but once the noise stopped we gave that up as well.

◄o►

Late at night, I dreamed of her, not the doubled half of the girl we had, but the doubled half we didn't. I saw her, miles above us, in air rarefied and thin, not breathable by common means at all, floating within their vessel. There she was, a girl who, no matter where you turned, always faced you. A girl who bared her teeth and stared, stared.

THE CASTELLMARCH MAN

RAY CLULEY

A top Raiders Hill in Radnorshire stands a solitary stone that some believe resembles a weeping figure. According to folklore, the shadow it casts as the sun goes down points the way to a cave of hidden treasure, stolen goods hidden by thieves waiting for a safe time to sell. Whether the stone figure weeps because it was never able to find this bounty, or because it grieves some greater loss, nobody knows, though of course there are stories to accommodate both possibilities. There are certainly plenty of caves in the area and the hills and mountains make for rewarding hikes.

◄◦►

Geo-cache findings: a toy car, a single glove, and a tarnished silver ring.

◄◦►

The Hayward Stables Guesthouse was a converted farmhouse with similarly renovated outbuildings, sturdy stone structures with heavy wooden mantles and beams. The door frames forced you to duck and the sash windows rattled in their frames when the wind was high, but it was cosy. All of the rooms were tidy, with instantly forgettable décor. Upstairs was carpeted thick enough to muffle footsteps whereas downstairs was all stone floor. A wide parking area extended around the back, and further down the track was an old stable that had been converted into a large storage shed, or barn, Charlie supposed. In the year since his last visit very little about the place had changed. Even the weather was the same: rain, rain, and more rain.

The food, though. That was different. Then again, perhaps the food was exactly as it always had been and he simply couldn't remember right; most food tasted bland to him these days, although he would have expected farmhouse fare to have been hearty and full of flavour, whatever his mood. The wine, of course, was fine. He'd worked his way through most of a bottle of red already. He'd probably order another.

It appeared there were only two other sets of guests staying at The Hayward Stables, judging by who had come to dinner. Maybe others had opted for bed and breakfast only (and maybe there was someone bedded down in the old stables—ha!). A large stone-floored dining room had been set with rows of mismatched tables and chairs, each piece of furniture up-cycled from something tatty to something deliberately dishevelled and shabby-chic. A young couple were trying to coax one child into eating and another into settling down, and they weren't doing a bad job. Another couple, middle-aged, sat only a table away from Charlie and bickered in hushed tones. The focus of their altercation was hidden beneath the noise of the nearby children and the persuasions of the parents, but the man seemed to be taking most of it, drinking his dark ale and listening, interjecting whenever moved by a particularly forceful point. The woman was a stern kind of beautiful, but maybe that was unfair. Maybe that was only because of her current mood: maybe she was usually more serene. Charlie used to get quite aroused whenever Lyndsey was angry, he didn't know why. He'd never told her that. Perhaps he should have.

Occasionally the husband caught sight of Charlie noticing and smiled politely, embarrassed by the quiet argument. They had bonded earlier over a complaint about the slow service, though neither party had voiced their concerns to anyone else but each other. While they'd waited for their food the man had joked, "Shame the stables are empty, I could eat a horse," and Charlie had laughed far too much. The man had noted the half empty wine bottle while Charlie raised a glass to toast his agreement, and to excuse his own reaction.

He pushed a piece of sausage around the gravy on his plate and loaded it with mashed potato but found he was no longer hungry. He never really had been. He laid the fork down just as the bickering woman wiped her mouth with a napkin she cast down like a gauntlet before excusing herself from the table. Charlie admired her legs briefly. The man made a half-hearted attempt to call her back, his volume restricted by public company. He looked around to check if they'd caused a scene. The young couple were far too busy with their own family but Charlie had nothing better to do and he offered a tight-lipped smile in sympathy.

"She doesn't like the weather," the man explained.

Charlie looked at the window but the curtains had been drawn against the dark. He knew it would be raining, though. Or had just been raining. Or was about to rain. It had been raining for days. Mostly only brief showers and a pathetic drizzle that was more like mist, hanging in the air, but it was all still rain just the same. "Welcome to Wales."

"Is it always like this then?"

"I'm not from here," Charlie said, and remembered the man in the barn, though he tried not to. "I think this is fairly typical weather, though, yeah."

"We're having a bit of a stay-cation," the husband said.

"Ah."

Charlie didn't care much for conversation, but the new silence between them felt uncomfortable so he said, "Well, there's plenty worth seeing around here. Lots of interesting places if you know where to look."

"What brings you here?"

My wife, Charlie thought.

"Treasure-hunting," he said. The man tilted his head for more, so Charlie added, "Geo-caching?"

"Sorry."

Charlie waved the apology away. "Bit of a hobby," he explained, and took another sip of wine.

It had begun as a joke, a nerdy pastime to get them both out of the house, away from the sofa and the TV. It gave them weekends of fresh air and exercise that was more fun than the gym. It gave them a chance to get to know each other again as they drove around the country, looking for geo-cache "treasures." Charlie told the man some of this.

"There's a website that provides coordinates for wherever you decide to explore, and a GPS will take you to each concealed geo-cache," he said, pausing to refill his glass. "Just a Tupperware tub or something, filled with an assortment of keepsakes. You take something, you leave something, you sign the notebook, and then you look for the next one."

"And this is a thing? People do this?"

Charlie nodded. "It's fun."

It had surprised Charlie to discover how much he enjoyed finding these secret places. Lyndsey had admitted the same, so it was to their mutual amusement that what had begun as a joke became something of a more serious pursuit, with weekly jaunts up and down the country. There were geo-caches hidden everywhere. They found them in trees, under hedgerows, submerged in ponds and rivers. They found them hidden behind road signs, tucked beneath old stone walls and concealed in ruined buildings. And as they searched, so they came to know hidden areas of the land, beautiful places off the beaten trail. They became tourists in their own backyard, learning more about their country. It always surprised Charlie just how much there was to discover. Every nook and cranny of Britain held a secret, it seemed.

"There are these clues," Charlie said. "Sometimes just coordinates to follow but sometimes something more cryptic. Those were Lyndsey's favourite. She liked to figure things out."

She had *me* all figured out.

"Lyndsey? That your wife?"

They both looked at the empty seat opposite Charlie. The plates were clean, cutlery still napkin-wrapped.

"Yeah. We came here this time last year. This is sort of an anniversary."

"Well, congratulations."

Charlie smiled a thank you into his wine, thinking, *not that kind of anniversary*. He tapped the wedding ring he still wore against the glass. He'd recently had it engraved with GPS coordinates. It represented their lives better than dates. The place where they met and the place where they parted suggested a journey that was both literal and metaphorical. Dates, he thought, would have seemed too much like an epitaph.

Charlie took a pouch of tobacco from the pocket of his chair-backed jacket and excused himself for a cigarette. He offered the pouch but was glad when the man declined. He didn't want to know him any better than he did already, and he'd shared too much about himself as it was. He left his wine and jacket to make it clear he was coming back, but he hoped the man would be gone by then.

◄◦►

The Church of Saint Brynach in west Dyfed, Wales, was founded in the sixth century. Its churchyard boasts the Nevern Cross, which dates back to the tenth century. Fashioned from dolerite, the cross stands 13 feet high and is beautifully carved, knotwork and ringwork and geometric patterns making it one of the most impressive carved crosses in Britain. The first cuckoo of the year is thought to land on this cross to announce the coming of spring. Also in this churchyard is "The Bleeding Yew." Its trunk bleeds a red resin believed to be the blood of a monk wrongfully hanged from its branches.

Geo-cache findings: a plastic bird, a colouring book of Celtic designs, and a packet of sweets (out of date).

It wasn't raining, but Charlie still sheltered beneath the small roof at the back of the guesthouse because the sky was thick with cloud. The moon appeared occasionally but only briefly. There was plenty of light, though, thanks to an automatic security bulb that had come on as Charlie stepped outside. It illuminated a vast puddled stretch of gravelled ground and four parked cars. One of them was a people-carrier which he guessed belonged to the young couple with kids, or maybe the owners of the guesthouse, though there was also a mud-splattered Land Rover that he thought might have belonged to them. The Audi was probably the bickering couple's car. The other vehicle was his. For a moment he thought there was someone sitting inside—on the passenger side, Lyndsey's side—but it was only the coat he'd draped over the seat. Not his new one, just his old waterproof, pale grey with bright orange reflective strips up the sides and arms, and absolutely hideous because those were the rules, according to Lyndsey, right up there with good hiking boots and a packet of mint cake. Every rambler, hiker, and apparently geo-cacher, had to have a vile waterproof jacket of clashing colours, preferably something that folded to the size of a handkerchief or packed itself away into its own pocket somehow. Lyndsey's had been orange and pink. It made her look like one of those sweets you used to be able to get from the corner shop, a rhubarb and custard. No, a fruit salad; rhubarb and custards were the other ones, the ones that lasted forever.

He rested the tobacco pouch on a nearby windowsill and set about rolling a cigarette. He tried not to look at the old stable but failed, glancing up at the dark shape of it several times between stages of the cigarette's construction. He would take another look inside before he left. He didn't particularly want to, but he was retracing his steps and the stable was a big part of that. Plus he needed to check if there was anybody in there.

He looked at the car again instead, hoping once more for that illusion of a passenger on Lyndsey's side, but the coat draped over the seat was just a coat.

Lyndsey didn't drive, but she was a fantastic navigator. Rather than rely on any conventional kind of sat-nav, Lyndsey used an app on her mobile phone with the volume down and provided her own range of voices, using outlandish, often terrible, accents, mimicking celebrities and sometimes people they both knew. Sometimes she made up characters, like Farmer Jones (*that be the wrong way, lad*) and Lady Wetherby (*oh, do be careful, driver*). She changed the voices whenever Charlie laughed. It was a game they had.

"Oh. No," she'd say, her voice overly robotic. "You do-not. Want. To-go. That. Way." Or she'd urge, "The other way, *the other way!*" in a voice filled with feigned panic, all the while calm as she looked out of the passenger window at whatever part of the countryside they were passing through.

"This is *not* the right way."

"It is."

"At the traffic lights, make a U-turn."

"There are no traffic lights."

"At the next junction, go off-road."

"In this car?"

"At the next dealership, purchase a new vehicle."

That's how she was.

"Warning: we are low on fuel."

"We're fine."

"Warning: we need coffee and chocolate or we will become annoying."

"*Become* annoying?"

"Advisory: coffee and chocolate will lead to sexual gratitude."

"That would be tempting if you weren't Stephen Hawking."

She'd laughed at that, loud and sudden and surprised, then covered her mouth with both hands. "Oh, that's wrong."

"I just don't find him attractive."

"You're not supposed to find *anyone* attractive."

"What about—"

"Anyone *else* attractive." Then, serious, "You do still find me attractive, right?"

Charlie smiled. He was standing outside, in the cold, smoking in full view of the stables that marked the beginning of the end, but he was also back in the car, back with Lyndsey who was asking, "Are we there yet?"

"Nearly."

"What about now?"

"Nearly."

"What about—"

"*Lynds . . .*"

He looked over at the converted stables.

It was a large but surprisingly squat building, with a sloping roof of cor-rugated metal. He remembered how it drummed with the rain. Inside was a vast open space. If there had ever been stalls for horses they were gone now. In fact, there was little to suggest they were ever stables at all, other than the name of the guesthouse, and he supposed that could have been a deliberate misnomer, something quaint and countrified to lure the tourists. The inside had smelled wet and warm, bales of summer-baked hay wrapped in plastic yet somehow releasing an aroma so that rain seemed to mix with sunshine. There was a metallic smell, too, and oil, from a vehicle that was not quite a tractor sitting guard in the open double doors, the tines of its threshing machinery like some medieval war machine to keep people out. It hadn't deterred them, though. If only it had.

Those doors were closed now, the machine tucked away inside, if it was there at all. Charlie exhaled a final stream of smoke with a sigh. If the fucking thing had been parked away properly in the first place, the giant doors shut, then they never would have gone inside. They'd have forgone the novelty of the setting and had sex back in their own room instead, only yards away.

Charlie dropped what remained of his cigarette and twisted it dead under his heel.

You look angry.

It sounded like Lyndsey's voice, but it was only in his head. Still, it made him smile. "You look angry" had been one of their geo-cache clues last time they were in Wales. It had looked like a code at first—*Ydych yn edrych yn ddig*—but it wasn't long after crossing into Wales that they'd realised it was simply Welsh. *Ydych yn edrych yn ddig*, you look angry, became a game so that whenever one of them said it in the car, thinking aloud, trying to figure it out, the other would offer a reply. *It's just the way my face looks. You stole the covers last night. I'm trying to fart.*

Not all of the locations came with clues or riddles, but those that did were Lyndsey's favourites, and she never Googled the clues or read the message boards in the community forum, nothing like that. She never cheated, not when it came to geo-caching. They figured them out together, just like they did everything else.

"You look angry" was a clue for St. Brynach Church.

"St. Brynach Church, named after—*wow*—St. Brynach," Lyndsey said. "Sixth century chapel, famous for the Nevern Cross or Great Cross of St. Brynach, one of the finest in Wales, thirteen feet high . . ."

Lyndsey liked to research everywhere they went, but only after they'd arrived, to avoid what she called spoilers. While she read to him from her phone, Charlie used his to take pictures. He'd usually manage a few secret ones of Lyndsey before she spotted him, and then she'd strike ridiculous poses or give him the dreaded duck-face pout. At St. Brynach's she hadn't noticed for ages, too busy searching among the gravestones, so after he'd taken a few shots of her bending over he turned the phone around for a secret selfie or two he'd send her later.

"You look angry."

As Charlie was contorting his face into an ugly sneer he'd assumed she'd caught him, but looking up, still sneering, he saw that she had her back to him among the graves. She patted one of them before turning to face him.

"You look angry," she said again. "Cross. Angry is cross. Get it? The Nevern Cross, probably. And you is probably yew tree. The one I told you about, the one that bleeds." She pointed and said, "*Yew* lead the way."

Charlie gave her one of his pity-smiles.

"Shut up, I'm hilarious."

Among the gravestones, Charlie said, "Honey, I love doing this with you, but I'm not digging up a grave. I've got my limits."

Yet here he was, a year later, digging up what should probably be left alone.

He contemplated another cigarette but it began to rain again, so he went back inside.

◄•►

Dryburgh Abbey, in Scotland, stands as a remarkable complete set of ruins. It contains paintwork that dates back to its construction in 1150 and remains one of the most beautiful examples of Gothic architecture.

According to legend, a woman who lost her lover made a home in one of the vaults and swore never to look upon the sun again until her lover returned. Learning he had died, she only ever came out from the vault at night, living a half-life of loss and loneliness.

Geo-cache findings: a heart-shaped fridge magnet, a novelty pen, an ornate thimble.

Whatever the couple had been bickering about was either resolved or temporarily forgotten by the time Charlie returned to his room. He was reminded of how thin the walls were by the sounds of their passionate make-up sex. Or maybe it was angry sex. "Fuck you" sex, Charlie thought, unamused by his own pun.

You look angry.

It sounded like good sex, whatever it was.

Charlie undressed and stretched out on his own bed. He matched his rhythm to the sounds from next door, masturbating to the squeak and creak of their bedsprings and looking at a photograph of Lyndsey he had on the bedside table. Eventually the woman's climax drew a scowling one from him and he was able, at last, to sleep.

◄•►

Croagh Patrick is a holy mountain that rises 765 metres above sea level and overlooks Clew Bay in Ireland. It is believed that St Patrick made his way here from Aghagower and spent 40 nights on its summit praying and fasting and casting out demons. Time has altered the legend so that demons have become snakes instead.

Geo-cache findings: none (not yet visited).

In the morning, Charlie skipped breakfast and went out to his car for the geo-cache he'd left on the back seat, a little of the secret life of Lyndsey and

Charlie West. Deliberately awful poems Lyndsey used to leave for him around the house (*I love you like blue loves sky, oh me, oh my*). A strip of photo booth pictures, Lyndsey flashing her boobs (never breasts, *never* tits), pictures they used to keep on the fridge and had to remember to take down every time they had visitors (and forgetting on more than one occasion). A length of rope (look out for snakes!). He'd considered leaving his wedding ring too but he couldn't bring himself to do it, not yet. There was no comments book inside either because this would be a geo-cache he never registered online. If anyone ever found it, it would be the owners of The Hayward Stables during some clean up or sort out. Putting it here was entirely for his own benefit. Like flowers on a grave.

The car was still wet from last night's rain. Puddles the size of small lakes blotted the gravelled drive and the early morning air held the smell of wet grass. Charlie took a deep breath of it and looked to the sky. Grey, but not raining, and somehow clean looking, as if grey was its usual colour and it had just needed the blue washing out.

Charlie hadn't bothered to lock the car—there was nothing left he couldn't bear to lose—and he was glad not to ruin the peace of the country morning with the electronic blip-blip of central locking. He retrieved the container from the back seat and closed the door again, its soft thump the only sound to disturb the quiet except for the crunch and scrape of gravel underfoot as he made his way to the old stables that might never have been stables.

The large doors were closed. Would they be locked, though? Were they more careful since the Castellmarch man? He doubted it. As he neared, Charlie looked out for a coil of chain wrapped around the handle grips or a large padlock clasped closed, or both, but there was no such thing. He tucked the Tupperware box under his arm, wedged high into his armpit, looked around for anyone who might see him, and gripped the door with both hands. It was a large one that slid across, essentially a moving wall more than a door, and he expected it to be heavy, but it moved easily and quietly, its bearings well-oiled. He opened it only enough to step inside and closed it again behind him.

For a moment it was pitch black dark. He heard birds waking up above him somewhere and smelled the damp sweet aroma of hay and feed and maybe manure, the sharp tang of petrol and machine oil, but he saw nothing. Eventually his eyes adjusted to the gloom, grey light filtering in through rusted holes in the metal walls and roof and through the sheets of newspaper that had been stuck over a large window. Most of the floor space had been taken up by a temporary holding pen made up of boards held between breezeblocks. There was no sign of any livestock, but as a veteran geo-cacher Charlie recognised the pellets of sheep droppings. At the back of the building, a stack of stored hay. That was where, a year ago, he and Lyndsey had enjoyed a private moment, a secret moment that turned out to be less secret than they had supposed. And over there, between the hay and a workbench cluttered with tools, that had been where the Castellmarch man had loitered. Unseen, at first, bedded down in a spill of hay and bundled blankets and tarp.

They'd been walking the grounds, exploring the fields just before dusk. It had been good to just walk together without searching for a geo-cache—there weren't any locations nearby, not then—and they had held hands and talked and made new promises to each other. To try harder. To do more fun stuff. She would be faithful, he would be more spontaneous. As they'd neared The Hayward Stables, Lyndsey had picked up the pace, claiming she wanted to get back before proper dark and the inevitable rain but walking with an urgency that suggested something else.

"You need to pee, don't you?"

"Maybe."

They only made it as far as the stables or barn or whatever the building was before Lyndsey had to relieve herself. She squatted behind a plastic rain barrel and a leaning stack of wooden pallets.

"Watch out for ropes," Charlie had warned.

Back when they'd first started geo-caching, one of the treasure boxes had been hidden among the roots of fallen tree. Lyndsey had crouched beside the trunk, reaching for an opening in the soil, but before she could finish a feeble joke about *rooting* around she'd leapt away with a scream of "Snake!" and the two of them had fled. The "snake" turned out to be a length of dirty rope, some coiled excess from what had been used to secure the geo-cache container to the tree stump. Charlie had teased Lyndsey about it forever since. This new teasing as she peed saw her hand come up from behind the water barrel to give him the middle finger.

"You look angry," Charlie said. An old joke by then, but one they still used occasionally.

"There aren't any snakes in Wales," Lyndsey said, standing and pulling her jeans up with her.

"You're thinking of Ireland."

She'd put her hand to her chest in mock distress, gave him another one of her voices, temporarily Irish. "You mean there *are* snakes in Wales?"

"Baby," he'd said, "Wales has fucking *dragons*."

Worse than dragons.

While Lyndsey buttoned up, Charlie joked that she shouldn't bother. At least, it had started as a joke. But because she'd stopped to "joke" back—"Oh yeah? Why's that?"—instead of simply dismissing his suggestion, he'd taken her by the hand and pulled her towards the open door. Her only protest had been an unconvincing, "We can't," but it turned out they could, and they did, rougher and wilder and louder than they had been in a long time. Proof, if any was needed, that they still had something. Reassurance, for Charlie, that she was still interested in him beyond the comfort and companionship of a long term relationship. Reassurance for her, he supposed, that he could still be passionate and commanding.

Afterwards, panting from where she lay bent over a collapsed bale of hay, Lyndsey had expressed surprise and gratification with the exclamation, *"Fuck."*

"Again? Okay, five minutes."

She had made a pathetic backwards slap at him without looking, exhaling a laugh that had little sound as she tried to catch her breath, but Charlie had already stepped away from her to get dressed again. He swatted her behind, gently this time, and placed her clothes beside her. He kissed her back, and when she rolled over with an exaggerated sigh, he kissed her breasts until she sat up. They were criss-crossed with lines from where she'd been pressed against the hay and strands were stuck to her sweaty skin. He helped her brush them away until she brushed *him* away, slapping at his hands.

"If you want to help you can find my shoes."

They had been such a struggle to remove in the heat of the moment, stuck in her jeans, that Charlie had thrown them aside when they were finally off.

"Charlie?"

"Yeah, I'm looking."

He was peering into the shadows on the ground when Lyndsey called to him again, quieter this time, but with a new tone that made it sound more urgent;

"*Char*lie." She had her t-shirt on but also held her arm across her chest while the other hand pushed her jumper and jeans into her lap, between her legs.

"Lynds?"

She didn't answer or turn to face him and finally Charlie saw what she was looking at. *Who* she was looking at.

The Castellmarch man.

He was wearing a hat, that fucking stupid hat with the flaps that came down over the ears. He was wearing an old army jacket, too, the type that was fashionable when Charlie was young if you wanted to prove how alternative or grungy you were. Army surplus with deep pockets, faded green (and if you were particularly rebellious or quirky, maybe you had a foreign flag stitched into the shoulder). His jeans were scruffy. Charlie couldn't see the man's boots properly but they were probably DMs.

"Oh, shit, sorry," Charlie said, "we just—"

"It was raining," Lyndsey said, slipping down from the hay bale to hide the lower half of her body. When that part of her was out of view she immediately stepped into her jeans, underwear be damned. It hadn't been raining, not quite, but it was now. It drummed loud against the roof.

The man exhaled forcefully from his mouth so that his lips trembled. Charlie couldn't tell if it was disbelief or amusement or anger or what.

"Sorry," Charlie said again, casting a quick look around again to ensure they had everything. He saw a pile of makeshift bedding, tucked away in the dark. A spill of belongings were spread across the ground nearby.

The man scratched at what he had of a beard and said, "Not from here." Charlie didn't know if he meant them or, judging by the rough bedding, himself.

"No, we're just . . . no. You? You staying here as well?"

Partly Charlie was trying to ascertain whether he and Lyndsey were in any kind of trouble. He was fairly certain the man was not one of the owners, and though there was a chance he was a farmhand or something, Charlie supposed the man was actually homeless, or a traveller, bedding down for a night out of the rain. Whatever and whoever he was, Charlie wanted to distract him from Lyndsey who was subtly trying to dress herself.

The man stamped one foot a couple of times and dragged it back across the floor as if trying to scrape something from his boot.

"I'm from *Castellmarch*. I *told* you."

Lyndsey shared a look with Charlie. It was a mildly judgemental look, as in she'd judged the man was mildly mental.

"I mean, I didn't tell you I was from Castellmarch," the man said, "just that I'm not from here. 'Not from here.' I said that."

"Right."

The man nodded. He looked at Lyndsey, dressing.

"So, is that in Wales then?" Charlie asked. "Castellmarch?"

"Castellmarch is in Abersoch, across the sea." He pointed in a direction that meant nothing to Charlie.

"Oh, right. Is it an island?"

The man laughed. "Abersoch's not an *island*." He looked at Lyndsey who had just plucked items of underwear from the ground, bunching them into a tangle of lace and straps and bra cups which she tried to hold casually. He grinned at her as if they shared a private joke or secret intimacy. "He thinks Abersoch is an *island*."

"He's not very clever," Lyndsey said, with a quick smile.

"Hey," said Charlie, "I'm right here."

"It's not an island," the man explained. "It's across the bay."

"Okay."

"I'm going to Carreg Castle."

"Okay."

Lyndsey was looking for her shoes. Charlie made a show of helping her so that he was too busy for further conversation.

"How about some music?" the man asked. He reached down to the array of things scattered on and around his bed. Charlie expected a radio but the man produced a flute, no, a whistle, a recorder or something, but surely he wasn't going to—

The man began to play.

The look Lyndsey gave Charlie was loaded with amusement, a smile in her eyes that acknowledged just how strange all of this was turning out to be. They would have fun, later, talking about it, the look said. She'd probably add this man to her repertoire of sat-nav character voices, Charlie thought.

The whistling was shrill but the open space of the large building seemed to soften it a little, lending a haunting echo that wasn't exactly unpleasant within the drumming sound of rain. There was a melody, and the man played with a burst of enthusiasm that made it lively at first, but his joy dwindled quickly and he stopped as abruptly as he had begun. "Do you know that song?"

Lyndsey shook her head. Charlie said, "No," and wondered if they'd been expected to sing along or dance or something. He wondered if they'd offended him somehow.

The man's scowl was only for his whistle, though. "That wasn't the song I meant to play," he said, pocketing the instrument. "I think it's broken."

Lyndsey laughed, partly in case it was a joke and partly because this was all just too weird. Charlie laughed a little with her, glad when the man smiled because now it meant they were laughing with him instead of at him. Kind of.

The man withdrew a pouch of tobacco from his coat pocket. He offered it but they both shook their heads no.

"Don't smoke," Charlie told him.

"What are you looking for?"

Lyndsey said, "My shoes."

The man put his tobacco aside and crouched out of sight. When he stood again he had two hiking boots, one in each hand. He held them by his sides.

"Great," said Lyndsey, "Thanks."

The man made no move to offer them, though. "Want to hear a joke?" he said.

"We better get back inside," Lyndsey said. She reached for her shoes. The man made an underarm gesture with one of them. He did it a second time but didn't throw.

"Go on, then," Charlie said. He meant go on, throw the boots, but the man used it as an excuse to tell his joke, Lyndsey's boots held by his sides.

"Two men in a pub, right? One of them, he goes to find a table, see, and the other one gets the drinks in. 'Pint for me and my donkey.'"

Charlie nodded—clearly they had to listen to the joke as some part of an exchange—but when the man kept repeating the character's drink order, Charlie nodded again to hurry the man along.

"So this happens a few times, same one going to the bar and saying 'pint for me and my donkey,' until eventually the other guy comes to the bar instead. Before he can order, the barman says, 'Your friend over there keeps calling you his donkey.' And the customer, he nods and says—"

Charlie knew the joke, he realised, but it had taken until now for him to remember the punch line. The man still surprised him, though.

"'Oh, *hee*-aw! *hee*-aw! *hee*-always calls me that!'"

The man brayed loud enough that each *hee*-aw! sounded like a scream, a shrill then guttural cry bouncing around in the confines of the barn. The sudden noise and volume startled both of them, as did the way the man thrust his head forward for each outburst, his lips peeled back against large slabs of teeth. Lyndsey had recoiled, pressing herself against a wall of stacked hay bales, wide-eyed. Charlie took her hand.

"Do you get it?" the man asked them, and without waiting for a response he said again, "He always calls me that. *Hee*-aw!" The final cry dissolved into laughter and Charlie laughed as well this time. Not at the joke, but in a kind of anxious release.

The man wiped tears from his eyes, still offering the occasional chuckle and sigh.

"Okay," Charlie said, "boots now, yeah?"

The man nodded. "You have a spirited filly," he said.

"Sorry, what?"

"Spirited," the man said. He looked at Lyndsey. "This filly likes a good ride."

"Hey," said Charlie, and, "Fuck," said Lyndsey.

The man laughed again. To Lyndsey he said, "Eager filly!" and to Charlie, "You ride her well," and then he tossed the boots. He threw them underarm, but he did it quick and Charlie had to twist and turn to try to catch them, missing both. Lyndsey gathered them up and pulled them on quick, laces loose, and Charlie turned her by the shoulders, guiding her outside and away, pushing her ahead of him. Behind them, the braying laughter of the man followed them out into the dark.

Charlie reported him to the owners. He did that much, at least. He gave them a slightly edited version of events in which he swapped post-coital surprise for seeing someone sneaking into the outbuilding and in the morning their breakfast was served with the reassurance that the man was gone. As to whether he'd been sent on right away or asked to leave that morning, the owners had been rather vague about that. "It happens sometimes," the wife had said, adding, "we should really keep it locked, I suppose."

Well, they still don't lock it, Charlie thought, and he was glad. He found a place behind the workbench where a metal brace and a supporting beam crossed (*x marks the spot*) and there, in a small nook close to the wall, he stowed his geo-cache of memories.

-o-

Sadie's Lane in Dorset, England, is reported to be one of the most haunted roads in the county. It came by its name in the early eighteenth century when a farm girl called Sadie Young allegedly rode her horse to its death as she raced to meet a lover who had abandoned her. Pitched from the fallen animal, Sadie was also killed and is said to haunt what is now a busy relief road. The location has since attracted several other ghosts, each of them linked to tales of heartbreak and loss. It is now a popular suicide spot.

Geo-cache findings: a selection of pressed flowers and a chess piece (rook).

Leaving the outbuilding, stepping from the dark into a morning still fresh and clean and grey, Charlie was greeted by last night's couple approaching their car (the Audi). The woman smiled, the kind of polite smile you give to strangers with whom you share a certain level of intimacy, like those in the same train carriage or a doctor's waiting room. If she'd known just how intimate they were, now, after last night, she probably wouldn't have smiled, Charlie thought. Or maybe she would. Maybe she was well aware of how loud they'd been. Today she was dressed in a jeans and jumper ensemble that was practical yet still somehow stylish, more town clothes than country. Charlie admired how the denim fit her.

"Beautiful, eh?" the husband said to Charlie. "That fresh country air."

Charlie nodded, more in hello than as an answer. "Morning," he said, stepping to his own car.

"Thought we might look for some of those interesting places you mentioned," the man said. He waved a folded leaflet to support his point. Charlie had seen a limited selection of them fanned out on a table in the dining room.

"Be sure to visit Carreg Castle," Charlie said, slipping the name in with little fanfare. The man opened up the leaflet to look but Charlie gave him directions anyway, hearing in his head one of Lyndsey's wonderful sat-nav voices in echo. "Just heading there myself, but I recommend you try it around sundown. It's a bit spooky, but beautiful. Romantic."

"Thanks," said the woman, and this time her smile was a little warmer.

"Yeah, appreciate it," said her husband.

Charlie prepared a cigarette, concentrating on the task until he heard the double *thunk* of car doors closing, then he watched them for a moment, a silent movie behind the windscreen. They seemed happy now, but then so did many couples. Anyone could look happy if they buried their secrets deep enough. Charlie watched them reverse out of the parking area. For a moment, when she turned around in her seat, the woman looked like Lyndsey. That quick profile and final look at Charlie that disappeared as they turned away and were gone.

Charlie smoked his cigarette. He didn't smoke in the car because Lyndsey wouldn't have liked it, but seeing her waterproof parcelled up into itself on the backseat he leaned in to retrieve it, careful to hold the roll-up outside the whole time. He turned the coat out, unzipped it open, and shook it into shape. He draped it over his on the passenger seat. From the corner of his eye perhaps it would seem as if she accompanied his drive. It was a pathetic hope, but strangely soothing.

"Okay," he said, finishing the cigarette, and though there was no one to say it to but himself, added, "let's go."

For a lot of the journey the roads passed through open country-side, fields dropping into valleys or climbing into hills, distant sheep scattered like chewed lumps of gum. Tiny towns or perhaps villages passed so quickly that moments later Charlie wondered at their exis-tence. Eventually, though, the hills closed in and the road cut its way through trees and shadow. The lanes became choked with mud and vast puddles made sections into shallow rivers. The hedgerows pressed close, sometimes scraping the car on tight corners. Charlie tried to focus his attention on the road, assessing when to slow down, when to speed up, balancing the risks of soft ground and floods by fluctuating between two speeds in a sort of compromise against getting stuck and losing control. He rushed through puddles in a shushed-thunder of spray that drummed underneath the car and spread in sheets either side.

On the back seat, another geo-cache container rattled as it slid left and right with the corners and jumped with the bumps and dips of the road. There was only one item inside.

He'd been hiding geo-caches up and down the British Isles for most of the last six months, building up to this moment. Little boxes of their life together, here and there. Their old GPS from back before they simply used apps on their phones. A half-eaten mint cake, which neither of them liked because it made their teeth feel funny but which they bought anyway because it was one of the rules, like the hideous waterproofs. He wondered how many people had walked past them, these secret geo-caches, never knowing what was there, and he thought, *well, life's like that, isn't it?* Everybody has a story you don't get to hear. Even in a relationship, there were things you didn't learn until far down the line together, or things changed, and maybe you didn't always like what you found. Lyndsey had thought she knew all there was to know about Charlie, and he used to think the same of her. For him, that familiarity brought comfort. For her, it was different.

He slowed the car just as an oncoming vehicle turned into the road ahead, blocking the entire width. The driver made a token effort to move aside, but there was no way they were going to squeeze past each other. Charlie checked behind and manoeuvred the car backwards.

"Attention: this vehicle is reversing."

That's what Lyndsey would have said as Charlie manoeuvred the vehicle back. "*Bleep! Bleep!* Attention: this vehicle is reversing." Then the warning again. And then the bleeps. And then the warning again, and then the bleeps, until—

"Lynds."

Her name sounded lost with no one to answer it. Charlie looked at the empty seat beside him but the waterproof there remained simply a waterproof, hanging like a thin corpse. An empty shroud, trying too hard to be bright and cheerful.

The other car followed Charlie, keeping close as if Charlie might change his mind, pushing him back. As soon as there was room, it pulled out and passed. If there was a thank you, Charlie didn't see it.

"You're welcome."

He changed gears from reverse to first and the car rocked in place. That was all. For a moment he thought he was stuck—"Come *on*"—but all he'd done was stall it. Overcompensating with the revs, he sent a fantail of mud spraying behind as he pulled away again. Better to lose control than get stuck in place, he thought, hurrying towards something he'd never find with nothing left to lose but himself.

⟨o⟩

Carreg Cennen Castle can be found in the village of Trap about 4 miles from Llandeilo in Carmarthenshire, Wales. It stands on a limestone precipice and within its bowels there is a tunnel which leads to a well said to hold mystical healing properties, particularly regarding ear and eye complaints. Visitors to the castle often cast corks and bent pins into the water in order to be healed.

Geo-cache findings (four out of five caches): a novelty key ring, a decorative bookmark, a plastic toy knight, a packet of crayons, a rubber sheep, a deck of pornographic cards, a two-pound coin, two bottle openers, a candle.

The first time he'd seen Carreg Castle was between the stutters of the windscreen wipers, leaning forward to peer through the glass as if a few more inches would allow him to see it more clearly. Back then, the sun had barely been out all day and what there was of it was sinking behind the hill the castle stood upon, the sky taking on the deepening blue tones of early evening with some red shining behind and between the ruined walls. Part of the hill dropped away as a sheer cliff so that the castle walls on one edge seemed to merge seamlessly into the precipice.

"Spooky," said Lyndsey.

This time it looked postcard-picture-perfect. The sky had cleared by the time he'd reached the castle, the sun having burnt away the misty haze of the early hours to reveal a sharpening bright blue sky dotted with clouds that hung motionless in a panorama that was beautiful and all so completely wrong. It should have looked ugly. It should have been pissing down and miserable and the end-of-the-world.

There had been a sequence of geo-caches here. It happened that way sometimes, especially with popular landmark locations. Clues to one revealed clues to another, and so on, giving you a good walk while building to what usually turned out to be an anti-climax. But then geo-caching was never really about what you found at the end. It was the journey, as clichéd as that seemed. The spending time together. It was learning more about your own country, the secret spectacles of home. Learning more about each other, and hoping you liked it.

They'd found the first geo-cache easily. Some of a stone wall had fallen and tucked amongst the rocks was an ice cream container bearing a strip of masking tape across its lid that declared, simply, "geo-cache." Inside they'd found yet another Welsh key ring (this time a flat rubber oval with Carreg Castle in bas-relief), a decorative bookmark (or quitter's strip, as Lyndsey used to call them), and a plastic toy. The toy was an armoured knight. He held a lance before him and his legs were unnaturally bowed, a half-circle scoop as if there had been a horse below him as well at some point. They took the horseless knight and left the key ring and bookmark, adding a yo-yo for whoever came next. Take something, leave something, move on. Another strip of masking tape inside the container provided a new clue and they followed it to the next location, and then again, and so on, until they were at the castle. It had become something of a silhouette in the fading light, and a cool evening breeze tousled Lyndsey's hair as she looked down at the glowing phone in her hand.

"We better get a move on if we want to get the last geo-cache. It's in the castle somewhere and it'll be closed soon."

The castle was privately owned but still open to the public. "It has a tea room and everything," Lyndsey told him, scrolling through information on her phone, offering Charlie the highlights. She gave him details about the accidental sale of the castle, gave him particulars of its history and structure, its six towers, the drawbridges, the chapel, all of it, speeding through centuries.

"It's mostly limestone here," she said, "and there's an underground tunnel that'll take us to where the last cache is, I think. '150 feet of tunnel leads you to a well, believed to hold mystical healing powers.' That's what it says. You throw corks or pins in and make a wish. It's particularly good at healing ear and eye complaints, apparently. Which is why I think the cache is there, because of the clue. 'You'll do well to keep your eyes open.' Which is a crap clue but it makes sense."

"Why corks and pins?"

She shrugged. "Doesn't say."

Charlie wondered at what else it didn't say as he made his way towards the castle again. As he walked among the shake holes, sunken depressions in the soil and cracked stone, he also wondered how Lyndsey made her decisions about what to share and what to not, and would she have left him anyway if it hadn't been for the Castellmarch man.

At the castle, Charlie descended into a gloom that suited his mood. The stone stairs were slippery with old rain and the castle's outer wall close beside him seemed like it was leaning, as if it wanted to push him over the edge. He imagined falling. He'd imagined it lots of times. But he didn't fall, and soon he was standing before a long narrow gash in the cliff face. Hardly any light penetrated the passageway, especially with his body blocking what there was of it, and he didn't have a phone this time to illuminate the way; he'd never replaced his, and the police still had Lyndsey's. Knowing how much darker it would become, he didn't bother waiting for his eyes to adjust and simply plunged right in.

"Here we go."

He was swallowed into nothing by the darkness. Arms out at his sides, he used the walls to guide him deeper. The stone was smooth and dry but very cold. He stooped, remembering how low the passageway became in places, and sometimes he was more comfortable turning sideways, but eventually he came to the standing pool of water where Lyndsey had joked about Gollum. She'd hissed "My *precious* . . ." into his ear in the dark.

"I expected an actual well."

Charlie backed up a few steps and sat. He was wearing his new coat, which was long enough to offer him some protection against the cold stone. In one of its deep pockets was the Tupperware geo-cache he'd brought, shallow but long, perfect for what it held. He checked his watch, its light casting an eerie green glow that only seemed to make the dark darker.

He was early.

He waited.

Charlie had shone the light of his phone around the perimeter of the pool that first time. There were shapes floating on the surface and gathered at the edges. Corks. Some of them had pins pushed through them. Back then he'd had to psych himself up to put his hand in the water, and he'd gasped at the temperature. This time he merely reached out and caressed the surface of the pool, making small waves in the darkness. He felt a cork or two against his palm. He had stabbed himself last time on pins at the bottom of the pool, reaching for a geo-cache they never found. He'd dropped his phone, swearing. For a moment the light had stayed on at the bottom of the pool, and he'd grabbed it up again quickly, as if speed could stop it from becoming *more* wet. Tried to shake it dry.

"What?" Lyndsey asked. "What?"

"Dropped my fucking phone."

"Yeah, but why?"

"Well I didn't mean to."

"I mean, did you hurt yourself? Did something bite you or something?"
There'd only been the brief sting of pins. "I'm okay."

"How's the phone?"

It was fine, until he pressed a button to check if it was fine, and then the
screen went black and the torchlight went out.

"Shit."

"Well done."

"Ssh."

"You shush." Lyndsey had lit the tunnel with her phone instead but Charlie
took it from her and plunged them back into the dark. He found Lyndsey's
arm. Her hand. He pulled her close and found something else and she'd
said, "Hey!"

"We'll have to grope our way out."

"Funny man."

And they had kissed. He remembered that very well. Sometimes,
when he couldn't sleep, he'd close his eyes as tight as he could to
replicate the utter darkness of that moment and he'd remember the
kisses they'd shared under the castle, buried in its rock. He couldn't
tell any more if they only felt like final kisses now, in retrospect, or if
he'd known it even then.

"We should pick up some rice when we get out," Lyndsey said, breaking
away. "For your phone."

"Does that actually work?"

He felt her shrug. "Saw it on Facebook so it must be true. Absorbs the
water or something. You remember Jenny from—"

"Ssh."

"No, I'm telling you a fascinating story."

"I think someone else is here. Listen."

They strained their ears to hear. Charlie turned his head and, for some
reason, opened his mouth. He found that helped sometimes. This time it did.

"Hear that?" he whispered.

"Yeah, someone's coming."

And yet neither of them felt relieved. Maybe because whoever was coming did so without a light.

As if they'd agreed it between them, neither of them called out or made any noise, and though Charlie had Lyndsey's phone he didn't even consider using its light. He backed away, deeper into the passageway, pulling Lyndsey with him, keeping close to the wall.

It was the Castellmarch man, of course. For a while he was only the scrape of footsteps, but somehow they'd known. Why else would they have remained so quiet? Why else had they tried to hide, when the normal thing to have done would have been to greet whoever else had come to this special place?

He was singing something softly to himself. Welsh words, unfamiliar, but Charlie thought he recognised the tune.

Lyndsey's breath was warm in Charlie's ear. Her mouth was so close that he felt her lips on him as she said, "It's him." He went to turn his head, to whisper back, but she held him still and said, lips to his ear, "It's the Castellmarch man."

The voice in the darkness with them was suddenly quiet, and though Charlie hadn't been able to follow the song properly he could still tell it had stopped mid-line.

"Somebody's there," said the man.

Lyndsey squeezed Charlie's arm tight but the two of them remained quiet. There was nothing to be afraid of, he thought. Not really.

"Who's there?" the voice called. "Why are you spying on me?"

They waited, silent, holding their breath and each other's hand.

"WHO'S SPYING ON ME?"

Charlie said, "We're *not* spying," and lit up the dark with Lyndsey's phone. Her grip on his arm tightened and they saw, together, the man crouching at the pool, that hat in his hands, and—

Charlie thought he saw . . . He thought, but he must have been wrong. He thought he saw the man's ears, long and pointed and furred, twitching at Charlie's voice. Horse's ears. Then everything was a chaos of movement and noise. The Castellmarch man leapt to his feet, literally bounding up and across at them on all fours. He knocked Charlie aside and into the wall, hitting him harder than he'd have thought possible for a man of such build. Charlie dropped the phone, but not into the pool this time. Its light stayed on, but the device was kicked several times in the to and fro of a scuffle. Lyndsey cried out, and swore, and Charlie yanked at her and pushed at the other, and they splashed through the shallows of icy water as the man cried out, "You saw me!" his voice bouncing around and back at them in the confines of the tunnel. "You *saw* me!"

Up close, Charlie saw the man definitely had horse ears. They stuck up from lank hair that swept from his head and down his back like a mane. He had one arm around Lyndsey from behind and then he leapt up so that he was on her back. Charlie tried to grab him, push him away, pull him down, and Lyndsey turned around, tried to run, tried to shake the man off. The Castellmarch man gripped her firm, though, fierce, his legs around her waist now. He reached down between her breasts with one hand, holding a bunch of her jumper in his fist, gripping at her ribs, and the other held a tangle of her hair, and he was laughing or he was screaming, it was hard to tell, all his noise coming out shrill and echoing back at them. His eyes were wide, and he frothed at the mouth, Charlie thought, and he rocked against Lyndsey's back, urging her on, pulling at her hair to guide her direction as she tried to run from him though he clung to her. Charlie saw her stagger the way they'd come and he pushed after them as the man's cries whinnied back and forth in the dark.

Near the entrance they became a hectic silhouette. Lyndsey was bent under the man's weight but still on her feet, ricocheting off the walls of the tunnel either side as the man held himself fast against her, upon her, one hand twisted in her hair and his groin rocking against her as if dry humping her back, playing giddy-up. In a panicked pirouette, Charlie saw his wife's head turn, saw her look at him a final time, the Castellmarch man leaning over with his cheek against hers and his ears, those stupid fucking twitching ears, and then the two of them were gone. They dropped away into open space and Charlie had to pull up hard to stop from following them over the edge and down.

Charlie had called out his anguish then, but now it was little more than a soft mewling sound in the dark as he remembered. Take something, leave something, move on, he thought. Lyndsey had been taken, he had been left behind, and if anyone had moved on then it wasn't him.

There had been no bodies down there, but in his dreams there were. Sometimes Lyndsey's, sometimes his own. Sometimes he saw her carried away, the Castellmarch man's bandy legs striding in great bounds. Sometimes it was Lyndsey who fled, carrying this strange man with her. The police found no trace of either person. They probably weren't even looking any more, but Charlie was. Leaving his geo-caches with clues only Lyndsey would understand, looking for her up and down the country. He wondered if she was looking for him. Just as he wondered, sometimes, about that final look she gave him. Sometimes he remembered fear. Other times, excitement. Occasionally what he saw, or thought he saw, was relief.

Charlie removed his wedding ring and, sitting on the ground, traced his finger over the engraving inside, the coordinates marking their life together. One of them was this one, Carreg Castle, where the water was said to hold mystical healing properties. The eyes and the ears and maybe, Charlie hoped, the heart.

He cast his ring into the water. There was barely any splash at all when really it should have thundered. Then, from his pocket, he took the final Tupperware container. He was wearing a new coat and the pockets were deep. From another he took the hat.

In that struggle a year ago he had torn the Castellmarch man's pocket and something had fallen from it. He had it now, in this final container. His wooden flute, or whistle, or recorder, whatever the fuck it was.

He took the instrument from its box and put it to his lips and played. It didn't take him long to get the tune right. Maybe it would call them back, isn't that how it worked in the old stories? Maybe *one* of them, at least, would come. Someone.

Anyone.

He played and he played until, finally, he thought he heard something. Voices, coming to him in the dark. He raised one of the flaps of the hat he'd put on and turned his ear to listen.

Yes. Voices. A man and a woman. He thought perhaps they were bickering, but that was okay. That might be better, actually.

He pocketed the whistle and the hat and stood. Take something, leave something, he thought. He pressed himself against one of the walls, hiding in the dark it made, and he waited.

◦►

In Abersoch there is a seventeenth century mansion that goes by the name of Castellmarch. According to legend it was once the home of one of King Arthur's knights, March Amheirchion, who had the ears of a horse. He kept them hidden, but occasionally someone would discover his secret and March (whose name means horse in Welsh) would be forced to kill them. He hid the bodies in a nearby bed of reeds. His true nature was finally discovered when a boy made a flute from one of the reeds and the only song the flute could play was "March Amheirchion has horse's ears." Nobody knows what became of March Amheirchion, but it is believed he had several children and that his line continues to this day.

THE ICE BENEATH US

STEVE DUFFY

The sound of the ice never used to bother me. You get accustomed to it in the course of a day's fishing, the creaking and shifting under the cabin as the frozen lake beneath you groans and settles. Claude and me, we've fished Bent Iron Lake every year since we started at Boeing, back on the old Vertol assembly. Back since before I got married, since the two of us got all white-collar and respectable—and now since Esther died, what is it, five years ago? Every January, it's been Claude and me out on the ice. You'd surely think I'd be used to it by now.

Bent Iron Lake is up in the high passes of the Snoqualmie National Forest, in between Mount Baker and Lake Chelan. You don't pass it on the way to either of those places—you don't go near it unless you're headed there, and nowhere else. It's at the end of an old logging track, around five or six miles north of Downey's Bunkhouse, which is the motel where Claude and I always stay. Days, we rent a cabin on the lake and fish for walleye and crappie, pass the Jim Beam between us, and tell tall tales of the ones that got away. Evenings, we doze in armchairs by the log fire at the Bunkhouse, like the old poops we've become. At least, that was the way it used to be, before last year.

So, here we are back on the lake, same old cabin, same old Claude and me . . . and yet somehow not the same. There's something else to contend with now, that thing that binds us closer even as it comes between us. That thing that happened the day of the snowstorm.

◄◦►

The whole day seemed to play out in twilight, I remember. All the way from sun-up to sunset there was a shroud cast over everything, heavy storm clouds piling up on top of Mount Baker, a cold wind blasting down off the slopes. It began snowing around midday, and by half past two it was already so dim inside the little cabin on the ice that we'd lit up the storm lanterns. Nothing moved in the snowstorm, no creature, no vehicle, and inside the cabin there was only the usual cracking and splintering beneath our frozen feet, an occasional bubble of air plopping in the borehole where our lines were cast. I remember we were talking over whether we ought to call it a day and head on back to the Bunkhouse, in case the roads became impassable. "Goddamnit, you could drive that Hummer through a six-foot drift," Claude was insisting, when we heard it, from outside, in a sudden lull between the buffets of wind that slammed against the thin cabin wall. The sound of footsteps through snow, crunching across the ice. And then a knocking at the door, as if the wind and all its bluster had hardened into a dull dead fist.

◄◦►

"Yeah, I'll take a pull," says Claude, and he holds out his hand for the Jim Beam. We've been knocking it back since midday, but for once it hasn't affected me any, not in the slightest. I'm not feeling the least bit lit up, and the warm place it usually makes in the pit of my stomach is noticeably absent—worse luck.

Claude, though, looks pretty loaded. There's a glitter in his eyes that I just don't recognise, though I've known him longer than I knew my late wife, and till last year I'd have unhesitatingly named him as my best and oldest friend, for all he's a crabby, waspish old fart that could pick a fight in an empty room. I'd still say that now, I guess, even after everything; but I might just hesitate beforehand, the way I did right there. At our age, what you're left with is pretty much all you've got. You've earned it, it's yours.

"Here's to crime," says Claude, and takes a long swig. Wipes his mouth with the back of his hand, sets the bottle down on the bench alongside him. "Oops."

I don't say anything, just carry on baiting my hook.

"What you got on that?" he asks. Knowing very well what I've got on it, of course.

"I was favouring an eye-drop lure," I tell him. "Just this second put on a doodlebug."

"Bullshit," he says, as he generally does. "How many goddamn times do I have to tell you? You wanna fish this lake? Spoon and a fathead. Pinch 'er off at the gills there," and he demonstrates the action.

"Well, that's one way," I say, as I generally do, and finish tying off.

Between us, framed by the trapdoor at our feet, the hole we cut in the ice this morning gives a brief gurgle, and peaty black water laps up at the duckboards. Claude answers it with a boozy chuckle of his own.

"Reckon I oughta know this lake by now. Your panfish? Your walleye? They're in and out of those weeds down under." He gestures through the hole, down into the deep green water. "They're in the last of the salad, the tangleweed there. It's been good feeding for 'em in there this last year, and they're loath to move on." He pauses, as if thinking about what he's just said, and laughs again, much too loud for such a small cabin. "Damn good feeding, you betcha."

I purposely don't catch his eye. All day he's been riding me, unable to let things be. We shouldn't have come back—I shouldn't have let him talk me into it. But he said it'd look bad if we didn't, people would begin to ask why. And now, ever since we got here, he's been needling away at it.

He waits for me to acknowledge what he's said, then with an annoyed little grunt—"ah, what the hell"—he takes another jolt from the Jim Beam. "What's done is done, right, Bob? Am I right?"

"That's right, Claude," I agree, and let my baited line sink down into the darkness. The ice creaks a little. Away up in the trees, there's the lonely winter sound of crows.

◂◦▸

We looked at each other, taken a little aback I suppose. At first I thought it might have been a park ranger, telling us we had to come off the ice because of the weather. You know, part of me thought that was just fine, and was more than ready to spend the rest of the day in front of a log fire at Downey's Bunkhouse. Anyway, there was no way of knowing who it was without one of us opened the door. Groaning a little—we had taken a little whisky that day, to keep the cold out of our old man bones—I got up and laid my hand on the door handle. But our visitor beat me to it.

He stood there in the doorway, filling it almost, a gaunt gangling scarecrow of a man with long black hair flying in the wind. He was an Indian, Native American I mean. Whether he was Wenatchee or not I don't know; I think of him now and it seems like he could have come from anywhere.

Even in that instant of being taken by surprise I noticed he wasn't properly dressed for the weather. He had on only a light Army camouflage jacket over sweater and jeans, was all, so that his thinness was accentuated in silhouette against the falling snow.

"Cold out there," he said, and with that he was inside. He left the door open behind him; I shut that, mostly so we wouldn't freeze to death while we found out who the hell he was and what the hell he wanted.

No sooner had I closed the door than we could smell it, both Claude and I. Whoever he was, the stranger, he'd been up to some pretty raw work. Filtering through the cabin came a stench—a rankness I remembered from hunting trips up in the mountains as a kid, passing by the butcher slabs in the yards of back-country cabins, the locals staring at you over the split rack of a jacked deer. It was the wrong side of gamy: putrid and maggoty and hot somehow, like fever. The stink of spoiled meat and rotten carcasses. The smell of death.

⟶

Claude sets down his rod. "Nothing biting today," he grumbles, and gets up from his bench to stretch. I might have told him the most he'd catch with that setup was a cold, but you know Claude: he wouldn't have listened anyway. 'Specially not today: he's been even more pig-headed than usual, if such a thing is possible.

I look around the four walls of the cabin, as familiar to me as my old office at Boeing. The ancient girlie poster opposite the door, the smudged sooty eyes of the soft-focus hippie chick staring back at us with the devastating bluntness of the young. The dusty shelves, the wooden storage chests, the smeary window with its scratched-up view across the lake. Unbroken white of the ice and snow, and beyond that the blackness of the trees. Behind the door, another poster, new since 2001: the twin towers of the old World Trade Center, brave in morning sunlight from the last millennium, and a legend, NEVER FORGET.

Claude stretches both arms wide apart, rocks on the balls of his feet, subsides again with a boozy exhalation and a grunt. He goes to look out the window, and accidentally kicks something over alongside the bench. Accidentally, maybe. It's the little McCulloch chainsaw we brought with us to cut our fishing hole in the ice.

"Hah," he says, picking it up and hefting it experimentally. "I got a good deal on this, you know? It's a good tool. Reliable." He waves it through the air as if he's sawing something, before setting it down on top of the storage chest. "Could have used this last year, know what I'm saying?"

"Last year we had the auger still," I say, and regret it almost immediately.

"Well, yeah, the auger," Claude says, sitting back down directly across from me, the ice hole between us once more. "The auger came in pretty handy too, huh? Did a job." He holds up a finger, spirals it once or twice before pointing elaborately down at the hole. "Heavy, that was the thing."

"Yeah, it was heavy all right," I concede, picturing it in my mind's eye. Picturing it slipping down into the ice hole.

Claude reaches behind him, groans an old-man groan. "You know, I pulled half the muscles in my goddamn shoulder with that? Couldn't put my shirt on without a twinge back there for weeks. Months." He grimaces. "Face it! We're not as young as we used to be, Bob. You and me."

I don't say anything at first. There he goes again, drawing us both in. Making it so we're linked, caught up in this together. Conspirators. And yet who started it I really couldn't say; nor yet who ended it. Perhaps it hasn't ended.

"Just fish the damn lake," I say in the end. "Quit grousing." I figure that way I can maybe defuse the tension that's between us, the tension that's been there since we stepped back in the cabin this morning. Our first time back on Bent Iron since that day a year ago, the day it snowed, the day Jimbo came a-knocking.

—◦—

"Jimbo," he said, when Claude asked him the second time. He was sitting on the storage chest, his back to the window, the light of the storm lantern falling from above his head, making him look even more cadaverous. "I go by Jimbo, you know?" An incredibly deep voice: it seemed to come from someplace lower than his boots. Up from the ice, maybe.

"Jimbo, huh? Well, okay, you wanna tell us where the hell you get off just waltzing into here like you own the joint, Jimbo?" Claude was staring at him in that bellicose Irish way of his, pale blue eyes the colour of washed-out winter skies.

"You got a problem out there?" I chipped in, not wanting to provoke any confrontations, but anxious to find out what the hell it was he did want. "Is it the weather?"

He considered a while, then said: "Storm coming up," as if that explained everything quite adequately.

"Snowstorm, yeah," I said quickly, wanting to break the silence that followed this remark before Claude could. "You having trouble on the roads?"

"Ain't been on the roads," he said, in that gravel-pit voice of his. "I been out in the woods." He gestured east, it might have been any distance.

"In the woods, huh? You huntin'? Trappin'?" Claude continued to stare him down.

It didn't seem to faze Jimbo any. "Huntin'?" It seemed to be the punchline to a joke he was sharing only with himself. He laughed, a rumble from deep in his chest. "Huntin's what I do, yeah."

"Permit?" Claude was in the mood to push it.

"I don't need a permit, man," he said, his eyes suddenly, startlingly wide. "This here is my permit." And he jabbed a finger at the veins in his wrist. "It's in the blood."

Claude snorted. The man held his stare for a few moments, then laughed and stretched out his considerable frame, totally at ease, it seemed. He grunted in satisfaction, and I could almost hear the creaking of his sinews as he flexed and relaxed. Perhaps it was the creaking of the ice put it in my mind.

"Look, we don't so much mind you getting someplace out of the storm," I began, seeing that Claude was about ready to take it up a notch or two. I was hoping mostly to defuse the situation without things taking a turn for the physical. "But, well, it's like Claude was saying, you breeze on in like you, I don't know, almost like you own the place—you didn't knock, you didn't wait for so much as a by-your-leave—"

"I been taking shelter here the last few nights now," Jimbo said, scratching at his rumpled bird's-nest of thick black hair. "Out on the ice, you know?"

"Have you, by God? Well, I guess you'd better find someplace the fuck else to take shelter, then, hadn't you, fella? Seeing as this happens to be our cabin."

"Your cabin?" As if that was another mighty funny joke to which he alone knew the punchline. "Okay, I'll tell you a story about that . . ."

◄○►

"You seem a touch snappy there, Bob." Claude's just determined to ride me. I was afraid this was how it'd play out.

"I'm fine," I say. "Isn't this the way it always is? The two of us, out here on the ice? Quit picking at it."

"Picking at it? Hey, we could pretend it never happened."

"It didn't," I tell him flatly. "Nothing happened. Nothing ever does."

He was looking at the poster of the twin towers. "I wish that were true, Bobby boy. I wish to fuck that was the way of it. But you and me, we know better. We *saw*."

I'm seeing even as he says it, even as I cut across him, "Saw jack shit is what we saw. Maybe it's about time you just dropped it, Claude."

"Goddamn, you've got a hair up your ass today," Claude says, and turns those unsmiling Irish eyes back on me, full beam. "Since when did you get so high and mighty, anyway? I guess we'd better talk about the weather, less we upset your delicate feelings."

"*I've* got a hair up my ass? I'm not the one who sounds like something out of a bad Charles Bronson movie. I'm not the one who keeps bringing it up, over and over again. All's I'm saying is, you'd better drop it, that's all."

"Drop it? *Drop* it? Lucky for you I did drop it," and I see there's no hope. He's determined to haul it on out like the biggest goddamnedest fish that was ever pulled out of an ice-hole on Bent Iron, whether it's so I can properly acknowledge his heroism, or the two of us can share a chuckle about the way we showed that punk a lesson, or whatever. "Lucky for you I dropped that motherfucker right slam in the basket. Lucky for you I took control—"

"Not so lucky for him, though, huh?" All the while I see the look on Jimbo's face, that sudden, almost comical look of surprise as he slumped forward.

"Him?" There's nothing remotely humorous in Claude's laughter. "You're crackin' me up here. *Him?* Yeah, well, maybe his luck had just about run out. Say, maybe he had a story about that as well! You think? Once upon a time—"

◄○►

"In the old days, in the days of longago, our people lived in lodges in a great clearing in the forest," said the big guy from outside, Jimbo. It seemed to surprise

Claude into silence for a moment, and I was just too taken aback by the whole shouting match to interrupt or do much of anything.

"Hundreds of tiny lodges in that great enormous clearing," Jimbo continued, "and all around, nothing but the forest for thousands of miles, a thousand days' march, clear out to the edge of the world. And the season it was always autumn, fruit on the trees, game in the forest, honey in bees' nests, a great yellow moon that rose above the trees and turned everything to silver. And it was never winter, and the snow never came to the clearing, nor the frost either."

Claude was sitting open-mouthed, as if he couldn't believe any of this, as if he'd been picked up from the twenty-first century and dumped into a fairy tale of the ancient days himself. As Jimbo continued he turned to me and mouthed what the fuck?

"Until the coming of the black crow king. Not a Crow—" you could hear the capitalisation in his voice—"I don't mean a man of the Crow tribe. This was the days before the tribes: back then there were only our people, and no others. Not even the wasichu. Only our people, the people of the clearing, and away off in the forest, the black crow king. Always outside, always waiting.

"The frost came ahead of him, see? It turned the fingers of the trees to icicles, and it turned the ground to stone, and some of the old people and the babies, they died even before he came. Even when he was just a smell on the wind, a red flush in the evening sky.

"And then one day the first flakes of snow began to fall on the clearing, and in the flurry of that snowfall he was among us. Down through the snow he flew, and he landed on the poles of the first lodge he came to, and he let out a caw. And if you looked at him one way, he was a bird still, but he spoke with the voice of a man, and sometimes when you caught sight of him from the corner of your eye, it seemed like it was a man up there. So, was he a bird that had magic and could trick your eyes into seeing him as a man, or was he a skinwalker that took the shape of a bird? No one knew.

"And he hopped down off the lodge pole and went into the lodge, and he took it as his own that evening. And in the night, the man who owned the lodge, the people all around heard him out in the clearing, and sometimes it sounded like the howling of a wolf, and sometimes the screaming of an eagle, and sometimes the roaring of a bear. But no one dared go see what was happening out there. And when the sun came up the next day, and the people came out of their lodges, they saw blood on the fresh snow, and they saw bodies, the bodies from out of the *black crow king's lodge, the woman and the children, all slaughtered and torn to pieces and fed on, so it seemed. And there amongst them was the man from the lodge, sitting there in the middle of the carnage, looking at his hands and weeping like some old grandmother. And there was blood all around his mouth. And up on the poles of the lodge behind him, there was the black crow king, and he cawed once like laughing, then flew up into the sky.*

"And the brother of that dead woman, he went up to the husband, and he took his axe and he smashed it into the husband's head. And that was the first time that any one of the people had raised his hand against another, and killed him. For the first time, fear had come among the people, and revenge, and guilt and anger.

"And later that day, when it came evening again, the people heard a cawing around the camp, and they looked up into the sky, and they saw the black crow king had come back. This time he went into the lodge of the man who'd killed his brother-in-law, and the same thing happened again. They heard the screams in the night, and in the morning they found him among the bodies of his family. And this time it was the man's own brother that killed him.

"And so it went on. Each night, he'd come back and choose somewhere new, the black crow king, and each morning they'd see the carnage out there in the snow. And each day it brought new fighting among the people, more killing and revenge. And in the end, the people said, "We have to leave this place, because the black crow king, he's chosen it for his own. Maybe if we go away, we can outrun him."

"And so the people broke camp for the first time ever, and gathered up their belongings, and they burned their lodges where they stood, and they set out into the forest. And they walked for a thousand days and more, on through that enormous deep forest till they came to this world, the world of here and now. And sometimes on the trail, when the evening came, they'd hear the sound of the black crow king away off in the trees, and it sounded like he was laughing at them. Like he was sitting up there mocking them."

◄o►

"Like we'd fall for his bullshit," says Claude. He laughs. "Crows and Injuns."

I don't say anything. I started the day with a headache, and it's been getting worse and worse.

Claude laughs some more, then he gets up from his bench and leans over the hole in the ice. "Hey, Chief," he yells. "That was a bunch of *bullshit!*"

"Will you for Chrissakes just leave it be?" I say. But he won't.

"Say, Bob," and he's still peering into the hole: "Reckon he's all the way stripped yet? I'd imagine this lake doesn't ever heat up all that much, you got your altitude, you got the streams off the mountain feeding in that cold, cold melt water all year round. That's a goddamn deep-freeze right there, once you're under the surface. If it wasn't for the fishes—"

"You goddamn ghoul," I say, my patience finally at an end. "Why don't you cast for him and bring him the fuck up, so's you can ask him yourself?"

"Maybe you could do it for me, Bob?" He's upright now, staring at me with those piggy little eyes. "Go ahead! Why don't you drop in your famous fucking eye-drop lure and your everlasting fucking doodlebug, and haul him on up? Oh—I forgot. Because you can't catch jack shit in this lake, buddy Bob, less I show you how it's done. Is that about right? Is that about the height of it? Because when it comes right down to it, I've always been the one who gets things done round here—and I mean, all the fucking years I've known you. Haven't I?"

"You can call it getting things done, Claude. I call it cold-hearted godless fucking murder."

"Murder? *Murder*? How about saving your stumbling fucking lilywhite ass, huh? How about we call it by its *right* name? I mean, hell, Bob, you saw him! You heard him! You were right here in this cabin, sat there on that bench—I mean, you could smell the dirty bastard, he was so close! You could smell it on him! Goddamn—" he's right up in my face now—"I mean, he probably rolled around in it for a week. Make a liar out of me, Bob. Tell me you couldn't smell it on him. Go on!"

-◦-

And of course that was nothing more than the truth, because the smell had been there in the cabin all the while Jimbo told his tale. It might have been the warmth inside made it seem stronger by the minute, or it might have been something else, something I wouldn't be so quick to put a name to. But by the time he stopped speaking, and sat back and looked at us with that big wolf's grin of his, you could barely breathe for it. The slaughterhouse reek of death.

"Mister," I said, breaking the silence that fell inside the cabin. "Mister, I hope you don't mind me mentioning it, but you appear to have gotten some blood on you." You couldn't rightly see what colour his rough knitted sweater was, underneath his tattered combat duds. It looked to be the colour of rust. Or

dried blood. But there were dark sprays and splotches all over the camouflage pattern of his jacket that weren't anything to do with concealment, except in the very grimmest of circumstances. Maybe when the wolf put on Grandmamma's clothes as a disguise to trick Red Riding Hood, they kind of had the same look about them.

"I been hunting," he said, and his smile was like an axe split in his face. "Messy work, you know?"

"What do you hunt up here?" I asked him.

He laughed. It was not a pleasant sound. "Can't you guess?" he asked. "Your buddy there, I think he knows. Why don't you ask him?"

Claude was looking at him in a way that suggested he did know, or at least that his suspicions were pointing in the same direction as my own now were.

"I know something, all right," he said. "I know it's about time you got your ass up off that bench and got the hell out of our cabin, that's what I know." His face was flushed brick red, and instinctively I half rose to my feet, ahead of the trouble I knew would come any second now.

"Whose cabin?" Jimbo said, still with that awful animal grin across his face. "Whose cabin now?"

And just at that moment, three things happened in quick succession.

The first thing that happened was a bang at the cabin window, and we all three of us must have jumped about a foot in the air. Hard up against the frosty glass, there was a furious rush of blackness in the flying snow. It blotted out the light for an instant, and then it was clear again, and then there was the black again, all of a flurry against the panes, and it took us a moment to realise what it was.

It was a huge black crow, battering itself again and again against the window, pecking at it with its big cruel beak, all the while cawing shrilly and angrily.

The second thing that happened was that Jimbo came up on the balls of his feet, smooth and easy, crouched slightly at the knees as if he was ready to pounce—that's the best way I can describe it. I think he was laughing—I can't swear to that.

The third thing that happened was that Claude grabbed his big old metal bait box from the floor beside him, and threw it underarm like a bowler, only upwards—straight at Jimbo's face.

The impact of it snapped his head back, slammed him against the wall of the cabin, his feet knocked out from under him when they hit the bench behind. He slumped to a sitting position, and in amongst all the mess from the bait box and the blood from his wounds, you could just about make out his face.

You might have said he was smiling still. Or you might have reckoned it was more of a snarl, split lips peeled all the way back to show his shattered teeth. Here and there stray hooks and lures were caught in the skin of his face. They made him look like some blood-spattered barbarian, a wild man out of the ancient days. He groaned once, and then he opened his mouth as if to speak, but all I heard was the cawing of the big black bird outside as it beat against the pane with all its force.

Jimbo swatted a hand at the barbs stuck in his flesh as if they were so many no-see-ums, ripped them out heedless of the damage they were doing. He grinned again, opening up the fresh wounds around his mouth, so this time it really did look as if the grin was splitting his face in two. And I swear to God that mouth was black like crows' feathers. "Oh, you done it now," he said thickly, spitting out the words in a spray of blood. "Look what you done. You're gonna be so-rry." A comedy inflection, up and down.

He began to get to his feet, and I had no doubt whatsoever that if he got upright, then it would be the worse for us, that we would indeed be sorry and worse than sorry by the end.

That's when I reached for the auger.

◦

"I know exactly what happened, Claude," I say. In my mind's eye it's as fresh and clear still as if we'd only just cleared the place up.

There in the boards of the cabin wall is my permanent reminder: the hole left by the auger's point. I remember how he staggered back; I remember the sound it made as he tried to force his body forward again, maybe still not realising what had happened to him. It was the sound of a knife stuck in meat and gouged around and around. I remember how long it took for the last of the spark to go out of his eyes, how all of a sudden he groaned, and voided a rush of thick dark blood from out his wounded mouth, and his head slumped down till it was almost touching the shaft of the auger buried deep in his chest. I remember too the way it felt when we finally managed to tear our eyes away from his body, and look at each other.

Claude took charge of everything, in his usual can-do way except maybe even more so, filled with a terrible bright kind of vigour. It was his idea to get rid of the body and the murder weapon alike in one fell swoop; he laid out Jimbo's body on he floor of the cabin, wrapped his dead arms around the auger, then bound it all around and around with fishing line. Then the two of us manhandled it upright, and slid it down into the fishing hole in the ice. We figured the weight of the auger would make sure it didn't come up, even in the spring when the corpses of the drowned are apt to rise; it would keep it down at the bottom while the low feeders did their work.

And now, up above where Jimbo's body lies bound to its doom, we sit in our old familiar cabin, Claude and I, bound even more tightly to our own.

The ice beneath gives out such a long, groaning creak, and I can't help but think of the noise that came out of Jimbo's throat as he fell forward that last time. "I can't do this anymore, Claude," I find myself saying. "It has to end. We've got to end it, one way or the other."

"End it?" There's a devilment in his eyes, in his voice. It reminds me of something I'd much rather forget, only I know I never will. "I thought we *had* ended it, once and for all. You don't think so?"

"No, I don't," I tell him. What else can I say?

"Sweet baby Jesus. Well, then. What's to be done, Bobby boy? What are we gonna do now?"

I can't answer. In the back of my throat there's a taste of blood, maybe the memory of a taste. If I open my mouth to speak, I'm not sure what would come out. I'm not even sure this blood I'm tasting is my own. All I know is that I've tasted it before, that it doesn't seem strange to me. Not now, not in this instant. I swallow hard, but it won't go away.

And there, right on cue, comes a flurry of snow at the window, and with it a shriek and a caw as the big black crow comes scrabbling for a hold with his sharp mean claws, his strong beak pecking hungrily at the glass.

ON THESE BLACKENED SHORES OF TIME

BRIAN HODGE

saw it happen, watched the street open up and swallow my son whole.

I understand human stress response, how it works. When violent chaos hits you without warning, the mind has to catch up. It lags behind to make sense of things. Four seconds, on average. Your world can end in those four seconds.

When I replay the moment in my head, in those four seconds I do superhuman deeds. I spring into action a nanosecond after the pavement starts to buckle. I cross the cul-de-sac at the end of our street in a blur. I catch Drew's car by the bumper, so it teeters on the brink long enough for him to scramble out and jump to safety before I let go, then hold him tight as we watch the taillights plummet down the sinkhole.

In those four seconds, I'm not a former Special Agent with the Bureau. I never went into the private sector for the money, giving corporate seminars on better business through reading body language. None of that. In those four seconds, I'm the superhero my boy grew up believing me to be.

Instead, while out front threading a new length of hose onto the soaker line in the flowerbeds, I looked up at the sound of his Mazda and watched it happen without moving a muscle. When Drew got within thirty feet of the cul-de-sac, the street gave way as his car's front end rolled over the weak spot. The Mazda tumbled into this freshly opened wound in the asphalt, nose first, tail end flipping into the air, then out of sight with the sound of grinding.

Then I ran. Four seconds of eternity later. By the time I got there, Drew was already gone, and all I could do was stand on the lip of the chasm and gape into the blackness that took over a few dozen feet down. I couldn't even see the car. It was as if the earth had yawned and opened a gullet years in the making.

Come to find out, it was. This was a calamity that had been built in stages, over time.

Two years ago, for the newest piece of it. Nearly a century for another.

Beyond that, we're into the millions.

-o-

The neighbors were kind, as neighbors are when one of their own succumbs to fate, and for a time there was hope. We clung to it because we all knew the way these incidents were supposed to turn out in neighborhoods like this. The toddler gets pulled out of the forgotten well. The puppy is rescued from the storm drain. Watch enough TV news and you'll be trained to expect it.

"They'll get him out, that's how this day is going to end, you wait and see," our next-door neighbor Dale told me. I'd always seen something of the high school and college athlete gone sedentary in him, thick in the middle now and florid faced, a man built for sweating. A Saturday's worth of ginger stubble covered his cheeks the same as it covered half his skull. "The air bag should've gone off, that would've cushioned him on the way down." Dale stared at the flurry of activity around the hole and nodded, as if he could will it so. "They'll get that winch down there. They'll knock out the back window and pull him out that way. You wait and see."

I wanted to tell Drew this myself, but whenever I tried his cell phone, it went straight to voice mail, as if he weren't in range. Which could have been a consequence of the earth itself, insulating and interfering, but then it didn't seem as if this sinkhole should be any worse than the average sub-basement or parking garage.

My hope was that he would already be standing on our lawn by the time Ginny got home from teaching her Saturday morning class down in Scranton. It wasn't to be. The first I saw of her, wiry and shorthaired, she came sprinting across the lawns from where she'd had to park up the street, because the intuitive part of her already knew. I caught her and we dropped to the spring grass, and I held her until I was sure she wasn't going to dive down the hole after him.

Plan B, then: Drew would be up and out by the time his sister got here. Katee was across the state in Pittsburgh, a sophomore at Carnegie Mellon, and would be home by evening.

"It's Drew, isn't it?" was how she answered her phone. They'd always been like that with each other, Katee more so than her brother, but it still went both ways. *It's a twins thing,* they would tease. *You wouldn't understand.*

Over the morning, our ill-fated street filled up with uniforms and barricades, flashing lights and vehicles with various department logos stenciled on the doors. All we cared about was the wrecker big enough to handle a semi-truck, and the spooled cable it fed into the hole, and the man in coveralls riding the giant hook down, like a child standing on a swing.

From a hundred feet away, we watched them work, another man operating the winch and a woman on a walkie-talkie, her free hand pressed to her other ear. I didn't know how much cable was on that spool, but eventually they came to the end of it. There was no place left to go but in reverse, and after a few moments in which it felt as if I'd lost the last moorings that kept me upright, the spool began to rewind.

We didn't need anyone to come over and update us. All the apprising Ginny and I needed was in their body language.

They hadn't even found the car yet.

◂◦▸

There may have been dozens of places in Pennsylvania coal country where this could've happened, but it had happened here. Our neighborhood—which came as a bitter surprise to one and all—had been built over the Tecumseh Mine #24. What had given way beneath Drew was the opening of the main shaft.

We learned this in our living room from a geologist with the state's Bureau of Abandoned Mine Reclamation. Her name was DeSalvo, and by now it was Sunday morning. With her graying hair gathered loosely at the back of her head, she looked as if she hadn't slept since she'd awakened the day before. Katee was home now, and none of us looked any better. We sat on the sofa—the Whitesides, family of three now—and DeSalvo across from us, as if she were the firing squad and we were the targets.

The mine had been closed in 1927, when the location was more remote than it was now, decades before the town of Carbon Glen had grown out to absorb it.

Even then, ample regulations governed how a mining company was supposed to close a site. But what are regulations for, if not to be circumvented? Tecumseh Mining had closed #24 fast and on the cheap. They'd either made it look right enough to pass inspection, or bribed somebody to avow that it had.

They'd demolished the headframe built over the shaft, along with the hoist house and additional shacks. All this would have required was dynamite. Then they tossed these broken timbers and the rest of the rubble down the hole until it caught in the shaft like fishbones in a throat. A few tarps, too, to catch the soil and rock they finished it off with. Pack it, level it, job well done. What should have been a proper seal instead amounted to a cork in a bottle.

"What worked it loose after all this time," DeSalvo said, "was the flooding you folks had here a couple of years ago."

Most people think of floods as happening only around rivers, lakes, oceans. But those of us who live with mountains can know something about them too. What you sometimes get with peaks and valleys is a network of funnels, capable of taking a heavy rain from across a wide region and draining it into a narrow area. On rare occasions, under freakish circumstances, enough rain might fall in a short enough time to overwhelm its normal channels.

Two autumns ago, it started raining one September morning and didn't stop for four days. Rather than blowing through toward the Atlantic coast, the storm stayed put and slowly circled overhead. It acted, meteorologists said, like a tropical storm.

Our neighborhood was lucky, on high ground. The worst we saw was soggy lawns and battered gardens and a few poorly sealed basements turn into wading pools.

We couldn't have known that rather than washing over us, millions of gallons of water were thundering through a system of tunnels far underground. The region is honeycombed with mineshafts known and forgotten, and it's likely that some ended up newly connected, even though they were never meant to be.

Tecumseh #24 among them.

Although it had taken only a few days to dismantle what had held intact since 1927, the blockage hadn't washed away all at once. More likely, it had gradually subsided in the nineteen months since, until all that was left was a scab of pavement that could no longer bear the weight of a car. Then it was just down to chance: *Who's going to be the unlucky one?*

"How deep is it?" I asked. "If you haven't even found Drew's car . . ."

DeSalvo stiffened at this. They'd found it, or thought they had.

"Six hundred feet for the main shaft. We have the map that was registered in the twenties, but it doesn't appear to be complete." DeSalvo could tell we expected more, even if it was bad. "There's the main shaft. That's vertical. According to the map, they went four levels down. Those are horizontal. They follow the coal seams, so they split off, into what are called galleries. But eighty feet down, there's what's called a slope shaft branching off the vertical, at a forty-degree incline. That's not on the map. I don't know if they dug it at the same time, or if it was an earlier shaft they ran into, or what. If it's an earlier shaft, there's no longer any sign of a matching opening on the opposite side of the vertical. So I don't know what to make of it. I just know you dig one or the other. Vertical or slope. You don't do both."

"And the car's in the slope shaft. That's what you're getting at?"

"It's the only possibility. If the car had dropped straight down the main shaft, it should be at the bottom, in the sump. But it's not."

Perched on the edge of the couch the whole time, Katee had had enough. "How? How does a falling car change directions like that?"

"The only thing anyone can figure is it got diverted by debris on the way down. Some of those pieces from the headframe are bigger than railroad ties. The headframe is the framework that supports the elevator cage for the miners, and the coal cars going up and down, so these supports had to be heavy duty. If one or two were angled across the main shaft, in the right place, they could've acted as a ramp. They're not there now, but they could've been dislodged on impact after the car went into the slope shaft."

"You're telling us this like it's still a theory," Ginny said, her face sharp and her eyes narrow. Most days she looked more like Katee's older sister than her mother. Not today. "That means you still haven't actually seen the car."

And here it came: "There's been a partial tunnel collapse at the opening to the slope shaft. At least twenty feet in. It's fresh, they say."

I could still think, in a wobbly, groping way, but I could no longer feel. It wasn't really me. Somebody else was doing the thinking and I was the numb one watching. Conceivably, Drew's car could have rolled all the way to the bottom, a distance no one even knew. This really was a worst-case scenario.

"I'm sorry," DeSalvo said.

This was when my hopes began to get dragged down the shaft too, and the idea of seeing Drew again began to slither from my grasp. Nobody was giving up. I knew that. But now this may have been a recovery operation for a body. Like any challenging rescue operation, it would take time, time Drew didn't have. Because I knew this much, too: If he could have left the car, he would have. He would've crawled back up the incline and clawed through as much muck as possible and yelled his lungs out until somebody yelled back.

This was the Drew we knew and loved.

"That's all I can really tell you right now," DeSalvo said, clearly wanting to leave, but hesitant, as if it would be rude unless she had our permission.

"One more thing," I said. "Do you know why they were in such a hurry to seal off the mine?"

Nearly a century ago, men had cut corners and it had led to this day. I didn't want to always wonder why. I wanted my hatred of them to be fully informed.

"I mean, was it greed? Were they just lazy? Some other reason?"

DeSalvo sat with the question awhile. "They did it a few months after the mining riots of 1927. Do you know about those?"

I didn't. But if you go back far enough, you'll often find trouble around a mine.

"Then why don't you let it keep for another day. You all have enough weighing on you now. I'm not the best one for the details anyway." She gave her phone a few pecks, then jotted something on the back of a business card. "This is who you should talk to. Wesley McNabb. He's a mine historian. He'll tell you whatever you want to know."

I walked her to the door, recalling the look in her eyes from moments earlier, and how her jaw had tightened. She hadn't wanted to get into it in front of a mother and twin sister who were already bearing more than they could handle.

But now that we had discretion going for us: "It's that bad?"

"Somebody mentioned you used to be with the FBI. If you're like everyone else I've met with that kind of background, you've seen enough to have . . . oh, a diminished assessment of humanity in general, let's call it. Or am I wrong?"

I shook my head no. "You're not wrong."

She made that expression where the lips curl inward and the mouth turns grim. "Tecumseh twenty-four should finish it off entirely."

◄◦►

We stayed hidden and watched them work from our windows.

The news vans had converged from the beginning, because their crews knew better than anyone how this was supposed to end. I grew increasingly annoyed by the crowd of onlookers, treating this like their day-off entertainment. They gathered on lawns until the property owners shooed them away, then drifted to others. Most seemed the type who hoped the worst, to make their trip worthwhile. Our neighbor Dale got into a shoving match with two of them, a scuffle with another.

The one they really had to fear was Ginny. They just didn't know it. She taught women's self-defense from here to Allentown, gave all-day seminars as far south as Philadelphia. She could've laid out any of them. She would seethe at them through the windows, then turn away. She was disciplined. The sinkhole was all that mattered.

"The people responsible for this," she said. "I want to dig up their graves and throw their bones down that hole."

The rescuers finished clearing the slope shaft's blockage Monday morning and worked their way to the car, which had traveled more than a quarter-mile down the incline. As quickly as our hearts soared at that news, they plummeted again upon learning that Drew wasn't in it, or anywhere near it.

They plumbed the sump at the bottom of the vertical, in case he'd been thrown clear of the car, but I knew they wouldn't find him there. He was good about wearing a seat belt. No, he'd gone into the slope.

"Maybe he wasn't thinking straight," Katee said. "If he hit his head, maybe he was going on instinct. If you get in trouble . . ."

Work your way downhill.

Those would be the instincts of a skier, dazed and in the dark. Drew had been on skis since he was six. Now he was a strapping, shaggy-headed kid who taught other six-year-olds how to snowplow and slalom. When the twins graduated high school, Katee knew what she wanted to study, and where, but Drew wasn't sure about college and couldn't say when he would be. Over a lifetime, what was a year or two to know himself better?

He loved skiing, though, and sharing his enthusiasm for it, and was ridiculously patient with kids, so it was the slopes of the Poconos for him. The season had stretched into the first week of April, and he'd been home a week. Where we always thought he was safer.

Work your way downhill. Because downhill is where help is.

The problem with that, in this rogue slope shaft, was that at a distance equivalent to two city blocks past the point where the car had stopped, the slope plunged into water, probably a remnant of the flooding nineteen months earlier.

So now our hopes began to drown, as well.

They brought in the world's gutsiest diver, experienced with exploring sunken caves, who deemed the conditions the worst he'd ever seen. His lights couldn't do much in such black, sludgy water. No map, pitch dark, visibility of inches, the possibility of another structural collapse? Nobody had to tell me this was the most dangerous thing he'd ever done. And for us. Our peace of mind.

When he packed it in after a few hours without recovering a body, I had nothing left in my heart to argue with.

By the end of the week, there was no closure anyone could provide. There was just a big, inconvenient hole in the street that needed filling in. They started with truckfuls of rock and earth, then pumped in mixer after mixer of concrete.

"You can't let them do this," Katee kept telling me, frantic to the point of tears. "Drew's not dead. I'd *know* if he was dead."

There can't be any worse feeling of failure than to reveal to your children how fallible you really are. No superhero to my son. Now, to my daughter, ineffectual before bureaucracy, and trying to use logic to get her to accept the unthinkable. I wasn't giving Drew up for dead. Just admitting he would've been down there waiting for rescue if he could have.

"You're wrong. You're so wrong," Katee told me. "Would it be easier for you to accept I know this if we were identical? If I was his brother or he was my sister, and we looked exactly alike?" She shook her head, giving up on me, if not Drew. "It's still a twins thing. You still don't understand."

You take your consolation where you can, and for me, the only source came from watching the spectators drift away without a payoff.

No body for you, you goddamn league of ghouls.

◂◦▸

Adjustment went slowly.

For weeks, Ginny drifted more in silence than not, barely within my reach. She would curl onto Drew's bed for hours. She would open his closet to bury her face in his clothes, her grief on an animal level, taking in his scent as if it might help her track him down. I began to fear I would never get her back all the way.

She came most alive when Katee called, in Pittsburgh again and trying to finish a semester that had gotten away from her. I could tell from our end that Katee spoke to her about Drew as though he were still alive. Did it help? I had no idea what was healthy anymore.

You should move, people told us. I knew what they were thinking. Every trip along the street, Ginny and I would be rolling over our son's grave. How are you supposed to do that and get past it? As for the neighbors, maybe selfishness was involved, too: If we stayed, we would be a reminder they were doing the same.

Ginny and I talked about it, if only to get it out in the open and confirm that we couldn't bear to do it. It would be like trying to erase him, outrun his memory.

That's not Drew down there, we decided. *He's gone. Whatever part of him that's stayed behind, it's in the house. This house. It's in the yard. This yard. That maple tree out front, we planted the sapling when he was five, and I remember the day, how he thought he was helping. We can't take that with us. Out back, that was his first ski slope, when he was six, and he'd pack every fresh snowfall into a ramp for three seconds of joy at a time. The bedroom, that's his color, we let him paint it himself when he was fourteen, and remember how frustrated we got when he had to paint it five times in eight months to find the perfect mix of blue and white. That's all him. We can't turn it over to strangers. Not now.*

So we stayed, and no one was more adamant about it than Katee.

How was Drew supposed to find us again if we didn't stay put?

⊸⊶

Our cool spring gave way to a summer whose wet heat fell on us like a boiled blanket. We were weeks into it when I decided the time to know had come. The anger still burned and always would. I hated men who'd left this world decades ago, whose company had been defunct since before the Second World War. I needed to know who and why.

I slid the card the state geologist had left me out from beneath its refrigerator magnet and called the number on the back. Her mine historian, Wesley McNabb, had been expecting it. He agreed to meet me at his home in Wilkes-Barre, a tidy two-story tucked back from the street behind some very old trees.

"I'm sorry for your loss," he said in the doorway. "That godforsaken mine, still causing misery to this day."

McNabb canted to one side when he walked, clumping along on a left leg that was clearly a prosthesis. He had the unruly beard, more salt than pepper, of a man who needed reminding to trim it, and the dull, weathered cheeks of someone who'd spent a lot of time in bad elements.

He led me to a big bedroom turned office. Tidy ended at its door. This had been a man cave since long before anyone had thought to coin the term, stuffed with cabinets and bookshelves, and an ancient rolltop desk with enough cubbyholes to serve a rural post office. Archaic pickaxes hung mounted on the walls, along with square lanterns made of battered tin. Shelves held flat-brimmed helmets with early electric lamps, and even older caps made for carbide lamps. A room like this took decades to accumulate.

And it wasn't made for company. The chair I took had come from a kitchen.

"They first sunk her in 1919, the spring after the Great War," McNabb began. "I'll tell you what's in the public record, and agreed upon, more or less. Then, if you want, we can get into the rest."

He gave names of owners and foremen and labor leaders. None of them meant anything, just characters in a story that started normally, most inclined toward peace after years of machine guns and mustard gas in Europe. But, eventually, everyone's true nature reverts to form.

The riots of 1927 had begun with labor strikes. Better pay, conditions, safeguards—the usual. You couldn't fault them for it. Digging coal had always been one of the worst jobs in the world, and maybe the slowest to improve.

Negotiations didn't last a week before the mine bosses cut them off and brought up a trainload of scabs from Philadelphia. McNabb ventured that the bosses never intended to settle in the first place, but were merely giving the appearance of it while they rounded up replacement workers.

"And to a striking miner," McNabb said, "there's not a lower form of life on earth than a scab. A man willing to take his job, and do it cheaper and probably not as good."

Hence the welcoming committee at the train station for the new arrivals. Those who preferred a longer reach showed up with axe handles and ball bats; leather saps and knuckle-dusters for those who liked to get in close and dirty. The bosses weren't stupid, and knew what to expect. They'd hired security accordingly, railroad bulls with clubs and saps of their own, and shotguns if needed.

The heaviest clashes went on for ten days. Six men went to the cemetery, dozens to the hospital, and Tecumseh #24 became an armed camp. But against a fixed number of local miners, and with a war chest for imported muscle, the company was always destined to win. After that, the violence dwindled to isolated brawls, mostly when scabs got caught outside the perimeter, their need to go whoring outweighing their sense of safety.

Seven weeks into the strike, the locals' resolve began to crack—nothing gained, too much lost, and ready to ask for their jobs back. And that was when a cave-in on level four went chain-reaction, causing a secondary collapse on level three.

"That's where they all were, those bottom two levels," McNabb said. "The mine had been going for eight years. Levels one and two were played out. Level three was getting there, but there were still some working it. Most were down on four. Three men, that's all that got out. They'd just brought a carload to the shaft. Everybody else, killed or trapped."

It was assumed there were more survivors than casualties. Cave-ins usually meant tunnel blockages rather than a collapse of the entire roof. Most of the men would simply have been on the wrong side of tons of rock and earth, timber and ore, with a limited supply of food, potable water, and maybe air.

"Under any other circumstances," McNabb went on, "you'd have the entire townful of men working to clear the blockage, as soon as they could get down the shaft. Not this time. Scabs, remember. No lower form of life on earth."

"Jesus," I whispered. "You mean they just . . ."

"Left them right where they were. Because scabs got what was coming to them. I understand the contempt. But bottom line, this is a situation every man who goes down a mine fears. He needs to know that if it happens to him, the ones up top have got his back. That's the bargain. So how a man sits in a church pew doing double duty as a meeting hall, looking Jesus in the face, and votes to do nothing . . . I don't know. But they did it. Unanimous. *'You brought 'em in, you dig 'em out'*—that's a direct quote from the strike leader to the company."

"Did they?" I asked.

"Tecumseh? No. They weren't any more eager to do it than the strikers, they just had different reasons. They claimed they had evidence there were no survivors, and if there were, they wouldn't survive as long as it would take to get to them anyway. They said all the right things . . . we regret the loss of life, don't want to endanger any more, blah blah blah. More likely, they didn't want to spend the money. And the scabs, they weren't union, so United Mine Workers didn't touch it.

"So that, more than anything," McNabb said with an air of wrap-up, "explains the haste in closing the mine, the half-assed job they did blocking the shaft. A thing like that becomes a shame over an entire community. It wasn't their tragedy, so there was nothing to memorialize. They didn't want to keep anybody's memory alive. The sooner they covered it over, the sooner they could get to pretending it never happened."

I wondered how collective the decision really was. If it had been genuinely unanimous, or a mandate issued by a few, everyone else encouraged to go along with it if they knew what was good for them. Even then, it was a decision with a point of no return. You couldn't change your mind two weeks later, asking *what have we done*, and make it right.

It took a lot to appall me, but this managed it. Our neighborhood was built over the bones of men who'd boarded a train to take whatever job they could get, and died clawing at the dirt.

-◦-

In retrospect, I wasn't sure what I expected from the meeting. It only validated a hatred I was going to feel anyway for men whose evil came not from some grand design, but cost-benefit analysis and spite. It didn't bring Drew back. It didn't dissipate the pall of mourning that settled over our home like a cloud that might never leave.

Most of all, it was never going to dissuade Katee of her notion that Drew was not dead, a fixation she persisted in nurturing as the months went by. To her, everyone had conspired out of a growing sense of inconvenience to bury her brother alive. It put me in the worst position imaginable—hoping Drew had died within the first hour of the accident, that he'd staggered dazed from his car and tumbled to a swift and merciful end in the cold black water at the bottom of the shaft. Better this than lingering to dehydrate and starve.

Only Katee didn't see it happening that way, either.

"He's alive," she said in late April. "I'd know if he wasn't."

As Ginny and I felt like the enemy, reminding her that denial was a normal phase of loss, and would pass.

"He's alive," she said in May.

As Ginny and I wondered if we shouldn't get her to a grief counselor.

"He's alive," she said in June and July.

The question was, was Katee, anymore?

This was her nineteenth summer, and it bore no resemblance to the previous eighteen. It was as if she no longer had friends, nor anyone she wanted to date. She had secured no job or summer internship, not even with me. Last year, I'd hired her as my assistant while on the road from seminar to corporate seminar. Not this year—but then, I'd cut my schedule to the bone.

Katee had her bedroom, and that was all she wanted. Its window overlooked our street, but she now rejected the view, and covered the glass with black construction paper. When we asked if she didn't want to paper over it with a poster, something with a view of a beach or ski slope, she pointed at the solid black and said, "Why? That's what Drew sees now."

As Ginny held her through some very long nights.

Me, I mostly wondered how to bring her back.

She'd always been the most forward-looking person I'd ever known. Her course of study at Carnegie Mellon was called Transition Design. Katee wanted to steer cities and systems and products toward sustainability rather than using everything up and throwing it away as fast as possible.

Now her sketchbooks gathered dust.

We'd all gone down that hole, and one way or another, had to find our way out.

Wesley McNabb probably understood this as well as anyone.

As for the rest of what he'd had to say, the parts that came down to sup-position and rumor, I wasn't sure what I believed and what I didn't. Or rather, what I wasn't *prepared* to believe.

Ginny, however, had taken a lot more on board than I realized that July evening I came back from Wilkes-Barre with the ugly history behind Tecumseh #24. She held it inside herself and gave it time to grow. I perceived none of this until the August morning I discovered her side of the bed empty and assumed she'd spent another night with Katee.

Wrong. Sometimes it felt like I'd been trained to catch every miniscule detail of everything except what was going on under my own roof.

I found her at the kitchen table, behind her coffee. She was dressed in charcoal-colored tactical pants, and a tank top and sports bra combo that showed off her cable-tight shoulders and arms. Her ass-kicking clothes, I called them. This was the uniform she wore whenever she taught women how to find their strength, how to dig in and fight, how to kill if that's what it took.

Only she wasn't in teaching mode. She was beyond, in *doing* mode. She looked like a mother, worried and committed and sleepless and fierce.

"What have you done?" I asked.

-◦-

The uncertainties surrounding Tecumseh #24 began with the cause of the calamity. Nobody could definitively say what it was.

"Even in 1927," McNabb had told me, "mining was a lot safer than it was twenty years before. That's mainly down to the switch to electric lamps instead of working by open flames, waiting to hit a pocket of methane. Even cheapskates like Tecumseh could get behind that. But those three survivors said they heard explosions, at a time when there weren't any scheduled. Not just one, but two. As miners, though, they were green, and scabs to boot, so their word was suspect. It made things sound deliberate. One of them, a fella name of Alvin Barnsley, went so far as to say he heard men fighting down on level four before it went to hell. No little scrap, either, but a big sudden uproar. That was part of the rationale Tecumseh had for declaring everybody dead already."

"How likely is that? Green or not, they had to be smarter than to let some disagreement get that out-of-control on the job."

McNabb tossed his hands up. "Anything's possible. What makes it suspicious is that, not long after, very much on the quiet, Tecumseh deeded over six acres to Alvin Barnsley, within a mile or so of the site, right up against the hills outside Carbon Glen. Why? Can't say. I don't know if it was for backing the company line, or what, but if that doesn't look like a payoff, I don't know what does."

"Wouldn't money be even quieter?"

"You'd think. But maybe under the circumstances it was the most disposable capital they had to work with. It was a strange situation all around." McNabb took a breath, going slower, as if accessing a new databank. "See, once they've been active long enough, and gone deep enough, sometimes mines start to develop their own mythologies. Miners start to see things, hear things. Tommyknockers—maybe you've heard the term? They're spirits down in the earth, up to no good most of the time, tapping on the other side of rock walls that shouldn't have anybody over on the other side of them.

"Well, those last weeks Tecumseh #24 was operational, it turned odd. They were supposedly pulling some peculiar things up out of there. But it's all just rumor, mostly. These weren't local men, letting their families in on a secret. It's scabs making pillow talk with whores. So consider the sources."

"What do you mean by peculiar things?"

McNabb folded his knotty hands together, turning pensive as he looked at the far wall. Through the wall. "When a mine turns strange on you, it's not necessarily the *what* that makes it strange. It's the fact that something's down there at all. Nothing's strange about an iron kettle or some crude old hammer. You look at them, you know what they are. What makes them strange is that they're embedded in the coal. Shouldn't be there. But there they are."

I couldn't detect a hint of lying, nor even exaggeration. He believed every word.

"Is that the kind of things they were finding?"

McNabb shook his head. "No. Stranger. This time, it's the *what*, too."

He slipped a photo from one of his desk's cubbyholes and handed it over. It looked old, felt old, on yellowed, edge-curled stock thicker than a postcard. It showed what, lacking scale, I might have identified as some eccentric collector's idea of a Bowie knife. Except it was laid next to a yardstick, and was a tad longer.

"That's the only picture I'm aware of, of anything that came up."

The weapon was half blade, half handle, and I couldn't fathom how someone could comfortably wield it. The handle looked like the tip of a large drill bit, a deep-set flange curving up and around the central shaft—three times in eighteen or twenty inches, as if something were meant to grasp it by wrapping inside the groove. The blade was nearly as unusual, with sweeping curves and small barbs, an altogether cruel-looking instrument.

I flipped the photo over. On the back, in pencil whose penmanship had an old-fashioned flourish: *Pulled from Tecumseh #24, June 16, 1927.*

"Supposedly they found some carvings, too. Statuettes. And items nobody even knew what to call. It would've been an ideal time for bringing things up and keeping them to yourselves. The company had its hands full trying to keep peace with the locals, get that situation resolved. They wouldn't have wanted to know. As for the hired goons, their curiosity likely didn't go any farther than how big a knot they could raise on someone's head."

A scenario came together in my head, greed meeting opportunity. The pieces were rough, but if you pressed hard enough, they might eventually fit.

"Is it possible that a bunch of guys started thinking of themselves as treasure hunters rather than miners?"

McNabb returned the picture to the cubbyhole. "Then turned on each other? That would fit the narrative the company preferred. But there's one more factor . . . the most outlandish, but it's there. The rumor was that two days before the accident, they hit a wall. I don't mean in the usual rock wall sense, a natural formation. I mean artificial. Constructed. With engravings on it, so that's how they knew it was something more. Huge, supposedly, but that may have been exaggeration."

"How is that possible? That can't be possible."

McNabb tapped the end of the photo. "If you accept this one, you have to consider the possibility of the other. I don't take a position. I just make note of the talk from back then, and this picture came from the local Carnegie library. They'd had it forever and never knew what to do with it, so they gave it to me. My theory? Whatever these men ran into down there, they tried to blow their way through it, or into it, and didn't know near as much about what they were doing as they thought they did. That accounts for a lot of things, assuming the survivor, Alvin Barnsley, was telling the truth. The collapse, the two explosions, the fighting and uproar." McNabb grinned, more challenge in it than mirth. "If you can put it all together into something that makes more sense, you're welcome to try. I do hope you'll share it with me."

He was right. It ticked a lot of checkboxes. Except, for me, a significant one.

"Do you know if Barnsley turned around and sold the land they deeded to him?"

I was still bothered by that. If he'd only wanted money, it seemed as if Tecumseh could have sold the acreage faster, and the payoff would've stayed quiet. It wouldn't have been a matter of public record.

"He did not," McNabb said. "He moved onto it. Apparently he wanted to give farming a try."

"A scab miner moving into a community that would've hated him. Did he have a death wish? The cave-in didn't kill him, he thought the locals might?"

"A farmer might not have thought it was worth the risk. But a treasure hunter could've." McNabb waved off the specter of him, leaving no doubt of his contempt. "The man was desperate enough to be a scab and fool enough to brag on what they'd been pulling out of the mine. It follows he may have been fool enough to believe he still had a future there."

◄o►

It had been a month since I'd gone to see McNabb and brought his stories home. For me, it had been the end of something—not closure, but at least an understanding of the chain of tragic events.

For Ginny, though, it had been a beginning.

I began to see the past month differently. The times when she'd taken longer than usual to come home from teaching a class. The increased hours she'd spent on her computer. Another man might have looked at such symptoms and suspected an affair. But Ginny wasn't the type to sneak. She was sufficiently blunt that she would've told me I was fucking up badly enough to get her thinking in this direction. Regardless, an affair was the last place she would have channeled her grief, her worry over Katee.

"I should've believed her," Ginny told me at the kitchen table, with her coffee and her ass-kicking clothes. "From the very start, I should've believed her." She laid a hand over her belly as if, even now, she could feel a kick within. A tapping on the other side of her uterine wall. "They spent nine months together in the dark. In here. If Katee says she'd know if Drew really was gone, then I should've had more faith that she knows what she's talking about."

Herself, she was stressing. Not me. The processes she was describing could *never* have included me. The three of them had been bound together in flesh and blood and water and, if you wanted to go that far, spirit. Even as her husband, their father, I was still on the outside. And I'd had to learn the hard way that sometimes the better part of fulfilling those roles meant knowing when to shut up and listen.

Ginny pushed her phone across the table to me. "Do you recognize him?"

The photo in the display showed as much as a mug shot, with an indistinct background that might have been a living room. Its subject looked several years older than we were, fiftyish, or maybe it was bad living: a man with thinning hair and meaty cheeks and a bowed, prissy mouth. I found something unsavory about him. He had a look I'd seen accompanying too many case files about men who'd spent years filling crawlspaces with bodies.

He hadn't wanted his picture taken. I could tell that much.

"No," I said. "I don't."

"You should. He was in the street outside our house for most of that week in April. We're practically neighbors. He's less than two miles from here."

"Is his name Barnsley?"

Ginny nodded. "Otto. He's the grandson. Third generation on the same property. Who does that anymore?"

Ginny drained her coffee, then came around the table and leaned on me with her arm strong and tender around my neck.

"You need to eat something, Trevor," she said, her chin resting on the crown of my head. "I got this far on my own and kept you out of it. I'm not doing the rest by myself."

⟨◦⟩

It seemed unwise to leave a car untended for hours in a place we didn't belong. We covered the distance on foot, the summer heat building in that first quiet hour of daylight as we skirted the backsides of homes and neighborhoods that petered out against the hills.

The Barnsley land was six acres of nothing much. Enough traces of outbuildings and fences remained to show that, decades ago, it might have passed as a small farm. Now it was a rundown pocket of decay, a pustule of times past clinging to the land. The house, two stories and shabby, was in need of paint and new shingles, and matched the unsavory impression I'd gotten from Otto Barnsley's candid snapshot.

And Ginny had come here alone.

"It bugged me that McNabb might not have been giving Alvin Barnsley as much credit as he should've," she told me along the way. "His intention all along was getting back into the mine. That much seems obvious. I started wondering if he didn't know something more than he should have. He either knew of another way in already, or thought he could find it."

The thought had crossed my mind even before Drew's car had been recovered. Another way in—it's the kind of thing you pray for, and the answer's always no. I'd still asked, and DeSalvo had double-checked her department's archives. When she said there was no such route, I believed her. Even though she hadn't known about the slope shaft, I trusted her.

Because the alternative—that a back way existed, but no one knew where to find it anymore—was too terrible to live with.

Maybe it had taken someone like Ginny to disregard the experts.

"Sometimes mines link up with cave systems, or older mines. Or something happens to connect one thing with another," she said. "Do you remember hearing about the Knox Mine Disaster, growing up?"

The name was familiar, but had no details attached.

"It happened around here too. 1959. The Susquehanna broke through into one mine gallery and flooded God knows how many others between Port Griffith and Exeter. They were digging where they shouldn't have. So yeah, things link up, even when they're not supposed to."

To our left, from where we stood on this derelict homestead paid for with blood and starvation, the hills rose and rolled away, green and thick with trees festooned with the last tatters of morning mist.

"The water that washed out that shaft underneath our street had to come from somewhere. It didn't come from our storm drains. Whatever's upstream of there, it has to extend a long way." Ginny pointed into the hazy hills. "It may not start here. But it runs through here."

She said this like there was no question about it. She *knew*. Maybe not yesterday. But today, after whatever she'd done in this house last night, she knew.

"I've seen the map."

"You didn't think about going through official channels on this?"

She looked at me as if, for the moment, she was forced to suffer a fool. Every husband knows that look. "Channels are what got the sinkhole filled in inside of a week. Channels are what left those miners down there to die. Channels would be less concerned with what I found and more with how I found it. So fuck channels. I'm here for Drew and Katee."

I followed her across the sagging boards of a creaking porch, inside.

The house put me in mind of Wesley McNabb's office, but that was one room. Here it consumed everything, and must have taken lifetimes, a single obsession passed down through generations.

The walls were hung with maps. One appeared so archaic a museum might have valued it at a small fortune, but it detailed no geography I could recognize, its text in no alphabet I knew. The newest, global, bristled with pushpins—one at our location, and three dozen more across every continent from west to east, from Antarctica to Siberia. Others showed Earth's land-masses in different stages of continental drift: Pangaea, then Gondwanaland and Laurasia, and onward, the later ones appended with a vast island in the South Pacific that had no existing correlate. *R'lyeh*, some ornate hand had labeled its work.

Photos? Those too, spanning decades of excavations and expeditions, in deserts and jungles, forests and mountains. A man with slicked-back hair and a machete stood over a litter of ferns beside an idol that might have been worshiped by maritime pagans. A sepia-toned team stood atop a jumble of stone blocks, dwarfed by them, in the cleft of a remote alpine valley.

Books? God, yes. Innumerable volumes on archaeology, geology, anthropology, astronomy, biology, metallurgy, advanced geometry and mathematics. An entire shelf was devoted to human anatomy, including textbooks on autopsies. Another was themed around ritual magic. They were supplemented by notebooks and legal pads beyond counting. I could think of bureau profilers who would've loved to spend a month combing through everything.

And all this was just along the path to where Ginny had secured Otto Barnsley hours earlier, his right wrist lashed to his left ankle with a zip-tie cuff. Another secured his right ankle to the iron leg of a woodstove. She used these plastic cuffs in her classes, teaching women how to fight with their hands bound; how to break the cuffs if they were strong enough. She'd never used them with bad intentions.

Just like that, it occurred to me: *We are on the wrong side of the law here. And right now I don't care about that, because I don't know* what *he's on the wrong side of.*

"Oh my," Barnsley said when he saw me, in feigned alarm. "He's a big one."

"I came here hoping I could appeal to his sense of decency," Ginny told me. "He doesn't have one."

Otto Barnsley peered up at us as if studying curiosities. Although the hours may have left him uncomfortable, he was not afraid. He was a soft-looking man, something larval about him, wholly unwholesome, the kind of person whose handshake would send you looking for the nearest faucet.

"I have other virtuous attributes." He glanced at Ginny, then down at his predicament. "Some evidently need a little more work."

The side of his face was bruised. I'd never known Ginny to go on the offensive. But she was an easy one to underestimate at first glance, with no second chances.

"What did he do?" I said. "What did he *try?*"

"I handled it." She laid a steadying grip on my arm. "Keep your set point. What we're here for."

We locked eyes, and she didn't let go until I calmed my breathing again. She was right. I wasn't ready to know what this man had thought he could get away with. Not yet. Details gave you reasons to snap.

Instead, I focused on this: Otto Barnsley didn't seem the type who ventured out to gawk at tragedies. He had to have been engrossed in the sinkhole itself, enough to show up every day with a vested interest in what the crews might discover. I suspected he'd gone home relieved.

"The map's over here," Ginny said, and retreated to the nearest dingy corner.

She'd removed it from its frame and spread it across a tabletop: yellowed paper the size of a poster, lined with a faint grid and filled in with what looked like ink over initial tracings of pencil. It was creased with enough folds to reduce to pocket size, but felt as if it had been a long time since it had been anything other than flat under glass.

It showed an entrance and a meandering channel that periodically branched off to other passages or ballooned into chambers. Near the south, it doglegged down into a linkup with Tecumseh #24, overlaid shadings depicting the various galleries of the mine's third and fourth levels.

This point of connection between the mine and the rest was the real anomaly. There weren't many straight lines on the map. But here, where the passage linked to the mine, was a square. I wasn't sure what the map's scale was, or if it was even accurate, but in context, this feature appeared to have the foundational dimensions of a house.

They'd hit a wall, McNabb had told me. Nothing natural, but constructed.

I tapped the map. "What is this square?"

Barnsley grinned, mocking. "What indeed?"

Ginny touched my arm. "If he decides to tell you anything more than he told me, fill me in. I need to round up some things for us on the back porch."

She folded the map and took it with her. Barnsley watched it go as if this was the first thing to cause him distress. I caught it in that split-second he tensed and squinched his eyes. A form of what's called eye-blocking.

"My grandfather thought his fortune was going to come from artifacts," Barnsley said. "In time, he realized it was in knowledge, instead. Knowledge being the true pearl of great price. But that structure down there was one thing he never understood. My father fared no better in his short life. It was a discovery ahead of its time."

"But *you* understand."

"I believe I do. Not without help. I'm just its humble custodian. There are people and organizations who've been studying the eclipted mysteries since long before Alvin Barnsley came north to steal a man's job and found a new path in life."

"What is it, then?"

Otto plainly loved to hear himself talk, but now he dodged. "Are you a godly man, Mr. Whitesides?"

"Not especially."

"Oh, what a pity. It's always delicious when someone's celestial illusions are shattered." Now Barnsley was the one reading me, that I had ceased to follow him. "Sometimes you brutish types who go into career fields where you get to legally hurt people have a crusader mentality. You have the kind of devoutness that leads you to conclude your god made you big for a reason. You break all the harder for it." He sighed with disappointment. "I would've enjoyed seeing that."

"Not a godly man yourself, I take it?"

"To the contrary. I have many gods. The kind that are worthy of the title because they have no use for it. Or for me. It's a big universe out there. What kind of worthy god would stoop so low as to concern itself with jabbering apes like you and me? Worthy gods only care about worlds. Not their inhabitants. Worthy believers don't care about worship. Only transfiguration."

It was a relief to hear Ginny calling up the hallway from the back of the house. Barnsley, I had decided, was the type who liked to appear cooperative, but only to steer a conversation where he wanted it to go. All I needed to know was this: If that structure in the mine was artificial, then Barnsley and his fathers had taken what was potentially the greatest archaeological find in history and kept it to themselves. Or, going by the evidence on the walls, between themselves and a clandestine network whose beliefs were beyond understanding. These were grotesquely selfish people.

"If you've got something to add, now's the time," I said. "It's getting late."

"Before you go, would you do me the kindness of cutting these oversized bread ties she's trussed me up with?" He looked at the clock. "You've reached the point of inhumane already. And there's a possibility you won't be coming back—not anytime soon, anyway—so there's no reason to compound the inhumanity by leaving me like this to perish. We wouldn't want that on your conscience, would we? Or are you as deficient of conscience as I am of decency?"

When I hesitated, he knew what that meant.

"You think I want to stop you from this mission? Not at all. You'll be the first newcomers in years who wanted to go in there willingly. I'm as curious as you are to see what happens next. I'm happy to share."

I'd heard enough. I followed Ginny to the back of the house and found her in a storeroom off the porch, furiously scouring the inside of a pair of facemasks with alcohol swabs. More safety gear was stowed here than one man alone would need. Barnsley had called himself the mine's custodian, had alluded to groups coming to study it as far back as his grandfather's day, and this much I could believe. This house was a way station for strange people with stranger agendas.

"We've got a decision to make," I said. "Do you have the cutter for his cuffs?"

Ginny didn't want to release him. But neither did she want to be the kind of monster who left him this way indefinitely. It wasn't a proud moment for either of us.

I cut him loose.

"You were somebody's son once. I just want to get mine back, if he's there to be found. Whatever condition he's in. Even if it's just bones. You get that, don't you?"

Barnsley stretched and massaged the ligature creases in his plump skin. "What's not to get?"

"Have you *seen* him?" I leaned close enough for Barnsley to smell murder on my breath. "When's the last time you were down there?"

"I tried once after the flood. Still too mucky for my tastes. And now . . . ?" He shrugged. "My ankles swell. As hikes go, it's not what my British friends call a doddle."

I drew back again. "What *is* that structure down there? Is it a room, a vault . . . ?"

He looked at me with bloodshot eyes, watery and puffy, but dreamer's eyes nonetheless. I'd seen these eyes on killers with trails of graves behind them, driven by a calm conviction that they were so far ahead of the rest of humanity they might as well have been recognized as a more advanced offshoot of the species.

"I've come to regard it as a machine," he said. "The oldest machine in the solar system. One of the engines of creation."

And if I wasn't sure what to make of that, I believed one thing he'd said: He was happy to share. But whether he thought he was sharing it with us, or us with it, I couldn't tell.

⊸⊶

We found the entrance where the map and Barnsley's elaborations said it would be. Even then, it wasn't easy. We trekked over the first steep hill behind the farm, then halfway down the other side. No trail, no signs, just landmarks amid trees that all looked the same.

It was screened so well a hiker could have passed by five feet away and not known it was there. Saplings had sprung up generations ago as the first rank of cover. Vines and ivy then hung like a curtain over a recessed doorway—a framework of huge, black timbers anchored into the hillside. If it hadn't been the entrance to a very old mine, then it had been built by people who'd wanted to give that impression. If you got this far, a Danger sign was there to warn you away, bolted to a door stout enough for a medieval hall. It was secured with a padlock as big as a tuna can, whose shackle was thick enough to shrug off bolt-cutters.

Barnsley had given Ginny the key. I hurled the lock downslope as far as I could, in case he'd thought to come up later and secure it behind us.

The door opened inward, on quiet hinges, something that could only have come from decades of oiling. I shined my flashlight on the back of the door, unsure whether I wanted to see evidence of someone having clawed at it to get out, unclear whether I was relieved that I didn't.

We were enveloped by an age-old smell of earth and stone, minerals and must. A claustrophobic corridor led in, braced by wood cut and cured when our grandparents were children. It ran level for yards, past the reach of daylight, then plunged down into a darkness more absolute than I had ever known. It was more than an absence of light. It seemed a solid substance, letting our flashlights cut it because it knew it would heal instantly.

Time to gear up. All we'd brought from home were pullover sweatshirts, while the back room at the Barnsley's had provided everything else: knee-high rubber boots to slip over our shoes, and flashlights and hardhats with mounted lamps running to battery packs on our belts. Around my neck I dangled a multigas detector. If we hit a hazardous level of methane or carbon monoxide or hydrogen sulfide, we had the facemasks she'd cleaned and a small air tank on our backs.

At the top of the steps, Ginny touched my arm. "Is it even possible? That Drew could still be . . . ?"

Her defenses were coming down. The shell had cracked and she didn't have to pretend anymore. There was just me now. But I think I was still the one who needed to hold the other more.

"I want to believe so," I said. "Even if I don't see how."

We began the descent, down steps carved into rock and fashioned from wooden slabs, until we hit a point where the way was smooth underfoot, the natural floor of a passage that undulated along like a serpent frozen in a slow, steady dive. Our hardhat lamps pushed ahead, squeezing the dark back. The air was cool and moist, like a cellar closed to the world, with the steady temperature of a late autumn day. The walls were grim and unfinished looking, nothing like weathered stone on the surface, known to the sun and moon.

"Do you hear that?" Ginny stopped and said at one point. "Do you *feel* it?"

I had to follow her lead, but yes—I did. It was an ambience on the threshold of awareness, like the sound of time and the weight of the hills bearing down atop us.

Our only sense of distance came from the map, charting our progress by a chamber, a turn, a branch peeling off to someplace that hadn't been worth the cartographer's ink. In time, the floor became permanently damp, a layer of muck sucking at the soles of our rubber boots.

And the air turned warmer.

Hundred of yards later, we were funneled to a cleft in the rock, an ancient fracture whose walls were just far enough apart to let us scoot through sideways. Along the way we'd passed spots that left me wondering what was natural and what might have been worked, but by the end of this claustrophobic passage there was no doubt it had been widened, with scars in the rock and matching chunks of rubble on the floor.

As we emerged from the passage, an expanded sense of space swallowed our voices and our headlamps turned feeble, without the closeness of the walls to contain them. We switched on our flashlights, too, and it became clear we'd emerged into Tecumseh #24's northernmost gallery, glints and glimmers reflecting from the unmined anthracite as if the darkness had turned glossy.

But to our left . . . ? Despite our reason for being here, the only thing that mattered, we could only stop and stare. Here was the very definition of out of place and time. We swept our flashlight beams up and down it, and from side to side.

Miners kept their ceilings from collapsing by leaving pillars of coal in key locations, but that didn't explain this. It was too big, too square, and it wasn't coal. This was something else entirely, fashioned from harder stone, thirty feet on each side and painstakingly chipped free of whatever coal had once entombed it.

Its walls were flat, on the smooth side of rough, except in three equidistant places where the entire structure was circled by bands of bas-relief carvings—pictographs or hieroglyphs or ideograms that didn't connect with anything I knew or ever wanted to. Some of them might have been text. Some might have depicted life forms known only from fossils, things that scuttled, swam, and flew, chiseled with a stylized sense of aesthetics I couldn't begin to grasp.

It looked to stand at least twenty feet tall, jutting through the low ceiling into the level above, but this was only the visible part. It didn't appear that our own level ground was its base. Where its sides met the floor, it looked as if someone had made an attempt to excavate further down. The trenches they'd left behind were now filled with slurry carried by the floodwaters of two years ago.

Ginny traced her finger down one corner edge. "It's not perfectly straight up and down. See how it slopes in toward the top?"

She was right. It wasn't a pyramid, though. More like an enormous pylon.

"No seams, either," she said. "This wasn't fitted together. It's all one piece."

"Barnsley called it a machine, though. An engine of creation, he called it."

"Do you believe him?"

"I don't know yet."

But consider the implications of how far down we were. Consider what this monolith was anchored in. Whatever its purpose, coal had formed around it. Meaning it had stood in the swampy forests of a primeval world, watching over the growth and death and decay of vegetation by the ton, until it was buried. Millions of years. Tens of millions.

Snippets of old science classes came floating back. The Carboniferous Period, I remembered that, and that the latter half was called the Pennsylvania Period. Just the sort of thing local science teachers enjoyed relating.

An incomprehensible 300 million years ago.

Yet before any of that could have happened, *this* had been shaped with purpose and design, and set in place for a reason.

And the air around it felt warm. It shouldn't have been warm.

"Trevor?" Ginny whispered. That's what you did in the presence of such a thing. "Whatever this is, it's not going anywhere. Let's get moving. We'll have time later to wrap our heads around this."

Farther into the mine, freestanding water had pooled, the last remainder of the flood that had washed our lives from underneath us. A few inches deep at first, until we were wading in chilly black water that swirled near the top of our knee-high boots.

Pale things slipped and slithered through it, away from us—wormlike creatures that wriggled in the flashlight beam, then submerged as if to escape the glare. Okay. Okay. Maybe they'd washed down here from a cave system, a place where they'd always been.

Even so, the more we saw of the mine, its galleries and corridors, the less any of it was what we'd expected. The water's surface was strewn with patches and swirls of lavender pond scum, algae that had learned to feed on something other than daylight. The rocky walls were slimed with growth. Gray fungus clung to stone and coal, and climbed frameworks of century-old timbers that helped secure the ceiling. This wasn't a defunct mine anymore. It was becoming an ecosystem, hundreds of feet from the reach of the sun.

In the main tunnel I stepped on something that shifted beneath my boot, then gave with a crunch. I probed with my foot, too much rubber in the way to discern anything, so I pushed up my sleeves and plunged my hand into the cold water. When it came up with a length of spinal column and a rib cage, I flung them away in disgust.

Ginny stared after the splash. "One of the miners? Almost forty of them died down here. Those poor men couldn't all have buried each other. And these Barnsleys don't seem like they were ever the type to do right by the dead."

It was obvious she hadn't seen the bones as well as I had. In that glimpse I'd caught in the headlamp, they didn't seem right, something malformed about them. The spine was overly long and twisted, as if from scoliosis. The rib cage had seemed wider, flatter. To me, it was only human because of expectations. Actually, I wasn't sure it was human at all. But I wasn't going to dredge it up again for another look.

We kept going, calling out for Drew as our lamps bounced off the disturbed water to make the walls ripple with shadow and light. It brought this place alive in the worst ways, the movement tricking us into thinking we weren't alone, that something was trying to flank us.

We cleared one gallery, then another—not hard, here where the water came to our knees. However Drew had gotten in from the slope shaft, he would've sought higher ground, dry earth.

We were slogging our way to the next gallery when a new sound began to creep up on us: a growing hum, low and steady, like a ground loop in a loudspeaker. Or the discharge around high-voltage towers. Since it was originating from behind us, there seemed only one possible source.

Whatever the so-called engine of creation was doing, I decided I'd rather know than not. I splashed back up the main tunnel, following my lights as they bounced around the curves, until I could see this aberration again. The hum had been joined by a second sound, a hollow, resonant grinding like stone or metal dragged across itself.

As Ginny splashed along behind me, we came in sight of the engine as it began to emit a pressurized hiss. A miasmal fog jetted from rows of narrow vents that had opened along the bands of carved symbols. It drifted along the roofline, then began to disperse and descend. It may have been no more than water vapor . . . but this was nowhere for misplaced trust.

"Masks," I said, and Ginny was already ahead of me. We opened the valves of our air canisters, then backed away from the cloud and resumed the slog ahead. At our backs, the warming air felt thickened, soupy. The multigas detector around my neck didn't make a peep—a relief, and the truth was, whatever the engine was generating, we'd probably been breathing some degree of residue this whole time.

Because this event couldn't have been a one-off. Undoubtedly, the structure had been doing this for a long time. Maybe it had reactivated during the flood. Maybe it had been running for decades, triggered by the miners' discovery of it. Or maybe it never stopped, and had continued to operate in its tomb of coal, venting fumes through minute cracks, all the way to the surface and bubbling through the groundwater.

It outgassed for three or four minutes before falling silent again. Only then did I think to activate the timer function on my watch. Depending on how much longer we were here, I could see if it was random, or had a pattern.

Further south, we found a shoreline along this stagnant black lake, where the next gallery led up to dry ground. In its farthest recesses, our lights swept across a row of heaped debris. When we saw what looked like filthy rags, we glanced at each other, and through our masks I saw that Ginny's eyes looked as stricken as I felt.

The air, I imagined, was vile here. What lay before us was mostly bones, many of them, all long past stinking, but there were bodies, too, putrid with advanced decay. The bones were caked with mud and wrapped with rotten vegetation, the fibrous debris that gets swept along with floodwaters. Their arrangement was too orderly to be anything but deliberate. Someone had pulled these jumbled skeletons from the water, piece by piece, after the chaos had calmed. The kind of thing a survivor would do. As for the bodies, I counted eight, but these were newer casualties. Decaying for two years sounded about right, as if they'd perished in the same deluge that had scattered the bones.

As if men given up for dead long ago had, in defiance of every natural law, clung to life all this time.

I just couldn't tell what their corpses were supposed to be. Not anymore.

"No," Ginny said. Only that, and nothing else. "No. No. *No.*"

If someone—Otto Barnsley, maybe—had assured me they'd been men once, miners all, I would've said okay. I can see that. But then what? What *happened* to them? What happened to their skulls, to flatten the cranial domes? Why did their jaws seem to jut, uppers and lowers alike? Why did their teeth look like ivory pegs now, and why had their limbs shortened? What made their rib cages look squashed in, flattened out, as if no longer meant for people who walked, but instead, for things that crawled?

Never in my life would I have thought that for men abandoned by the world, starving and dehydrating in the dark would've been the merciful thing.

I took Ginny's hand, so we could finish what we'd started.

And when we spotted him in the next gallery, even from a distance of many yards away, I knew it had to be Drew, because the heap along one rough wall was so much smaller. Just one person, lost in perpetual darkness, swathed in dirty clothes I never thought I would see again. How he'd loved that blue flannel shirt.

My boy. Oh, my beautiful boy.

Ginny ran to him, the way only a mother would, stripping the mask from her face and letting it dangle by the tube to bang against her legs. Her helmet clattered across the ground, the beam of light cartwheeling as she dropped beside him. To touch him, hold him, as only a mother could.

I took my mask off too. *Where you go, I go.*

But as a father, god forgive me, I was slower, because I was terrified of what I would find, then appalled by what was there.

Drew was beyond pale, with the pallor of skin no longer meant for a world with a sun. Our lights caused him pain, made him flinch and recoil, but even that movement looked clumsy. What happened inside when bones softened, when sinews relaxed? This. *This* happened. This puddled bag of reconstituting skin and bones that struggled to sit upright. He recognized the voices beside him, weeping and trying to soothe him, but he had trouble saying anything in return. *We're here*, we told him. *We're here.* He croaked and sobbed and made sounds unlike anything I'd ever heard from a person. And where was the grin I remembered, the smile that could brighten rooms? Gone, along with most of his teeth and half of his once shaggy hair.

I dropped at his other side, so that Ginny and I looked at each other across him, the way we would when he was bedridden and tiny. Chicken pox. Mumps. Fevers and colds. He always got better. We'd always feared he wouldn't. No reason, it's just the way you worry when they're little. You never quite lose that fear, even after they've grown so robust they seem immortal.

And for all I knew, that's what he was now. The corpses next door were proof of that. Barring calamity, he might live for ages. Just no longer in a form I would recognize as anything that had come from me.

He wouldn't want this. He couldn't want this. We couldn't leave him to it. Not our Drew. And not Katee, either, because a part of her would always be caught down here with him in the timeless black.

Ginny touched him so much more readily than I could. She stroked his cheeks until he could open his eyes. She put her face close so he would know how much she loved him. She found the kind of smile I would've thought she'd left above. She wiped away both their tears, making mud of the grime on their cheeks. She touched her lips to his clammy forehead, and held his hand so gently, because it seemed as if one good squeeze might crush its bones.

I'd never known such shame, because it was all I could do to rest my hand on his sinking chest, feeling its shallow, panting breaths, fighting the sort of disgust that strains the very fabric of a love you thought was inviolable.

And she knew. Ginny knew. She knew everything that mattered right then.

"Why don't you go?" she said after a while. "Back out to the tunnel. You should go." When I protested, a whisper: "I don't want you here for this."

For a few more moments I curled on the floor beside him, shaking, and so did she. I kept my eyes shut. It was purely presence then, the ineffable spirit of someone you love that you could never mistake for someone else. And it was Drew. My boy. My beautiful boy. But fading away, into something else.

Then I kissed him and left them together, for as long as it would take Ginny to do what we both knew I couldn't.

Time to wrap our heads around things later—that was the promise. Right now, it was all I had to keep my mind from cracking in two.

I sat by the edge of the black lake, the surface as still as a sheet of obsidian. These were the shallows, but there had to be depths, too, a gradual decline or a sudden drop into a cold chasm. The diver who'd searched the bottom of the slope shaft had found as much, even if he hadn't been able to navigate a way through it.

Yet Drew had. The two sides were connected, and Drew had found the way. Tumbled from his car downhill, all the way into the water at the bottom, and instead of crawling back up the shaft toward daylight, he'd emerged over here. Hurt, disoriented, in darkness, without an air tank, he'd accidentally done what a trained diver couldn't?

I couldn't believe that at all.

But I could believe he'd been brought by someone who already knew the way.

As recently as the flood, survivors from the cave-in had been alive down here. *Don't ask how, not yet, just go with what I can say for certain.* There were survivors. I'd seen the bodies. Bodies and bones that someone had cared for. So there had been at least one survivor from the flood, as well.

Good god. Imagine that. Entombed alive. Nine decades of abandonment, betrayal, mutation. I couldn't imagine anything lonelier than being the sole survivor after your pitch black world was inundated and the last of your fellow exiles have drowned. If even one spark of humanity remained, you'd do anything to not be alone anymore.

What a gift Drew must have seemed.

Back in the gallery, Ginny was singing to him, a cradle lullaby I hadn't heard in eighteen years. The acoustics made it sound as if we were in a church instead of a tomb.

At my feet, on the shore of this stagnant lake, the black glass surface rippled, as if disturbed from far away. I moved nothing more than my eyes, scanning the shadows as far as they let me see.

It may have only been the flipping of one of those pale eels I'd seen earlier. But I didn't think so.

So with one ear I followed Ginny's song, and with the other listened for a splash.

I let the grief in deeper and imagined how she would do it. She knew how to break people, but knew how to put them to sleep, too. She knew how to wrap her arm around someone's neck from behind, how to notch their throat in the crook of her elbow and squeeze so the blood stopped flowing to the brain. It's only uncomfortable for a few seconds. Then the lights go out.

That's when you should release the choke. Unless you intend lasting harm. To kill the brain, all you have to do is keep holding the person close and not let go, for the longest few minutes of your life.

Up the tunnel, back where we'd come in, the engine of creation hummed to life again. I checked my watch—thirty-six minutes—then reset the timer and debated putting my mask back on. Could be it was too late already, because we'd breathed the air down here before we'd ever switched to the tanks.

I hoped it took more exposure than that. Days of it. Weeks of it.

It was the key to everything, though. If something could rightly be called an engine of creation, then it could just as easily be an engine of *re*-creation.

Terraforming—that was the word that came to mind. Paving the way for life as something altogether *other* knew it.

I pictured the monolith as it must have been, a mysterious and indestructible pylon squatting in the forested hush of our world at its most primeval. Humming like a swarm of dragonflies the size of condors and spewing its fumes to the wind, casting seeds of life and metamorphosis. One of dozens, assuming this was what was marked on that map on Barnsley's wall, pinned with sites from pole to pole.

Its vast antiquity was beyond questioning. Only who had put it here was up for grabs. Barnsley's many gods, I had to guess—the worthy gods that cared only about worlds and not their inhabitants. Least of all, a few poor scabs who thought they'd found their fortune.

Near my boots, the waterline rippled again, as somewhere out in the darkness, drips and drops plinked to the surface. Down the tunnel I glimpsed a pale shape, like the inverse of a shadow, rising from the water, then descending again.

I wished I'd worn my old sidearm. But there were rocks.

You poor bastards, I thought. Mythology was full of heroes who lamented that we were only the playthings of fickle gods. The miners would know better. They weren't even that much, just casualties to a process that had never factored them in in the first place.

Behind me, the lullabies were no more.

My family. Oh, my beautiful family.

Still, I wondered if those miners hadn't battled like heroes just the same.

For months, one thing had bugged me about that slope shaft. The only apparent opening was the one Drew had been diverted into. The rescuers hadn't found any sign of a corresponding opening on the other side of the vertical. But nobody could afford to worry about that at the time.

So what if it had never been a long-forgotten shaft sunk from the surface at all? Suppose it had been dug from below, by something trying to get out. Whatever the miners were becoming, and scabs or not, some may yet have known how to excavate a tunnel that wouldn't collapse on them. They'd only misjudged, and run into the blockage that Tecumseh had dumped down the main shaft.

Maybe by then they'd realized they didn't have time to try again.

Christ—how had they lived even that long? Water could have been seeping in even then. And for a time, they might have fed on their dead. Beyond that, I didn't want to know. The engine of creation had made them its own soon enough.

One thing was certain: By the time Alvin Barnsley had found his way back in, his comrades were no longer fit for the topside world. Otherwise, they would've left.

I knew it was done when Ginny sobbed, a sound ripped from an imploding core, and something in me broke too. We had no son anymore. Katee had no brother. We had only memories now, until our minds might unravel and let them spill with all the rest.

For a moment I intended to rejoin her, then reconsidered. No. She would want these moments to herself, as well. This I knew. Sometimes it felt like I knew her so well I had no idea who she actually was anymore.

As for whatever had been watching from the deepest darkness of the mine, and must've fled when it heard us coming, it understood what had just happened as well as any of us. It must have been waiting for this moment.

At first it was merely ripples coming toward me, a V-shape gliding through the water, the vague suggestion of something's back. Then it hit the shallows and struggled to find its feet again. I caressed the rock in my hand.

And if one good thing could come of such a terrible moment, it was that I could feel peace over what we'd spared our son.

In it, you could still see the man it had been, even if it was a man reshaped by the archaic reptilian forms lost to a world 300 million years gone. The connection wasn't in its eyes, though. It had none, only vestigial bumps where they'd been. It found me by sound alone. It wasn't in the shape of the face, either, with the flattened crown of its skull and the wide, jutting jaw brimming with peg teeth. It wasn't in the grotesquely lengthened torso, or the stumpy limbs, or the skin so pale it looked blue against the black. And it certainly wasn't in the thick, tapering tail it was trying to hide.

No. It was in the pride he took in trying to stand. *There* was the man. In his pride, and the way he carried the ancient miner's pick in the clawed appendage that had been his hand.

I let my rock drop to the floor.

Even across 300 million years of speciation, in a creature I'd never seen, I knew his body language. I knew exactly what he was begging for.

He offered me the pick, then plopped to the ground, on all fours, half in the water and half out, where he looked so much more at home. And with his head at my feet, he waited.

I should have hated him for what he'd done to us. I should've condemned him to a life of renewed solitude. But I couldn't. He'd only wanted what we all want. Wretched as he was, he had only wanted to not feel so alone.

In my hand, the pick's handle felt rough and rotten, sloughing off splinters. The iron end curved like a rusty crescent moon. I squeezed it until my knuckles went as pale as he was, then hoisted the tool over my head.

I could think of nothing crueler in the cosmos than gods that cared only about worlds.

It took an inhabitant to care about mercy.

HONORABLE MENTIONS

Allan, Nina, "Maggots" (novella), *Five Stories High*.

Barron, Laird, "An Atlatl" (novella), *Limbus Inc. Book III*.

Barron, Laird, "Oblivion Mode," *Children of Lovecraft*.

Bell, Peter, "Southwold," *Phantasms*.

Boatman, Michael, "Christmastime in Zombietown," *13*.

Bonfanti, Daniele, "Game" (novella), *The Beauty of Death*.

Boston, Bruce & Manzetti, Alessandro, "Slade, Mary And Pet" (poem), *Sacrificial Nights*.

Braum, Daniel, "How To Make Love and Not Turn to Stone," *The Beauty of Death*.

Collings, Michael R., "Catacomb" (poem), *Corona Obscura*.

Gardner, Cate, "We Make Our Own Monsters Here," *Shadow Moths*.

Hargadon, Stephen, "Mittens," Black Static #53, July/August.

Headley, Maria Dahvana, "Little Widow," *What the #@&% is That?*

Hill, Susan, "The Front Room," *The Travelling Bag and Other Ghostly Stories*.

Hirshberg, Glen, "Freedom is Space for the Spirit," Tor.com, April 6.

Hodge, Brian, "The Weight of the Dead," Tor.com, June 1.

Johnstone, Carole, "Wetwork," Black Static #52.

Jones, Stephen Graham, "Eternal Troutland," *Children of Lovecraft*.

Jones, Stephen Graham, "The Night Cyclist," Tor.com, September 21.

Kiernan, Caitlín R., "Excerpts for *An Eschatology Quadrille*," *Children of Lovecraft*.

Kiernan, Caitlín R., "The Line Between the Devil's Teeth," Sirenia Digest 130.

King, Michelle Ann, "My Sister, the Fairy Princess," Black Static #52, May/ June.

Langan, John, "Anchor" (novella), *Autumn Cthulhu*.

LaValle, Victor, "The Ballad of Black Tom" (novella), A Tor.com Book.

Larson, Richard, "Extraction Request," Clarkesworld January #112.

LeFanu, Sarah, "Fran Nan's Story," *Uncertainties Volume 1*.

Lloyd, Rebecca, "For Two Songs," *Ragman & Other Family Curses*.

Manuel, Derek, "Five Things Successful Clowns Must Do," Clowns: The Unlikely . . .

Matheson, Richard Christian, "Sea of Atlas," *Zoopraxis*.

Matsuura, Thersa, "The Carp-Faced Boy," *The Beauty of Death*.

Morris, Mark, "Full Up," Black Static #51.

Neal, Harmony, "Dare," Black Static #53, July/August.

Nickle, David, "The Caretakers," Tor.com, January 20.

Oates, Joyce Carol, "Big Mama," EQMM March/April.

Oates, Joyce Carol, "The Crawl Space," EQMM Sept./Oct.

Runge, Karen, "My Son, My Son," *Seven Sins*.

Sanchez-Izenman, Jeanette, "She'll Only Come Out at Night," Black Candies.

Schweitzer, Darrell, "We Who Have Encountered Monsters" (poem), Spectral Realms #4.

Sharma, Priya, "Inheritance, or the Ruby Tear," Black Static #53, July/August.

Shi, Eve, "Blood Like Water," *Asian Monsters*.

Slatter, Angela, "Finnegan's Field," Tor.com, January 13.

Taylor, Lucy, "He Who Whispers the Dead Back to Life," *Into Painfreak*.

Thomas, Scott, "The Girl with Pennies on Her Eyes" (poem), Spectral Realms #4.

Warren, Kaaron, "All Roll Over," *In Your Face*.

Wehunt, Michael, "October Film Haunt: Under the House," *Greener Pastures*.

Weighell, Ron, "The Letter Killeth" (novella), *Pagan Triptych*.

Wellington, David, "Lacey," *The 3rd Spectral Book of Horror Stories*.

Williamson, Chet, "That Still, Bleeding Object of Desire," *Cemetery Riots*.

Wise, A. C., "When the Stitches Come Undone," *Children of Lovecraft*.

Wong, Alyssa, "You'll Surely Drown Her If You Stay," Uncanny 10.

ABOUT THE AUTHORS

Gregory Norman Bossert grew up in Cambridge, Massachusetts, but has settled just over the Golden Gate Bridge from San Francisco. He started writing on a dare in 2009, at the age of forty-seven; his story "The Telling" won the 2013 World Fantasy Award for Short Story.

On weekdays (and all too many weekends) he works for Industrial Light & Magic, most recently on *Rogue One: A Star Wars Story* and Steven Spielberg's adaptation of *Ready Player One*.

"Between Dry Ribs" was originally published in the February 2016 issue of *The Dark*.

––◦––

Nadia Bulkin writes scary stories about the scary world we live in, three of which have been nominated for a Shirley Jackson Award. Her stories have been included in volumes of *The Year's Best Dark Fantasy and Horror* and *The Year's Best Weird Fiction*, and in venues such as *Nightmare*, *Fantasy*, *The Dark*, and *ChiZine*. Her debut collection, *She Said Destroy*, will be released by Word Horde Press in August 2017. She grew up in Indonesia with her Javanese father and American mother. She now has two political science degrees and lives in Washington, DC.

"Wish You Were Here" was originally published in Nightmare 49, *People of Color Destroy Horror*.

––◦––

Christopher Burns is the author of six novels: *Snakewrist*, *The Flint Bed*, *In the Houses of the West*, *The Condition of Ice*, *Dust Raising*, and *A Division of the*

Light—and a short story collection, *About the Body*. He lives in Whitehaven, West Cumbria.

"Numbers" was originally published as a chapbook by Nightjar Press.

◄◦►

Siobhan Carroll is an associate professor of English at the University of Delaware. When not plotting world domination, she studies nineteenth-century board games, polar exploration, and the history of geo-engineering. For more fiction by Siobhan Carroll, visit: voncarr-siobhan-carroll.blogspot. com/p/fiction-poetry.html

"Nesters" was originally published in *Children of Lovecraft*, by Ellen Datlow.

◄◦►

Ray Cluley's work has been published in various magazines and anthologies. It has also been reprinted in Ellen Datlow's *Best Horror of the Year* (volumes 3, 6, and 8), Steve Berman's *Wilde Stories: The Year's Best Gay Speculative Fiction*, and in Benoît Domis's Ténèbres series. His story "Shark! Shark!" won the British Fantasy Award for Best Short Story, while "Water For Drowning" was short-listed for Best Novella and his collection, *Probably Monsters*, for Best Collection. You can find out more at probablymonsters.wordpress.com.

"The Castellmarch Man" was originally published in *Great British Horror 1, Green and Pleasant Land* edited by Steve J. Shaw.

◄◦►

Kristi DeMeester is the author of *Beneath*, a novel published by Word Horde Press, and *Everything That's Underneath*, a short fiction collection published by Apex Publications. Her short fiction has appeared in *Year's Best Weird Fiction* Volumes 1 and 3, in addition to publications such as *Black Static*, *The Dark*, and several others. In her spare time, she alternates between telling people how to pronounce her last name and how to spell her first. Find her online at kristidemeester.com.

"The Beautiful Thing We Will Become" was originally published in *Eternal Frankenstein*, edited by Ross E. Lockhart.

◄◦►

Steve Duffy's short fiction has appeared in numerous magazines and anthologies in Europe and North America. His most recent collection of weird stories, *The Moment Of Panic*, was published in 2013; it includes the International Horror Guild award-winning short story, "The Rag-and-Bone Men."

In 2016 Steve won a Shirley Jackson Award for his story "Even Clean Hands Can Do Damage," and he has been nominated on several occasions for a World Fantasy Award.

Steve lives and works in North Wales.

"The Ice Beneath Us" was originally published in *Uncertainties Volume II*, edited by Brian J. Showers, The Swan River Press.

◄◦►

Brian Evenson is the author of over a dozen books of fiction, most recently the story collection *A Collapse of Horses*. He has been a finalist for the Shirley Jackson Award three times. His novel *Last Days* won the American Library Association's award for Best Horror Novel of 2009. His novel *The Open Curtain* was a finalist for an Edgar Award and an International Horror Guild Award, and has just been rereleased by Coffee House Press. He is the recipient of three O. Henry Prizes as well as an NEA fellowship. He lives in Valencia, California, and works at CalArts.

"No Matter Which Way We Turn" was originally published in *People Holding*, spring.

◄◦►

Christopher Golden is the *New York Times* bestselling author of *Snowblind*, *Ararat*, *Tin Men*, and many other novels. With Mike Mignola, he co-created the cult favorite comic book series *Baltimore* and *Joe Golem: Occult Detective*. As editor, his anthologies include *Seize the Night*, *The New Dead*, and *Dark Cities*, among others. Golden has also written screenplays, radio plays, non-fiction, graphic novels, video games, and (with Amber Benson) the online animated series *Ghosts of Albion*. He is one-third of the pop culture podcast *Three Guys with Beards*.

"The Bad Hour" was originally published in *What the #@&% is That?* Edited by John Joseph Adams & Douglas Cohen.

⤙◦⤕

Award-winning horror author **Gemma Files** has also been a film critic, teacher, and screenwriter. She is probably best-known for her Weird Western Hexslinger series: *A Book of Tongues, A Rope of Thorns,* and *A Tree of Bones,* and has published two collections of short fiction, *Kissing Carrion* and *The Worm in Every Heart,* as well as two chapbooks of poetry. Her book, *We Will All Go Down Together: Stories About the Five-Family Coven,* was published in 2014. Her most recent novel is *Experimental Film,* which won the 2015 Shirley Jackson Award for Best Novel and the 2015 Sunburst Award for Best Novel (Adult).

"Grave Goods" was originally published in *Autumn Cthulhu,* edited by Mike Davis.

⤙◦⤕

Brian Hodge is one of those people who always has to be making something. So far, he's made eleven novels, 125 shorter works, and five full-length collections. His first collection, *The Convulsion Factory,* was ranked by critic Stanley Wiater among the 113 best books of modern horror.

Recent and upcoming works include his latest novel, *Dawn of Heresies; I'll Bring You the Birds From Out of the Sky,* a novella of cosmic horror paired with folk art illustrations; and his next collection, *The Immaculate Void,* will be out in early 2018.

He lives in Colorado, where he also likes to make music and photographs; loves everything about organic gardening except the thieving squirrels; and trains in Krav Maga and kickboxing, which are of no use at all against the squirrels.

Connect through his web site at brianhodge.net, Twitter (@BHodgeAuthor), or Facebook (facebook.com/brianhodgewriter).

"It's All the Same Road in the End" was originally published in *The Mammoth Book of Cthulhu,* edited by Paula Guran, and has been optioned for a feature film.

"On These Blackened Shores of Time" was originally published in *Children of Lovecraft,* edited by Ellen Datlow.

⤙◦⤕

Robert Levy is an author of stories and plays whose work has been seen Off-Broadway. A Harvard graduate subsequently trained as a forensic psychologist, his first novel, *The Glittering World*, was a finalist for the Lambda Literary Award and the Shirley Jackson Award. Shorter work has recently appeared in places like *Black Static*, *Shadows & Tall Trees*, *Strange Aeons*, *Autumn Cthulhu*, and *The Madness of Dr. Caligari*, among others. A Brooklyn native, Robert is at work on a number of projects in various media including a television pilot, a scripted podcast, and a new novel. He can be found at TheRobertLevy.com.

"The Oestridae" was originally published in *Black Static* #52, May/June.

◄◦►

Livia Llewellyn is a writer of horror, dark fantasy, and erotica, whose fiction has appeared in *ChiZine*, *Subterranean*, *Apex* magazine, *Postscripts*, *Nightmare* magazine, as well as numerous anthologies. Her first collection, *Engines of Desire: Tales of Love & Other Horrors*, was published in 2011 by Lethe Press, and received two Shirley Jackson Award nominations for Best Collection and Best Novelette (for "Omphalos"). Her story "Furnace" received a 2013 SJA nomination for Best Short Fiction. Her second collection, titled *Furnace*, was recently published by Word Horde Press. You can find her online at liviallewellyn.com.

"Bright Crown of Joy" was originally published in *Children of Lovecraft*, edited by Ellen Datlow.

◄◦►

Rebecca Lloyd is from the south of England. Her short stories have been collected in *Mercy* (Tartarus Press), which was nominated for the 2014 World Fantasy Award, *The View from Endless Street*, *Whelp and Other Stories*, which was a finalist in the 2014 Paul Bowles Short Fiction Award, and *Ragman and Other Family Curses* (Egeaus Press).

Her story "The Ringers" was short-listed in the Aestas Short Story Prize 2016, her novel *Oothangbart* was published by Pillar International Publishing. She is also the author of the novellas *Woolfy and Scrapo* and *Jack Werrett, the Flood Man*.

She is currently working on a Gothic horror novel set in 1851.

"Ragman" was originally published in *Ragman and Other Family Curses*.

⁓

Gary McMahon is the author of eight novels, and several novellas and short story collections. He lives with his wife, son, and two cats in Yorkshire, and likes to write about the horrors found in the cracks of everyday life.

Occasional musings can be found at his website, www.garymcmahon.com.

"What's Out There?" was originally published in *Uncertainties II*, edited by Brian J. Showers, The Swan River Press.

⁓

Adam L. G. Nevill was born in Birmingham, England, in 1969 and grew up in England and New Zealand. He is the author of the horror novels: *Banquet for the Damned, Apartment 16, The Ritual, Last Days, House of Small Shadows, No One Gets Out Alive, Lost Girl,* and *Under a Watchful Eye*. His first short story collection, *Some Will Not Sleep: Selected Horrors*, was published on Halloween, 2016.

His novels, *The Ritual, Last Days, House of Small Shadows*, and *No One Gets Out Alive* were the winners of The August Derleth Award for Best Horror Novel. *The Ritual* and *Last Days* were also awarded Best in Category: Horror, by R.U.S.A. Many of his novels are currently in development for film and television, and in 2016 Imaginarium adapted *The Ritual* into a feature film.

Adam also offers two free books to readers of horror: *Cries from the Crypt*, downloadable from his website, and *Before You Sleep* available from major online retailers.

Adam lives in Devon, England. More information about the author and his books is available at: adamlgnevill.com

"The Days of Our Lives" was originally published in *Dead Letters: An Anthology of the Undelivered, the Missing, the Returned* . . . edited by Conrad Williams.

⁓

Peter Straub is the author of seventeen novels, which have been translated into more than twenty languages. They include *Ghost Story, Koko, Mr. X, In*

the Night Room, and two collaborations with Stephen King, *The Talisman* and *Black House*. He has written two volumes of poetry and two collections of short fiction, and edited the Library of America's edition of H. P. Lovecraft's *Tales* and two-volume anthology *American Fantastic Tales*. He has won the British Fantasy Award, ten Bram Stoker Awards, two International Horror Guild Awards, and four World Fantasy Awards. In 1998, he was named Grand Master at the World Horror Convention. In 2006, he was given the HWA's Life Achievement Award. In 2008, he was given the Barnes & Noble Writers for Writers Award by Poets & Writers. At the World Fantasy Convention in 2010, he was given the WFC's Life Achievement Award.

"The Process Is a Process All Its Own" was originally published in *Conjunctions: 67 Other Aliens*, fall 2016.

◄o►

Steve Rasnic Tem's last novel, *Blood Kin*, won the Bram Stoker Award. His new novel, *UBO*, is a dark science fictional tale about violence and its origins, featuring such historical viewpoint characters as Jack the Ripper, Stalin, and Heinrich Himmler. He is also a past winner of the World Fantasy and British Fantasy Awards. Recently a collection of the best of his uncollected horror—*Out of the Dark: A Storybook of Horrors*—was published by Centipede Press. A handbook on writing, *Yours To Tell: Dialogues on the Art & Practice of Writing*, written with his late wife Melanie, will appear soon from Apex Publications. In the Fall of 2018 Hex Publishers will bring out his middle grade Halloween novel, *The Mask Shop of Doctor Blaack*. Visit the Tem home on the web at www.m-s-tem.com.

"Red Rabbit" was originally published in *Borderlands 6: An Anthology of Imaginative Fiction*, edited by Olivia F. and Thomas Monteleone.

◄o►

C.E. Ward mostly writes ghost stories, and is the author of three collections of them: *Vengeful Ghosts*, *Seven Ghosts and One Other*, and *Malevolent Visitants*.

"House of Wonders" was originally published in *Malevolent Visitants*.

◄o►

DB Waters is a writer and rare book dealer, specialising in signed modern first editions. Previous work has been published in *The Frogmore Papers*. "Fury" was first published in England by *Nightjar Press*. His most recent work is a

388   ABOUT THE AUTHORS

supernatural novella, *Gretina*, for which he is currently seeking publication. He lives with his wife and daughter in Shropshire, England.

"Fury" was originally published as a chapbook by Nightjar Press.

ACKNOWLEDGMENT OF COPYRIGHT

"Nesters" by Siobhan Carroll. Copyright © 2016. First published in *Children of Lovecraft* edited by Ellen Datlow, Dark Horse Books. Reprinted by permission of the author.

"The Oestridae" by Robert Levy. Copyright © 2016. First published in Black Static #52, May/June. Reprinted by permission of the author.

"The Process Is a Process All Its Own" by Peter Straub. Copyright © 2016. First published in *Conjunctions: 67 Other Aliens*, fall 2016. Reprinted by permission of the author.

"The Bad Hour" by Christopher Golden. Copyright © 2016. First published in *What the #@&% Is That?* edited by John Joseph Adams & Douglas Cohen, Saga Press. Reprinted by permission of the author.

"Red Rabbit" by Steve Rasnic Tem. Copyright © 2016. First published in *Borderlands 6: An Anthology of Imaginative Fiction* edited by Olivia F. Monteleone and Thomas F. Monteleone, Borderlands Press. Reprinted by permission of the author.

"It's All the Same Road in the End" by Brian Hodge. Copyright © 2016. First published in *The Mammoth Book of Cthulhu* edited by Paula Guran (Robinson). Reprinted by permission of the author.

"Fury" by DB Waters. Copyright © 2016. First published as a chapbook by Nightjar Press. Reprinted by permission of the author.

"Grave Goods" by Gemma Files. Copyright © 2016. First published in *Autumn Cthulhu*, edited by Mike Davis, Lovecraft Ezine Press. Reprinted by permission of the author.

"Between Dry Ribs" by Gregory Norman Bossert. Copyright © 2016. First published in *The Dark*, February. Reprinted by permission of the author.

"The Days of Our Lives" by Adam L. G. Nevill. Copyright © 2016. First published in *Dead Letters: An Anthology of the Undelivered, the Missing, the Returned . . .* edited by Conrad Williams (Titan Books). Reprinted by permission of the author.

"House of Wonders" by C.E. Ward. Copyright © 2016. First published in *Malevolent Visitants*, Sarob Press. Reprinted by permission of the author.

"The Numbers" by Christopher Burns. Copyright © 2016. First published as a chapbook by Nightjar Press. Reprinted by permission of the author.

"Bright Crown of Joy" by Livia Llewellyn. Copyright © 2016. First published in *Children of Lovecraft* edited by Ellen Datlow, Dark Horse Books. Reprinted by permission of the author.

"The Beautiful Thing We Will Become" by Kristi DeMeester. Copyright © 2016. First published in *Eternal Frankenstein*, edited by Ross E. Lockhart, Word Horde Press. Reprinted by permission of the author.

"Wish You Were Here" by Nadia Bulkin. Copyright © 2016. First published in *Nightmare 49*, People of Color Destroy Horror. Reprinted by permission of the author.

"Ragman" by Rebecca Lloyd. Copyright © 2016. First published in *Ragman & Other Family Curses*, Egaeus Press, Keynote Edition I. Reprinted by permission of the author.

"What's Out There?" by Gary McMahon. Copyright © 2016. First published in *Uncertainties Volume II*, edited by Brian J. Showers, The Swan River Press. Reprinted by permission of the author.

"No Matter Which Way We Turned" by Brian Evenson. Copyright © 2016. First published in *People Holding*, spring. Reprinted by permission of the author.

"The Castellmarch Man" by Ray Cluley. Copyright © 2016. First published in *Great British Horror 1, Green and Pleasant Land* edited by Steve J. Shaw, Black Shuck Books. Reprinted by permission of the author.

"The Ice Beneath Us" by Steve Duffy. First published in *Uncertainties Volume II*, edited by Brian J. Showers, The Swan River Press. Reprinted by permission of the author.

"On These Blackened Shores of Time" by Brian Hodge. Copyright © 2016. First published in *Children of Lovecraft* edited by Ellen Datlow, Dark Horse Books. Reprinted by permission of the author.

ABOUT THE EDITOR

Ellen Datlow has been editing science fiction, fantasy, and horror short fiction for more than thirty-five years. She currently acquires short fiction for Tor. com. In addition, she has edited almost one hundred science fiction, fantasy, and horror anthologies, including the series *The Best Horror of the Year*, *Fearful Symmetries*, *The Doll Collection*, *The Monstrous*, *Nightmares: A New Decade of Modern Horror*, *Children of Lovecraft*, and *Black Feathers: Dark Avian Tales*.

Forthcoming are *Mad Hatters and March Hares*, *Haunted Nights* (with Lisa Morton), *The Saga Anthology of Ghost Stories* and *Devil and the Deep*.

She's won multiple World Fantasy Awards, Locus Awards, Hugo Awards, Stoker Awards, International Horror Guild Awards, Shirley Jackson Awards, and the 2012 Il Posto Nero Black Spot Award for Excellence as Best Foreign Editor. Datlow was named recipient of the 2007 Karl Edward Wagner Award, given at the British Fantasy Convention for "outstanding contribution to the genre," was honored with the Life Achievement Award given by the Horror Writers Association, in acknowledgment of superior achievement over an entire career, and the Life Achievement Award by the World Fantasy Convention.

She lives in New York and co-hosts the monthly Fantastic Fiction Reading Series at KGB Bar. More information can be found at datlow.com, on Facebook, and on Twitter as @EllenDatlow.